Dear Peggy –

Wishing you
a speedy
recovery!
Love
Laura Agee

Lion's Bell

By
Lorraine Agnew

ISBN-13: 978-1494768355
ISBN-10: 1494768356

For Kristen, my daughter-in-law and friend, who creates beautiful covers for my books. Thank you for your creativity.

Lion's Bell

Chapter 1

World War II had ended and the promise of a peaceful tomorrow began for most people who survived the horror.

Anna Mary Deluca was not one of them. She suffered collateral damage and was left with so many emotional scars, all the hope and anticipation of a brighter future couldn't renew her spirit.

Her heart had been shattered and all that remained was a tiny piece, a morsel she maintained for her youngest daughter, Rosalie Catherine. Every other part had become decrepit, stained with the blackness of hatred and loss, and soaked with the stench of loathing.

For Anna Mary, to turn the other cheek seemed impossible.

She offered sentiments of mistrust, hatred and anger to Rosalie on a daily basis in order to steel her from future pain. What she did, instead, was steal her joy of childhood.

"Never trust anyone. Always be on guard."

"Never befriend a German. They're all Nazis."

"Don't open your heart to anyone or it'll just get broken."

To these rules, there were no exceptions.

Anna Mary's friends often passed unnoticed glances; a roll of the eyes, a slow shake of the head. While they didn't agree with her, they did understand from where her hatred had come.

"Maybe she's traumatized," Ruth Goldberg, her closest friend, would say. "It could be the result of losing too much to the war."

Ruth had fled Germany long before Hitter came to power. While she despised him for his actions against her people, she told Anna Mary that she couldn't share her view that *all* Germans were Nazis. Instead, in trying to remain a loyal friend, she attempted to justify Anna Mary's position.

Oddly, Anna Mary never expressed a hatred of the Japanese even though in 1937 it was Japan that invaded China and initiated World War II in the Pacific, not to mention the bombing of Pearl Harbor in 1941.

She also held no ire toward the Italians when in April of 1939 fascist Italy invaded Albania.

1

In her mind, when Germany invaded Poland, they became the sole perpetrator of the war.

"They started it all when they broke the Munich Agreement and it's the Germans who did the most damage. They killed millions of people, mostly Jews, and because of Nazi aggression under Hitler, my life was ruined."

To some extent, although slanted, most of what she said was true. History revealed as much.

Her life, in fact, was ruined, if not damaged severely, inasmuch as her son, Stephen, who was only eighteen, was killed in the spring of 1944 in a battle outside of Anzio, a town south of Rome, Italy.

Her husband, Guido, was just about to be shipped out to Europe when news of Stephen's death arrived. He was permitted to return home for several weeks to comfort his family and arrange his son's funeral.

Anna Mary, who was forty-one at the time, became pregnant as a result of her husband's extended visit. Shortly afterward, he was deployed to Germany. Before the year ended, though, men from the government were at the DeLuca's door.

Anna Mary would tell the story of how she opened the door expecting to find carolers – since it was a week before Christmas - and came face to face with two other men bearing sad news.

"Daddy lost his life during the Battle of the Bulge, the turning point of the German offensive," Anna Mary explained to her sixteen year old daughter, Carlotta, as though that made it more acceptable.

Before his body was returned home, the much-stressed Anna Mary gave birth to Rosalie, a month premature. She was born in Kings County Hospital in Brooklyn, New York, on New Year's Day, 1945.

By September, the war ended. Anna Mary and her daughters were forced to move into a tenement in Brooklyn. It was a three-story brownstone with eight apartments, two on each floor, including the basement. The elevated train ran past the window of their second-floor apartment.

Anna Mary returned to work as a receptionist for an insurance company in Manhattan. Raising two daughters on her own turned out to be more difficult than she thought possible, but she pushed forward.

In June of 1947, Carlotta graduated from high school.

"You should get a job, save your money, and go to college," Anna Mary insisted. "I'll help as much as I can."

Carlotta, however, had other plans. During the summer, she eloped with a young man she'd met while on vacation in Florida with her friends the summer before. They'd been writing letters throughout the course of her senior year.

Much to Anna Mary's dismay, the man was German. His name was Sigmund Lowe. His friends called him "Lion." The fact that he was a scientist with a bright future and held a good job with the government didn't sway Anna Mary's outrage. An argument ensued and Carlotta stormed out of the house. Anna Mary would never lay eyes on her daughter again.

Rosalie would often look at the photograph on her mother's bureau that showed Carlotta holding Rosalie on her lap when the latter was almost two with a small Christmas tree in the background.

Rosalie would study her sister's face. They shared their father's almond-shaped eyes and their mother's thick black curly hair. Both girls were petite in stature like their mother. Anyone viewing the photograph could see they were related. Even as a toddler, Rosalie had a thick crop of ringlets.

There was also a photograph of her father and brother.

When Rosalie viewed her family portraits, she became sad. She had a father and brother she'd never known. What was even sadder for the girl was that she had a sister who was still alive who she couldn't remember. Why, she often wondered, didn't she know her sister?

In early December of 1951, Rosalie asked her mother that very question. She had been preparing a list of people she wanted to invite to her seventh birthday party.

"Mama, can I invite Carlotta?" she asked, her deep brown eyes looking hopeful. "She never comes to see us. Maybe she'll come if I invite her."

Her mother became angry.

"No, never, and don't ever ask me again."

"But, why, Mama?"

It would be the first time Rosalie felt the rage that stirred inside her mother; a mother who, most of the time, was like a deep spring, gushing with love and patience.

"That one," Anna Mary had said, her face twisted with anger, "just snuck out in the middle of the night and eloped. Then she returned three days later with a thick gold band on her finger."

Anna Mary had stood and put her left hand on her tiny waist. She raised her right one with her index finger pointed. She was pretending to scold Carlotta. "How can you run off with a Nazi and get married after just losing your father to them. And it's because of *his* people that your brother is dead, too."

She then leaned closer to the frightened child. Their eyes met.

"Then your sister clenched her fists and insisted that he was not a Nazi. She said he was a scientist, like that made a difference."

Anna Mary's eyes were so filled with hatred Rosalie had to stop herself from bursting into tears. Anna Mary continued.

"They're all Nazis," she said through gritted teeth. "And I don't trust a one of them. So I told her they could forget about sleeping under my roof. I was terrified he'd kill us all in our sleep."

Rosalie gulped. She closed her eyes and the dark figure of her brother-in-law sneaking into her room to smother her with a pillow caused her to shiver.

Anna Mary continued.

"He's called Lion. What a ridiculous thing to call a man. And his family's rich, you know. And how do you think they got so rich?"

She paused, took a breath, and answered her own question.

3

"Oh, I'm sure it comes from their government. I just wonder what secrets they were relaying to the Nazis. Or maybe they're in cahoots with the commies."

Rosalie was used to her mother's use of the word "cahoots." Everyone who was scheming some diabolical plan was in cahoots, according to Anna Mary. Some of the other words weren't so easy.

Confused, she asked, "Mama, what's a commie?"

"Communists, Rosie. They're as bad as the Nazis."

Rosalie wasn't sure what a Nazi or a Communist was, but she learned that afternoon they were to be feared and never trusted.

"Your sister and I argued for a long time and then that little traitor stormed out of the house, taking everything she owned with her."

"Where do they live now?" Rosalie asked.

"They live in a suburb just outside of Atlanta, Georgia."

Rosalie had no idea where Georgia was, but she hoped it was far away. For days, she couldn't get the thought of her brother-in-law off her mind. She'd awaken in the middle of the night, sure the "lion" was lurking in the darkness.

By spring, however, it appeared Anna Mary had a change of heart. She had opened an invitation, read it, and called Rosalie to the kitchen.

"Your sister has had a baby. She has written and asked that we attend his christening. I won't go, of course. They're Lutherans."

"What's a Lutheran?"

Anna Mary rolled her eyes.

"You know that we go to a Catholic church, right? Well, she goes to a Lutheran church. She even changed her religion, that one."

"Is that bad?"

Anna Mary shook her head.

"No, it's not bad. It's just not Catholic. Anyway, I thought it over and I've decided to allow you go."

A knot formed in the pit of Rosalie's stomach.

"I have to go see the Nazi?"

"He won't hurt you."

"But you said he'd kill me in my sleep."

"Don't be such a nervous nelly. That's just an expression."

Her explanation did little to calm the child's fears.

Chapter 2

Sigmund Lowe was born on March 9, 1924. He was the only child of Reinhart and Herta Lowe. Reverend Lowe was the pastor at St. Paul's Lutheran Church in a small countryside town twenty miles from Berlin.

He could read by the age of three and astounded his parents with his ability to recall lists of names, dates and long rows of numbers. At four, they hired a piano teacher named Naussner, no first name, just Naussner.

"Your child is amazing," he proclaimed after the first few lessons. "I've never seen anyone take to the instrument so quickly."

By the time he was six, he was playing Bach and Mozart with the hands of an experienced pianist.

At eight, he was pushed into a higher grade at school.

"Reverend Lowe," said the school headmaster, "your son is getting into mischief because he is bored. He needs to be challenged."

Since he was tall for his age, he fit well into the upper class. That was where he met Otto Kramer, a lanky boy with hair so blonde it was almost white and faded blue eyes. He reminded Sigmund of the morning mist.

Sigmund was able to retain all of his lessons with acute understanding and could recall the information at will.

At the same time, unlike his new friend, he couldn't be persuaded to believe anything that didn't make sense to his logical thinking. At that time in Germany, intense propaganda became a daily ritual for the children. It had no effect on him.

"Papa, they say we should hate the Jews. This is wrong, yes?"

Reverend Lowe would nod.

"Keep your beliefs to yourself, son, but keep your beliefs."

While it seemed to Sigmund that his teachers were more interested in sports and building a strong body, he continued to outshine his classmates when it came to intellectual matters.

When it became obvious to his teachers that his ability far overshadowed his classmates, he was sent to a university to finish his studies. He graduated at fifteen with the highest marks in his class.

He was then sent to the University of Technology where he received a Bachelor's degree in mechanical engineering in just under two years. Interested in rockets and space travel and displaying a high aptitude, he was sent to the Friedrich-Wilhelm University of Berlin. He graduated two years later with a PhD in physics.

Before his nineteenth birthday, in 1943, he was summoned to Berlin for an interview for a position at a government-run laboratory.

"Father, the laboratory is far from here. I'm afraid I'll have to live within the confines of the facility that houses the laboratory. At a time like this, with so much turmoil in our country, I don't want to live so far from home. What if you and Mama need me?"

"Don't worry about us. I can take care of Mama. There is nothing here for you? You must go and follow your calling. You are a scientist."

The Lowes only justification for letting go of their son was he would be working alongside some of the most brilliant minds in Germany. Surely, they realized, he would be safe.

"And," Reverend Lowe told his wife, "it's either the laboratory or the battlefield. Surely, he will be better off there."

A week later, after kissing his mother and shaking hands with his father, the nineteen-year-old was escorted to a waiting vehicle by two soldiers.

As the sedan pulled away, he looked back to see his parents standing on the walkway that led to the church, waving and throwing kisses. Although they were still in sight, he could already feel the pain of separation. It wasn't like when he left for school. He had gone willingly, excited about the opportunity that awaited him. This, however, was different. He wasn't given a choice. It was an assignment from Adolph Hitler himself. On top of that, he could feel the animosity of the driver and his companion.

"We will have to blindfold you, Dr. Lowe. The facility is top secret," said the driver.

At that, the other officer leaned over the back of the front seat and tied a piece of black fabric over his eyes.

The drive to the facility took more than three hours.

"Where is this laboratory? Is it far from my family?" he asked from the darkness.

"It is in Germany," the man replied in an angry tone. "And that is all you need to know."

Eventually, Sigmund realized the smooth highway had turned into a bumpy road. After fifteen minutes or so, the same officer who had covered his eyes spoke.

"Lean forward and I will remove your blindfold."

Why, Sigmund wondered, did he seem so angry.

"Am I in trouble?"

"No, quite the opposite. This is not a punishment. This is a great opportunity. And you should learn to appreciate what the fuhrer is giving you instead of whining about leaving your family."

Sigmund settled back into his seat. A great opportunity? What, he wondered, was so great about being taken away from his family and forced to work in a secret location, a location unknown to him?

The car pulled up to a guard house where a soldier perused the documents he was handed by the driver.

"Everything is in order," he said and returned to the guard house.

The heavy iron arm that had blocked the road lifted quietly into the air and the car drove beneath it. After a few seconds, they came to a high chain-link fence. Another soldier slid a portion of the fence to the right, allowing the car to pass through. Sigmund looked out of the rear window and saw that it was immediately returned to its position, creating the barrier that would keep the unwanted out and, he knew, those who were retained there, in.

They followed a gravel road through a thick forest. Finally, they came to a clearing.

The first building he saw was a white marble, two-story, with long slits for windows that sat to the right.

"This is the laboratory," said the driver.

They passed a strange structure made from what he assumed was concrete. It was circular and consisted of several pillars. The top appeared as an open cap, joining the vertical posts.

"What is that for?"

"That, my good doctor, will be the secret you will be asked to keep. Just as the location is our secret, what goes on here is unknown to us," the driver said.

A need-to-know basis, he thought. Perhaps, he wondered, that was why they seemed annoyed with him.

"The living quarters are straight ahead," the driver said.

Sigmund noticed three smaller buildings, also white marble. Oddly, he realized that while all of the buildings in the complex stood majestic and well maintained, the grounds were naturally landscaped with nothing more than stone walkways between the structures. Of course, he thought, what gardener would be trustworthy enough to work at such a top secret facility.

The car stopped and the soldier in the passenger seat immediately got out and hurried to open the door for Sigmund. The driver opened the trunk and retrieved Sigmund's two suitcases, one containing his clothing, the other his books.

"Welcome, Dr. Lowe," a voice called.

Sigmund turned to find a man rushing up the walkway from the center apartment building. He, unlike the two with whom he arrived, seemed pleasant, almost joyful.

His round face and wide eyes made him appear jolly. He had a white beard and his hair reached to the base of his neck. Sigmund thought he resembled a photo he'd seen of a Christmas elf. He immediately like the man.

He put his hand forward and the man grasped it with both of his.

"I am Dr. Auman. It's indeed a pleasure to meet you. We've heard a lot about the prodigy, the brilliant Sigmund Lowe. And you are how old, son?"

"Nineteen, sir."

"Nineteen. My, my, that is most amazing."

Sigmund didn't notice that his riding companions had returned to the car until he heard the crunch of tires on the driveway. He watched as the vehicle disappeared around a curve in the road.

"Come, I will show you to your quarters. You can refresh yourself and meet me back here. I am ever so anxious to show you our facility. Oh, my dear boy, you are in for quite a treat, quite a treat."

"Thank you, sir."

He followed the jolly man, noticing that high fences topped with barbed wire surrounded all of the buildings within the complex.

"You will be in the first building," he said. "As you can see, there are three. Each contains four apartments, two on each floor.

"Each scientist, and there are twelve of us, is assigned to a fully furnished unit, complete with a living space, fully-appointed kitchen, bedroom and bathroom."

Sigmund's apartment was on the second floor. The furnishings, although sparse, looked new. The floors were covered with thick carpeting.

"Just in case the downstairs neighbor needs sleep," he said, making a motion to indicate that a carpeted floor would allow him to move about quietly.

Sigmund smiled and nodded.

"Behind the apartments," Dr. Auman added, "you will find a separate building that houses a gymnasium, sauna and library. There is an attendant on duty at all times."

Dr. Auman shook Sigmund's hand again and left him alone.

Sigmund appraised his new home and, to his own surprise, discovered a good feeling settled within him. He unpacked his suitcases and stored them in a closet in the bedroom.

He opened the refrigerator and discovered a quart of milk. He located a glass in a cabinet over the sink and filled it. In another cabinet, he discovered a box of sugar wafer crackers. He ate several, downing them with the milk. He realized he was hungry.

The clock on the wall over the kitchen table that had two matching chairs, told him it was almost dinner time.

"No wonder," he muttered and ate two more sugar wafers.

Although capable of eating more, he was anxious to see the grounds. He left the apartment and went outside.

He walked to the other building, the one containing the laboratories. There was a small structure that blocked the way to the main entrance. He was met by a burly man in the common military uniform, complete with the familiar swastika emblems on the jacket and hat. He was tall with a broad chest and reddish skin.

"So, you are the new one, eh?"

Sigmund nodded.

"Sigmund Lowe."

"It's nice to meet you, Dr. Lowe. I am Franz. If there is anything you require, ask me and I will see that you get it. You can use any of the facilities when you are not working. Your work day will begin at six in the morning until six in the evening. You will have a half hour break for your mid-day meal, however, you must remain in the laboratory structure. There is a cafeteria where you can eat.

"For your evening meal, groceries will be delivered to your apartment once a week. You will be given a list of available foods. You will put a checkmark by what you want."

"What kind of food?"

Franz laughed.

"Ah, so you don't cook, eh?"

Sigmund laughed and shook his head.

"No, I'm afraid not."

"Well, don't worry, everything will be to your convenience. You are one of the chosen. It is my job to see to it that you have everything you need."

The chosen? Sigmund wondered. Chosen for what?

He thanked Franz, received an identification badge and headed along the gravel walkway to the building that contained the laboratories. Once again, he was stopped at the double glass doors that refused to yield to his push. He noticed a large green button to the side. He pressed it.

Overhead, a screen that he hadn't noticed lit up and Dr. Auman's face appeared. The door made a clicking sound.

"Come in, my boy."

Sigmund entered and the door closed behind him and clicked again. He didn't take five steps when a door to his right, marked "Sicherheit", opened and Dr. Auman emerged.

"Come, come. I'm like a giddy child. We are working on the most amazing project."

Sigmund sensed his excitement and, although he was somewhat intimidated by the security and secretiveness of the facility, his heart began to beat a little faster. He quickened his gait to keep up with Dr. Auman as the elfish man took the stairs two at a time.

At the end of the hall, they stopped at two massive iron doors.

Dr. Auman placed his hands on the bar of each door and pushed.

"This is it," Dr. Auman said as light filled the space around them.

Sigmund's pulse raced even faster when he saw what was inside. The enormous room was brightly lit from overhead as well as with daylight that poured in from the window-lined walls.

There were several computers lined against three of the four walls. Sigmund had read about the first programmable computer invented by his fellow countryman, Konrad Zuse, in 1941.

"What are these? Are they Z3's?"

9

"No, these are far more powerful than the Z3."

Sigmund then focused on a large table in the center of the room. What sat on top of it caused him to hold his breath. It was unlike anything he'd seen before, yet he knew it was significant.

"Do you know what this is?" Dr. Auman asked.

"It looks like a space capsule," he said, his eyes scouring every inch of the thing. "What is this writing?"

He referred to a series of hieroglyphs that were etched into the bottom of the capsule. They looked like those found inside the pyramids in Egypt.

When he lifted his gaze, Dr. Auman was staring at him with a most peculiar smile.

"Egyptian?"

"Yes," he said, his grin growing wider. "And no."

Sigmund allowed a confused look to cross his face.

"Yes and no? What does that mean?"

"It is similar to Egyptian hieroglyphs, but where did they get them?"

"What do you mean, sir?"

Dr. Auman smiled.

"This inscription is a mixture of Egyptian and," he said, pausing just long enough to make Sigmund lean closer.

"And?"

Dr. Auman rolled his eyes upward and smiled.

"Them. It came from them."

"Them? Them, who?"

"Well, my boy, let me put it this way; about four years ago, a strange object came streaming out of the sky right here in the countryside of our beloved Germany. A month later, seventeen laboratory complexes like this one were built. Each one has a specialty. All on demand of the fuhrer himself"

"What is ours?"

"Time travel."

Sigmund laughed.

"Oh, is this my initiation? Are you trying to see how gullible the new guy is?"

He was surprised to find that Dr. Auman didn't as much as crack a smile. His joyful demeanor made a complete one-eighty turn. Instead, he held a frozen expression.

Sigmund wasn't sure what to make of the news. Time travel, he thought, was impossible. Has the fuhrer gone madder than people thought? Is he really wasting the country's resources on such nonsense?

"Within five years, the German military will have the most powerful weapons and we will govern the entire planet," Dr. Auman said. "You see this small bell-like structure? Well, we will build one larger and it will be launched from there."

Sigmund followed the finger that pointed to the cylindrical structure he'd seen upon his arrival. It was clearly visible through the tall windows.

"God has smiled on Germany, my boy."

Sigmund had heard that the German Faith Movement proclaimed God had not manifested Himself in Jesus Christ, but in Adolph Hitler.

Reverend Lowe had become enraged at such a claim. From that day forward, he told Sigmund, he'd work tirelessly against the Nazi regime and everything for which Hitler stood. Now, he thought, he had landed in the middle of the whole mess. Afraid to say the wrong thing, he became silent.

"Go home and rest, son, and think about what I just said."

Sigmund returned to his apartment, ate a sandwich with a glass of wine, and stared through the window pane at the gnarled barbed wire that, in his heart he believed, held him prisoner.

What did Dr. Auman mean when he rolled his eyes upward? Was he talking about extra-terrestrials or God? Either way, the thought that people followed a man like Hitler was frightening on its own, but to assume he was *chosen* by either a higher intelligence or God was downright terrifying.

He was reminded of a conversation he'd had with his close friend, Otto Kramer, about the imprisonment and extinction of those who didn't fit into Hitler's vision of a master race.

"They don't kill the Jews because they are a threat," Sigmund had argued. "They kill them because they aren't part of the so-called Aryan race. We all know the stories of many non-Jewish people who are being killed, as well. And this is wrong, Otto, wrong."

His friend had defended the actions of Hitler, hailing him for his *vision*. Now this, a declaration that the man was receiving assistance from a higher, other-worldly source.

Sigmund rinsed his dish and wine glass, dried them, and put them away. He showered and climbed into bed.

He didn't sleep that night, not for a single second.

Chapter 3

It was spring of 1945, two years since Sigmund arrived at the government facility hidden deep in the German countryside. He and his colleagues had made considerable progress in the field of time travel.

Then, less than a month ago, Adolph Hitler ordered the obliteration of all scientific projects and the execution of the men who worked on them.

It was by mere coincidence that Sigmund escaped the same fate.

For three weeks, the young man remained hidden in the forest. The once well-manicured gentlemen looked more like a wild animal. Being isolated at a secret government facility, he was permitted to let his hair grow longer than the accepted style of the era.

Now, dirty from nights of sleeping beneath the brush, his hair was unruly and unkempt. His coarse beard crawled over his face like weeds in an ignored garden.

From within the thicket of the bushes, his intense blue eyes searched the area. A small noise to his left caused him to crouch low. It was a red deer coming into a clearing, its massive body and antlers impressive. Sigmund reached for the knife he formed from a thick branch checking to make sure its point was still sharp. He stood and in that instant the animal sensed his presence and took off in the opposite direction.

"*Verdammt*," he seethed, his stomach grumbling.

He examined his makeshift weapon and smiled.

"This would hardly kill you, my friend," he said as the massive rump disappeared into the woods. "A poke, no more."

He reached into the small bag he constructed from the sleeve of his shirt and produced several small berries. He didn't know what kind of berry he had been eating, but he'd seen the birds filling themselves on the crimson treat and decided that if it was safe for them, they'd be safe for him. As he ate, he walked into the clearing.

"Come on back, mister deer, Sigmund is starving," he said, also in his native language. "Maybe you have a friend, a rabbit perhaps."

Sigmund, feeling defeated, sat by a tree, resting his head against its gnarly finish. He wondered how he was still alive. He kept telling himself it must be God's will. Surely, it was with Divine guidance that he narrowly escaped being slaughtered with his colleagues.

How long ago was that? He had lost track. And how, he wondered, did a smart boy end up being a hunted man and, worse, by his own people.

A crisp breeze climbed over the thicket of the woods. Sigmund shivered and pulled the collar of his lab coat tighter around his neck. He was seated with his back to an oak, his knees close to his chest.

He'd finished the last of the berries he picked from the bushes along the riverbank. At one time, he loved all kinds of berries. However, he had been living on them for the past three weeks and knew that if he made it home alive, he'd never eat another for the remainder of his life.

He looked at his wristwatch. It was just past three in the afternoon. Three o'clock. He smiled. Mentally, he was back in his lab. It was only a year ago, but it seemed like a lifetime.

He and his colleagues, who now included his childhood friend, Otto Kramer, had successfully moved a small, bell-shaped metal box containing a pocket watch with the time set to three o'clock.

He shook his head as he recalled the moment when he reached up and set the coordinates into the vibrational accelerator, a device that sat on a hanging shelf attached to the ceiling. It was set to move the object fifteen minutes into the future.

"Ready?" Dr. Auman had asked.

He and his colleagues nodded. There was an overwhelming sense of excitement as they moved behind a glass wall and watched as Dr. Auman pressed the large square button on the side of the accelerator. He hurriedly joined his staff behind the wall, watching and waiting.

"Oh, my God," whispered Sigmund as the space around the box began to shimmer.

It looked like a mirage as waves of air from above became more and more active around the box until it began to glow. The antennae-like rods attached to the accelerator began to spit out what could only be described as lightning bolts. After two minutes, the box itself began to shimmer and, in an instant, it disappeared.

"It's gone," Dr. Auman said, sounding triumphant.

"Yes, now let's hope it reappears," Sigmund said.

The others chimed in with their agreement. They waited, watching the clock on the wall, the minutes seeming to last hours. Then, as the taller hand met the number three, the area beneath the antennae began to shimmer. Static seemed to fill the room, and flashes of light beams bounced off the table.

The men stared in awe as the metal box reappeared in the exact location it had sat fifteen minutes ago.

Dr. Auman rushed to the table and flipped open the cover. He pulled out the pocket watch and held it up.

"Three o'clock," he said. "We have successfully moved an object through time, and the object has not aged, not even a second."

Sigmund shook his head at the recollection. What a triumphant day, he thought.

During his second year at the facility, the scientists had executed two more experiments; one that moved an hour in time and a third that didn't reappear until the following day precisely at noon.

The men had been locked away in the complex with no distractions from beyond the gates. If it wasn't for Otto Kramer, who had special permission to leave the premises, they would not have known that the war was not going well for Germany. The allied forces were closing in on Berlin.

Sigmund thought about the morning less than a month ago when Otto knocked on his apartment door. He'd been asleep.

"May I come in?" he'd asked. "I know it's early, but I have news."

"Yes, come. Were you able to contact my parents?"

Otto looked down for a long moment. When he lifted his gaze, his pale blue eyes were filled with tears. Sigmund felt a cold shiver. What *bad* news, he thought, was about to be handed to him.

"I'm afraid your parents were killed in a bus accident. You know with the war, one never knows when they will come in contact with a land mine. The bus containing several youths from the church overturned and tumbled down an embankment. It burst into flames. They were heading into the woods for a retreat. I'm so sorry, my friend, but everyone perished."

Sigmund couldn't move. Otto placed his hand on his shoulder and patted it.

"I remember when your parents took us on those youth retreats."

Sigmund nodded, recalling several trips with other boys where they'd sit around a campfire and discuss the Bible.

"They were good people and I am so sorry to give you this sad, sad news," Otto added. "You will be permitted to go home and claim their property. Perhaps take personal items."

He recalled how the next morning the same soldiers who delivered him to the complex escorted him to his father's church.

"You may stay until tomorrow," the driver had said.

"I'm not sure if that's necessary," Sigmund replied.

"Decide for yourself. We will be in the café at the end of the street."

Sigmund thanked them and watched as they drove to the corner.

He realized they'd left him in the spot where he last saw his parents waving and his mother throwing kisses. A hard knot formed in his throat and his eyes welled with tears.

When he walked through the double doors of the small church, it felt unusually cold, even though it was already April and the air warm.

"Sigmund," a woman said, her voice almost a whisper.

He turned to find his mother's closest friend, Elsa Stein, her tall, slim form coming out of the darkness.

"I barely recognized you," she said, gently kissing his cheek.

"We are very comfortable at the lab. Since we are kept inside the gate, many of us have let our hair grow and our beards, as well."

She hugged him tightly and whispered words of comfort in his ear. He nodded, returned her kiss and stepped outside. He stood on the walkway for a few minutes, recalling his childhood as the pastor's son.

He went into the residence where he and his parents had lived. Once inside, he packed all of the photographs, personal mementos, and legal documents that belonged to his parents. He had to admit, there wasn't much.

With a small suitcase in hand, he walked the length of the street.

"Here," one of the soldiers called, waving him into the café. He stepped inside and took a seat at their table.

"Have you decided? Are you ready to leave?" the driver asked. "As I said, you are permitted to stay overnight if you wish."

"No, that's not necessary. There is nothing for me here."

After a light meal, Sigmund was returned to the complex. He joined his colleagues in the laboratory just as Dr. Auman was holding a meeting.

"Tomorrow, we make history," he said. "We will move something an entire month forward. This is very exciting."

Sigmund couldn't feel the excitement as he had other things on his mind. After the meeting, he approached Dr. Auman in the hall.

"Where's Otto?" he asked.

"He's in Berlin with the fuhrer. He's a favorite, that one."

"When will he return? Will he be here for the experiment, too?"

"He's due back tomorrow morning. Don't worry, son, you'll be able to enjoy your triumph together. I know you are close friends.

"And, Sigmund, let me speak for myself and our colleagues, we are very sorry for your loss. But, at times like this, sometimes it's best to wrap oneself up in work and try not to focus on the past."

Sigmund thanked him and went to the laboratory to help set up the vibrational accelerator for the next day's experiment. They were expecting an entourage from Berlin. There was talk of Hitler attending the send-off.

He was barely able to sleep. He rose with the sun, took a shower and looked at his reflection in the bathroom mirror. His hair was already touching the base of his neck. His beard was thick.

"You need a shave and a haircut," he said to his reflection. "But not today. Today, we make real history."

He dressed and hurried to the laboratory. One of his colleagues, Dr. Holtz, was sitting at a desk in the far corner of the lab.

"Have you been here all night?" Sigmund asked.

"Yes. I was checking our calculations as they must be perfect. Remember, we are not only moving the bell into the future, we are also relocating it at our sister laboratory ten miles away. And, I'm pleased to say, everything is ready."

"Good. I am anxious. They say the fuhrer may come today."

Dr. Holtz shrugged.

"Yes, me, too; quite anxious. I am sure our leader wouldn't want to miss this amazing event. Our bell will travel through time and space."

Sigmund stepped to the window and peered at the place behind the laboratory. The large bell-shaped object, at least twenty feet high and ten feet wide, was tethered to its brace, the large cylindrical structure made of concrete. It had several openings around the sides, making it appear as an upside-down crown. From the top ledge, chains were strung across, meeting in the middle where it adhered to the top of the bell. It was deep bronze with a large swastika painted in the center, an exact replica of the one he'd seen upon his arrival.

The vibrational accelerator was poised to send the force needed to propel the bell forward.

"I'll be back shortly," Dr. Holtz said. "I want to get a quick shower."

When he left, Sigmund checked all of the connections. There was nothing left to do but wait. He paced the floor in nervous anticipation.

From a side window, movement caught his eye. He went closer and saw several jeeps approaching.

One of the soldiers in the last jeep jumped out and turned to face the small guard house. Franz emerged, his uniform tidy. He saluted the soldier and before his hand returned to his side, the soldier fired his rifle.

From the soundproof building, it was as though he watched a silent film clip as Franz moved backward with the thrust of the bullets and fell silently to the ground, his chest soaked crimson.

The jeeps moved toward the apartments. He wasn't sure what to do next. His palms were moist and his heart pounded so hard, it hurt.

He watched in horror as his colleagues were pulled outside, a few still in their pajamas, Holtz naked and wet. They were lined up and, without pause, shot to death, their blood staining the stark concrete.

Sigmund gasped, held his breath for a few too many seconds and let it out. Tears sprung to his eyes, spilled onto his face and down his neck; so many, he was forced to close his eyes tightly to control them.

"Oh, my God. What's happening?" he said.

When he opened his eyes, he saw a soldier, most likely the leader, moved along the bodies, making sure they were dead. His back was to Sigmund.

In order to get a better look, Sigmund rushed to Dr. Auman's office and peered outside. He watched as the soldier stopped at the spot where Dr. Auman lay and turned him over. He could see Dr. Auman's mouth move. The soldier leaned closer to hear the dying man's words. He said something and, without pause, pulled out his weapon and shot him between his eyes.

Again, Sigmund jumped. He stared at the doctor's lifeless body, wondering why the Germans would kill their most brilliant scientists.

He couldn't believe that so much horror could take place in but a minute's time. He knew he had to get out of the building and find a place to hide. From a small bathroom window that had been left open, he heard voices. He got on his knees and moved closer.

"There's one missing," the leader shouted. "Find him. No one can leave this facility."

Staying out of sight, Sigmund crawled back to the laboratory where he was able to stand. He looked around the room, his eyes wild with fear. Then, without further hesitation, he rushed to the vibrational accelerator. He heard footfalls in the main hall. There was no time to set the coordinates. Instead, he slammed the palm of his hand into the large square button.

Outside, the bell began to shake. Sigmund hoped to draw the attention of the soldiers long enough to make an escape. From his spot by the accelerator in front of the large observation window, bolts of lightning burst outward, creating a curtain of electrical currents around the bell. It began to shimmer.

"Go to the laboratory and shut that goddamned thing down! Hurry," an angry voice demanded.

Now it seemed every soldier was heading toward the laboratory.

Sigmund went back into the bathroom and climbed out of the window. Shielded by two pine trees, he balanced himself on the window ledge. He stepped onto a row of decorative marble tiles, his back plastered to the wall of the building. His heart racing, he moved along the edge where it met the corner. With nowhere to go, he jumped toward the last tree.

"Son of a bitch," he cursed in German, as he fell through the yielding branches.

He grabbed a thick branch and held tightly. Around the corner of the building, he could see the flashes of light and hear the crackling of static as it bombarded the bell. In a second, the area became silent.

The bell was gone.

He jumped to the ground and headed toward the perimeter. When he reached the fence, he climbed up and, wrapping the barbed wire with his lab coat, climbed over. His wrists were already bleeding from the places where the barbs tore through the material. He pulled at the coat, not wanting to leave it behind.

He ran as fast as he could, for as long as he could. Branches slapped at his face as though angry that he should trespass into their quiet domain. No one followed him over the fence and the forest was too thick to permit any of the vehicles. He was certain, however, soldiers were behind him, their weapons ready to end his life.

Keep moving. Keep moving and don't look back.

He had covered his trail as he moved. That was more than three weeks ago. There was nothing beyond the point he'd reached but a river.

He stood and walked to a spot, a pinnacle where he could see the movements in and out of the gate. There had been no activity for several days. Even the gatekeeper had been taken away and, he noticed, the gate left up. He found that odd.

Tired and hungry, he made the decision to return to the complex. By early evening of the following day, he reached the gate. He was so exhausted, he could barely walk.

As he got closer, he was surprised to see new activity. Jeeps and trucks passed freely through the gate.

"No swastikas," he mumbled.

He noticed a jeep parked on the road just beyond the guard house. It had the insignia of the United States Army. There was a man seated in the guard house smoking a cigarette and reading a magazine.

His head jerked upward when he heard the snap of a fallen branch, his pistol drawn. The man immediately lowered his weapon when he saw Sigmund.

"Holy shit! What happened to you?"

"I was lost in the woods."

The man gave him a thorough once-over and grabbed a walkie-talkie from inside the guard house.

"Hey, Captain, I think I found your missing scientist."

A crackling noise delivered a response. He settled his gaze on Sigmund and smiled.

"What does he look like? He sort of resembles the guy you've been looking for," he replied and winked at Sigmund. "But, to be honest, he looks like a lion, large mange, fuzzy face, piercing eyes."

The voice crackled again.

"Sure, you got it."

He turned to Sigmund.

"He wants us to wait here. I can't leave my post."

"You are American, yes?"

"Sure am, born and raised in the great state of Texas. Hey, are you hungry? I got some crackers in here."

He went inside the guard house and picked up a knapsack.

"Here you go, crackers. They have peanut butter on them."

Sigmund accepted the food. Without asking, the soldier handed him a canteen.

"It's just water, but you look like you could use it."

He drank hungrily from the canteen, then stuffed another cracker into his mouth.

"Thank you," he said.

"Cigarette?"

Sigmund nodded. Before it was half smoked, a jeep sped to the gate and three men jumped out, surrounding Sigmund.

"What's your name?"

"I am Dr. Lowe."

"Sigmund Lowe?"

He nodded and took another long drag on the cigarette.

"Well, we've been looking for you, Dr. Lowe. Looks like your pals murdered all of your colleagues."

"They are not my *pals*," he said, sounding angry.

"Well, that's real good to know because if they're not your pals, we won't have to shoot you."

Sigmund noticed a sense of lightness in his tone.

"What is your name?"

"I'm Melvin Gold."

"You are a Jew, yes?"

"Yeah, why? Oh, that's right, you people don't like Jews."

"I don't dislike anyone," he said. "Except for the bastards who killed my colleagues, that is."

Captain Gold laughed.

"I know what you mean. You know, we were hoping to find one of you alive. It seems we found two. All of the other scientists are dead."

"I know. I witnessed what happened. Who else is alive? Is it Otto Kramer? And what about the laboratory? And the bell?"

Captain Gold shrugged, indicating he had no answers. He motioned toward the jeep and Sigmund climbed inside. One of the soldiers got into the driver's seat. The others remained at the guard house.

"Are you hungry?"

"Starved. I ate peanut butter and crackers from the soldier in the guard house. It was very tasty."

"Well, there's a lot of food and water still in your apartment. We went through all of the units. I noticed that the Nazis rummaged through all of them. I don't know what they were looking for."

"I would assume anything related to our research. I have some files, but I'm certain they did not find them. They are sewn into the lining of my winter coat."

"Ah, very clever."

"Yes, my papa used to say to trust no man who could kill another simply because they are different."

"Your papa sounds like an intelligent man."

"Yes, he is."

"I can tell you this, they didn't leave a shred of evidence of the work done here in the lab. They emptied it out, down to the last tidbit of paper. To be honest, Dr. Lowe, it looks like nobody ever worked there.

"I'm assuming you did. Am I right?"

"Yes, you are correct."

"What were you working on?"

Sigmund wasn't sure how much to reveal, so he remained elusive.

"We were doing experiments."

"What kind of experiments? And what in all that's holy is that contraption over there?"

Sigmund knew he was talking about the concrete circle that had housed the bell. When he looked in that direction, he wondered if it moved forward in time or if the Nazis had taken it. Captain Gold got out and walked the perimeter of the concrete structure.

"Damn, this is the oddest thing I've ever seen."

"It has a purpose. Well, it had a purpose."

"I assume one day you'll tell me just what its purpose was, huh?"

"It held a vehicle. We called it the bell because of its shape."

"And what did this bell do?"

"As I said, it was a vehicle. It traveled."

Captain Gold shook his head, obviously reaching the assumption that he'd get no more information from the doctor. He changed the subject.

"How long have you been out there in the woods?"

"I think about a month. What date it is?"

"It's the middle of May."

"How is it that you are here and not the SS?"

"Because, my friend, we kicked their asses and sent them packing. The war's just about over. Hitler is dead. The Third Reich has fallen. We've been searching for the scientists who worked on Hitler's secret projects."

"Why?"

"Because we want you to come to America and bring your knowledge with you."

Gold got back in the jeep and as they drove on, he reached over and touched the driver's shoulder.

"Pull up to the unit on the end."

The driver stopped in front of Sigmund's building.

"Your friend is waiting inside your apartment."

Sigmund shook hands with Captain Gold and climbed the stairs. When he opened the door, he was greeted by Otto.

"Sigmund, you're alive. Oh, thank God. I was just about to pack up your things. You look terrible."

"Yes, I know. The American at the gate said I look like a wild lion."

At that, Otto, laughed.

"Then, that will be your new name, Lion."

He hugged Sigmund tightly. Sigmund was filled with emotion.

"Otto, my dearest friend, I'm so glad you were not here when the SS came. It was so horrible. I can't erase the images from my mind."

"I arrived as they were leaving," he said. "I pulled into the woods and waited. They took everything, everything!"

"What about the bell?"

At that, Otto laughed aloud.

"No, they didn't get the bell. I heard one of them say it disappeared right before his eyes. Sigmund, what happened?"

"I hit the button and sent it into the future. I believe it is at the second laboratory. I don't know where as only Dr. Auman knew its coordinates."

"No, it never arrived there. Luckily, it was not armed," Otto said.

"What did you say?"

"What did you think we were going to use it for? The bell, I've been told, was designed to house a particle accelerator. It could carry bomb grade uranium. Hitler planned to program it to land in the heart of any country that defied his demands."

20

"A bomb?"

"Yes, my friend, a bomb. What else would we want to deliver to the enemies of Germany? By the time they realized what power we had, there would be no one left but us, the Aryan race, the Nordic race, the master race. All others are dangerous to society and needed to be eliminated."

"And you agree with this?"

His angry words caused Otto to back up. He seemed to collect his thoughts, Sigmund surmised, weighing his response.

"We believed Hitler was our leader, delivered to us from God Almighty. The pure-bred Nordic leader. I've been taught this since childhood. Of course, now things have changed."

"Yes, things have changed. According to the American outside, Hitler is dead. The Third Reich has fallen."

Otto put his hand on Sigmund's shoulder.

"Sigmund, my friend, let us put all of this behind us. They want us to go to America and work for them."

"So, what will you do?"

"Hell, I'm going to America. And, in light of the death of your parents, I'd suggest you come along with me."

Sigmund smiled and said, "My parents are not dead. They are in Switzerland."

"What? How?"

"The bus accident was not real. The people on the bus were not from Father's church. They were Jews from our village. I spoke to Mrs. Stein. You remember her, yes?"

Otto nodded. Sigmund continued.

"She said the gestapo had been asking a lot of questions in the town about anyone hiding Jews. Obviously, even though they knew the war was coming to an end, they still wanted to rid Germany of Jews. Such nonsense.

"Nevertheless, Father knew many in his congregation were doing just that, hiding their friends in attics and basements. He and Mama planned the whole thing to get them out of Germany. As a matter of fact, she said the entire congregation was in on it."

"That's wonderful," Otto said, sounding somewhat insincere. "Well, why don't we get your parents and we'll all go to America."

Sigmund stared at his old friend and wondered about his motives. He would do anything Hitler asked. Would he be as dedicated to a new leader?

For the first time, he questioned the friendship that had bonded them throughout his life. He wondered if Otto Kramer could be trusted.

Chapter 4

On Thursday morning, Anna Mary put Rosalie in a taxicab belonging to her friend, Harry Pinella. He was heavyset with black hair upon which sat a dark baseball cap with the Yankees logo, a white "NY."

"Don't worry, Anna, she's in good hands," he reassured her. "Ready to go, Rosie?"

Rosalie kissed Anna Mary good-bye and climbed into the taxi.

"Hi, Mr. Pinella. Yes, I'm ready."

"So, you're going to visit your sister, huh?"

Rosalie nodded.

"You're gonna love flying in an airplane."

"I hope so. I'm a little afraid."

Pinella laughed.

"There ain't nothing to be scared of, little one. Airplanes are safer than cars. You just relax and you'll enjoy it."

After that, he didn't say much else during the trip to the airport.

When they arrived, he got out and hurried around the taxi to open the door. He tipped his hat to a woman wearing a blue uniform with a wings emblem on the pocket.

"Take care of my girl," he said, handing her Rosalie's ticket.

The woman accepted it, smiled broadly and took Rosalie's hand in hers. Rosalie realized the woman was chatting much like Mr. Pinella. She assumed that was how adults spoke to children. She noticed it was different from the manner in which they spoke to each other.

The airport was crowded. The woman weaved in and out of the throngs of people. When they reached the gate, she handed an attendant Rosalie's ticket.

Her eyes widened at the sight of the airplane outside the gated area. She followed the attendant to the movable stairs beside it.

"Have a good trip," the woman said.

Rosalie looked up. To the seven-year-old, the steps appeared endless. Her heart beat wildly all the way to the top where a flight attendant greeted her at the door of the airplane and led her to an assigned seat in the second row, next to the window. She clung tightly to a gift wrapped in blue paper with angels on it. An envelope addressed to Carlotta was taped beneath the bow.

"You can put that on the floor," the attendant said. "I promise, no one will touch it. Just slide it under the seat in front of you."

Rosalie placed the gift on the floor and pushed it forward with her foot.

She held her breath as the airplane raced up the runway and let it out as it took off. She enjoyed the feeling of lift-off. She never shifted her gaze from the window and imagined she was on a magic carpet flying above the clouds.

It seemed to take a long time to get to Georgia. When the airplane landed, another woman escorted her to a tall man with thick blond hair that had a natural wave to it. His eyes were a brilliant shade of blue and his complexion smooth. When he opened his mouth to speak, she noticed he had perfectly straight white teeth.

"Hello," he said, bending forward. "I am your brother-in-law, Sigmund Lowe. How are you?" he asked politely.

The sound of his accent caught her attention.

"I'm okay," she said.

She wanted to hate it, but there was something about it that intrigued her. He wasn't dark and foreboding; he was light and elegant.

"Where's my sister?"

"She's home, resting."

"Is she sick?"

"No, no. She was up with Stanley all night."

Stanley, she knew, was the baby's name.

As they walked toward the parking lot, he asked, "Did you have a nice flight?"

"It was okay," she answered in a low voice.

The truth was that she enjoyed every minute of it. For her, it was the adventure of a lifetime. She loved the way it felt when it took off. She couldn't stop looking out the window at the clouds. And when it touched down, she felt the thrill of speed as it headed toward the terminal.

He nodded and smiled.

"I like airplanes. I always have."

She wanted to talk about the experience but decided it was best not to become too familiar with him.

When she didn't respond, he didn't say anything until they reached his car, a long black sedan.

"Would you care to sit in the front or back?"

"I don't care."

He opened the front door. She wished she had opted for the back seat. When she hesitated, he asked, "The front is okay, yes?"

"Yes," she said and slipped into the passenger seat.

He took her suitcase and the gift and placed them on the back seat.

She peered through the window as they crossed two bridges, not speaking. The second led them to a long, winding road lined with trees that reached across to form a majestic green arch.

Rosalie leaned forward, looking up.

"It's nice, yes?"

She jumped.

"Yes. It's pretty."

"I like it here. This is my favorite roadway. It feels as though we're in a magical tunnel, no?"

"Yes, it does feel like that," she said. "Is the house much farther?"

"Just a little way. You are growing anxious to see your sister, yes?"

"Why do you add a yes and a no to your questions? Is that how na--, I mean German people speak?"

She wondered if he caught her near slip. When she turned to look at him, she saw that his view remained on the highway.

"I'm sorry. Yes, we often speak that way. I think it is because we are new to English. After all, Rosalie, I was born and raised in a place where German was spoken. Sometimes, it's difficult to speak English like an American. Forgive me."

Rosalie wasn't sure how to respond to his answer. She wondered if she had offended him. Her stomach began to hurt. She rubbed it and turned her head toward the side window.

"Are you alright? Are you going to be sick?"

"No, I'm fine," she said.

"It's not much further."

After a few minutes, Rosalie felt compelled to make amends.

"I didn't mean anything wrong. I don't mind if you ask questions like that, really. I was just asking."

"That's good because my parents often ask questions in that manner, too," he said.

Oddly, she noticed, he didn't seem angry. Rosalie could almost hear a hint of laughter in his tone. She looked at him and realized he was, in fact, smiling. She smiled, too.

"They do?"

"Yes. I hope you don't find it too annoying."

"No, it's okay. I don't mind. I sort of like it."

Now, he laughed.

"Oh, so you like how clumsy I sound?"

She didn't want to. She even tried to stop herself, but she laughed, too. And she especially liked the manner in which he spoke to her, unlike Mr. Pinella and the lady in the blue uniform.

After a few seconds, she turned to him.

"You're funny."

"Oh, heavens. Funny. No, I'm afraid not. Carlotta says I'm always too serious. She said I'm not fully Americanized."

"Is that why my mother said you're a Nazi?"

At first, he didn't say anything and Rosalie was sure she'd gone too far. She'd angered him and now she'd be in danger. However, he merely replied in a soft voice.

"Rosalie, I am not a Nazi. It's very complicated and I wouldn't expect a person as young as you are to understand. But, I assure you, my family and I are not Nazis."

Of course, he'd deny it, she thought.

"You believe me, yes? I mean, you do believe me, don't you? There, is that better?"

She wanted to smile, but she didn't dare. Instead, she lowered her head and shrugged. What, she wondered, would her mother think if she heard them sharing such a nice conversation.

"I don't know. Can we talk about something else?"

"No need. We are here."

They passed through an arch made of stone. On one side, it read, "Silver Peach Acres" in crisp silver letters. Once inside, she noticed a building with tall columns lined up along an open patio. Over the door, it read, "Clubhouse." Behind it, she saw a recreation area. There were tennis courts, a swimming pool and what looked to her like every outdoor play-set imaginable. She smiled, hoping to get to spend time there.

The streets were laid out like a large horseshoe with each house situated on one acre. Sigmund drove to the left of the clubhouse and followed the curve of the road until he came to the entrance of a driveway flanked with bronze lions. He turned in and pulled up to a spot where a brick-paved walkway led to an expansive house.

From her spot on the driveway, she could see behind the house where a row of four garages with a second floor apartment was located. The building reminded her of a motel she had visited on vacation as it had a full balcony that ran the length. A dark man was on the second floor smoking a cigarette. When he saw the car, he walked down the stairs and greeted them.

"Hello, Dr. Lowe," he said, a wide smile on his face. "Can I help you with anything?"

"No, we're fine. This is my sister-in-law, Rosalie. She prefers to be called Rosie."

The man leaned down and peered into the car.

"This is Mr. Johnson. He lives in the apartment above the garage. He is a gardener."

"A gardener?"

"Yes. He is the man who takes care of the grounds, cuts the grass and plants all of these beautiful flowers. He also takes care of the peach trees behind the house."

Even from inside the car, she could tell Mr. Johnson was a large man. His skin was dark brown and smooth. When he smiled, he had straight white teeth. He had the widest shoulders she'd ever seen. The white tee-shirt he wore seemed to stretch to its capacity to cover them. A pack of cigarettes sat within the folds of the sleeve, perched on his bulging arm muscle. When he spoke, his voice was as soft as a whisper.

"How do you do, Miss Rosie?" he said as he removed his straw hat and nodded politely. "Welcome to Georgia."

His hair, she noticed, was short and curly. Rosalie thought her hair would look the same if she cut it. Even at the tender age of seven, she could sense his kindness. She immediately decided she liked the gardener.

"Thank you, Mr. Johnson. And I really love peaches."

"I do, too," he said and smiled broadly.

Sigmund got out, walked around the car to open the door for Rosalie. Mr. Johnson opened the back door and retrieved her suitcase and the gift.

"Looks like the missus is chomping at the bit to see her little sister."

Sigmund smiled and agreed, accepting Rosalie's things.

"I think you are right on that."

"Enjoy your stay, Miss Rosie. Your sister's been looking forward to this all week."

Carlotta, who had been waiting at the door, rushed to the car as soon as Rosalie's feet touched the pavement and fell to her knees. She hugged her so long, Rosalie thought she'd never let go.

"Why did you move so far away?" she whispered.

"You're young and might not understand, Rosie, but I need a lot of distance between Mama and me or I would go crazy."

She had no idea what that meant, but she was glad Carlotta called her by her preferred name.

As if reading her mind, Carlotta added, "Ruthie told me you prefer to be called Rosie. That's right, isn't it?"

"You talk to Aunt Ruthie?"

"Yes. She lets me know how Mama's doing."

"Well, Mama put a letter with Stanley's gift."

Carlotta anxiously looked for the envelope. She removed it from the gift and slid it into the pocket of her sweater.

"Well, come on inside and I'll show you to your room. I fixed it up especially for you," Carlotta said.

Rosalie entered the house and found herself in a tiled foyer. To the left was a set of closed double doors. To the right sat a large living room. She could see a dining area just past a television and slightly around the corner, through an arched opening. In front of her was a hall that led to what she assumed was the kitchen as she could see cabinetry.

Carlotta turned down a hall that branched off to the left just past the double doors.

On the right, she noticed a nursery. It was definitely a boy's room, she thought, as she spied the blue walls, blue plaid curtains and a mobile featuring four brown stallions. On the dresser sat a lamp, its base was a matching brown horse.

Straight ahead, she noticed what appeared to be her sister's bedroom. The furnishings looked like things an adult would use.

Next to it, to the left, she saw another door.

"That's a guest bedroom," Carlotta said.

She stopped and opened a door to a fourth room directly across from the nursery. In contrast to Stanley's very blue room, everything was in shades of pink.

"You like pink, yes?"

"You sound like him," she said.

Carlotta laughed.

"Yes, I suppose I do. They do that a lot; make a statement and add a question to the end. It's funny. You're pretty smart to pick up on it."

Rosalie shrugged.

"Mama said you're just like them."

"Who?"

"The na--," she began and stopped herself. "Mama said you're just like them Germans."

"It's *those* Germans, not *them*, and, of course, that's not true. I'm my own person. It's just that when you live with people, sometimes you pick up their accent or turns of phrase.

"Anyway, *do* you like pink?"

"I suppose so."

Carlotta seemed irritated and began to tear nervously at a fingernail. Rosalie wondered if she hurt her sister's feelings.

"I-I'm sorry, Carlotta. And, yes, I do like pink and your house is really beautiful."

At that, Carlotta seemed to settle down, a bright smile replaced the look of strain that seemed to mask her face. Even at the tender age of seven, Rosalie could tell her sister was upset. She wondered why it was so easy to make her get like that. She wondered if it was because her sister was miserable living with Sigmund.

"Are you happy here?"

"Why, yes, of course. Why wouldn't I be happy? I have a wonderful husband, a beautiful son, a loving family and now my precious little sister is visiting me. I'm extremely happy right now. Why would a little munchkin like you even ask such a question?"

She leaned toward Rosalie and pinched her cheek.

"You're such a funny little one, you know."

Without waiting for an answer, Carlotta left Rosalie to unpack the few items she brought.

Rosalie placed them in a small bureau by the window. She pulled the curtain aside and noticed a play set in the backyard. Suddenly, her mood lifted and she decided to enjoy her time in Georgia.

Surely, she thought, the Nazi wouldn't murder her in her sleep with his baby son in the room just across the hall.

27

For Rosalie, her three-day visit turned out to be more pleasant than she'd anticipated.

On the first day, she met her nephew, Stanley Stephen Lowe, a chubby infant with bright blue eyes and a thick crop of yellow curly hair. Most of the time was spent talking to Carlotta who seemed to have a lot of questions.

What grade are you in? What school do you go to? What's your favorite subject, color, food? Rosalie enjoyed sharing her thoughts with her sister.

On Friday, Rosalie noticed Sigmund wasn't home and took the opportunity to speak more freely.

"Is your husband a nice man?"

"Oh, yes, of course," Carlotta reassured her.

"Where is he now?"

"Work. He works a lot. He's a scientist."

"I don't know what that is."

Carlotta laughed.

"Well, to be honest, I'm not sure what he does. I know he works in a laboratory. He's very smart; a genius, actually."

Still unsure of her brother-in-law's profession, Rosalie smiled and accepted the fact that whatever it was he did for a living was most likely not against the law.

On Saturday, Carlotta assigned her the task of arranging fresh flowers in tall glass vases. Once in a while, Sigmund would pass by and pat her on the head. He'd ask if she needed anything. As much as she tried to despise him, she found him to be a most agreeable man.

On Sunday, she met Sigmund's parents, the Reverend and Mrs. Lowe. He was a tall man with white hair, combed straight back, and light blue eyes. She was medium height with short brown hair and soft gray eyes.

"Aren't you a sweet little girl," Mrs. Lowe said.

Rosalie smiled and wondered if she was a Nazi, too.

The reverend seemed preoccupied with the baptismal ceremony. He checked his ideas with Carlotta who seemed agreeable with everything he suggested. After a service at St. John's Lutheran Church where Reverend Lowe was the pastor, a service that lasted more than an hour and followed by another twenty-minute baptism, they returned to the house.

Carlotta had hired a woman from a neighboring town to serve food and a man with a funny mustache to serve drinks.

The day seemed to fly by. When the party ended, it was time for Rosalie to leave. The grandfather clock by the front door made three gongs.

"Come on, little one," Sigmund said. "We must hurry. Get your things. Your plane leaves in an hour and a half and it takes almost an hour to drive to the airport."

She hugged Carlotta for as long as she could, crying into her shoulder.

"I'm gonna miss you."

Carlotta held her arms out straight, her hands resting on Rosalie's shoulders.

"Yes, me, too. Maybe Mama will let you come again during the summer when school's out. Would you like that? We can go to the lake. We have a small boat," Carlotta said.

"I'll ask Mama."

One last hug and she was on her way, once again rolling beneath the green canopy, over two bridges and straight into the airport parking lot. A woman was waiting for her by the entrance.

"I hope you'll come and visit us again," Sigmund said.

She looked into his face. Why, she thought, did he have to be a Nazi? If not, she was sure she could have liked him. It was as though he could read her thoughts because he allowed a sad frown to crease his brow.

"Maybe," she said. "Thanks for the ride. I-I mean, thanks for everything. It was real nice."

He nodded, his frown evaporating.

"You' are most welcome. We enjoyed having you visit."

The trip home was as exciting as the trip there. When she got off the airplane, another woman escorted her to the waiting taxi of Mr. Pinella. He pulled away from the airport and drove onto the highway.

"So, Rosie, did you enjoy your trip?"

"Yes."

"Did you have a good time at your sister's house?"

"Yes. I have a nephew."

"Yes, I know. Your mother told me. I've been friends with Anna Mary for a long time. We grew up together."

"Did you know my father, too?"

"Guido? Yeah, I knew him, too. Your daddy's a hero. You know that, don't you?"

"Yes, he died at the Battle of the Bulge," she said, repeating Anna Mary's words.

"Well, don't ever forget that he died so we could be free."

"Did you go to the war with Daddy?"

"I went to war, yeah, but I was down there in the South Pacific. I was fighting the Japs. Your father fought the Nazis."

Rosalie became quiet, wondering if the man was trying to make a point. After a mile, he spoke over his shoulder again.

"Don't let them fool you, Rosie. You can't trust a Jap or a Nazi, ever. And those commies are even worse. You just listen to your mama."

She nodded.

"Okay Mr. Pinella," she said.

After that, Harry drove in silence. For the first time, she noticed how drab the city was compared to the Georgia greenery. When she arrived home, Anna Mary was waiting on the front stoop of their apartment building. Harry got her suitcase from the back seat and handed it to Anna Mary.

"Thanks, Harry. I owe you one."

Harry patted Rosalie on the shoulder.

"Remember what I said. Don't trust anyone but your mother. Loyalty's important."

He pulled the taxi away from the curb and waved to them.

"Harry's a good man, a veteran," Anna Mary said. "He only has one leg. Thank God it's his right one or he wouldn't even be able to drive a cab for a living. That goddamn war."

A feeling of guilt seemed to crawl up Rosalie's back and wrap itself around her shoulders. It felt heavy and cumbersome.

Once inside their apartment, Anna Mary placed a bowl of chicken noodle soup in front of Rosalie.

"So, how did you get around down there?"

Rosalie, trying to muster her loyalty, replied, "The Nazi drove me in his new car."

Anna Mary smiled.

"And the little Nazi, what's he like?"

Rosalie pictured Stanley's cherub face and bright eyes.

"I don't think he's a Nazi, Mama. He's really little," she said, tears welling in her eyes.

Anna patted her shoulder.

"Okay," she said. "Don't get upset. I was only kidding."

Rosalie wanted to talk more about Stanley. It seemed the moment she set eyes on him, she fell in love. Carlotta allowed her to feed him and help her with his bath. She wanted to tell her mother about the experience.

Anna Mary, however, asked little else about the baby, glancing briefly at the photograph of him that Carlotta had given Rosalie. Anna Mary sat it on the table. She asked nothing about Carlotta, either.

"So, what's her house like? What does the Nazi do all day? What did you eat? Tell me everything."

"I liked it there. It's real quiet and all of the houses have grass around them. There's a park with a pool and swings. At the party, Sig, I mean the Nazi played music on the piano, and we ate strudel. It's German cake."

To Rosalie, her mother seemed disappointed. She felt as though she had failed her in some way.

"I'm sorry, Mama. I guess I shouldn't have had so much fun there."

Anna Mary patted her shoulder.

"Don't worry so much. Go, get ready for bed. You already missed two days of school because of your sister. You have to go in tomorrow."

"Are you mad at me, Mama?"

Anna Mary let out a long sign.

"No, Rosie, I'm not angry with you."

Rosalie went to her room, unpacked her suitcase, and got ready for bed. After a bath, she put on her nightgown and climbed into bed. Anna Mary came in and kissed her good night.

"Really, Rosie, you have to stop being such a worrywart."

Rosalie, tired from the long day, drifted off to sleep with visions of her nephew in her head.

In the days that followed, it seemed to Rosalie that her mother had lost interest in her Georgia adventure. When she asked Anna Mary if she could visit Carlotta again, the woman seemed annoyed.

"We'll see," she said and the subject was dropped.

The following year, a month after her eighth birthday, Anna Mary and Rosalie moved into a housing project in Brooklyn, New York; the same one where the Goldbergs lived.

For Rosalie, it was a move up. She was glad to be rid of the dark, smelly hallway and the trains that woke her in the middle of the night. She hated the building in which they lived. She hated the dark hallway that smelled as though too many types of food were being cooked at the same time. She hated the naked light bulb screwed into a yellowed socket with its wire exposed that hung from the ceiling at the top of the high narrow stairs.

"It's so dark I can hardly see the steps," she complained.

"It's a blessing," Anna Mary said. "That hallway is a mess. At least you don't have to see the ugly dark brown paint. And, although, I try, I cannot keep the steps clean. I was the only one in the goddamned building who took the time to clean them."

Rosalie wanted to protest. Her mother's version was something akin to a lie. She'd push the broom into Rosalie's hand and demand she sweep the steps. She held her tongue rather than receive a slap on the side of her head for sassing her mother.

Mostly, she was glad to be away from the rats she often heard scurrying about, scrounging for food. More than once, her mother had to call the building superintendent to set traps. She'd hear them snap in the middle of the night and immediately pull the covers over her head.

In the projects, they had a bright two-bedroom apartment with a small kitchen, a dining area and a nice-sized living room. Rosalie had her own room with a large window that overlooked the play area behind the building. Anna Mary, recalling Rosalie's description of her room at Carlotta's, purchased a bright pink bedspread.

Rosalie liked the projects. She loved her new room and the green grass and bushes that surrounded the three- and seven-story buildings.

Even though, at one point when she had asked several times, she was warned never to ask if she could visit Carlotta again, she was permitted to send greeting cards and an occasional letter. For that, Rosalie was thankful. At least, she thought, she could find out how her beloved Stanley was doing.

Chapter 5

It was summer of 1955. Anna Mary had taken a job as a secretary at the Northeast Presbyterian Hospital, a short half-mile from the project development.

With the country on the rebound after the war, the prosperity had filtered down to the struggling Anna Mary. Finally, she found a little extra money in the budget.

"We're going to go to Brighton Beach every week," Anna Mary had promised.

"Every week?"

"Yes, Rosie, every week. Saturday will now be our beach day."

For Rosalie, now ten, she was anticipating the best summer of her life.

Anna Mary kept her promise. For four weeks, they had a Saturday morning ritual. They'd eat breakfast, pack bologna sandwiches for lunch and head down to the train that took them to Brighton Beach Station. Rosalie would tell Anna Mary about whatever book she was reading as they walked the three long streets to the beach holding hands.

Anna Mary had even inquired about Stanley. Rosalie didn't know if it was the beach, the sun or the fun, but it appeared her mother was beginning to let go of some of her anger. More than anything else, she loved her beach days.

The Monday after their fourth outing, Anna Mary returned to work and came in contact with a pneumonia patient. By the following week, she couldn't get out of bed. By the last day of July, her body was so weak, she suffered a heart attack and died.

Rosalie watched, in horror, as Dr. Zimmerman pulled the sheet over Anna Mary's face right there in the apartment. Ruth Goldberg, her mother's closest friend, rubbed the girl's shoulder the whole time.

"You'll be okay, Rosie," she whispered. "God has a plan for you."

When the men came in an ambulance and took Anna Mary away, Rosalie sat on the edge of her mother's bed and wept until she felt sick to her stomach. Finally, after she spent every ounce of pain that had been bottled up inside, she looked into Ruth's wizened face.

"God has a plan for me? Then how come He took everyone away, leaving me all alone? It's just not fair."

Ruth didn't try to explain about the unfairness of life. Instead, she pulled the girl close and allowed her head to rest on her shoulder.

"I feel like a lost soul, Aunt Ruthie," she said. "What's going to happen to me? Can I live with you and Uncle Rudy?"

She looked into the mirror on Anna Mary's bureau and watched Ruth's reaction; a gentle shaking of the head.

"No, I'm sorry, honey," she said with a slight accent that colored her words. "Our apartment is too small. And, besides, you should be with your family. You will go live with your sister."

"But she's married to the Nazi."

Ruth locked gazes with her in the mirror.

"Now, don't be so fast to judge, little one."

"But his people killed your people." she said, repeating her mother's mantra.

"But Sigmund has killed no one."

Rosalie couldn't understand how she could feel that way.

"Mama said all the Germans were Nazis and not to be trusted. And even Mr. Pinella said so. He said not to trust Japs either. I think he means Japanese people."

"Now, now, don't say things like that. Besides, it's the law. You have to go live with your family. Remember, Rosie, while all Nazis may have been Germans, all Germans were not Nazis. Do you understand this?"

Rosalie nodded, still apprehensive of the new living arrangement.

"I wish you really were my aunt then the law would let me live with you," she said, her mouth pouting. "Aunt Ruthie, what's that mean, the law?"

Ruth smiled and kissed the top of her head.

"The government, sweetheart. The law is what the government tells us we must do."

"Oh, great. The government is sending me to live with my sister and her Nazi husband."

Ruth shook her head.

"Rosie, stop. You sound like your Mama. You're too young to hold onto such hatred. I'm telling you, it's that kind of thinking that caused your mother to have a heart attack. One should never burden themselves with so much hatred.

"Besides, didn't you have a nice time when you visited her when the baby was born? Didn't Sigmund treat you kindly?"

Rosalie shrugged.

"Yeah, he was nice, but that was because I was only visiting for a few days. I'm not sure if he'd be too happy to be stuck with me all the time. What if he makes Carlotta send me to an orphanage?"

"Oh, my goodness, child, Carlotta would never allow such a thing. I talked to her this morning. She said she's happy to have you live with her."

"What about the Nazi?"

"Listen, Rosie, it will not serve you to call him that. You must put all that behind you."

She cupped her chin in her hand so their eyes met.

"Now, give Aunt Ruthie a big hug. Don't be mad at me for sending you to Carlotta's."

For the first time in her short life, Rosalie felt like a victim. She hugged Ruth as tight as she could, her mouth close to the woman's ear.

"It's just not fair," she said, and began to cry again.

Chapter 6

The day of the funeral brought an onslaught of mixed emotions for the ten-year-old. Mostly, she was sad and afraid of what the future held for her now that she was on her own.

Her coal black hair hung in soft waves around her face. Normally, she wore her hair parted in the middle with pigtails or braids. Ruth had suggested something a little more formal for the funeral.

"You want to make your mama proud, don't you? Well, one way is to look your very best to honor her life."

Rosalie had sat quietly as Ruth set her hair in large curlers and had her sit underneath the hood of a hair dryer for an hour. Ruth removed the curlers and an entirely new hairdo sat atop her head. Her usually curly hair was smooth and wavy.

"I don't look like me," she said.

"Sure you do, only now you look a little more like your sister."

Rosalie thought about Carlotta; the way she looked when she'd visited her three years ago. She glanced at her reflection.

Yep, I do look just like her.

The Goldbergs drove her to the church.

"You can stay here and greet mourners or come and sit with us," Ruth said when they entered the vestibule of the church.

"I'll stay here," she said, remaining as close to the double doors that led to the street as possible.

Rudy patted his wife on the shoulder.

"Leave her here. She has to do this her way. Come on, let's sit."

"Are you okay, Rosie?" a familiar voice asked.

She turned to find Harry Pinella standing by the inside doors.

"Yes, I'm okay. I'm waiting for Carlotta."

"Hmm, I see. I suppose the Nazi is coming, too, huh?"

Rosalie shrugged.

"I suppose so."

He patted her shoulder and turned away, entering the church.

Rosalie remained by the door as a small parade of distant relatives and a handful of friends made their way down the long aisle and past the coffin. She couldn't go near it.

"Hello, Rosalie. I'm your father's cousin from upstate New York," said a middle-aged woman with stained gray hair and a small black hat with a veil that touched her long wide nose. "You look so much like your sister when she was your age."

She wanted to explain that it was because she was wearing Carlotta's hairstyle. Instead, she mumbled a short, "Thank you."

"You girls are so pretty. You look just like your daddy. Oh, yes, he was a handsome boy. We grew up together in Yonkers."

Rosalie had no idea of the location of Yonkers. To her it was foreign. Her father's cousin pinched her cheek and turned away. She watched as the heavy woman waddled toward the altar. She couldn't imagine the older woman as a child, small and thin, running about with the childhood version of her father. Then again, except for a few photographs, she had no recollection of her father. He, like her brother, was nothing more than a sepia image in a gold frame.

Rosalie had mixed feelings. She was angry at her father for dying at the Battle of the Bulge and leaving her mother to fend for herself with two little girls. She was angry with her mother for leaving her alone. She was angry with Ruth and Rudy for not allowing her live with them. And, she wondered, why couldn't she live with the second cousin?

Since she hadn't seen Carlotta since Stanley was an infant, three years ago, she wondered if she'd be glad to see her again. The last time she heard from her sister was a few months ago. She'd sent her an Easter card.

Rosalie felt as though she was unable to breathe. She stepped outside, just in time to witness the arrival of her sister and brother-in-law.

From afar, Rosalie thought Carlotta looked like a movie star. She wore a black suit with a crisp white blouse and high heels that had straps curling around her ankle. She had a heavy gold necklace draped around her neck and her wrists were laden with gold bangle bracelets. The sun reflected off her diamond earrings.

Carlotta walked toward the church with Sigmund at her side. He wore a black suit, too. His bright white shirt contrasted against the black tie and sparkling tie-clip that matched his cufflinks. The sun was bright that morning and it seemed to shine on them, making them sparkle.

As they approached the top step, however, Rosalie noticed Carlotta's face looked tired and drawn; dark circles spread well below the dark glasses she wore. Her long black hair was pulled back severely and tied at the nape with a black scarf.

"Hello, Rosie," she said in a sad voice. "Were you waiting for us?"

Rosalie immediately began to cry. It was as though it was bottled up inside like soda and someone shook her so hard she exploded.

"I can't go in there," she said, her voice sounding shrill.

Carlotta wrapped her arm around Rosalie's shoulder.

"Come on, we'll go in together. There's nothing to be afraid of."

As they walked toward the coffin, Rosalie began to tremble. As soon as she saw her mother's face, her knees buckled. Suddenly, Sigmund had hold of her other arm. She could feel him pushing her forward. She wanted to snatch it away and tell him to leave her alone. She didn't dare look at him.

As they approached it, Carlotta knelt on the padded kneeler that had been placed alongside the coffin. Sigmund stood behind her, his iron hand still wrapped around Rosalie's thin arm.

In her mind, she could hear Anna Mary's ire toward him. He wasn't to be trusted. Then Harry's words echoed in her mind. She had to remain loyal to her father's memory. He died fighting the Nazis. There was no way she could allow a Nazi to become a friend. She owed it to her parents. She was almost tricked into liking him when she was seven, she told herself, but she's ten now and he wouldn't fool her again.

She finally summoned the courage to yank her arm free. He stepped back as she knelt beside Carlotta.

"What am I supposed to say?" she whispered.

"Just pray that she's at peace."

Even at ten, Rosalie knew that wasn't happening.

"Peace? She was never at peace when she was alive," she whispered. "Aunt Ruthie said she was angry at the whole world."

"I know, but she's at peace now. She's in God's hands. She's with Daddy and Stephen."

Rosalie had no response to that. Her mind raced.

Mama and Daddy and Stephen are with God and I'm stuck here with no one to look after me. God, why don't you take me, too?

She blessed herself and stood. When she turned around, she noticed Sigmund standing to the left, his head bent. She suddenly had the urge to kick him in the shins.

He was the one who caused her mother so much stress. He was the one who was responsible for her father's death. And he was the one who snatched her sister away.

I hate the Nazi, too.

Carlotta was at her side, once again ushering her along the middle aisle to the first pew. They held hands all during Mass and, when it ended, they walked back to the vestibule arm in arm.

Several family members hugged Carlotta and told her how fabulous she looked. Rosalie thought she looked beaten down. That, too, she decided was the Nazi's fault.

Rosalie rode with them to Holy Name Cemetery where Father James said a few words. Afterward, everyone seemed to scatter in all directions. Rosalie stood by her mother's grave and stared at the coffin. It was made of a rich wood with large brass fixtures. Carlotta was at her side holding her hand as the coffin was lowered into the ground. When it reached its final destination, Carlotta said, "Come along, Rosie."

Rosalie lifted her face toward Carlotta.

"Where?"

"We'll take you home. We'll pack your things and you can come live with us in Georgia. You can have your pink room back. I kept is fixed up for you. I really thought Mama would let you visit. It's all still there."

While the thought of returning to the pretty room she'd used when she visited sounded like a good idea, Rosalie looked up at Sigmund and somehow knew she couldn't live under the same roof as a Nazi. She thought about her mother's warning that he'd kill her in her sleep.

With these thoughts bouncing around in her head, she felt the need to distance herself from him. She backed away and the heel of her foot missed the edge of the opening. She fell backward, almost tumbling into the open grave, on top of her mother's coffin.

"Rosie!" Carlotta exclaimed, her eyes wide. Her mouth made a perfect oval. She reached for her, but it appeared she was just out of range. Suddenly, a strong hand had her by her upper arm and was pulling her forward.

Sigmund literally lifted her off the ground and landed her next to Carlotta who hugged her tightly, rubbing her arm where her husband had grabbed it.

"Are you okay?" she asked.

Rosalie's heart was pounding.

"Crap. I almost fell in with Mama."

Carlotta suddenly burst out laughing. Rosalie wasn't sure why, but she began to laugh, too. She wondered what others thought seeing Anna Mary's only children standing by her grave laughing like hyenas.

She looked around and found that, thankfully, everyone had left.

Rosalie turned to thank Sigmund and realized he had walked toward the car. At the edge of the grass, he opened the front door and waited.

Carlotta walked toward him and got in. Rosalie stood there wondering if he'd hold the door for her, too. Much to her surprise, he opened the back door and turned toward her.

"Are you coming, Rosalie?"

His accent was still strong, guttural.

She didn't answer; instead she walked past him and climbed in the back seat.

"Thanks," she muttered.

"You are welcome," he said.

It sounded like "velcome." She wanted to spit at him.

She watched him through the rear-view mirror as he drove. Carlotta cried as she blew her nose and wiped her eyes.

"You must stop this, Carlotta. It is not good for you to stress yourself out so much."

"I can't help it. I hate to think that my mother died hating me."

"Let it go, Carlotta. Just let it go."

Rosalie wanted to speak up, but somewhere inside, she was afraid to disrespect her mother.

After a few minutes, they didn't speak of it and Carlotta seemed to settle down. At least, Rosalie thought, she stopped crying and blowing her nose. It was already red and quite sore-looking.

Every now and then, Rosalie would catch a glimpse of Sigmund in the rearview mirror.

If he wasn't a Nazi, I could see how a woman would be in love with him. He is handsome.

The three years since her visit to Georgia didn't seem to touch him. He still wore his wavy hair in the same style and his brilliant blue eyes looked as vibrant as she had remembered.

When he turned to look at Carlotta, she noticed his strong profile, his straight nose and nice full lips; lips that now seemed taught. In her mind she could almost hear Anna Mary's words.

"He looks as though it would kill him to smile."

Then again, she reminded herself, they *had* just come from a funeral.

When they arrived at the fourth-floor apartment where Rosalie had lived with her mother on Farragut Road in Brooklyn, Carlotta packed some of Anna Mary's belongings in cardboard boxes. She went to Rosalie's bedroom.

"Do you want anything of Mama's?" she asked.

Rosalie was seated on her bed, staring at the floor, shaking her head.

"I got her necklace," she mumbled, without looking up. "That's all I want."

A lone box sat on the floor by the door. It held Rosalie's sole possessions. There were four dresses, six blouses, five skirts, one orange sweater, a winter coat that was a size too small, a pair of sneakers and a yellow rain slicker.

The only dress shoes Rosalie owned were on her feet. She had a stack of eight books, most of which she received as birthday presents, a worn jewelry box made of cardboard with a faded picture of a Victorian lady on the top, a bag with her personal care items and a worn teddy bear whose ear was hanging on by a thin thread.

"This is everything?" Carlotta asked. "Where are the rest of your clothes?"

Rosalie shrugged.

"This is all I have."

"Oh, okay. Well then, I guess that's that," Carlotta said. "Let's go."

Sigmund picked up the box.

"I'll put this in the trunk."

A noise from the hall caught Rosalie's attention. It was Ruth. She stood in the doorway as she spoke.

"I filled out the paperwork at the Tenant Office already."

Carlotta hugged the woman and thanked her.

Ruth smiled and patted her hand.

"As I said, not to worry. My son, Ira, is coming this afternoon. He owns a small second-hand furniture shop on Fifth Street. He'll take everything."

Rosalie followed Carlotta back into Anna Mary's bedroom. Rosalie heard the apartment door open and close.

Ugh, the Nazi's back.

Carlotta handed Rosalie her mother's jewelry box.

"I really think you should take this, too.

There was a larger box sitting on the bed. Rosalie saw that it was filled with the family photo albums, a few records, mostly Frank Sinatra, and her mother's keepsake box.

"That's Mama's letters from Daddy," Rosalie said.

Carlotta smiled.

"We'll take it."

Rosalie spied her mother's straw hat sitting on the shelf in her closet.

"Can I have that, too?" she asked, pointing to it.

Carlotta reached up and grabbed the hat, looking it over.

"God, Mama really loved this silly old thing."

"Yeah, I know; that's why I want it. Is it okay?"

"Of course. You won't actually wear it, will you?"

Rosalie gave it a "once-over." It was tattered. The straw was broken in spots and the ribbon was faded from the sun. Overall, though, it still felt study in her hands.

"I might," she said.

Carlotta allowed an understanding smile to touch her lips.

"Okay, but not in public. Promise."

Rosalie smiled back. That was so typical of Carlotta, she thought. Her mother often complained that Carlotta was too vain and that she was always concerned about how she looked in public. She would say, "Carlotta doesn't dress to please herself; she dresses to please everyone else."

Rosalie wondered how her mother knew that since she never saw Carlotta. Nevertheless, the girl thought, based on her sister's attitude toward the hat, her mother was probably right.

"Ready, ladies?" Sigmund asked. "Our plane leaves in two hours and I still have to return this rental car."

His accent was so distinct that Rosalie wondered how she'd ever be able to live with him. It would be a constant reminder that her father died in a country where almost everyone talked that way.

He picked up the last box and left. Carlotta was right behind him.

Rosalie stood in her mother's bedroom and took one last look. Her bed had been stripped down and the curtains removed from the windows. Some of her clothes still hung in the closet. She walked toward it and touched the blue dress, her pink housecoat and her favorite beige blouse. She looked down at her shoes. Rosalie removed her shoe and slipped her foot in one brown pump, then the black dress shoe and finally a slipper.

She leaned forward and smelled the clothing. Closing her eyes, she could almost smell her mother. A tear ran down her face. She wiped it on the sleeve of one of the blouses. A movement by the door caught her attention.

"How long have you been standing there?" she snapped.

Sigmund stiffened, obviously not used to being spoken to in that manner. Yet, she noticed, his eyes took on a gentle look.

"Long enough," he said in a soft voice. "Come along. Your sister sent me back for you."

"This is hard," she said.

"Death is never easy, Rosalie."

"I prefer Rosie."

"Oh, yes, that is right. I will try to remember that."

They walked down the long hallway that led into the dining area. Ruth was still there. She hugged Rosalie, then pulled away so she could look into her face. Even though she was only ten, they were the same height. That was why everyone called her "Ruthie" as it suited someone small.

"Come and see me sometimes, Rosie," she said.

"She will be permitted to visit if she wishes," Sigmund said. "I will buy her a plane ticket."

Ruth planted a kiss on Rosalie's cheek.

"There you go. Your brother-in-law said he'll even buy you a ticket. So, there'll be no excuses."

She reached out her hand toward Sigmund.

"Take care of my girl," she said.

"We will."

Rosalie frowned. How dare he touch her when his people killed millions of her people! And his accent grated on her. She wanted to scream at him that w's had a "waa" sound, not a "vaa" sound.

She kissed Ruth and followed Sigmund downstairs, through the stairwell lighted with long windows. They walked through the courtyard in front of the building, past the benches and the play area. Several of her friends and neighbors were outside. They waved or patted her back as she passed.

"Don't be a stranger, Rosie," called Mrs. Dougherty.

By the time they passed the grassy area where she'd spent many hours playing with her friends and reached the sidewalk, she was exhausted. Even at ten, she knew it was only fear that sapped her energy.

Sigmund opened the back door again and waited until she took one last look around.

"I'm gonna miss this place. I wonder how I'll ever make it."

"You are starting a new life, Rosie. One day, you will look back and wonder how you ever lived here."

She wasn't sure what he meant. She'd always felt lucky to live in the housing project. Sure, they were poor; but so was everyone else. There was a

41

certain amount of crime; but crime was everywhere. She looked at the seven-story buildings clustered together and spread out as far as the eye could see; windows by the hundreds.

Yet, leaving the safety net of her "projects" felt uncomfortable. She knew what she had; she wasn't sure what was ahead.

For a moment, she wanted to jump out of the car and run back to the security of the apartment. She knew she couldn't do that. By next month, new people would be sitting in her kitchen and sleeping in her bedroom. There was no place for her on Farragut Road anymore. She felt as though she was being exiled from her home.

Her heart raced and her palms became moist. She was never so afraid in her life.

Chapter 7

The flight to Atlanta was bumpy. Several times Rosalie thought she would surely wretch into the funny little bag Carlotta had handed her.

"Don't be embarrassed. Lots of people puke on airplanes," she whispered.

She looked through the small window and focused on the fluffy clouds. It was peaceful, almost magical. The sky seemed to explode with the most vibrant blue she'd ever seen. Suddenly, her stomach seemed to settle down.

"Something for the girl?"

She turned to find a flight attendant, a young woman with long blond hair, looking in her direction.

Sigmund, who was in the aisle seat, leaned his head in her direction.

"Rosie, would you like some ginger ale. It is very good for an upset stomach."

She nodded and he placed the order. Ten minutes later, she returned with two coffees and a soda. The cool liquid did, in fact, make her stomach feel better. That, and the fact that the airplane now seemed to be gliding on silk.

Rosalie was falling in love with flying again, just as she had when she was seven.

Carlotta slipped into a nap. Sigmund read a newspaper. Rosalie studied them. Carlotta was as beautiful as she'd remembered. Her long eyelashes rested on her olive skin. Her full lips fell slightly apart as she let out a slight sound.

When she looked at Sigmund, he was looking at her. She jumped.

"Your sister needs to rest. It has been very difficult for her."

"It hasn't been so easy for me either," she said.

"I am sure. Do not worry, it will get easier. I promise."

As she looked into his eyes, she wondered how he got the nickname of "Lion." She thought about the time she had visited the Prospect Park Zoo and saw a lion there. Sigmund didn't look like a lion to her. He had no full mane or facial hair of any kind.

"Why do people call you the lion?"

He didn't answer right away. Instead, he seemed taken aback.

"Who told you people call me that?"

"Mama."

He seemed to think over his response. He turned his gaze toward the aisle, then to the front of the airplane, then outside, past Rosalie to the open space.

"Why? It's a long story. I am not sure it is one you could understand. One day, when you are older, I will tell it to you."

Although she wanted to hear the story, she thought he had a reason for wanting to wait. Whatever that reason, she believed there would come a day when he would tell her. In the meantime, she decided, she'd simply put her own spin on it.

It probably has something to do with him and his Nazi pals.

The airplane landed in Georgia on time and a car was waiting to take them home. As they passed beneath the canopy of tree limbs on the road to Silver Peach Acres, a feeling of familiarity welcomed her.

She began to feel excited knowing she'd see Stanley again. When the limousine pulled into the driveway, the Reverend and Mrs. Lowe, emerged with the child.

Rosalie was surprised at how much *he'd* changed. The tiny baby was now walking and talking and looking like a tiny version of Sigmund. He wore a red and white striped polo shirt and a pair of white pants that reached his knees. He jumped up and down when he saw Carlotta.

The Reverend and Mrs. Lowe welcomed her with open arms as Sigmund unloaded the luggage and the two boxes that had been tied with string. He carried them into the house. The family followed. It seemed everyone was talking at the same time.

"I'll put on a pot of coffee. Dinner is almost ready," Mrs. Lowe said.

She and Reverend Lowe disappeared into the kitchen.

"Papa, is this the girl who's gonna live with us?"

Sigmund picked up Stanley and looked into his eyes.

"Yes, this is the girl. Her name is Rosie and she is your aunt."

Stanley looked at Rosalie and smiled.

"Hi."

"Hi," she said and approached him. "You don't remember me, but I came here to see you when you were a tiny baby."

Stanley didn't seem impressed with his new aunt. Instead, he turned his attention to Carlotta.

"Mama, is Rosie gonna sleep in the pink room?"

Rosalie recalled the lovely room where she'd spent three days.

"Yes, the pink room belongs to Rosie."

Sigmund put Stanley down and picked up the box with Rosalie's belongings.

"Follow me," he said.

"Me, too?" Stanley asked.

"Yes, you, too," Sigmund said and winked at Rosalie.

Rosalie followed him and Carlotta, and Stanley followed her. She could hear him giggling the whole way and wondered what he was up to.

When Carlotta opened the door, she discovered the surprise. The room was similar to how she'd left it except that there was a banner draped across the wall that read, "Welcome Home, Rosie."

"I helped Mama and Papa with it," Stanley announced. "It says your name on it. See?"

Rosalie looked at him and, once again, fell madly in love with his face. This new living arrangement, she decided, was exactly what she needed, Nazi or not.

"Unpack your things and come to the kitchen. My mother has cooked dinner for us."

"Mama Lowe makes the best pork and sauerkraut," Carlotta added.

Rosalie unpacked her meager belongings and looked around her room. She put her comb and brush on the bureau, looked at her reflection in the mirror and decided this might work. It just might work.

Getting settled in her new life was much easier than she'd thought possible. The pink room was now her own and she was permitted to add anything that suited her taste. Above her desk, she hung a photograph of her favorite scientist, Albert Einstein, a prize she'd received for taking second place in her school's Science Fair the year before.

Stanley, on the other hand, seemed to demand ownership of her and his attachment to her served to take her mind off her mother's death. It was only at night that she felt the pangs of her broken heart.

Carlotta did everything she could to make her feel at home. She took her to a nearby shopping center where she bought her an entire wardrobe for the summer and fall that included shoes, boots and sneakers. She gave her money to buy things like hair ribbons and barrettes.

"Is there anything else you need?" she asked.

"I hate to ask for anything else?"

"No, no, you just ask away. Whatever you need, I'll buy."

"Could I get a tablet and an envelope so I can write to Aunt Ruthie?"

Carlotta led her to a small writing desk in the corner of the living room. She opened a drawer.

"This paper is for letters. And over here are the envelopes. Stamps are in that drawer."

Rosalie opened the drawer to find pens and pencils lined neatly, stamps, a box with paper clips and a pair of scissors.

"You see. Everything you need is here. You can write to anyone you wish."

Rosalie felt very much at home. The only room she was not allowed to enter was Sigmund's office. Carlotta had, at least, given her a peek inside.

Rosalie had looked around. It was dark, stuffed with rich mahogany furniture and high-back leather chairs. A huge desk sat on a red carpet with a lot of intricate designs. A shelving unit stocked with books and various statues and photographs lined the wall that separated the office from her bedroom.

"Sig does top secret work, so we never invade his private space."

Rosalie shrugged. She didn't mind. However, she had to admit, it did intrigue her. For now, she decided, she'd stick to the rules.

After that, the summer seemed to fly by. They went to the lake every other day where Stanley ran around, pulling her along. Several times they fished off the side of their small motorboat. They ate peanut butter and jelly sandwiches and Orco cookies.

The gardener, Mr. Johnson, seemed busier than ever. Every time she saw him, he was working, either driving the lawn mower or planting something. And every time they crossed paths, he'd tip his straw hat and say, "Fine day, Miss Rosie."

When summer passed, Carlotta enrolled Rosalie in the Bradford Elementary School where she was tested and placed appropriately in the fifth grade. On the first day, she made friends with a girl named Denise Perry and a boy named Joseph Barnes.

Denise was slim with light brown, almost blond hair that hung to her waist in waves and green eyes. Joseph was a stocky boy with brown hair and dark blue eyes.

Rosalie divided her days between school, homework, her friends and time with Stanley. Carlotta always seemed to be somewhere in the background doing things for everyone around her.

For Rosalie, her life had turned from misery to delight. She couldn't believe that she could be so happy. She was even beginning to feel comfortable around Sigmund.

As October turned the trees orange and gold, Carlotta's mood seemed to change. She seemed more on edge than usual. Then, in the middle of the night, Rosalie heard Carlotta crying, her sobs drifting through the quiet house.

Rosalie had been asleep so, at first, she thought she was dreaming. She laid awake in the dark and waited. After a few minutes, she heard Sigmund's voice, his deep tones muffled by the intruding walls.

She couldn't hear what he was saying. It was more like a low, steady hum. She sat and tried to concentrate on her sister.

What's he doing to make her cry so hard? Just when I was starting to get used to him.

She could hear the words in her head, but they sounded more like Anna Mary's. Her heart ached with the depth of her sister's sobs. After a few minutes, she could stand it no longer and jumped out of bed, making a mad dash into the hall. She made her way toward the master bedroom at the far end.

She stood outside. She could hear her sister's voice now, frantic, almost hysterical. She rapped on the door.

Sigmund opened it half way. She could see Carlotta sitting in the center of their king size bed. Her dark hair hung like a mop around her face; her eyes were swollen.

"What's the matter with my sister? What did you do to her?"

"Listen, little one," he said, a deep frown creasing his brow, "I have done nothing to harm her. Go in. Ask her yourself."

Rosalie stiffened her back, lifting an indignant chin. She was surprised, however, when he held open the door.

In one easy swoop, Carlotta pulled her close and nestled her head into Rosalie's slim shoulder. She continued to weep in gut-wrenching sobs.

"Carlotta, what's the matter? Are you sick?"

Carlotta nodded into Rosalie's shoulder.

"Did you call the doctor?" Rosalie asked.

"He is on the way," Sigmund replied.

She didn't realize he was standing right behind her. She stiffened when she realized he was so near.

"Go back to bed," he said. "I will take care of my wife."

His hand landed on her arm. Rosalie was just about to yank it free when the doorbell's ring snatched their attention. Sigmund quickly turned away and went to let the doctor into the house.

The activity had aroused Stanley and the boy called for his mother.

"Go," Carlotta whispered. "Please go in and take care of Stanley."

"Are you sure? Maybe I should stay with you."

Carlotta nodded. Stanley called again.

"Go, please."

Rosalie passed Sigmund and the doctor in the hall. By now, Stanley was screaming for Carlotta. Rosalie rushed into his room.

"Mama, Mama, I want my Mama," he wailed.

Rosalie sat on the edge of his bed and took his small hands in her hands and looked into his distraught little face.

"Why's Mama crying?"

"Don't worry. Mama has an upset tummy and the doctor is going to make her feel better. You can see her tomorrow. In the meantime, would you like it if I slept in here with you?"

Stanley's gaze moved past her, toward the hall that separated him from his mother. He seemed to consider her offer. He sobbed a few times and nodded, laying his head on his pillow.

"I'll get my pillow and be right back, okay?"

"Yeah, okay," he replied in a weepy voice.

She went into her room and grabbed her pillow. As she reached the door, she heard Sigmund and the doctor in the hall. They were whispering.

"She should be admitted tonight," the doctor was saying.

Rosalie's stomach tied itself into a knot. She listened for Sigmund's reply. In a moment of selfishness, she imagined having to live in that house with only him and Stanley.

"Can we see how she handles the new medicine?" he asked.

"Sure. It's not mandatory, Sig, but it is my suggestion. She needs help. She's on the brink of a nervous breakdown."

Rosalie could almost hear her mother's voice in her head.

What mind games is the Nazi playing on Carlotta? What guilt is she feeling for being with a man whose people murdered her father and brother? Was he experimenting on her with drugs?

Rosalie tried to shut them out, but she could feel her mother's anger gripping at her spirit.

She stepped into the hall. Sigmund turned abruptly and eyed her. Rosalie squinted her eyes, giving him the dirtiest look she could muster. She wanted him to know she was on to him. He wasn't going to get away with driving her sister crazy. She turned in a deliberate fashion and marched into Stanley's room, making sure to throw one last look his way.

He stared back at her, as though he wanted to say something. Whatever it was, she didn't want to hear it. Somehow or another, she believed, she had to get her sister and nephew away from him.

She climbed into bed with Stanley. He snuggled close, his hand holding tight to hers until he fell asleep. She remained awake for what seemed like a long time and, when she awoke, she heard the birds outside chirping at the new day.

Stanley was still asleep, his face toward the wall.

She rose and walked down to Carlotta's room. The door was ajar and the bed empty. She felt panic rise inside her chest as she rushed down the hall and into the kitchen.

Sigmund's parents were sitting at the table, a pot of freshly brewed coffee on the stove. Reverend Lowe had horn-rimmed glasses perched on the tip of his nose as he read the newspaper.

Mrs. Lowe smiled when she saw Rosalie.

"Where's my sister?" Rosalie asked from the doorway.

"Sig took her to the hospital. She is very sick, dear," Mrs. Lowe said.

"What kind of hospital? Do they do experiments there?"

They looked at each other as though confused by the girl's question. She decided to explain, hoping to inform the couple she couldn't be fooled. She frowned, her young face suddenly appearing old and wary.

"I know how you Nazis like to experiment on people. My mother told me all about you."

Mrs. Lowe stood up, a look of outrage on her face.

"How dare you speak to us in that manner, young lady!"

Now, Reverend Lowe was on his feet, scurrying around to his wife's side. Rosalie was sure he was about to pounce on her. Instead, he put his hand on his wife's shoulder and guided her back into her seat.

"There, there, now," he said, soothing his wife. "The girl is just upset. She doesn't know what she is saying. She's just worried about her sister."

Mrs. Lowe wouldn't be patronized.

"She has no right to say those things," she insisted, her accent strong.

"Please, my love, sit. Let me talk to the girl."

When Mrs. Lowe finally settled down and her anger seemed to abate, Reverend Lowe reached out his hand to Rosalie's. Instinctively, she wanted to pull it away, but the gentle look in his eyes mesmerized her.

"Come, Rosie. Let me explain what has happened to your sister."

He guided her to the chair he had occupied. He reached for a cup from the drain board and poured coffee in it.

"Do you drink coffee, little one?"

Rosalie nodded.

"Milk and sugar, too?"

Rosalie shrugged.

"Put milk in it, Reinhart, for goodness sake. A child cannot drink black coffee," Mrs. Lowe said in an annoyed tone. She stood and reached for the sugar bowl. "And sweeten it with some sugar."

As much as she had been taught to hate all Germans, Rosalie had to admit that she enjoyed the sound of their accents.

Mrs. Lowe reached inside the white paper bag on the counter and produced a long, golden strudel, sparkling with sugar. She took a knife and sliced it into several pieces, placing two on a dish and sliding it across the table.

"Here. Eat. Maybe this will sweeten your disposition. Nazis. We are not Nazis. Who told you such a thing?"

"My mother," she replied. "She said Sigmund is a Nazi, so I figured you must be Nazis, too."

"That is ridiculous. What do you think? Do you think every German is a Nazi?"

Rosalie wanted to tell her that her mother had, in fact, told her just that. Instead, she shrugged.

"I don't know."

"Mama, don't bully the girl. She just lost her mother and now her sister has been placed in an institution. She is only a child," Reverend Lowe said.

Again, Rosalie calmed at his gentle tone.

"An institution?"

"Yes, a place where they can help her."

She wanted to protest but his smooth, melodic voice seemed to settle her pounding heart. She looked from one face to the other, then to the strudel.

"Eat," Mrs. Lowe said. "You are nothing but skin and bones. I have to go in and wake up Stanley."

When she left, Reverend Lowe pushed the dish closer to Rosalie.

"You like coffee, yes?"

She nodded. She had been a coffee-lover since the age of two.

"And do you want milk and sugar?"

She nodded again, glad he asked her first.

He prepared her coffee and pushed the cup alongside her plate.

"There you go. Mama doesn't mean to get angry, but she doesn't like to be associated with the Nazis. They took everything we had. We escaped Germany with nothing but the clothes on our backs. Thankfully, Sigmund was able to get his hands on our personal mementos. Believe me, Rosalie, she hates them as much as your mother did."

Rosalie looked into his creased face, his light blue eyes stained with grief, the grief of losing everything.

"They made you leave?" she asked as she helped herself to the strudel.

"Oh, no. We, I mean my church, St. Paul's, was being used as a sort of 'underground railroad' for the Jews. You know what that is?"

Rosalie had learned about the Underground Railroad in America; the series of homes and other places where slaves escaping the South could find shelter. She understood his connection and nodded.

"We took a busload of Jews from the Nazis and escorted them out of Germany before they could be shipped off to a camp," he said, a sadness in his tone at the recollection of the event. "We made them think it was a youth group from the church and the bus ran off a bridge and down a ravine."

Rosalie didn't realize that she had stopped chewing. He reached across the table and gently closed her mouth, which was agape.

"Really? Did that really happen?"

"Oh, yes. After we crashed the bus, we ran and ran until we came across a caravan of gypsies who were traveling under the cover of night. They knew of my church and they took us with them. We travelled for five days, all the time trying to avoid soldiers. On the sixth day, we crossed the border into Switzerland, stayed there for a few months while things settled down. You see, the war was coming to an end, but still dangerous and it was best to stay put.

"After that, we went our separate ways. Mama and I were able to catch a train into Paris, where we had family. We stayed there until it was safe to travel. Soon after, Sigmund was brought to America by the government and, eventually, he sent for us. We love it here in America."

"But aren't you rich? My mother said you were rich."

He laughed at that.

"Yes, but not with money. We are rich with family and friends; with things that matter in life."

"But your house is so nice. And you have nice things. I remember from my visit. Remember, at the Christening?"

"Mama and I worked for everything we have. When we came here, the American Lutheran Church, provided me with a church, a house and a congregation. We were sent here. The congregation had already been established and it didn't take long for us to settle in."

Rosie's mind reeled with contradictions. Was this possible? It was as though the reverend could read her mind. He bent down so that his eyes were level with hers.

"Rosalie," he said in his softest voice, "you will have to trust me on this. Not all Germans are Nazis. If your mother told you that, then I am afraid she was mistaken."

Rosalie liked it that he didn't call her a liar. Instead, he suggested that she was mistaken. Everyone makes mistakes. Perhaps, she thought, her mother had, too. The guilt she felt because she was beginning to like the reverend seemed to subside. Suddenly, it was okay to like a German.

The one thing she knew for sure was that she loved Stanley, and he was half German. To like a full-blooded German, however, had seemed like an impossibility. Yet, there she was, sitting across from one. He was feeding her strudel and refilling her coffee.

Just then, Stanley burst into the room.

"Grandpapa," he said and climbed onto the older man's knee.

Rosalie watched as they hugged for a long time. She liked the way the reverend picked him up and kissed his face on both sides, not once, but three times. The whole time Stanley was laughing aloud.

"Cheerios?"

"Yeah, Cheerios."

"That's, yes, not yeah. You don't want to sound ignorant, do you?"

"Sorry, Grandpapa. Yes, please make me a big bowl of Cheerios."

Reverend Lowe stood and placed Stanley in the chair.

"Where has Grandmamma gone?" Reverend Lowe asked.

"She said she is going to make Mommy's bed."

With that, the whole episode from the night before flashed before Rosalie's eyes. She had been so engrossed in the reverend's story about their escape from Germany, she'd forgotten about Carlotta. The guilt seemed to rush in and remove the good feelings.

"Where is Carlotta?"

"She is in the hospital. She is sick," he said.

Mrs. Lowe entered and, as she passed Stanley, she tousled his blond hair. She took her coffee cup and refilled it, then sat at the table.

"Do you know what a nervous breakdown is?" she asked.

Reverend Lowe raised his hand as though trying to stop his wife from saying too much.

"What? She is old enough to know what is wrong with her sister."

"Yes, I'll be eleven soon and I want to know."

The reverend shook his head and sat at the opposite side of the table.

"Your sister has very bad nerves. She can barely sleep at night. She is a tortured soul, Rosalie," Mrs. Lowe said.

"Who is torturing her? Is it Sigmund?"

The Lowes looked at each other, both shaking their heads. Again, Rosalie looked from one to the other and then at Stanley. He was busy scooping cereal into his mouth. He didn't seem to mind that his mother was missing.

"This isn't the first time, is it?" Rosalie asked.

"That is correct. She has been to the sanatorium before."

"What's wrong with her?"

"We don't know. She won't say. Sigmund has had her to the best psychiatrists in Georgia. It's as though she is haunted by her past."

"Her past?"

"Yes. We, that is Papa and I, think something has happened to her that caused her great pain. Perhaps you can shed some light on your sister's past."

"I was only about three when she left home. I know she and my mother had a big fight. My mother told me that she gave my sister a choice, and my sister chose the Na …," she caught herself. "I mean, my sister chose Sigmund."

"Guilt?" Mrs. Lowe said to her husband.

Reverend Lowe shrugged his shoulders.

"Could be."

They finished breakfast and the subject of Carlotta didn't surface again until Sigmund returned two hours later. Rosalie was putting a puzzle together with Stanley in the living room.

"She's resting comfortably," he said. "I'm flying in a doctor from the west coast."

"Hollywood? My mother told me they were all nuts out there."

He didn't answer. Rosalie decided to put two and two together and in her ten-year-old mindset summed up that if they were all nuts on the west coast, that's probably where all the best doctors lived.

She decided to give Sigmund a point for at least trying to help her sister. Up until that moment, she was sure he was the reason for all of her problems.

That was a pivotal day for Rosalie. She was beginning to realize that things were not as they appeared, or as she had been taught to believe. She looked at him with new eyes. For some reason, she thought, he looked extra handsome.

The guilt washed over her like a cold Atlantic wave. She actually shuddered.

Was that Mama sending her disapproval my way?

She instantly recalled a story her mother had told her about a girl who was told to look after her younger brother by her dying father, a widower. Anna Mary said the girl didn't do as she was asked and one night she was awakened by the presence of her father standing at the foot of her bed. He reached down and grasped her toes and squeezed them until she cried out in pain.

"Take care of your little brother," her father's ghost demanded.

The next day she discovered that her toes were black and blue.

"Her father reached out from the grave and punished the lazy daughter," Mama had said.

Rosalie, feeling guilty for liking the Lowe's, decided to never sleep with her feet uncovered again.

Chapter 8

The next day, Sigmund took Rosalie and Stanley to All Saints Rest Home, a quaint Christian sanitarium affiliated with the Lowe's church.

Rosalie wore her best dress, a red one with a large white bow just below the collar. She braided her hair and tipped it with red bows.

"You look lovely, Rosie," Sigmund said when she came to the breakfast table. "I know you're nervous about seeing your sister at the sanitarium, but this is what's best for her."

"When will she be able to come home?"

"In a few days. She just needs some rest."

It was a short drive deeper into the Atlanta suburbs. To Rosalie, it looked like a posh country club. The main entrance was unlocked, its wide double doors open and inviting.

"This way," a woman in a white uniform said and led down a short hall.

Rosalie was shocked when she saw Carlotta. Her hair was pulled back into a ponytail and she wore no makeup. She had dark circles under her eyes. When she saw Stanley, she held out her arms. He ran to her and she held him close, kissing his head. She placed him on the bed beside her.

Rosalie approached.

"Carlotta," she cried and wrapped her arms around her sister's neck. "Carlotta, what's the matter with you?"

"I don't know, Rosie. I'm so filled with guilt and regret. Every time I think about Mama, my whole insides seem to churn into a volcano in my stomach. I feel like I'm out of control."

"You cannot control the past, Carlotta," Sigmund said. "You have to let it go."

"That's easy for you to say, Sig. Your parents adore you. My mother died hating me. Could you live with that?" she said over Rosalie's shoulder.

Rosalie could sense Carlotta's angst and was able to experience the sting of Anna Mary's actions. Her breath caught in her throat and she blurted out, "Mama sent you a letter, didn't she? Remember I brought it with me when I visited you before."

"The letter? The letter? Here, look at it."

She reached inside the pocket of her robe and tossed it on the bed.

"Read it. No, wait, I'll just tell you what she wrote. It said, 'Congratulations on your baby. From, Mama and Rosie.' That's all it said. After all these years, that's all she had to say. She hated me, Rosie."

"No, Mama didn't hate you. She loved you," Rosalie insisted.

Carlotta appeared taken aback. She lifted her dead eyes to Rosalie, a confused expression distorting her delicate features.

"Really? How do you know that?"

"Really. Mama loved you. She said she hated the Na - - ," she said, pausing, her thumb curled in Sigmund's direction. "She hated him."

"And obviously my son," she said, sobbing again.

Rosalie stood still for a few seconds, her hands on Carlotta's shoulders. She thought about the Lowe's and their story about escaping from their own home country. She looked at Sigmund. Maybe, she considered, he wasn't so bad. She thought about Anna Mary and how she called Stanley the "little Nazi."

"Listen, Carlotta," she began in a voice even she didn't recognize. It sounded like that of a mature woman, someone much older than ten. "Mama was a wonderful person, but she could also be mean."

She wasn't sure why she said that. A sudden wave of guilt engulfed her. There it was, the one feeling she feared most. Her mother was newly passed and here she was, talking bad about her.

She immediately looked at Sigmund to see if he was grinning, happy to know the horrible Anna Mary DeLuca had been exposed. She was shocked to see a sad look in his eyes. She turned her attention back to Carlotta.

"Anyway, Mama loved you and your son. She was just stubborn."

"Did she say that?"

"Yeah, all the time. Listen, I'm just a kid, but I can tell when a person is feeling bad. Believe me, Carlotta, she felt as bad about the argument as you do right now. She'd cry sometimes when she'd tell how it all happened."

Carlotta's disposition seemed to brighten. She sat taller and took Rosalie's hands in hers.

"Do you think Mama's forgiven me for marrying a German?"

She knew the answer. Anna Mary would never forgive what she considered a betrayal if she lived to be a hundred. When Rosalie looked into her sister's eyes, she knew what she *had* to say.

"Of course, she forgave you. Really, Carlotta, Mama loved you and Stanley. Like I said, she was just too stubborn to admit she was wrong."

Carlotta let out a long sigh, as though she was releasing all the pain that had been bottled up. She looked at Sigmund.

"Did you hear that, darling? My mother didn't die hating me. She may have held our marriage against me, but she didn't hate me. Oh, my God, I feel as though I've been released from prison."

She stood and walked to Sigmund.

"Take me home. Let's just forget all about the past and move forward. That's what Dr. Lerner says I should do anyway."

She was smiling, her eyes glistening with tears. She turned to Stanley and picked him up, swinging him high in the air.

"Your Grandma loves you. She's looking down on us and smiling from Heaven."

She grabbed her clothes from the closet, went into the bathroom and closed the door.

"Looking down from Heaven and smiling? What do you think, Rosie?"

Rosalie smiled. His sarcasm hadn't gone unnoticed.

"More like turning over in her grave like Aunt Ruthie always says. Anyway, she says that when she talks about dead people she knew."

Sigmund smiled and nodded. He stepped toward Rosalie and wrapped his arms around her slim shoulders as he bent lower.

"You are something else, little one. From this day forward, you will want for nothing. Whatever you need, you just ask me and I will see that you get it. Do you understand me? Think of me as your big brother."

Rosalie couldn't help but smile.

Stanley jumped on the bed and then onto Rosalie's back.

"Will you give me a horsey ride out to Daddy's car?"

"I sure can," she said. She turned to Sigmund and asked, "Can Carlotta come home now?"

"She sure can," he replied, repeating her response.

Rosalie laughed.

"It doesn't sound the same with your accent."

"No, I suppose it doesn't. But, I meant what I said. Anything you want or need, just ask."

Carlotta emerged from the bathroom looking as radiant as the noon sun.

"Let's go home," she said. "Let's go home."

For Rosalie, the next few months were what she called a total transformation, a word she learned from her brother-in-law. Carlotta had become involved in several groups at the reverend's church.

It seemed no matter what situation arose, Sigmund handled it with care and dignity, another of his words. Rosalie delighted in a newfound peace.

Christmas of 1955 was fast approaching and she asked if she could send a card to Ruth. Carlotta gave her a card with "Happy Holidays" scrawled across the front. The inside was blank.

"Here you go, sweetie; you can write her a letter."

With pen in hand, Rosalie set upon her task.

"Dearest Aunt Ruthie," it began. "My life has completely turned around. I'm almost eleven and can't believe my good fortune. When Mama passed away, I felt as though my life was ending. I now have a bright new outlook. I can hardly remember what life was like on Farragut Road.

"The only way I can explain it is that most of my memories are in black and white, like an old photograph that's faded and cracked around the edges. That is, until I moved into Carlotta's house.

"It was a little difficult adjusting at first, but after Carlotta recovered from a nervous breakdown, anyway that's what Sigmund called it, it seemed as though a rainbow crawled from beneath the city sidewalk, climbed high into the sky, and arched back down to earth, landing on Carlotta's green lawn.

"But, as lovely as the surroundings are, Aunt Ruthie, what I love best about living with my sister is my nephew, Stanley. When I wake up in the morning, I can't wait to see his face. He laughs a lot and that makes me laugh. When I go to sleep at night, I thank God that this special little boy is in my life.

"Thank you for making me come here. I hope you and Uncle Rudy are doing fine. Say hello to Ira for me. Tell him I said that girls are still better than boys."

She chuckled at that, recalling how Ira used to tease her about boys being bigger, stronger and smarter. She hoped he'd remember their ongoing joke.

"I love and miss you."

She signed the letter and placed it in the envelope, making a face when she licked the foul-tasting glue. She wrote the address on the envelope and paused when she had to write the return address, her address.

"Wow, this really is my home," she said to herself.

The months that followed brought even more excitement. Rosalie finished fifth grade with straight A's on her report card.

In summer of 1956, Carlotta, now displaying an aura of self-confidence and happiness, announced she was pregnant.

As the holidays approached and Rosalie celebrated her twelfth birthday, it appeared to her that her sister's stomach would surely burst. By February, she seemed to waddle. As Carlotta's pregnancy wore on, Rosalie spent more and more time with Stanley.

Finally, in April of 1957, Carlotta and Sigmund's second child was born. Rosalie sat in the waiting room with the Lowe's and Stanley, who chatted endlessly. The double doors opened and Sigmund entered with a huge smile on his face.

"Where's Mama?" Stanley asked.

"She's inside with your new little sister. We've named her Catherine."

"That's my middle name," Rosalie said.

"Yes, Rosie, we know this. You will be her godmother, yes?"

Rosalie beamed.

"I'd love to be her godmother, yes," she said and hugged Sigmund.

"Would you like to meet Catherine?" he asked.

"Yeah, I want to meet my little sister," Stanley said.

Rosalie nodded, a look of utter contentment on her face. She opened her heart to her brother-in-law and let him in. For that, she was a happier person. And Sigmund couldn't do enough to make her feel at home. This was her family now.

The christening, much like the one for Stanley, was a day-long event. Being the godmother, she and one of Sigmund's friends, a man named Otto

Kramer, stood up for the child. She especially liked the part where the pastor lifted Catherine high in the air and offered her soul to God and the angels for love and protection.

This time, however, Rosalie didn't have to fly back to Brooklyn. She was at home and it was at home she was happy to remain.

The summer of 1957 promised more fun than she could have imagined. The family had been preparing for a Fourth of July celebration. Rosalie and Stanley hung red, white and blue banners throughout the yard. They matched the red and white geraniums and the bluebells Mr. Johnson had planted.

The Reverend and Mrs. Lowe arrived before noon, bringing with them platters of potato and macaroni salad. Rosalie was beginning to think of them as her grandparents, too. When they brought gifts and treats for Stanley and Catherine, they always made sure there was something special for Rosalie.

The barbecue turned out to be one of the best days of Rosalie's life. She had adjusted to her new life and never entertained negative thoughts about Sigmund. She had made a conscious decision to make up her own mind about people. That was until later that night when she overheard something that had the capability to tear her new world apart.

The excitement of the day caused Rosalie to stir, unable to fall asleep. When the clock struck midnight, the soft gongs from the grandfather clock in the foyer announcing its arrival, the frustrated girl got up and sat on the window seat beneath her bedroom window. There was a small patio situated on the other side of a hedge where Sigmund often went to smoke his pipe. On this night, the aroma wafted into her room.

Hmm, he can't sleep either.

"I am worried," she heard a man say.

She didn't mean to eavesdrop, but she recognized Otto's voice. She mistrusted him, even though she couldn't put a finger on the reason, and this caused her to wonder what *worried* him.

He spoke in secretive whisper.

"In the day, we would just throw these people into a camp."

"What is it that worries you?" Sigmund asked with an annoyed tone.

"These people and their riots and protests. Why does Carlotta have to get involved with them? She must stop. What will happen to us?"

"First of all, Otto, I would never tell my wife not to support anything related to civil rights. And, even if I did, she would tell me to go to Hell. She does what she wishes. She follows her heart. And I support her."

"But what do they want, these Negroes?"

"Equality. They are Americans, too. They've been living here a lot longer than us. Carlotta fought to allow Mr. Johnson, our gardener, to live in the apartment over the garages. The Homeowners Association tried to stop her. She wouldn't hear of it. The man is a veteran who defended his country and she wasn't about to allow small minds to tell him where he could live. I admire her for that."

"Yes, Lion, I see what you mean. But now they are talking about forcing their way into a school in Arkansas that only allows white children. Tell me, what would the fuhrer do with such insolence?"

When Rosalie heard him use the word "fuhrer," a chill ran down her spine. Was he talking about Adolph Hitler? She leaned her head out of the window to ascertain that she would hear Sigmund's reply.

"The fuhrer? Otto, those days are gone."

"We were stronger then. Now, we are at the mercy of this government. Everything we do, they take and hide. We work hard and receive no accolades for our efforts. They hired us, but they hate us."

"We aren't dead, are we?" Sigmund snapped.

"That's because no one knows we're Nazis."

Rosalie stopped breathing. She was frozen in time and space.

Nazis? Mama was right. He is a Nazi.

"Listen, Otto, forget about what's going on. It has nothing to do with us. Why can't you understand that?"

"But what if the government decides to take action against them? Tell me, do you think they will treat us kindly with your wife helping them? Perhaps they will place us in camps, too."

"Don't be a fool. We are safe here. No one is going to a camp. You must stop this nonsense. It's foolish."

Otto's voice became more irritated.

"These are uncertain times, Lion, and if you are too stubborn to realize that we are in danger, then I say you are a foolish man. I'm telling you, if this government cracks down on these people, we will all be put before a firing squad. These Negroes are going against the law and your wife is helping them."

"Enough of this talk," Sigmund said. "You are making the mountain from the mole hill. I am telling you; stop this."

Rosalie's entire body seemed to shiver. While overall, it appeared Sigmund said all the right things, the one thing he didn't say was that he wasn't a Nazi. Why? She sensed a crushing feeling in the center of her chest.

My heart is breaking. Sigmund, just when I was beginning to like you. Say you're not a Nazi. Please. Say it.

When he didn't say it and seemed only to want to put an end to the conversation, her mind began to reel.

Mama was right. Mr. Pinella was right.

Somehow, she had to take action. How, she wondered, was she going to save her sister and the children? And why, she asked herself, did she allow herself to become enamored by this man with his phony kindness?

She shut the window and laid across her bed. She stared at the ceiling catching the lights from the street as they formed strange shadows across the room. She wondered if she should tell Carlotta about the conversation. Maybe she really didn't know he was a Nazi. And what about all those things her mother had insinuated about his loyalty to Russia? Could it be true he was a spy, selling American secrets to the Communists?

She turned on the small lamp by her bed and went to the bookshelf by her desk. She scanned the titles and grabbed her history book. As quickly as she could, she located the chapter on communism.

"The government owns everything. Wow, no one is allowed to own property," she said. "I don't think I like the sound of that."

She closed the book. She began to formulate a plan to expose Sigmund and Otto. She told herself she had to be smart about it. No one, not Carlotta, not even her closest friends, Denise or Joseph, could know her plans.

"What I need is proof," she whispered.

She climbed back into bed and pulled the sheet up to her neck. She fell asleep thinking about ways to spy on Sigmund, thereby taking him and Otto down.

When morning arrived, bringing with it a bright sun and a gleeful bird chirping outside her window, Rosalie opened her eyes. She didn't notice the sunlight or the bird's song. All she could focus on was how to convince Sigmund that he should allow her to go to work with him. It was as good a place as any to begin her work. She got up, dressed and hurried to breakfast. Carlotta was feeding Catherine.

"Good morning, sleepyhead," she said. "You must've been pretty tired. It's already nine."

Rosalie looked at the clock on the wall, a black cat's face with eyes that went from side to side with each second.

"Did Sigmund go to work already?"

"Oh, my goodness, yes. He left at seven. Why?"

She took two slices of bread and slid them into the toaster, trying to sound as casual as she could.

"Well, I was wondering if he'd take me to work with him. I'd love to see where he works. I've never seen a laboratory before."

She stared at the red filament, not daring to look into Carlotta's face. Surely, her sister would be able to recognize her lie.

"When he gets home tonight, you should ask him. He might like to show you his lab. But, Rosie, I'm just a little curious. Why?"

Rosalie waited before answering. She had to think before she spoke. She had to sound honest and unsuspicious. Just then, the toast popped up and she grabbed the slices of bread.

"Oh, ah, hot, hot, hot," she said, dropping them to the counter.

She took a plate and placed them on it, then moved to sit at the table across from Carlotta.

"Rosie, why?"

She didn't look straight into her sister's face. Instead, she busied herself lathering butter on her toast as she spoke.

"I think I might like to be a scientist one day," she said. "I did win a picture of Albert Einstein at the Science Fair at my old school."

At that moment, she realized that science was actually one of her best subjects. She would use this truth to persuade her sister of her interest in

Sigmund's work. She lifted her eyes and looked directly at Carlotta who was placing the baby in the small bassinette by the table.

"And, I got an 'A' in science. So I was thinking, I might be good at it."

"That's true. Your teacher said that it's your strongest subject."

Now Rosalie was beginning to feel comfortable with her plan. She smiled and nodded.

"Yes, it is."

"When Sig gets home, we'll ask him. Or, if you like, you can ask him yourself. I'm sure he'll say it's okay. He loves his work and, surely, he would love to share some if it with you."

Carlotta seemed comfortable with her compliance, so Rosie took the next step.

"Do you know anything about his work?"

She wished she had a notebook and pencil to jot down any information she could obtain from Carlotta.

"Heavens, no. I'm a dunce when it comes to science. History's my strong subject."

"We were learning about the Communist Party," Rosalie said, hoping to get a reaction from her sister.

She was disappointed when Carlotta merely smiled and poured milk into a tall glass. She placed it in front of Rosalie.

"There you go. Drink up. It's good for your bones."

She wanted to press the question about communism, but Stanley entered wearing his own version of a Superman outfit, a pair of red and blue pajamas and a "cape" fashioned from a pillow case.

"Truth, justice and the American way," he said, his hands on his hips.

"Hurry," Carlotta said. "We've been invited to lunch at the Lowe's today."

She picked up Stanley and nuzzled his ear.

"Come on my little super hero. We're going to see Gran and Pop Pop today."

At that, Stanley threw his hands in the air and yelled, "Yay!"

For the first time since hatching her plan to expose them, Rosalie felt a pang of guilt. No one, not even her own mother, had treated her as well as Carlotta. Yet, somewhere at the back of her mind, she could hear the words of Harry Pinella who had warned, "Don't let them fool you, Rosie. You can't trust a Jap or a Nazi, ever. You just listen to your mama."

Chapter 9

Sigmund ran his hands through his thick blond hair. He barely slept the night before as Otto's words repeated in his mind.

"We were stronger then. Now, we are at the mercy of this government. Everything we do, they take and hide. We work hard and receive no accolades for our efforts. They hired us, but they hate us."

"We aren't dead, are we?"

"That's because no one knows we're Nazis."

For Sigmund, he didn't consider himself a Nazi. He never believed in the superiority of the Aryan race. He hadn't realized his time-travel experiments were designed to destroy everyone but them.

His supervisor, Dr. Auman, often made reference to the Germans as the future of mankind. He was sure the man died believing he worked to improve the world for everyone, with Germany leading the way.

"With this, we can do much good," he'd said.

Sigmund shook his head at the thought of the massacre.

He took pride in the fact that he was loyal to his new government. He remained a man of his word. He'd made an agreement with the American government. If he'd come to the United States and continue the work he had been doing in Germany, he would be protected. The government, thus far, had treated him fairly.

The business with the new civil rights activities had nothing to do with his work. The fact that Carlotta supported the cause was something to which he gave little thought. He was proud of her for standing up for her beliefs.

He felt safe because he never killed anyone. He was a scientist, working in isolation with several others.

The fact that he and his colleagues were working on high-level projects, some that had the capability of giving Germany the upper hand in the war, had been forgiven in exchange for his knowledge and continued efforts, this time on behalf of the Americans.

Surely, Otto was over-reacting to the recent protests against the government. They were becoming more and more widespread and, it seemed, the media covered every sit-in or demonstration.

Although Carlotta was an active participant, he believed her actions would, in no way, affect his agreement with the government.

What did worry him, though, was his long-time friend.

Otto had been close to Hitler. He had been offered many opportunities because of that affiliation. When the war was coming to an end and the soldiers were sent to kill all the scientists who had been working on Hitler's secret projects, while he tried to believe in his friend, he often wondered if it was a coincidence that Otto had been called away only to return after the execution of his colleagues. Also, he recalled the look on Otto's face when he told him about his parents and the bus accident.

Who, he wondered, now held Otto's loyalty? He was almost certain it wasn't the government of the United States. He constantly complained that their achievements were never shared with the scientific community.

"Perhaps these Americans are planning a world takeover. With what we are developing, they would definitely have an upper hand," Otto had said.

Sigmund had no way of knowing what the government planned. During the last decade, what he did know was that their efforts were focused on rebuilding the vibrational accelerator.

Without their original team, the ones slaughtered by the German military, Sigmund and Otto struggled to create it again. They were close, he knew. The Americans he worked alongside were brilliant. They, however, never had access to any information other than what he brought with him.

If they succeeded in replicating the vibrational accelerator, he wondered, what would Otto do with the information? Would he keep the project a secret or sell the technology to whoever bid the highest?

He knew Otto was angry at the American government. There was no way of knowing of what he'd be capable in retaliation for what he perceived as its unfairness.

There was a Cold War going on with Russia. This, he know, could add to his concerns about Otto.

He stood and went to the window. Beyond the complex, he could see a small park about a quarter of a mile away with a waterfall. It looked peaceful.

Otto, my friend, why do you have to complicate matters?

He watched as the sunlight reflected off the waterfall. He promised himself he'd keep a close watch on his friend.

Adding to the stress of a sleepless night and long day at work, that evening when he arrived home, Carlotta asked him to take Rosalie to his laboratory. The girl had appeared excited at the prospect.

"She wants to do a summer project for school; something about getting extra credit in science. I think we should support her," Carlotta said.

"I'll ask, but remember, dear, this is a secret installation. I am not sure they would welcome visitors."

Carlotta and Rosalie appeared satisfied with his promise to, at least, ask for permission.

The next morning, he arrived at the laboratory and immediately headed to his supervisor's office. He hoped to put this behind him and focus on more important matters.

Armand Bennett looked up when Sigmund rapped on the door that was slightly ajar.

"Come in," he said.

He was a heavy-set man, so much so that when he walked it looked more like a waddle. He had thin black hair, tinged with gray. He pulled some of it from the side of his head and combed it over the top, barely covering his scalp. His eyes were deep brown, almost black. He sported a mustache and short beard that matched the salt and pepper of his hair.

He held more degrees than seemed possible for a man in his fifties. They lined the walls of his office, some framed in gold, some in thick black and some in wood.

Sigmund took the seat opposite Bennett. The latter leaned back, a huge smile on his face.

"So, are you here to tell me that you've completed the vibrational accelerator?"

Sigmund raised his eyebrows and smiled.

"I wish it was that easy," he said.

At that, Bennett tilted his head to the left.

"Oh, this is worse than telling me that we still do not have our prize?"

"Much worse. My wife wants me to bring her little sister in to see where I work. She is at the top of her science class."

Dr. Bennett nodded.

"Oh, I see. Well, let me think about this. Does the child wish to become a scientist one day? Is that what this is all about?"

"I don't really know. I've already told my wife it would be impossible, but I promised I'd ask. And I did."

Sigmund stood to leave.

"Hold on, doctor. I haven't refused. Tell me, how old is the girl?"

"Twelve."

"Twelve, hmm," he said, scratching his chin. "Dr. Lowe, do you talk about your work at home?"

The fact that Dr. Bennett was calling him by his surname caused Sigmund to feel uneasy. He allowed a serious expression to settle on his face.

"Sir, I never talk about what goes on here outside of these premises."

"Hmm, and what about Dr. Kramer. I know he's bitter. The advances we've made so far are not being published and I know this disturbs him."

Sigmund recalled the recent conversation with Otto. How, he wondered, did Dr. Bennett know? He wondered if Otto had shared his opinion with the supervisor.

Just say she can't come and let me get out of here.

Dr. Bennett seemed to be formalizing his response.

"Sure, next week. We'll have her tour the facility, the ground floor only, of course. We'll take her to all of the laboratories on the main floor. The child doesn't need to know what we do two floors beneath the earth."

Sigmund let out a long sigh. It was not one of relief. This, he thought, had the capability of making matters more complicated. He forced himself to sound pleased.

"Really? We can do that?"

Dr. Bennett laughed.

"Of course. We are a government facility, paid for by the taxpayers. The last thing we need is for your sister-in-law to return to school in the fall and tell her teachers that she was being *kept out* of a government facility. No, I think it's a good idea to let her come in and have a look around. Besides, what harm could it do? She's just a kid."

Rosalie was ecstatic that Sigmund would take her to his laboratory. It would give her a chance to take notes and do follow-up work after the visit. Whatever he was up to, surely, she thought, she'd see it.

She was barely able to sleep the night before the visit. She'd written the conversation between Sigmund and Otto in a small marble notebook.

She read her notes beneath her sheet, a small flashlight lighting the pages.

"Otto said that now, they're at the mercy of this government. Everything they do, the government takes and hides. They work hard and receive no 'something or other' for their efforts."

Everything they do? What is it they do that they don't tell anyone about?

She jotted a sentence across the top of a blank page.

"Look for things that aren't normally found in a laboratory."

She closed the book and stuffed it between her mattress and box spring. She took a sip of water from the glass on her nightstand and returned the glass to its spot. She shut out the light and laid in the darkness. Every now and then a car would pass and its lights would cast strange shadows on her ceiling.

It gave her an idea. Just like her room, there was a place for everything and everything was kept in its place. That was normal. The strange shadows that were crawling across her ceiling didn't belong there. She decided that's how she'd discover what went on at Sigmund's laboratory.

She awoke with the rising sun the following morning. She dressed quickly as she wanted to be ready to leave on time with Sigmund. Stanley and Catherine were still sleeping as she quietly made her way to the kitchen.

Carlotta, looking sleepy, poured coffee in Sigmund's cup and slipped bread in the toaster. Sigmund entered, kissed her and sat across from Rosalie.

"Hey, if you guys don't mind, I think I'll go catch a few more winks. It's not that often the kids sleep in," Carlotta said.

She didn't wait for a response. She patted Rosalie on the shoulder.

"Have fun today and make sure you eat before you leave."

"Well, Rosie, are you ready for the big tour? You know, they don't usually do this. But I told Dr. Bennett that you are an 'A' student in science and he said he'd welcome an aspiring scientist."

Rosalie smiled and reached for the now popped-up toast, placing one slice on her dish and the other on his. She buttered it as she spoke.

"Carlotta said you do top secret work. Will I be able to see that?"

"Top secret? Really? I wouldn't necessarily say it was top secret. However, as with all research, we have to keep certain things a secret until we are ready to make them public."

"Why?"

"So no one steals our ideas."

That made sense to Rosalie. Still, she knew, she was doing more than touring the lab, she was doing research that would one day expose Sigmund and Otto for the Nazis or, she corrected herself, the Communists they were.

The laboratory was housed in a long building made of smooth white concrete. When they arrived at the parking lot, Sigmund showed his identification badge and a guest badge he'd gotten from the security officer the day before for Rosalie.

"Welcome, miss," the guard said and allowed the heavy gate to open, sliding to the left.

Inside, two guards stood watch, one on either side of the road.

"Wow, look at them."

"This is a government facility, Rosie. They are military men. They protect the grounds and those inside. I hope the sight of guns doesn't alarm you as you will see many more guards."

Rosalie wasn't the least bit alarmed. Seeing them gave her trip an added sense of excitement. Whatever was going on there, she was sure, she'd get a good look at it.

Sigmund parked the car and came around to open the door for Rosalie. She took her notebook and pen out of her school bag.

"Am I allowed to write stuff down?"

"Sure, that is no problem. You will do a report for school, yes?"

By now, she was used to his backward questions, as she called them.

"Yes. My principal said that whatever we did over the summer we could present to the class in September. Like I said before, I'll get extra credit."

"Very good idea," he agreed.

They entered the glass doors, three sets wide. A guard checked their identification badges. Sigmund introduced Rosalie to the man.

She smiled sweetly and followed Sigmund to his office, a small space at the end of the hall, all the time making mental notes about her surroundings.

"I'm not in here very much," he said.

She looked around. Everything that should be in an office seemed to be there. There was a desk, a chair, a table behind the desk that had fancy legs and photos of Carlotta, Stanley, Catherine and, surprisingly, herself, on it. She liked that one. It was Christmas and she was sitting on the floor with Stanley in front of the fireplace.

"Hello."

The voice came from the direction of the hall. She turned to find a man with sparse black and gray hair standing in the doorway. He reached out his hand and said, "Welcome, Rosalie. I'm Dr. Bennett. I've heard many wonderful things about you."

She shook his hand, amazed that he was so friendly.

In her mind, she was taking notes she'd later put in her secret notebook. *Note to self: Dr. Bennett seems way too friendly.*

Sigmund motioned for her to follow him. Dr. Bennett led the way, Sigmund behind him. The hall was eerily quiet. She expected to see more people rushing about, doing important government work.

The first room they reached contained rows of machines. They were tall and had what looked like tapes playing.

"This is our computer room. It is kept very clean," Dr. Bennett said. "No food or drink is allowed in here."

It was cold and noisy and, to her, the machines seemed to be working hard, but at what she couldn't imagine. She looked at each one, unimpressed.

Note to self: Computers don't tell you anything.

"Where are all the instructions for your experiments?" she asked.

"Ah, that's a good question," Dr. Bennett said. "All the information that supports everything we do is contained in this computer system. It also stores everyone's name and personal information, background and experience. It matches the right people with the right experiment. I can pull up all the information I need on a screen in my office."

"Can I see it?"

"Oh, no, dear, it's all confidential. We must protect our scientists."

"Protect them against what?"

She noticed that he gave Sigmund a quick look before answering her question.

"Well, we don't want anyone stealing our ideas."

Note to self: They seemed to have agreed that their main goal is to keep things a secret so no one steals from them.

"Come along," Sigmund said when Dr. Bennett moved back into the long hall that seemed to stretch into oblivion.

She followed him as he identified the offices. There were several that belonged to doctors. She assumed he meant scientists like Sigmund, not like her pediatrician. Some had people in them and some were vacant.

They made a left turn and came to another long hall. She followed the men into a room with a sign over the door that read, "Mechanical Shop."

Inside were four long tables, silver with small machines scattered atop. At the far end, a man was soldering something onto one of the small machines. He stopped and removed the odd-looking hood with the glass front as they approached.

Note to self: It's a mechanical shop but there are no cars.

"This is Dr. Jacoby," Dr. Bennett said.

He smiled and shook her hand.

"What are you doing?" she asked.

Dr. Bennett laughed and nodded to Dr. Jacoby.

"I'm soldering a rod to this component."

She wrote it down.

"Why?"

Again, she noticed he looked to Dr. Bennett for permission to answer her question.

"This rod," he said, identifying the piece, "will transmit electricity when this button is pushed."

The index finger of his left hand was on a square button.

She wrote that down, too.

"Where will it transmit the electricity? I mean, will it look like a little bolt of lightning?"

She noticed that Sigmund seemed taken aback with her question. Had she asked too much? In her mind, she was only trying to link the electricity to lightning as she was taught in school about the weather.

"Yes, it will," Sigmund said. "And it will then be able to give other machines a charge of electricity that they need. One machine works off another and another."

That sufficed as an answer. She jotted it in her notebook. They left the shop and walked along the corridors. Most of the rooms looked the same. It seemed to her that every scientist she met was trying to produce lightning.

"Well, that's pretty much what we do around here," Dr. Bennett said as he glanced at his watch. "I have a meeting. If you like, you can show Rosalie the cafeteria."

He shook her hand and left. She watched as he disappeared around a corner. She looked up at Sigmund who looked a little too uncomfortable.

Note to self: He's hiding something.

"Come this way, Rosie. I'll buy you a cup of coffee. You can say you were on a coffee break. Would you like that?"

Her eyes grew wide.

"Yes!"

The cafeteria was at the far end of the building. It seemed to take a long time to get there. Once inside, she discovered, it was much like the one at her school with rows of tables and benches, a kitchen area and a lot of windows.

Sigmund chose a seat by a window that overlooked a small waterfall, the one he could see from his office that was just outside of the complex. The sun was causing the water to sparkle like diamonds.

"It's nice here," she said and drank some coffee.

"Do not tell Carlotta about the coffee or I will be in her dog house for a month," he said, smiling.

"Don't worry, I can keep a secret."

"So, how do like this place. Nice, yes?"

She smiled and said, "Real nice. But, Sig, where do you guys do the top secret experiments. I saw an elevator at the end of the hall and I noticed this building has only one floor. Where does that elevator go?"

Sigmund hesitated a little too long for Rosalie.

"To the basement … where we keep the supplies … nothing to see down there."

Note to self: He's definitely hiding something.

She finished her coffee and accompanied him back to his office. She waited, looking over the photographs, as he made a few telephone calls. After a few minutes, he excused himself.

"I must go and speak to Jacoby, Dr. Jacoby. You know, the man with the little lightning machine. I will be right back."

Rosalie nodded and asked if she could sit in his chair.

"Of course, you can be the doctor today."

When he left, she began snooping through the drawers. There were several folders standing in a deep drawer with colored tabs. One had Dr. Jacoby's name.

She reached in, pulled it out and opened it to find an unattached page. It was called a "memo." To her, it appeared to be some sort of a letter to Sigmund. She couldn't understand what she read. Although it was in English, it used words she had never seen before. She grabbed her pen and opened her notebook.

"Vibrational Accelerator," she mumbled as she copied the words. "Super Collider. Fusion."

She heard footsteps outside the office and quickly replaced the folder. She saw someone pass the office through the opaque glass in the door. She quickly put her notebook back into her small tote bag and returned the folder.

She stood and looked down the hall. Sigmund was nowhere in sight. She decided to head in the direction of the elevator.

She heard voices and slipped into a narrow opening backing up into something round and hard. When she turned, she discovered it was a doorknob. She opened the door and realized it led to a stairwell. The stairs only went in one direction – down.

Her curiosity seemed to overtake her senses and she ran down the two sets of stairs. When she reached the bottom, she came to a thick gray door made of heavy steel. She pushed on the handle and it opened easily, almost too easily.

Her heart was pounding like a drum as she made her way along the dimly lit hall.

Note to self: Now this is out of the ordinary. Not normal.

She came to a glass wall beyond which two men appeared to be fidgeting with an odd-shaped contraption. It looked like a bell with a door on the front of it. The men had their hands on a round object inside the bell.

"Try it now," one of the men said.

Note to self: Sigmund is doing secret experiments that maybe even Dr. Bennett doesn't know about.

Her eyes grew wide as the other man stepped behind a panel and was just about to push a button. Suddenly, a strong hand landed on her shoulder. She let out a scream. One of the men in the room looked in her direction, an angry glare drilling into her face.

"Rosie, what are you doing down here?"

"I was l-looking for you," she said.

Sigmund waved to the men inside the room.

"It's okay. The child is lost. I'll take care of the situation. Go on with your work," he said.

He stuck his head in the door and said something to the men that she couldn't hear. The men hesitated, nodded, and returned to their task. Sigmund backed into the hall and hooked her arm, then practically dragged her down the corridor. He took her up the same way she had come down.

"I'm real sorry, Sig, really I am. I was just looking for you and I saw the stairs and I thought maybe you had to get something from the basement."

He didn't answer. Instead, he escorted her to his office and motioned for her to sit. His look seemed to warn that she was to remain in her seat.

He went through a small pile of telephone messages and placed them in a box on his desk. He stood and motioned for her to stand. She obeyed.

"Are we going home now?"

"Yes."

"But it's not even lunch time. Are you angry with me?"

He didn't answer. She followed him as he hurried along the corridor toward Dr. Bennett's office and waved to the older man.

"I'm leaving for the day," he said. "I'll be working at home."

Dr. Bennett nodded and stood, approaching them.

"See you in the morning. And, Rosalie, it was a pleasure having you visit our little facility today. You can come back again whenever you like."

She smiled, shook the hand he offered and followed Sigmund outside. The whole time, he didn't say a word. When they got to the car, he opened the door and waited for her to get in. Once inside, he shut the door and walked around the car. He got in, but didn't slip the key in the ignition.

"Sig, are you mad at me?" she asked again.

He stared straight ahead, a stern look on his face.

She shivered. Surely, he was devising a plan to kill her. She had seen too much. The Nazi was going to murder her for discovering his evil deeds.

He put the key in the ignition and started the car, still not uttering a word, not even as much as a growl which, at this point, she would have welcomed. He was being too quiet for her taste.

When they left the facility, he drove her to a nearby park. She recognized the small waterfall and realized they were behind the laboratory complex. He stopped the car, got out and walked around the car to open her door. When he did, she pressed her back into the seat.

He's going to drown me under the waterfall.

"Rosie, come out of there," he said.

Nervously, she turned sideways and let her feet fall to the pebbled ground of the parking space. He shut the door and walked toward the waterfall. She followed, although she really wanted to run away.

"Rosalie Catherine DeLuca," he said as he bent down so he was face to face with her.

She gulped and nodded.

"Do you swear that you will never divulge what you witnessed today in the basement laboratory?"

She stiffened as he grasped her right hand and raised it.

"Swear to God, Rosalie. Swear that you will never tell another living soul what you've seen."

She wanted to ask what would happen if she didn't swear, but thought better of it.

"My right hand to God, I won't tell anybody, ever."

"Listen, little one, people have been arrested for doing what you did today. That," he said pointing to the squat building that sat within view of the waterfall, "is a government facility. That is a place where secret projects are developed and tested. If anyone knew you were down there, we both could be in a lot of trouble. Do you understand?"

"Y-yes. What about the two men."

"They will not say anything to anyone."

"Is that what you told them, not to tell anyone, when you stuck your head in the door?"

He nodded.

Note to self: He has his own people working there.

"Rosalie, I know you can be trusted. Don't let any of what you saw go into your school report. In fact, let me read it before you hand it in."

She realized she didn't have a choice, so she nodded her agreement.

"I'm really, really sorry. But, Sig, I'm not even sure what I saw. Can I say it now, to you?"

He nodded.

"It looked like a bell. Is it a bell?"

"No, it is just shaped like one."

"I guess you can't tell me what it is, huh?"

He stared at her for a long time.

"Why are you so curious?"

Because I think you're a Nazi and you are probably telling the Communist Party everything that's going on in America.

"I don't know, I just am. I guess deep down inside I'm a scientist, just like you. I want to know everything."

He smiled at that. Maybe, she thought, he's smiling because he remembers being as curious when he was her age.

"Yes," he said, "I know that feeling. Come on, let me take you home. Remember, Rosie, a promise is a promise and should never be broken."

She got in the car, her head feeling jumbled from the demands the adults in her life had put on her. First, her mother and Harry made her promise to never trust a German or Japanese person. And, as soon as she began to trust one, she discovered he was a Nazi. Or, at least, he didn't deny it.

Now, Sigmund was making her promise not to tell anyone what she saw. Although she promised, she knew in her heart, she would eventually find someone to trust and she'd reveal his secret.

Note to Self: After today, I'm not going to make another promise to another person.

Armand Bennett sat back in his chair. A red light attached to a screen on his desk had blinked. He pressed the button next to the light and the screen came alive.

He focused on the girl, Rosalie, creeping along the quiet hall.

"She's a curious one, that one," he said to himself.

"Sir, a low voice whispered from the speaker next to the screen, do you see this?"

"Yes."

"Dr. Lowe's guest is breaking security protocol. Shall I send someone?"

"No, I can handle this. She's a child; a little too curious, but no threat to the facility. Let's see where she goes."

He watched as she opened the door to the stairwell. Almost instantly, a new picture appeared on his screen. It followed her down the stairs. He pressed another button and the lock on the second door released. Rosalie, unaware she was being watched, opened the lower level door and slipped through.

Again, the picture instantly changed to the hall where she gingerly crept along, staying close to the wall.

Dr. Bennett shook his head and smiled. He watched as she came upon the laboratory assigned to Sigmund Lowe and his staff. She peered through the wall of glass. He could see her eyes widen as streaks of what looked like lightning flashed.

A hand landed on her shoulder and she spun around to see her brother-in-law, her expression one of shock. At that, Dr. Bennett smiled again.

"Gotcha," he mumbled to himself.

He watched as Sigmund Lowe escorted the girl back to his office and out of the building. A new screen displayed their exit from the parking lot.

"Sir, they're gone," the voice said.

"Thank you. Save the tape," Dr. Bennett said.

"Yes, sir," came the reply and the red light disappeared.

Dr. Bennett stared into the ether. Sigmund Lowe had broken the rules. No one, not family nor friend, was permitted below the main floor. He shouldn't have left her alone. Also, he should've marched the precocious twelve-year-old right into his office.

Instead, he took it upon himself to usher her out of the building as quick as the lightning-type electricity he invented.

"You're mine now, Dr. Lowe," he said in a low voice. "You're all mine."

Chapter 10

When Rosalie returned home, she immediately went to her room and locked the door. She pulled out her marble notebook and moved to sit at her desk. She jotted down all of the "notes-to-self" she had stacked in her mind.

Note to self: Dr. Bennett seems way too friendly.

She wrote: "First, while I found Dr. Bennett to be friendly, I'm not really sure if he can be trusted."

Note to self: Computers don't tell you anything.

She wrote: "Somehow I have to find out how to get information from a computer. This could take a while."

Note to self: They seemed to have agreed that their main goal is to keep things a secret so no one steals their ideas.

She wrote: "Dr. Bennett and Sigmund may be hiding something. Find out what it is."

Note to self: It's a lab but there are no test tubes.

She wrote: "Go to the library and find out what other tests are done in a laboratory."

Note to self: He's hiding something.

She wrote: "Find out what it is."

Note to self: Now this is out of the ordinary. Not normal.

She wrote: "What was that secret place underneath the building and why did Sigmund act so strange?"

Note to self: Sigmund is doing secret experiments that maybe even Dr. Bennett doesn't know about.

She stopped and, tilting her head to the side, had a new thought.

If Dr. Bennett did, why didn't he have a guard down there?

She wrote: "I better not say anything to anyone until I find out who is hiding stuff from who."

Note to self: He has his own people working there.

She wrote: "Maybe those guys down in the basement are all Nazis or Communists, but who would I tell. Maybe Dr. Bennett doesn't even know they're down there."

Note to Self: After today, I'm not going to make another promise to another person.

She wrote: "Mama and Harry made me promise not to trust people. Now Sigmund is asking me to promise not to tell anybody what I saw."

After she'd written her final comments, she reviewed her list of notes and what she thought she could do about it.

She sighed heavily and leaned back in her chair. She took each item one at a time, trying to formulate her next step.

She heard Carlotta's voice coming from the kitchen.

"Rosie, lunch."

She quickly returned her marble notebook to its hiding place and smoothed her bedspread.

She didn't want Carlotta to send Sigmund for her. The last thing she needed was for him to see the look of utter guilt she was sure covered her face.

"I'm coming," she called.

She stood in front of her bureau and looked at her reflection. She fidgeted with her hair, securing a bobby pin that was assigned an unruly curl that insisted on laying over her ear.

"There," she said to her reflection. "All back to normal."

Sigmund heard Carlotta's call to lunch. He'd returned from the laboratory with Rosalie and immediately went into his office, locking the door behind him.

He pulled out the bottom drawer to his desk so far that the front leaned on the floor. He slipped his hand past the back of the drawer until it bumped against a flat metal object. He then reached for the latch that was held down by a flat face combination lock. Unable to see it, he pressed the appropriate numbers and it gave way beneath his fingers.

Inside sat a folder. He stopped for a moment.

"Tell me, Dr. Lowe, do you talk about your work at home?" Dr. Bennett had asked.

Sigmund had reassured him he didn't. Yet, here, stashed away behind his heavy wood desk drawer was a set of plans that could get him fired, if not imprisoned.

Sigmund pulled out the folder and laid it on his desk. He checked the windows, making sure no one could see inside. He flipped open the folder and looked at the top page. There was a swastika in the middle of the page. Stamped across the top were the words "*STRENG GEHEIM.*" Top secret.

He flipped the first page and studied the early schematics of the Vibrational Accelerator. It was the basis upon which the final version had been built; the very one Rosalie had seen in the basement laboratory.

He leaned back in his chair and thought about what had just occurred. How was she able to access the basement? The halls are monitored by an in-house security system. Also, the doors are always kept locked, only to be opened in the event of an emergency. Yet, his guest was permitted to make it as far as his lab.

"What is that all about?" he whispered to himself.

He looked at the page again. Aside from the folder he'd sewn into the lining of his overcoat and eventually turned over to the Americans after the Nazis confiscated everything else, the schematic was all he had left. The reason he had it was because he had been comparing the basic design against the one in the laboratory when Otto barged into his apartment to inform him of his parents' assumed demise.

He'd stuffed it in the pocket of his lab coat when he heard Otto at the door. After his ordeal in the woods, he went to his apartment to shower. It was then that he realized it was still in his possession. He slit the lining of his suitcase and slid the page behind it, then packed his clothes and personal items.

No one, he thought, not even Dr. Bennett, knows it exists.

The Americans believed that everything the Germans brought with them was in that folder or stored in their minds. He felt he should've revealed that he had the original schematic of the bell, but after the way the Nazis turned their backs on their fellow countrymen, he trusted no one a hundred percent.

The only reason he never told his parents or Carlotta about the schematic was so they could remain innocent of its existence.

Plausible deniability, he thought. One cannot be held responsible for something of which they have no knowledge.

He focused on the page again. Below the drawing was a series of steps he'd taken since his arrival in the United States more than a decade ago, each one building on the basic design.

"Rosalie," he whispered. "What am I to do about Rosalie?"

On the way home, after he'd made her promise to never tell anyone what she witnessed, she seemed to burst with too many questions.

"What's it for?" she asked. "Why is it kept in the basement?"

"No questions," he'd said.

"But, I want to know," she insisted. "Is it allowed?"

He didn't quite understand her meaning at first.

"Oh, do mean legal?"

She nodded.

"Yes, of course. It's what we do out there. But it is not for public knowledge. One day, when we know what we have and how to use its power, we will reveal it to the world."

"And what about Dr. Kramer? Does he know about it?"

"Yes, of course. We are a team."

"I didn't see him. Where was he today?"

"I don't know, Rosie. Please, stop asking so many questions."

She had quieted down, but Sigmund could tell she was like a simmering pot, ready to boil over. Finally, when they returned home, she thanked him and rushed to her bedroom. He'd heard the click of the lock on her door.

Whatever the girl was up to, he knew he'd better keep a close watch on her. One wrong word to the wrong person and he could be in a lot of trouble, perhaps even to the extent that he'd be deported. The thought of returning to Germany sickened him.

He knew Rosalie had a report to write for school. Hopefully, she'd keep her promise and allow him to read it before she handed it in.

"Sig, lunch is ready," Carlotta called.

He quickly returned the file to the fireproof box at the back of his desk drawer and locked his desk.

"Coming, dear," he said and headed to the kitchen for lunch.

Armand Bennett had spent most of his adult life working for the United States government. He'd had three positions, one in the CIA, and two in secret government facilities similar to the one in which he now headed.

What his scientists were working on, he knew, was so valuable it could bring millions of dollars to the right person; a person who would turn his back on the United States, a traitor.

The Germans, as he often referred to Sigmund Lowe and Otto Kramer, were working on an invention that had originally been sought by Adolph Hitler.

While Otto Kramer played a large part in their progress, Armand Bennett knew it was mostly accomplished by Sigmund Lowe.

Somehow the brilliant scientist had been able to recall the specifications of what the Germans called the vibrational accelerator, a device that enabled time travel. It was the accelerator that had the capacity to propel an object into the future.

He smiled as he recalled the first time he'd seen the schematic the two had drawn, every detail from memory. Just thinking about that moment made his heartbeats quicken.

Otto had explained the process.

"We used a wristwatch in a titanium box the first time and it moved fifteen minutes forward without a mar on it."

Sigmund had nodded, assuring Dr. Bennett that Otto's story was true.

"At first," added Sigmund, "the box in which the wristwatch sat began to look as though it were a mirage. There was a wall of air waves that shimmered. They became more and more active until, all of a sudden, the entire area around the box also began to glow like a dim light.

"We had built antennae-like rods and attached them to the vibrational accelerator. These rods had sent small lightning bolts, for lack of a better description, that surrounded the vehicle.

"After a few minutes, the box also began to shimmer and, in what seemed like a flash, it disappeared. Fifteen minutes later, the box reappeared in the same spot inside of the vibrational accelerator. When we checked the time, it was still set at three o'clock."

Armand Bennett recalled the description of the experiment word for word. Those words were what kept him arriving early to the laboratory every day, oftentimes on the weekend as well.

The vibrational accelerator, a square device no larger than the common breadbox, with one side open for viewing the object to be transported, had been completed. It had the capability to break down anything placed inside of it into pure energy and propel it forward in time.

"Brilliant," he'd said, patting the men on their backs.

"Now, all we need is the proper containment vessel in which to move an item forward. The atoms must remain in a close proximity so that when the object arrives in the future, it can be reconstructed perfectly," Sigmund had said.

Armand Bennett listened closely, taking notes. He had worked long enough for the government to know he'd need specifics for the three-part requisition form. Even someone of his stature was not exempt from the requirements of bureaucracy.

"It has to be made of a specific material so that it won't melt under the heat intensity of the faux lightning," he wrote. "Cost should not be an issue."

The titanium was delivered within the month. The container was shaped like a small bell or capsule. It could contain whatever was locked inside.

Dr. Bennett told his supervisors in Washington that, like the original experiments, they planned to start small. He'd almost shivered with anticipation at the prospects of such an achievement.

He was assured that a larger bell-shaped vehicle could be built and that it would be capable of moving a human being forward in time.

"How about back in time?" he'd asked.

They simultaneously shook their heads.

"We are not sure. The war was coming to an end and all of our work had been destroyed. Who knows how far we could have gone if the fuhrer had not instructed all discoveries be destroyed," Otto had said.

"We can rebuild it and we can go from there," Sigmund Lowe had said.

"Yes, yes," Armand Bennett had agreed. "We can start from there. We only have to catch up. Baby steps; it's a matter of baby steps."

Armand Bennett relaxed against the back of his chair and looked toward the ceiling. That conversation had occurred a long time ago, more than three years, in fact. He was beginning to think they'd never regain what had been lost. Finally, however, Sigmund Lowe announced that they had caught up.

"Soon," he'd promised, "we will test the device. We will use a timepiece so that we can monitor the movement of the hands."

That conversation took place last month. They were now ready to move an object ahead in time. The vibrational accelerator sat waiting to move forward with its interrupted progress.

A slight smile curved his lips. Rosalie DeLuca had seen it, he thought, and she had no idea what she was viewing. He hoped this "slip" in protocol would expose any would-be traitors.

While he kept those in Washington up to date on the progress, he made a conscious decision to filter what he reported.

"We're close," he'd say when asked. "We're very close."

That seemed appropriate as the funding came rolling in without hesitation. He knew those at the Pentagon were hoping for a powerful weapon. A time machine could be just that weapon.

With so much at stake, Armand Bennett had sworn to make certain everyone involved in the process was kept under his surveillance.

He knew it from the minute he was assigned his post. When the Germans had arrived and were assigned to his charge, he set the wheels in motion. Using his CIA connections, he made sure their homes were under constant surveillance. That included everyone, even the secretaries who brought them coffee in the morning and filed their papers.

He thought it unfortunate he was only able to monitor visual and verbal activities outside of the houses.

Another matter that had been brought to his attention was a reference to visits from "other worldly" entities. Although he'd heard of such visits before, he wasn't convinced it was possible. True or false, he decided not to take any unnecessary chances. He had the homes of the two German scientists monitored for any and all electrical anomalies.

So far, and as he expected, there was no activity reported.

The general surveillance, however, proved helpful. Just last week, he was able to eavesdrop on a conversation between the men that took place in the Sigmund Lowe's yard. He was able to see and hear them on the film that was collected on a daily basis.

He shook his head at the thought of Otto's words.

"No one knows we're Nazis," he'd said.

Of course, Sigmund Lowe didn't agree or disagree with his close friend and colleague. Dr. Bennett opened their files and spread them on his desk.

Perhaps, he thought, Sigmund Lowe doesn't consider himself a Nazi.

He focused on Lowe's file. His parents were Lutherans. His father, a pastor, had secretly rescued several Jewish people, leading them out of the country and into safe hands in Switzerland.

He shifted his eyes to the folder on Otto. He, on the other hand, was one of Hitler's favorites. He'd often dined with him, most likely asking questions about the project.

"Adolph Fucking Hitler," he whispered, shaking his head.

As much as he hated the man, there was a part of him that understood his unrelenting search for newer and more powerful technologies, especially those frowned upon by academia. He'd been ridiculed for his efforts.

"These projects are nonsense," one of his colleagues said when he told him he'd been offered a position with the German scientists. "They were all shot because they couldn't develop a single idea that met the approval of their *fuhrer*. Believe me, they're all a bunch of lunatics."

Armand Bennett smiled, recalling his colleague's smug face.

Yeah, they're lunatics, all right. That's why I have in my facility a machine that can move objects into the future. Who's ridiculous now?

Armand Bennett allowed his gaze to move from one file to the other. He reviewed their backgrounds again.

"Which one of you will betray this country?" he asked.

It was a major concern because he'd recently received intelligence that someone, possibly one of the scientists, had communicated with a known associate of a high-ranking Communist.

As he sat in his office anticipating an experiment that could change the world, he couldn't help but wonder about his fellow scientists.

"Which one of you will run to our new enemy, Russia? Otto Kramer, you are the obvious choice, but Sigmund Lowe, you could surprise all of us."

Chapter 11

Rosalie spent three days on her science report. It focused on the security at the laboratory. She was sure to use proper grammar and her best handwriting.

She rapped lightly on Sigmund's office door. It was slightly open and she could see him at his desk. He looked up and smiled, motioning for her to enter. She smiled broadly and handed him the two-page report with the bright yellow cover with the words "My Summer Vacation: A Trip to a Government Laboratory."

He seemed pleased as he eyed the colorful presentation. He lifted the cover and read.

"The scientists keep their discoveries secret so no one can steal their ideas. How much fun it would be to become a scientist and create wonderful things for mankind. We must always remember, though, that business is business and it's competitive. That includes projects run by private companies as well as those from the government."

She knew it was complete, yet remained vague at the same time.

When he was finished, he allowed a long sigh to escape his lips.

Good, he's relieved. Mr. Brilliant Scientist hasn't got a clue as to what I'm up to. You're going to jail, Nazi.

"This is very good, Rosie. You seem to have understood the process of discovery and the importance of secrecy. I like that you compared it with private companies. I think you will get an A+."

She smiled and took the report.

"I hope so. Well, I'll see you tomorrow. I'm going to bed."

He stood and walked around the desk.

"Thank you for your discretion."

She wanted to ask him what the word meant. Instead, she allowed him to shake her hand.

"You're welcome."

As much as she wanted to hate him, it was at times like this that she found it almost impossible. He treated her with respect and dignity, two more words he'd taught her.

She went to her bedroom and stuffed the report in her school bag. She placed it in her closet. She still had six more weeks of summer. She closed the door and caught a glimpse of her reflection in the mirror.

She had grown two inches since she'd arrived and now wore her hair in a neat ponytail. She wore expensive clothing and shoes, had her own television in her room and, she thought, what a room. It was so much better than anything she'd ever had.

Carlotta prepared delicious food and made sure she had everything she needed. She was as good to her as Anna Mary had been.

Rosalie knew she couldn't ask for a better life after losing her mother. She lived in a beautiful home and went to a progressive school where she had many good friends.

She heard Stanley make a squealing noise from the bathroom where he was playing in the bathtub. He and Catherine were her family, along with Carlotta and, yes, even Sigmund.

She stared into her own eyes.

How could you betray them? And what will happen to Carlotta and the children once her Nazi husband is exposed?

Filled with guilt, she went toward her bed. There, tucked between the mattress and box spring was all of her evidence to date. Soon, she knew, she'd have enough and that would be the end of Sigmund Lowe and Otto Kramer. She wondered what Dr. Bennett would think of their conversation.

She closed her bedroom door and pulled out the book. When she opened it, Dr. Bennett's card fell out.

It's not time to call him, not yet.

She placed it back in the book and closed the cover.

I shouldn't do this. I should burn this book.

She held it in her hands, the black and white marble design faded to gray as tears filled her eyes.

What should I do? Maybe I should just tear it apart.

She returned the book to its hiding place. As she did, she could hear Harry's words.

Never trust a Nazi or a Jap.

"Or a Communist," she whispered to herself. "Then, who can I trust?"

For Rosalie, summer seemed to move at top speed. Between trips to the lake with Carlotta and several day trips with other kids from the church, time seemed to fly by. When not involved in those activities, she spent her free time with Denise Perry and Joseph Barnes, her two closest friends.

As August neared its end, it didn't seem possible that she was making plans with Carlotta for a back-to-school shopping trip. She had not written a word in her marble notebook and, she admitted to herself, it helped ease her feelings of guilt. Those feelings, however, stirred one night when she, once again, overheard Sigmund and Otto talking.

"Now that the test was successful, I think it's time for us to receive the credit we deserve," Otto said.

"Successful. No, we've only passed the first hurdle. We still have a long way to go. You must stop looking for personal accolades, Otto. Can you not look at the big picture? This is important work, work that can change the world. And we, you and I, are in the middle of it. The day will come when we will get what we deserve."

"And if it doesn't?"

When Sigmund didn't reply, she stuck her head out of the window. She made a noise, catching their attention.

"Someone might be listening," Otto said. "It is best we do not discuss these matters here. If we do not get the satisfaction we deserve, then it will be up to us to take it."

Rosalie pulled her head inside and became irritated that their voices had lowered so much the sound from the patio was nothing more than a garbled mumble.

I knew those two were up to something.

September arrived pulling her into a new school year. She handed in her report for which she received a high grade. It seemed, however, none of her classmates were particularly interested in what went on at a secret government facility. She didn't care. That wasn't really her main goal.

She got what she wanted, a notebook filled with incriminating evidence. She smiled to herself. She was learning more and more words from Sigmund, words she'd use to send him and his traitor friend straight to jail.

As much as she tried, after that night she discovered there were no opportunities to gather information on them. They stopped meeting outside her window, much to her dismay, and without secret conversations between them, she had nothing new to add to her marble notebook. She wondered if she'd reached the end of her investigation.

It seemed Carlotta had arranged her life in such a manner that her time was being pulled in an entirely different direction with school, music lessons and Bible study.

Could Carlotta be in on it? No, Rosie, don't think that way.

She pulled out the notebook but couldn't bring herself to write words that could incriminate her sister.

The holidays brought a wide array of joyful experiences. She attended a Halloween party at school and helped Carlotta prepare a Thanksgiving meal.

"Now you know how to cook everything from soup to dessert," Carlotta said as they pulled homemade pumpkin and apple pies from the oven.

Christmas, much like the years before, was the busiest time. Carlotta and Sigmund showered the children with gifts. And with every one she opened, a tinge of guilt caused her mouth to go dry.

Rosalie turned thirteen on New Year's Day of 1958 and, once again, Carlotta and Sigmund showed her how much she was loved. They surprised her with a party that included several of her school and church friends.

With the new year, Sigmund, it seemed, spent more and more time at work. She asked if she could visit, but he informed her that they were at a critical juncture and a visit would be impossible.

Rosalie almost laughed when he told her because, while something inside told her that she should be building her case against him, whether from guilt or confused feelings, she was glad she had an excuse to remain still.

During spring break, Rosalie was allowed to visit Ruth Goldberg.

"Aunt Ruthie said to be prepared. Uncle Rudy had a stroke in February and he's not going to look the same."

"What's a stroke?"

Carlotta explained what had happened to Rudy Goldberg and what the girl should expect. The day after Easter, Sigmund drove Rosalie to the airport. He kissed her cheek and put her on a flight to New York.

"Take care of my little sister," he told the flight attendant.

As before, it was Harry Pinella, still donning his Yankees baseball cap, who met her at the airport.

For Rosalie, the ride felt strange. She'd grown so used to Georgia that the hustle and bustle of New York seemed overwhelming. She hadn't been there an hour and was already feeling homesick for the robust green lawns and rows of bright flowers that described her new home.

Harry seemed older and more worn, too. She noticed that his black hair had turned gray above his ears where it was visible as he still wore the blue hat with the NY logo for his favorite team, the Yankees. It, too, looked old and worn.

What she noticed most was that his limp was now more pronounced. She knew he was a veteran and had lost his left leg in the war, but when she last saw him, two years ago, his tendency to lean to the left seemed less noticeable. She wondered if it was always like that or if she had simply become more aware now that she was almost a teenager.

"How's life with the Nazi?"

It'd been a while since she heard those words said aloud. It almost felt as though he were insulting her.

"It's good."

"What does he do all day?"

"Works. I went with him to his laboratory once."

"Really? How come?"

"For school. I want to be a scientist when I grow up."

"Oh, so now you're taking after your brother-in-law?"

A wave of guilt flooded the back of the taxi. Rosalie could barely catch her breath.

"N-no, no, I would never," she said, sounding defensive.

"What did I tell you, Rosie? Do you remember? Just because he allows you to live there, remember he's only doing it because your sister wouldn't have it any other way. He's not to be trusted."

"I don't trust him," she blurted out. "I'm trying to find out what he's up to and when I do, I'm going to report him to the cops."

She caught Harry looking through the rear-view mirror at her. He seemed to have a look of approval on his ace.

"Well, be careful. Them pigs are dangerous."

Somehow, calling Sigmund a "pig" felt wrong. She didn't know why, but she wanted to defend him. She was glad when the car stopped and he got out to open the door. She was back in the projects, the taller buildings, the crowded streets, and the noise. It felt overwhelming.

"Well, here you go, dear," Harry said as he handed her the suitcase she'd received from Carlotta and Sigmund for her birthday. "I'll be back in four days to pick you up. Tell Ruthie I said hello.

"Hey, you still remember what apartment she lives in, don't you?"

Rosalie nodded and thanked Harry, a deep desire to move away from him gnawing at her stomach. For that, too, she felt guilty.

"Okay, thanks Mr. Pinella."

As he drove off, Rosalie made her way to Ruth's apartment. She knocked on the door. When it opened, Ruth stood with her arms wide and a bright smile. Rosalie remembered her as a small woman, but now she appeared tiny, almost lost in the opened doorway.

"Rosie, how are you, darling?"

She hugged her for a long time. Rosalie could smell the scent of Chanel No. 5, her signature perfume.

"Oh, my God, you're taller than me now. Look at you. You seem all grown up. Come, Uncle Rudy is dying to see you."

As predicted, he looked small and frail. He was seated in a wheelchair by the window that overlooked the playground at the back of the building. He seemed to brighten when he spotted Rosalie.

"Come and give your old uncle a big hug."

She bent and hugged him. He felt brittle beneath her hands.

"Hi, Uncle Rudy. How are you feeling?"

"I'm good. I can't walk or lift my left arm, but I'm alive," he said with a wide smile.

Rosalie felt as though she would cry if it hadn't been for Ruth hooking her arm and easing her toward the sofa.

"So, how's life in the South?"

"It's beautiful there," she said, and told Ruth about her new life in Georgia. "We eat a lot of peaches."

At that, Ruth laughed aloud.

"I bet you do."

The visit seemed long and boring to Rosalie. While she loved the Goldbergs, there was nothing to do but sit around and watch television.

At breakfast on the third day of her visit, Ruth handed her a toasted English muffin.

"My goodness, I can't believe you're going home tomorrow. This week went by so quickly. I miss you already."

Rosalie, who couldn't wait to get back on the airplane and go home, merely smiled and nodded, quickly biting off a piece of her muffin.

"Harry will be here at noon," Ruth said. "Are you homesick?"

Yes. I'm homesick. I'm bored to tears. I want to go home.

"A little. I miss the kids. They're so much fun," she said, not entirely lying.

"I'm glad you are happy with your sister, Rosie. And I'm glad Sigmund treats you good."

Inside, something stirred; a mixture of affection and guilt.

When she didn't say anything, Ruth asked, "He does treat you good, yes?"

At that, Rosalie laughed, sending a small piece of her muffin flying across the table.

Ruth looked stunned.

"What? What did I say?"

Rosalie swallowed her muffin with a hard gulp and followed it with a long drink of orange juice.

"I laughed because that's how Sig talks. He always ends a question with a yes or a no."

"English is not an easy language to learn. You don't know because you were brought up here."

"That's what he says."

"Do you like him now?"

"Sometimes," she admitted for the first time in her life.

"Good, good."

Rosalie frowned.

"Aunt Ruthie, is it okay to like him? I mean, knowing what he is."

"And what is he, honey?"

Rosalie couldn't bring herself to say the word aloud.

"You know."

"I do know. He's your family; that's who he is."

"But Mama said - -," she began.

"Rosie, don't. Your mother, God rest her soul, was the salt of the Earth; a good woman. But she was tormented by hatred. Don't live like that, child. Whatever Sigmund was or did is in the past, he's a new man now, an American, working for the government. You have to stop holding a grudge."

Rosalie looked into Ruth's soft brown eyes; eyes that pleaded with her to change her way of thinking.

"But even Mr. Pinella says I should never trust a Jap or a Nazi. He said they're not to be trusted."

85

"Harry Pinella is a bitter man. I remember him when he was young, before the war. He was always angry at someone. One day, he called Uncle Rudy a cheap Jew bastard because he didn't give him a big enough tip."

Rosalie's eyes grew wide. Ruth nodded.

"Can you imagine such a thing?! And poor Rudy was so embarrassed. He explained that he'd left his wallet at home and promised he'd make it up to him on the next trip."

Ruth paused and balled up her fist.

"I told him he should've punched Harry square on the nose."

Rosalie laughed.

"Aunt Ruthie, you're so funny."

Rosalie settled down and sat back, folding her hands on the table. She became thoughtful.

"What is it?" Ruth asked. "Tell me what's bothering you, honey?"

"Don't you want to see the Nazis punished for what they did?"

"I let God decide who deserves to be punished. As for me, I try to forgive. It's difficult, make no mistake about that, but I try."

Rosalie suddenly felt bad that she'd be leaving so soon. She'd forgotten how loving Ruth had always been. She spent the remainder of the day playing Mahjongg with her and Rudy.

By the time Harry arrived, Rosalie felt like a new person; a more mature person. She hugged Ruth and Rudy for a long moment and kissed their creased faces. Somehow, she knew in her heart, she'd never see them again.

She didn't speak much on the return trip to the airport. Instead, she listened with new ears as Harry complained about the trouble with the "negroes." She decided Aunt Ruthie was right; Harry was just an angry man.

As the airplane touched down in Georgia, Rosalie decided she'd live her life differently and it would begin the moment she stepped off the airplane.

"Rosie! Rosie! Over here!" called Stanley.

She could see him jumping up and down and waving his arms above his head. The look on his face was pure exhilaration.

Sigmund stood behind Carlotta holding Catherine on his shoulders. They were all smiling. She rushed to them, enjoying their embraces.

"Did you have fun?" Stanley asked.

"Yeah, it was great," she said, finally free to admit that she loved to fly.

"Mama says we're going on vacation and we're all gonna get on the airplane," he said. "Ain't that right, Mama?"

"Isn't, Stanley; not ain't," Sigmund said, tousling his blonde hair.

"Oh, yeah, I forgot. Daddy says ain't ain't a word," he said, laughing.

Sigmund pursed his lips and shook his head.

"Welcome home, Rosie," he said.

Carlotta hugged her tightly for a long time.

"I missed you," she said.

Rosalie got on her toes as Sigmund leaned forward so she could kiss Catherine.

"Roe, Roe," the child said.

"She said my name, right?"

Carlotta leaned toward Rosalie and whispered in her hear, "Sigmund's been teaching her all week. I think the big lug missed you, too."

At that moment, Rosalie made a decision to tear the marble notebook to shreds. She could barely stand the anticipation. Fearful thoughts crept into her mind.

What if someone found it already? What if they send Sigmund to the gas chamber, whatever that is?

When they arrived home, however, she was distracted by the Lowe's and several neighbors, as well as Joseph and Denise.

"Welcome home," they yelled as she stepped out of the car.

With her thoughts on other matters, she found that, once again, time seemed to rush forward at top speed. It seemed that in no time at all, she was already cramming for her June finals.

The marble notebook remained hidden between her mattress and box spring, out of sight and out of mind for Rosalie.

One afternoon, just as summer vacation inched closer, she wondered if, before she destroyed the book, it would be wise to discuss her suspicions with Denise and Joseph. They were, after all, sworn to secrecy.

"Let's decide right here and now," Joey had said one day during lunchtime, "that anything we say to each other is not to be shared with anyone else unless permission is granted."

The three hooked pinkies and made the deal final.

When summer arrived, Rosalie discovered a plethora of outdoor events that included another barbecue that seemed to go on and on.

It wasn't until well past nine that most of the guests left. As usual, it was Otto who remained behind.

Rosalie, exhausted from an exciting day, kissed Carlotta good night and headed to her room.

"Tell Sig I said good night. I'm too tired to wait for him," she said.

She slipped into her pajamas and climbed into bed. She thought about the marble notebook but decided it was safe as long as she was sleeping in her bed.

Tomorrow. I'll tear it up tomorrow.

Just as she was about to drift off to sleep, she heard the low murmur of voices outside her window, coming from the spot where she'd overheard Sigmund and Otto before.

Although she felt too tired to get up, she forced herself to move to the window. She lifted it a few inches higher and crouched below the windowsill. She wanted to cry when she heard Sigmund's voice. He was speaking so low, she could barely make out his words.

Otto, on the other hand, who was closer to the window, spoke a tiny bit louder.

"Bennett wants another test. I'm telling you, he's really putting on the pressure. It seems we are no closer than when we first arrived. What are we missing? I thought we had it all worked out. What if they send us back to Germany?"

Sigmund said something, but his voice was so low, Rosalie couldn't make sense of it. She was sure, however, she heard him mention Russia.

"Some will pay whatever is asked for this technology," Otto said.

The knot returned to the pit of Rosalie's stomach.

Who? Who will pay? Is he talking about the Russians?

Again, Sigmund said something that sounded like a curse. Rosalie wasn't sure. She waited a few minutes in silence. She peered over the windowsill and saw the men walking away. She turned and sat on the floor, her back to the wall.

Why? Why? Please, God, don't let it be.

She got back into bed and pulled the sheet to her neck. She thought about her marble notebook.

After all that I've been through, I think the Nazis really are Communists now. I'm almost sure I heard him say something about Russia.

Rosalie's dreams were filled with turbulence. Night after night, she'd see Sigmund dressed in the Nazi military uniform, or she'd witness him handing notes to strangers, no doubt Russian spies.

It was exhausting.

Even after a late August visit to Disneyland in Anaheim, California, a vacation she never could have imagined, she still couldn't shake off the conversation she'd witnessed between Sigmund and Otto.

Before she knew it, Rosalie was thick into the school year. It seemed her history class did little to dissuade her from her mission to expose the "Commies" as she now called them.

On a crisp autumn afternoon, while walking through the wooded area behind her house with Joseph and Denise, Rosalie made the decision to let them in on her plans.

"Holy shit!" Joseph said. "Who would've thought such a thing could be going on right under our noses."

Denise gave her head a slow shake, the pony tail of her waist-length hair swaying from left to right.

"You guys are crazy. They're not Communists. My dad said he knows them both since the day they arrived in America. He said they're patriots."

Rosalie repeated their conversations.

"Patriots?" she asked, sounding controversial. "I don't think so."

"I think you're jumping to conclusions."

"Oh, don't listen to her," interjected Joseph. "She's always trying to be the voice of reason. She's been like this since kindergarten."

Denise shrugged, turning up her nose to them.

"Say what you want, but you're going to see I'm right, and you're going to get into trouble."

"We could spy on him," Joseph said. "My dad showed me how to set up a camera without anyone knowing it's even there."

The thought of having to deal with photographs seemed like a dangerous idea to Rosalie.

"Can we just spy on him without taking pictures?"

Denise became adamant.

"Don't do it, Rosie. It's not right to spy on people."

"There she goes again," Joseph said. "Denise, why don't you just go home and let us adventurous types handle this situation."

Annoyed, she stomped off, grumbling over her shoulder.

"Crazy fools."

Joseph waved her off.

"Go," he said.

They headed straight to Rosalie's room. She was glad her sister wasn't at home. Joseph looked around and his eyes grew.

"Ha, I have a great idea. We can make a hole in the sheetrock between your bedroom and Sigmund's office. At least you could see what he's up to."

Rosalie wasn't sure about drilling a hole in Carlotta's wall. She kept the house immaculate and would surely detect that someone made a mess.

"She has dirt radar. She can find a speck of dust on the ceiling."

Joseph, on the other hand, wouldn't be stopped. He removed the photograph of Albert Einstein on the wall above the desk.

"What's against the wall in his office?"

"A bookshelf."

"Open shelves?"

Rosalie thought a moment and smiled, nodding.

"Good. I'll be right back."

Twenty minutes later, he returned with a hand drill. He set the point against the wall and began to turn. Within seconds, he pierced the first layer of drywall. He pushed past the empty space between the wall in Rosalie's room and the office. A few seconds later, the second wall surrendered to the drill bit.

"You're going to have to go in there and clean up any plaster," he said.

Rosalie ran to the foyer. The door to Sigmund's office was closed. She heard Carlotta outside with the children. When she peeked through the glass side panel by the door, she could see her getting them out of the car. The grandfather clock by the door made a single gong.

She pulled the doors apart and ran into the office, directly to the bookshelf. She calculated the height of the hole and quickly found it.

"Joey, can you hear me?"

"Yeah. What's it look like on that side?"

"There is some white stuff on the shelf."

"That's plaster. Clean it up."

Rosalie obediently cleaned up the plaster with the sleeve of her blouse and stepped back. Without the photograph of Einstein covering the hole, she could see a small shaft of light penetrating the otherwise dark office.

"Joseph, cover the hole."

He did and the light disappeared. She strategically placed a bookend of an angel holding a harp so that the hole allowed a straight line view to the center of the room.

She went into the foyer to check on the whereabouts of Carlotta and the children. Carlotta had stopped to chat with Mr. Johnson. Rosalie hurried back to her room, climbed on her desk and slid the photograph to the side.

"Perfect! It's a clear shot right to his desk."

Joseph puffed out his chest.

"See, I told you. I'm going to be a spy when I get out of school. I'm going to work for the CIA. Now remember, be as quiet as a cat and he'll never know you're here."

Rosalie was only half-listening. All she could think about was what would happen to her if Carlotta discovered she was spying on her husband. Surely, she told herself, they'd put her in an orphanage.

"Hey, I gotta get home. I'll see you at school. Good luck with your snooping," Joseph said.

Rosalie stared at him for a long moment. He simply smiled, shrugged and turned to leave.

"Joey, do you think I should fill it in?"

Joseph paused at the doorway and turned to face her. He had an odd expression on his face, one not suited to a teenager. At first, he didn't speak and this made Rosalie shift uncomfortably from her right foot to her left.

"Well?"

"The way I see it is this," he began, a frown creasing the tender skin of his brow. "If he isn't doing anything wrong, then who's going to even know about it? If he is, then you caught yourself a spy and you'll be a hero."

"But what if they find out?"

Again, he seemed to give her question a lot of thought.

"Rosie, if they catch you, just tell them you're spying on him just for the fun of it. Say that you want to be a spy and you wanted to see how long you could go without being found out."

Rosalie contemplated his answers. Finally, when she didn't add anything to their conversation, Joseph shook his head and pursed his lips.

"Rosalie, you really worry too much and I gotta get home. I'll see you tomorrow."

She walked with him to the front door. With his handy drill tucked beneath his shirt, he strolled past Carlotta and Mr. Johnson.

"See ya, Miss Carlotta, Mr. Johnson," he said and waved.

Rosalie, who was standing on the front step, merely shook her head.

"He's a cool one; that's for sure."

She went back to her room and practiced climbing on her desk to view Sigmund's office. The trick, Joseph had said, was to move like a cat and breathe as little as possible.

This became her nightly ritual; put on her pajamas, wash her face and hands, brush her teeth, shut off all lights, and spy on Sigmund.

Chapter 12

Months of surveillance yielded no results. It was beginning to look as though she'd made a mistake in judgment. There was no nefarious activity in his office.

Then, on an early spring night in 1959, Rosalie, now fourteen, had followed her ritual and climbed into bed. Just as she was drifting into sleep, she heard her sister's voice. It sounded frantic.

"Sig, Sig, come here."

Rosalie kicked off her blanket and rushed to the door, opening it wide. She heard Stanley crying and coughing. It sounded like a bark.

As Sigmund passed, she asked, "What's the matter?"

She followed him into Stanley's room.

He didn't answer. He knelt beside the boy's bed and leaned down so that his lips gently landed on Stanley's forehead.

"He's hot," he said, his accent sounding more pronounced than usual. "We have to take him to the hospital."

Carlotta turned to Rosalie.

"Can you stay awake and listen for Catherine?"

Rosalie nodded as she tried to see Stanley's face now hidden by Sigmund's shoulder.

"Is he going to be okay?"

"Yes," Carlotta said.

To Rosalie, she didn't think her sister sounded convincing.

The two rushed the child out of the house. Rosalie pulled the door shut and locked it, then moved to the living room window. She watched as the car, a new Cadillac with rocket-shaped lights at the back, pulled out of the driveway, onto the street, and disappeared around the bend in the curve.

For the first time since her arrival, she was alone with one of the children. She thought about Catherine, her safety in the hands of a teenager.

I can do this. I'm responsible.

With confidence, she went to Catherine's room. She was lying on her back, her arms spread out in innocent abandon, her mouth slightly open. Her stomach rose and fell with deep, rich breaths.

Rosalie kissed her index finger and gently touched Catherine's cheek. "Don't worry, little sister, Stanley's going to be okay."

She went to the living room and waited by the telephone, ready to answer it on the first ring. Thirty-five minutes later, the news arrived.

"It's the croup," Carlotta said. "They're going to keep him in the hospital for a day or so. He's in an oxygen tent and breathing much better. Sig and I are going to stay here for a while longer. Is Catherine okay?"

"Yes, she's sleeping."

"Okay. How about you? Are you okay? Are you afraid or anything?"

Rosalie stiffened.

"No, of course not. I'm not afraid at all. I'm fourteen; I'm not a baby. I'll just sleep on the sofa until you guys get home."

She could hear a slight chuckle in Carlotta's voice.

"That's a good idea," she said. "And Rosie, thanks. I'm so glad you're here. I know Catherine is in good hands."

Rosalie liked the idea of that, being in charge, being the one on whom her sister could depend. She'd done so much for her already and for Rosalie, this was a small way to pay back for the kindnesses shown to her by not only her sister, but her brother-in-law, too.

"I'll see you soon," Carlotta said and the telephone line went dead.

Rosalie went to check on Catherine one more time, then to her room for her pillow and blanket. She put them on the sofa, double-checked the lock on the front door, and laid down. After a few minutes, she realized she was too amped up to sleep.

She got up and went to the kitchen. She poured milk into a tall glass, returned the bottle to the refrigerator, picked up her drink and headed to the living room. She was about to turn on the television when she realized the doors to Sigmund's office were open, wide open.

The dim light on Sigmund's desk cast an eerie yellow streak across the rug-covered office floor and onto the cream tiles of the foyer. Something inside urged her to inch ever closer.

She knew she shouldn't enter. Yet, there it was, an open door, an invitation to get a first-hand look at the documents he kept secret.

She crept even closer to the opening, her slight frame feeling tiny as she stood in the doorway where both French pocket doors had disappeared within the walls on either side.

It was too much temptation for the girl.

She stepped inside. On his desk sat an open folder. Her heart began to beat a little faster. She bit her bottom lip and ever so carefully took another step forward. Her eyes settled on what lay on his desk.

Secret documents?

She placed the glass on the edge of the desk and walked around it. Her curiosity urged her to examine the pages before her. She discovered the first four pages had been turned over as though Sigmund had been flipping through them. On the fifth page, she saw a sketch of a bell-shaped object with numbers written beneath it. She'd seen something similar when she'd visited his laboratory when she was twelve.

She picked up the pages, one at a time, and examined several more. There were notations written in German. These, she assumed, were from his laboratory; perhaps the very documents he and Otto were going to sell to the Russians.

She hurried to her room and retrieved the camera she'd received on her birthday in January, a small Kodak DualFlex IV that had a flash attachment. She inserted the flash bulb and hurried back to Sigmund's office. She laid out the pages in order and, with shaking hands, began snapping photographs.

From the far corner of the room, which was cloaked in darkness, she heard a crackling sound. She looked up, squinting into the inky blackness, her eyes still adjusting to the light from the flash.

She heard a stir, as though someone had entered through the bookcase. Then, as if from the ether, a man dressed in black from head to toe stepped into the yellow light. She noticed he also wore dark glasses, which he didn't remove.

Rosalie jumped and dropped her camera on the desk. She instinctively stepped backward. The edge of Sigmund's chair caught her and she fell into the seat. Her mouth opened but nothing came out.

The visitor remained still.

After a few silent seconds, she muttered, "Who, who are you? Are you some kind of a spirit or something?"

Without a reply, the man rounded the large desk and gently pressed his first two fingers to her temple. It felt more like the flutter of small wings than an actual touch. In her mind, she was able to see her own life history play itself out like a movie. Was it possible, she wondered, that the stranger was reviewing her past, learning who she was and from where she'd come?

She tried to pull away, but discovered she'd lost the ability to move. Her breathing became shallow and a feeling of lightheadedness overtook her. After a few seconds, he stepped backward, his image caught between the dim light of the desk lamp and the darkness of the corner.

Her heart pounded so hard she felt as though her entire body was responding to each beat. Her palms felt moist and a strange taste crept onto her tongue.

Again, she asked, "Who are you?"

"My name is not important," he said in a deep voice. "What is important is that you cease your activities immediately."

"I wasn't doing anything," she said. "I was just curious about my brother-in-law's project."

Then, thinking quickly, added. "I want to be a scientist like him when I grow up."

"Lies can only get you in trouble, Rosalie. Or do you prefer I call you Rosie?"

Rosalie closed her eyes tightly. So much had occurred in her young life over the last four years. The loss of her mother, moving to Atlanta, and coping with her own suspicious nature.

This, she knew, was something she'd never dreamed possible. It couldn't be possible. And, yet?

I'm dreaming. Wake up! Wake up!

"There are strange things in the Universe, Rosie; things you cannot even imagine with your young mind. But I can tell you this, you cannot control your environment. We, however, can control matters and know this, *we* have the power to take from you everything you hold dearest."

Her eyes opened, wide and frightened.

"Like my family?"

"Exactly. Be warned, girl. Your fate is in your own hands. Do as you are told and you and those you hold closest to your heart will be protected. Disobey and you will live to regret your curious mind."

She swallowed hard and, in a weak voice, asked, "What do you want me to do?"

The stranger became silent. She closed her eyes again.

I'm dreaming. Wake up. Wake up!

She was sure she'd fallen asleep on the sofa and was in the midst of an exciting dream and when she opened her eyes she'd see only the ceiling above the sofa.

"Rosalie Catherine," the man said. "Open your eyes."

Oh, shit. Oops!

She opened them to find the stranger still standing in the same spot.

"Where did you come from?"

"You are a curious little one, aren't you," he said, more of a statement than a question.

Still, she felt compelled to respond.

"Yes, yes, I am. But I didn't mean any harm. I'm just curious about Sigmund's work."

"Lies don't become you, young lady. We know you are gathering information against Sigmund Lowe."

He leaned closer.

"What do you have against the Lion?"

She had forgotten that his friends called him by that name.

"I don't have anything against him. He's been very nice to me. But I was taught that being a patriot was important and if I trusted anyone who wasn't American, I was just being fooled."

The man shook his head.

"Ah, yes, the famous warning of one Harry Pinella."

"Y-you know Mr. Pinella?"

"Indeed we do. He warns that you are never to trust a -- how does he say it – oh, yes, a Jap or a Nazi. *He's* the fool."

Hearing him repeat Harry's warning made her feel uncomfortable, as though she knew it was wrong.

"Yes, well," she stuttered. "Well, that's what he said."

"Don't listen to such nonsense, Rosalie. He's an angry, frightened man."

"And who should I listen to? One person tells me one thing and then someone else tells me something different. I overheard Sigmund and Dr. Kramer talking and I think they're Communists."

Now the man stepped forward, almost touching the front of Sigmund's desk.

"Rosalie, you should believe your instincts. You've had a notebook filled with what you call evidence for years and still you've done nothing with it. And why? I'll tell you why. Because you know in your heart that Sigmund is a good man. I believe you overheard him say something about 'rushing' matters and assumed he said something else."

Rosalie didn't know how to respond to that. After all, the stranger was correct about the book. A feeling of overwhelming guilt washed over her.

"I'm sorry, really I am. I'm just confused."

"We understand," he said.

"I'll rip up my notebook and throw it away," she said. "But, please, don't kill me or anything. I'm in charge of my niece and she's too little to be home alone."

"We won't harm you. You're just a child. However, we believe you are filled with regret for your actions. A little guilt, perhaps? Thankfully, no harm's been done. And, because you deserve an opportunity to make restitution, we're going to give you a chance to make it up to the Lion."

He reached down and, without touching them, flipped the pages until he came to a place where a formula lay unfinished. He pointed to a pencil.

"Write this down in that spot."

She followed the direction of his pointed finger.

"Here?"

"Yes, please."

He began to call out numbers, running them off as if from memory. She wrote as quickly as she could. Several times he used words like "lowest transfinite number" and "contour integral" and, somehow, she knew what symbol to use.

"I don't know how I know these words and these funny little drawings. I've really never seen or heard them in my whole life. How am I doing this?"

"With my help," he said.

She continued jotting down several lines of equations until she filled the page.

"Should I try to read them back?"

"Please."

She did, using the correct terminology.

"Wow! That was amazing. Please tell me how I was able to do that?"

When the visitor didn't reply, she looked up, surprised to find the room empty. She reached up and turned the lamp shade, directing the dim light toward the bookcase.

"Where'd he go?"

She looked down and noticed that the folder was still open, but the page on top was the one with the bell-shaped object. She flipped through the pages that followed, looking for the one with the long string of numbers and equations. Before she could find it, she saw the reflection of headlights in the driveway.

She quickly returned the folder to the original status and grabbed her camera. She rushed to her bedroom and stashed it under her bed.

As quickly as she could move, she ran to the living room and leaped onto the sofa, pulling the sheet tight around her neck. No more than a few seconds passed when she heard the key unlock the front door. Through narrowed eyes, she watched as Sigmund entered, sat his keys on the small table by the door and kicked off his shoes.

She leaned on an elbow, rubbing her eyes as though just waking up.

"Is Stanley okay?"

Sigmund walked toward her and sat on the other end of the sofa, inches from her feet.

"Yes, he's going to be fine. The doctor said he can come home tomorrow."

"Where's Carlotta?"

"She decided to stay with him. He was scared. He's just a child."

"Yes, I know. He acts like he's all grown up sometimes, but he's just a little guy. I think I'd be a little scared, too."

Sigmund smiled.

"I'm sure."

Rosalie sat and pulled up her knees.

"How's Catherine? Did she sleep the whole time?"

"Yes. She's good."

"Did you sleep here the whole time?"

She suddenly remembered the glass of milk on his desk. The entire incident with the strange man caused her to shiver.

"What's wrong?"

"Nothing. Yes, I did stay here, the whole time," she said.

Sigmund leaned back and let his head rest on the back of the sofa. He closed his eyes.

Rosalie watched, wondering what he'd do next. She was terrified he'd remember his files and go into his office. He didn't move. She watched as his mouth fell open a little and his breathing became steady and deep.

She got up and tiptoed across the foyer. Looking into the office, she spied her glass on the edge of his desk. She rushed in, picked it up, and walked through the small hallway to the kitchen. She sat the glass on the counter and let out her breath in a relieved sigh.

"Would you like some Bosco in your milk?"

Rosalie jumped at the sound of his voice and, she realized, it hadn't gone unnoticed.

"Oh, I'm sorry, Rosie. Did I frighten you?" he asked as he removed the milk bottle from the refrigerator and the syrup from the overhead cabinet.

"I thought you were asleep, that's all."

He poured out the milk, stirred in the thick brown liquid, and sat on one of the stools by the center island. He placed the bottle in front of her.

She shook her head.

"No, thank you."

She took a sip from her glass, a white line formed on her upper lift. She wiped it away.

He sipped his drink and eyed her the whole time. Somehow, she thought, he knew. After a few minutes, he stood.

"You can go to bed now, Rosie. I am sure you are tired. You did a great job tonight. We're lucky to have you here."

Rosalie smiled.

"Thanks. Well, good night."

She gulped the rest of her milk, peering over the rim of the glass as he headed to his office. She put her glass in the sink, reclaimed her pillow and blanket from the sofa, and headed to her room. She closed the door behind her.

Be a cat. Be a cat.

In the darkness, she climbed on her desk and removed the photo of Albert Einstein, holding her breath the entire time. She aligned her eye with the hole until she could see the dim yellow light change from a long empty shaft to the outline of a tall man. She let out a long, almost nonexistent breath. Slowly, she inhaled and held her breath as Sigmund moved around the desk and sat.

She watched as he flipped through the pages as though only half-concentrating. Surely, she thought, he was also thinking about Stanley. When he arrived at one of the last pages, he seemed to come alive, shifting in his chair. He reached for the lamp and adjusted the yellow light until it was two shades brighter.

She watched as he perused the page with the numbers that she had been told to write. He picked up the pencil, looking at it as though it was a foreign object. He seemed frozen for a long time, then relaxed into his chair. Rosalie thought he looked confused.

Shit, I wasn't dreaming.

Sigmund looked up, his eyes aligned with hers. Her heart began to pound. He appeared to be looking directly into her eye. Then he looked at the page again, scratched his chin, a habit she noticed he practiced when in contemplation, and began to write on another sheet of paper.

After a few minutes, he lifted his head, his eyes squinted. He was thinking. Rosalie had seen that look before, too, and knew without a doubt that *that* was his thinking *look*.

He rose and left the office. Rosalie quickly returned Albert Einstein to his hook and crawled beneath her bed covers.

Chin-scratching, squinty stares. He's too smart to fool.

She heard his knock on the door. She wasn't sure if she should open it or pretend to be asleep.

"Rosie, are you awake?"

She laid perfectly still. She saw the light from the hall slip between the door and the jamb. She wished she'd remembered to lock the door.

"Rosie."

"Wha-what's the matter?"

She sat up, feigning grogginess.

"Rosie," he said and moved to sit on the edge of her bed. "Did you hear any sounds coming from my office tonight?"

He doesn't know. He really doesn't know. He's confused.

Relief surrounded her like a warm blanket.

"Hear anything? Like what? Did something fall and break?"

"No. It's nothing like that. Were you in my office?"

She shook her head. He nodded.

"Well, it looks as though *someone* has been in my office. And you were the only one here. I wonder if it's possible that someone else could have gotten past you. You heard nothing, yes?"

"Yes. I mean, no. I didn't hear anyone."

He shook his head slowly as if trying to contemplate the events that led to his discovery.

"You see," he said, again scratching his chin, "I had some papers in a folder, papers I usually keep under lock and key, and it seems someone has written on them."

Rosalie was torn between telling him what had happened and sticking to her lie. When she did neither, he turned so that their eyes met. The light from the hall felt like a spotlight strategically placed to keep her from hiding anything from him.

"Rosie, it looks like your writing, the way you form your numbers."

"Really?"

He nodded.

"The numbers written represent a complicated sequence that solves a big problem I've been having with my project at work. Yet, it seems you wrote them."

Again, he became quiet.

"Did you have a dream, perhaps?"

She didn't answer right away. Instead, she let the dream explanation play itself out.

"Yes, I did. I had a weird dream that a man came to the door and said that I had to write down a whole bunch of numbers or someone would come and take Catherine. After I wrote the numbers down, he told me to go back to sleep. I remember that I ran down the hall to make sure Catherine was still in her crib. Wow, that's strange, isn't it. Did I actually write down numbers?"

He nodded.

"Sig, do you think it wasn't a dream and that it really happened?"

"I don't know what to think."

"Will the man in the black suit come back for me?"

"A man in a black suit?"

She paused, cursing herself for saying too much.

"Yes."

"Anything else?"

She shrugged.

"Dark glasses?"

She nodded.

How does he know this stuff?

Finally, she couldn't take it any longer and she blurted out a question of her own.

"How do you know about this man? It was just a dream."

Sigmund appeared stunned.

"The question is how do *you* know about this man?"

Rosalie could no longer contain her anxiety. She bolted upright in her bed and allowed the truth to pour from her mouth.

"Because I was snooping around in your office and he stepped out of the corner, out of the darkness, and he scared me to death, and he just seemed to crackle and appear."

Sigmund's eyes grew wide. A wide smile crossed his face.

"Yes, that's how they do it," he said, excitedly. "That's exactly how I've heard they've appeared to people in the past. This is astonishing."

"Where do these people come from?" she asked.

He smiled and pointed his index finger upward.

"Really? Space aliens?"

"I think so, but I'm not sure. They could be aliens from outer space or, perhaps, inter-dimensional travelers."

"Either way, they're aliens, right?" she asked, needing to identify her frightening experience.

Sigmund nodded.

"Really, Rosie, your guess is as good as mine. Nevertheless, this is extraordinary," he said, still smiling.

He stopped, the smile faded, and he frowned.

"But Rosie, why in Heaven's name were you snooping around my office?"

Rosalie was on the brink of hysteria. The events of the evening had her trembling. She knew she'd never fall asleep unless she confessed. She jumped out of bed and rushed to her desk, climbed on it and removed the photograph.

"I've been spying on you ever since I got here. Last year, I put this hole in the wall so I could see what you were up to. I'm a terrible person. Please don't put me in an orphanage."

Sigmund stood and rushed to her side. He leaned over her desk and looked through the hole.

"I thought you were a Nazi and were selling secrets to the Communists."

"Oh, my God, Rosalie! Oh, my God!"

She'd never seen the usually "calm and collected" Sigmund so rattled. Her eyes grew wide and she nodded her head so quickly she looked like a bobble-head doll in the rear window of a car.

"I know. I know. I'm so sorry. I never told anyone. I wrote everything down in a notebook, but I never showed it to anyone."

Sigmund began to pace. He rubbed the back of his neck, stopped, turned to Rosalie, said nothing, and paced some more.

"Sigmund, I'm so sorry; really I am. Here," she said, reaching beneath her mattress to produce her marble notebook. "Take it. Rip it up."

He took the book, flipped through pages and looked Rosalie straight in the eye.

"Did you tell your friends?"

"Joey and Denise?"

He nodded.

She wanted to lie, but the time for truth was at hand and she knew the only way out of the mess she'd gotten herself into was to tell the truth and nothing else.

"Yes, I told them."

"Rosalie, Rosalie."

Oh, crap, he's calling me by my real name.

"I never showed them the book. I only told them I thought you and Dr. Kramer were selling secrets to the Russians."

Now, he stood before her, tall and menacing. She was sure he was about to hit her. Instead, he placed his right hand on her shoulder and bent forward so their eyes met again.

"You brought Otto into this, too?"

She gulped and nodded.

"Who else?" he asked.

"No one, I swear."

"And you told no one about this book, yes?"

"No one."

Sigmund looked at the book in his left hand, turning it over as if the answer was somewhere on the back cover. Rosalie glanced at the marble design.

"Rosie," he began, then paused.

At that, she let out a long sigh of relief. Surely he wouldn't call her Rosie and then murder her. When he spoke, his voice was soft.

"Rosie, you must tell your friends that you're mistaken. Tell them it was just a suspicion because I came here from Germany. Tell them you hate all Germans and wanted to hurt me. Tell them you saw a television program where the girl's brother-in-law was a spy. Tell them anything you wish, but tell them you no longer suspect me or Dr. Kramer of any wrong-doing. Can you do that?"

Rosalie nodded.

"Good."

He turned and headed toward the door. He stopped and turned to face her.

"Promise me, Rosie."

"I promise; cross my heart and hope to die."

She realized he'd never heard that expression as he seemed taken aback by her oath.

"Fine," he finally said. "Fine."

Once alone in her room, she hung up the photograph of Albert Einstein. She stood looking into his face, his wise eyes seeming to look into her soul. She could almost hear him tell her not to do it, but she did it anyway. She climbed on the desk and peered through the hole.

Sigmund was at his desk, the marble notebook in front of him. He seemed to be reading her notes. Every now and then, he'd shake his head. Once or twice, he actually smiled. Finally, when he'd reached the end, he closed the book. He lifted his eyes to the bookcase, to the place where Rosalie watched.

"Good night, Rosie," he said and shut off the lamp.

She jumped at that, her heart pounding.

Shit, he saw me. He knew I was watching.

Then, as quickly as she could, she replaced the photograph and climbed into bed. She was exhausted. Tomorrow, she promised herself, she'd figure it all out. Tomorrow.

Chapter 13

It had been several days since Rosalie's frightening experience in Sigmund's office Monday night. She wanted to ask him who the strange man was and from where he'd come.

She stayed home from school on Tuesday while Sigmund picked up Carlotta and Stanley from the hospital.

Rosalie was still anxious about the experience and needed to spend time alone with Sigmund.

"We will talk later," he promised.

On Wednesday, she had to return to school and he was called away to Washington, D.C.

"I have an important meeting at the Pentagon," he explained to his wife. "It's business as usual. The DOD always needs reassurance that their project is progressing."

That, thought Rosalie, was his lame explanation to Carlotta. Somehow, she knew it had something to do with the mysterious man. She knew the DOD stood for the Department of Defense.

On Wednesday at school, as promised, she informed Joseph and Denise that she was over her fascination with Sigmund and Otto. It turned out to be easier than she thought.

"I figured Denise was right," Rosalie explained. "It was just my overactive imagination."

Denise had looked at Joseph and gave him a grin of satisfaction.

"See, I told you."

Joseph merely shrugged.

"Whatever."

At home, however, things were a little tougher. Stanley, she discovered much to her own dismay, was a terrible patient. The minute she got home from school, his demands began. They were relentless.

"Rosie, come in and read to me."

"Rosie, come in and keep me company."

"Rosie, let's play Go Fish."

On Thursday, Carlotta finally let him roam the house. He seemed to like the idea of spending the entire day in his pajamas.

By the end of the week, Rosalie was wound as tight as a top. She felt as though if she didn't talk to Sigmund soon, she's surely spin out of control.

"When's he coming home?"

Carlotta seemed beside herself with a sick child and a rambunctious three-year-old who seemed to have unlimited energy.

"Tomorrow," she said as she prepared lunch. "Why are you so anxious to see him?"

She wanted to tell Carlotta about the man, then decided it was best to keep quiet. She shrugged.

"I just need some help with a report."

"Well, he'll be home around noon tomorrow, just in time for Easter."

Trying to distract her anxiety, Rosalie headed to Denise's house where her friend was trying on her new Easter outfit, complete with straw bonnet.

"Looks nice," she said.

"Did Carlotta get you a new outfit?"

"Yes, a blue dress and white hat."

"I love Easter," Denise said, rattling on and on about how her family celebrates the holiday.

Rosalie couldn't concentrate on her chatter. It seemed mundane to discuss Easter outfits and jelly beans. She stood and headed for the door.

"What's the matter? Where are you going?"

"Denise, I just remembered something. I gotta go."

She sprinted out the front door much to the shock of her friend.

Easter bonnets and colored eggs and chocolate bunnies. Really? I've been visited by space aliens. Who cares about jelly beans!

When she arrived home, she found Carlotta boiling eggs.

"We'll dye them tomorrow when Sig returns," she said.

I can't wait. I can't wait.

She could barely sleep that night. She tossed and turned until her exhaustion overtook her overactive brain. Dreams of men in black turned into dreams of bell-shaped flying saucers.

By morning, Rosalie was well rested despite the fact that the strange man seemed to visit her in her sleep. At first, she thought it had all been a dream. She got out of bed and lifted the mattress. The book was gone. It was no dream.

"Rosie, are you awake?"

She slipped her feet into her slippers and wrapped her bathrobe around herself, tying the belt at her waist.

"Yes, Stanley."

Without asking, he burst into her room. He was getting tall, she thought, as she watched him stride across her room and plant himself on her bed. At seven, he *really* looked like a small version of his father. His blonde hair was cut in a crew cut and his brilliant blue eyes seemed to shine, especially when he was excited and, with Easter only a day away, he was definitely excited. His words seemed to explode from his mouth in rapid succession.

"Papa's coming home today and the Easter bunny is coming tonight and tomorrow, at church, we're going to have an Easter egg hunt. I can't wait."

Rosalie remembered the event from the previous years. Since arriving in Georgia, she was given the choice to remain in the Catholic Church or join the Lutherans. The latter seemed like the easiest option.

"After all," Carlotta had said, "we're all Christians."

"Are you excited, too?" he asked.

She kissed the top of his head.

"Yes, I'm excited, too."

"C'mon, Mama made us pancakes with blueberries and she knows how to make a face with a big smile with them."

Rosalie followed him to the kitchen. Carlotta, she thought, looked especially stunning. She had her hair pulled up in a ponytail that sat on the top of her head and seemed to dance from side to side as she moved about.

Rosalie watched as she placed a dish with a smiling blueberry pancake in front of Stanley.

"See," he said. "I told you so. Look, my pancakes are smiling at me."

At that, Rosalie laughed and accepted a dish with three smiling pancakes from Carlotta who winked at her.

As she ate, Rosalie watched as Carlotta orchestrated her life. She poured milk into a small cup for Catherine and proceeded to help her manage it, a loving smile etched on her exquisite features.

She's so beautiful. If only she knew what was going in her house; a strange man appearing and disappearing. I'll never tell her. I wouldn't want to be the one to burst her bubble.

Carlotta, she thought, seemed to float in her sea of tranquility.

After a few minutes, Carlotta turned to Rosalie.

"What's up, girlie? Why are you looking at me like that?"

"Like what?"

"I don't know; sort of funny. Is there something on your mind?"

At that moment, Rosalie's heart seemed to fill with love for her sister. She wanted to repay her for her kindness. With the burden of trying to expose Sigmund as a traitor lifted, she suddenly felt light and full of joy.

"I love you, Carlotta. I probably should've said that before. You've been so good to me. I just want you to know I appreciate everything you do."

Carlotta stopped, her body seemed to freeze. She turned to face Rosalie who noticed that, while she appeared frozen in time, a tear rolled down her cheek. It seemed as though a mere second passed and Carlotta was at her side, hugging her and kissing her cheek.

"Mama loves you, Rosie," Stanley said.

"Mama loves Rosie," Catherine repeated almost verbatim.

"Very good, Catherine," Carlotta said. "Good girl."

Rosalie finished her meal and went to her room. There, she made her bed, hung up her pajamas and robe, and dressed in a pair of red slacks and a red and white checkered blouse. She slid her feet into her white Keds.

The grandfather clock by the door reminded her it was ten o'clock. When, she wondered, would she be able to speak to Sigmund? Surely Carlotta, Stanley and Catherine would demand his attention. She was beside herself with anxiety. She needed something constructive to do. She went into the kitchen.

Carlotta had just finished washing the dishes. She removed her apron and hung it on a hook by the back door.

Stanley and Catherine were in the family room watching television. She knew it was cartoons as squeaky voices seemed to fill the space between the rooms.

"Can I help you with something?" Rosalie asked.

Carlotta appeared surprised by her offer.

"Like what?"

"I don't know. Tomorrow's Easter, I figure you probably have a million things to do"

"Yes, I do have something you can help me with. I have so much to get ready for the children, my children, anyway. And we're having a party after services tomorrow. I could use some help preparing mini-baskets for the kids at church."

"That sounds like fun. Sure, what do you want me to do?"

"Go into Sig's office and get the box on the third shelf of his bookcase. It's marked "St. J" and, I promise, it's not heavy. It only has baskets made from colored cardboard and Easter grass inside of it."

Rosalie involuntarily cringed, recalling her recent encounter.

"Don't worry. I know Sig usually doesn't want anyone in his office, but he means the little ones. I'm sure he won't mind if you go in and get the box. Just don't touch anything on his *precious* desk," she said, smiling at her own remark.

"Okay," she said and headed toward the double doors, now closed to intruders.

She grabbed the handle on the right door and slid it open. As she stepped into the darkened space, her pulse quickened. The heavy drapes had been pulled shut and the closest light was the lamp on his desk.

Rosalie crept eerily toward it and, just as she was about to turn on the lamp, she heard the crackling sound. The door, now five feet behind her, slid closed on its own, a gentle "click" completing the task.

"It is you?" she asked.

Silence surrounded her. She wondered if she'd only heard the wind on the window, or perhaps a breeze that caused the door to slide shut. She wanted to turn and flee. Something inside urged her forward. She took a few more steps until she bumped into the corner of the desk.

"Damn," she whispered.

She slid her hand across the smooth finish, feeling for the base of the lamp. Just as her pinky touched it, it went on. It was then that she realized she wasn't alone, although she couldn't actually see anyone.

"Look, mister, I'm allowed in here. I'm helping my sister."

She jumped when a woman's voice spoke softly.

"Rosalie, where's Dr. Lowe?"

She'd never heard anyone refer to him as Dr. Lowe except for Dr. Bennett.

"Who are you?"

"That's not important. We must speak to Dr. Lowe."

"He's in," she paused, wondering if she should tell this new arrival he was in Washington D.C. "He's not home."

"Where is he? We cannot locate him."

Rosalie wasn't sure what that meant, but she replied, "I'm not sure."

"You began to say where he's gone, Rosalie. You really don't want to lie to us. I have an important message for him."

Rosalie didn't like her tone at all. While her voice was soft and low, her warning sounded terse.

"I'm not lying. Look, he'll be home at lunch time. I'll tell him you asked for him, whoever you are. I'm sure he'll know what to do."

Rosalie had been staring at the lamp the entire time, afraid to turn her face toward the visitor. Her hands began to sweat.

"Don't be afraid, child. No one is going to hurt you."

"I'm not afraid," she lied.

The woman made a soft laugh.

"Really? How old are you?"

"Fourteen."

"Look at me," the woman said. "If you're not afraid, stop staring at that lamp shade and look at me."

Rosalie realized that fourteen or not, she was terrified. Yet, something inside her seemed to rise up. It seemed to slide into the base of her spine and force its way to her neck, straightening it. Now, standing taller than she realized she could, she turned and faced the mysterious woman.

She jumped when she realized no one was there. The light from the lamp reached across the room, past the wing-back chair, and onto the bookcase. There, on the third shelf, sat the box.

"St. J," she whispered.

She hurried to the bookcase and grabbed the box. Without shutting off the lamp, she went to the door, pulled it open and fled into the foyer. Her heart was pounding. She felt as though she had just ran all the way home from school.

"Rosie, what's the matter? You look like you just saw a ghost," Carlotta said. Then, in the same tone, added, "Oh, good, you found the baskets."

She took the box and headed to the kitchen. Rosalie watched as she disappeared around the wall. She could hear Bugs Bunny coming from the family room. The front door opened and Sigmund entered. Rosalie, still shaken, turned with a start and said the first thing that seemed appropriate.

"What's up, Doc?"

It had been a long, difficult week for Sigmund. It all began when Carlotta summoned him to Stanley's room. There, he found the boy wheezing and barking like a dog.

He was so upset he left important papers on his desk; papers that were meant for his eyes only, and one a particularly secret document.

Once his son was tucked away in an oxygen tent, his wife at the boy's side, he returned home. There, he discovered a strange man had visited his sister-in-law in his office. Her story sounded surreal, but he knew it was true.

He'd heard many stories of the ether people. Most of the time they wore black suits and dark glasses. Rumor had it that the reason for the dark glasses was because they were beings of light and if they didn't wear them, beams of light would shoot from their eye sockets.

She'd been shaken by the experience and admitted that she'd been spying on him since she arrived. He knew of her past influences, a mother with a distinct hatred for anyone of German heritage, and understood the girl's feelings, but he never thought she'd go so far as to plan his demise.

She swore she'd drop her investigation and apologized over and over again. There was no reason to think she'd do otherwise as the visitor appeared to have scared her tremendously.

The next day, after retrieving his family from the hospital, he remained at home, locked away in his office. He reassured Rosalie he'd discuss the visit.

"I need some time to review what you've given me. Tomorrow, I promise. We'll talk tomorrow."

He went over the new formula, step by step, and wondered how Rosalie had the ability to write it.

On Wednesday, when he arrived at his office, he was called into Dr. Bennett's office.

"Sigmund, we have a problem. We have reason to believe you've been visited by them."

He nodded his head as if to indicate the "them" he spoke of came from somewhere above, perhaps outer space. The jury wasn't in on their origin yet.

"How do you know this?"

"So, it's true?"

Sigmund mentally cringed. He'd asked the wrong question.

"I didn't see anyone," he finally blurted out.

"Really? Well, that's strange. As you know, we keep an electronic surveillance monitor here. It picks up any anomalies in the entire area. When we checked the map, it appeared the disturbance came from your home."

Sigmund knew about the monitors. Actually, he was one of the scientists who designed the system. It measured any unusual electrical activity on a grid. Whatever these beings were, they packed a lot of power when they visited. To his knowledge, they'd popped in on several of his colleagues when he was in Germany. However, since their arrival in the states, nothing has been detected. He was beginning to think either they were no longer willing to share their knowledge or, perhaps, they really didn't exist.

Then, out of the blue, one appears to his teenage sister-in-law, of all people. His mind reeled with the implications of the visit. A clearing of the throat reminded him Dr. Bennett waited for his response.

The last thing he wanted to do was drag Rosalie into the middle of the intrigue.

"I didn't see them. I was at the hospital with my son who has the croup. When I arrived home, I realized someone was in my office."

"How did you know?"

Sigmund pulled out a sheet of paper upon which the new formulas were written. He handed it to Dr. Bennett who examined the writing.

"Who wrote this? I dare say, it looks like your handwriting."

Think fast, Sigmund, think fast.

"Yes, it is mine. It was written on a mirror and I copied it."

"A mirror? How clever of them. What did they use?"

"A crayon."

Dr. Bennett raised his eyebrows.

"A crayon?"

Sigmund nodded and smiled.

"Yes. Can you imagine that? These beings have the ability to travel throughout the universe, or so we believe, and they use a crayon to relay an important formula."

"Where's the crayon now?"

"It's on my desk at home."

"I think we should examine it to see if there is any radioactive material on it."

"I'll go home and get it."

Dr. Bennett seemed excited.

"Yes, yes, do that."

Just then, Judy Mason, Dr. Bennett's secretary, entered.

"DC's on the line."

Dr. Bennett picked up the receiver. Before he could utter a word, the person at the other end must have been speaking as Dr. Bennett merely listened, nodding his head and uttering a couple of 'Yes, sirs'. He hung up the receiver and looked across the desk.

"We're going to Washington. I've notified the DOD of what we detected and now they want our asses up there."

"When?"

"Now. Go home and get that crayon, pack a clean shirt and meet me back here in half an hour. I'll call Dr. Kramer."

Less than an hour later, Sigmund, Otto and Dr. Bennett boarded a helicopter that took them to a private airfield, then a private airplane that whisked them off to the capital. On the way, Sigmund told the story to Otto, who merely nodded as he listened.

As close as the men had been throughout their lives, Sigmund couldn't bring himself to tell him about Rosalie. Somewhere, way in the back of his mind, he still had reservations about Otto's loyalty.

His history had tainted him. When he was thirteen, his mother and younger brother were killed en route from Paris to Germany when the train on which they travelled took a curve too fast and was thrown off the tracks and down a deep, rock-strewn embankment. He was left to fend for himself with a father who remained in allegiance with Hitler's henchmen.

Otto had watched as his father, a high-ranking SS officer, escorted his childhood friends and their families away, each time being reassured that it was for the good of the country.

No, Sigmund thought, he had become too damaged during his formative years to have a clear vision.

He would keep Rosalie out of it for as long as possible; forever if necessary.

Upon their arrival at the Pentagon, home of the United States Department of Defense in Arlington, Virginia, Sigmund handed over the crayon to Dr. Bennett's supervisor, another scientist named Saul Hartman.

An examination revealed no signs of radioactivity. Sigmund knew it wouldn't. He'd snatched one from Stanley's room before packing his clothes. This, too, Sigmund kept from Otto.

The formula, on the other hand, proved to be of much more significance. It set the basis for accelerated movement through time. Unlike his previous experiments where objects were thrust into the future and slowed down in the same dimension, this formula had other properties, those of which he wasn't sure. It hinted at the possibility of either another dimension or, perhaps, a property not yet anticipated.

The trip to Washington turned out to be nothing more than a visit to a think tank. Sigmund, Otto, Dr. Bennett and seven other scientists spent the better part of two days attempting to decipher what appeared to be a coded formula.

"Let's take a break," suggested Dr. Bennett. "We'll meet in Georgia first thing on Tuesday, my office. I want to see all of you there by eight. I'll bring the doughnuts."

His last remark met a round of laughter. Sigmund, however, didn't as much as break a smile. What, he wondered, was he to do about Rosalie? He didn't appreciate the fact that the stranger left the formula with her. What did she have to do with any of this? She's just a child, he thought. Yet, at the same time, the visitor felt it necessary to warn her about exposing anything about her brother-in-law's work.

On Saturday, he left Washington and headed home. He was confronted by the girl who asked the strangest question the moment he walked through the front door.

"What's up, Doc?"

With raised eyebrows, he repeated her question.

"What's up, Doc? What does that mean?"

Rosalie had smiled and shrugged.

"I didn't know what else to say. I just had another visitation and I was so scared and I heard Bugs Bunny on the television and you walked in the door. It all happened at once. That was the only thing I could think of."

Her explanation sounded trivial, especially compared to the news that she'd received a second visitation. What she reported was more disturbing.

"Another visit?"

Rosalie nodded.

"I think this one was a lady."

"A lady? You mean a woman appeared?"

Sigmund was just about to pull Rosalie into his office when Stanley entered the foyer and ran toward him, his arms wide.

"Papa, Papa's home," he squealed.

Sigmund scooped him up and hugged him.

"You are feeling better, yes?"

Stanley nodded.

"Yes, lots better."

Carlotta entered the foyer, too, with Catherine in her arms.

He bent his head to place a kiss on her mouth.

"Welcome home, Love."

He smiled, realizing this was all that mattered. His family. He lowered Stanley to the floor and took Catherine from Carlotta. He nuzzled her ear causing her to giggle.

"Papa's girl."

"Well, we're just about to have lunch. Are you hungry?" Carlotta asked.

Sigmund nodded. In fact, he was starving. With so much that had occurred during the past week, he barely had an appetite. Now, being with those he loved and recalling the details of Otto's past, more than ever, he knew his main goal was to protect his loved ones. That, he reminded himself, included Rosalie.

"Ten minutes," she said and turned toward the kitchen.

Stanley took Catherine's hand and led her into the family room.

"C'mon, Bugs is going to steal all the carrots."

Catherine happily followed.

Alone in the foyer, Sigmund focused on Rosalie.

"My office. Now. Tell me everything."

Rosalie felt like an erupted dam once again, spewing every bit of information she could recall with the utmost force, every detail, every emotion.

"But when I turned around, she was gone. I know I heard her. It wasn't just my imagination," she said as she slowed to a more peaceful stream. "Sig, do *you* think I just imagined it?"

She didn't know why she asked that question, except she wanted to be certain he believed her.

"No, I don't think you imagined any of this. These visitors, they are strange beings. We only knew of men who appeared. However, think about this. Perhaps one of them appeared as a woman so that you would not become too frightened. That sounds reasonable, yes?"

"Well, it didn't work. She scared the crap out of me. But, Sig, what I want to know is why me. Why do they visit *me*? I'm a nobody and I don't know anything about science."

Sigmund nodded his head as he scratched his chin.

"That, my dear girl, is the million-dollar question. I have been asking myself the same thing all week. Why Rosie?"

"Did you tell Dr. Bennett?"

At that, Sigmund seemed to stiffen, his accent more exaggerated.

"No, I have not told Dr. Bennett. As a matter of fact, I have not told Dr. Kramer either. Rosie, listen, you must tell no one about the visitors. For now, let's keep this between us. I think it is best for you and your safety that no one knows you are involved. "

Rosalie liked the sound of that. She nodded in agreement.

A soft knock on the office door informed them lunch was ready. When they emerged, Stanley stood looking up at his father.

"How come Rosie's allowed in there, but not me?"

Rosalie wanted to tell him that he should be glad he wasn't allowed in the office. Lately, it's been a scary place with strange visitors from another world popping in and out. Instead, she leaned down and patted his head.

"Because I'm already fourteen and I'm going to be a scientist soon. Right, Sig?"

Sigmund nodded.

"Yes. When you are fourteen, you will also be permitted in my office. In the meantime, I do not want to find cartoons drawn on my important papers."

As he spoke, he tickled the boy's chin. Stanley laughed, accepting his fate.

"Okay, Papa. C'mon, Rosie, after lunch we're gonna color Easter eggs."

"Going to, not gonna," Sigmund corrected.

Rosalie smiled.

Sig might just be a good guy. Just to be sure, the next time one of those strange beings visits me, I'm going to ask why they chose him. I hope I like the reply. I'll just die if he turns out to be a real Communist, especially now that I might be starting to like him again.

Chapter 14

After Easter services on Sunday, Rosalie headed to the Recreation Hall with the other children at St. John's. It was a large multi-purpose room at the back of the long, narrow building.

Rosalie could tell that Herta Lowe was delighted to see her. She hugged her tightly and assigned her the task of hiding three dozen colored and designed eggs in the church garden.

"The little ones will be out of Sunday School soon, so we have to hurry."

As she placed the colorful eggs around the garden, Rosalie could hear "Hallelujah Chorus" coming from inside the church from the second service.

A few minutes later, the garden and the church sat silent, waiting for the next round of celebration. Rosalie sat on a small stone bench by a fountain.

The music began again and this time when it stopped, a stream of little Lutherans emerged from the double doors and into her quiet space. Each had a brightly colored cardboard basket for which to gather their eggs.

She noticed Stanley at the far end of the garden. He'd found the egg she hid beneath a butterfly bush. His face seemed to light up.

After all of the services ended, Reverend and Mrs. Lowe joined the family for dinner. The holiday passed with the same festivities as the year before. It included good food, a lot of treats and happy, normal conversation. However, sitting in the back of her mind, larger questions loomed; questions that weren't normal

She wondered for what her brother-in-law searched. She knew, sooner or later, he'd reveal his goal and clarify her confusion. In the meantime, she only wanted to be a teenager with a week off from school for spring break.

She spent Monday morning with Carlotta and the children cleaning up at the church. Just before noon, she went home to finish a homework project that was due upon her return the following week. She noticed the door to Sigmund's office was pulled open about six inches. She peered inside and found him at his desk, reading.

"Hi, Sig," she said through the small gap. "I didn't know you had off today."

"Hello, Rosie. Yes, I'm going over that formula. It's quite amazing that you were able to write this."

Rosalie smiled and shrugged.

"I don't know how I did it either."

"What are you doing today?"

"I have homework, a project to finish. Carlotta and the kids are still at your dad's church."

"Okay. And, Rosie, thank you for helping them. I know my father appreciates it."

"No problem," she said. "Well, I have to do my homework. I'll talk to you later. Do you want me to shut the door?"

"Yes, please. I want to go over this again."

She pulled the right door until it clicked into the left. She spent the rest of the afternoon cutting out various cloud images from a magazine Sigmund had given her on meteorology for her science project.

She spent Tuesday with Denise and Joseph. She hadn't seen them since Thursday, the last day of school before spring break.

Joseph had spent that time in Philadelphia with his grandparents and returned that morning.

"So, what have you guys been up to while I was gone?" he asked.

"Oh, nothing," Denise replied. "You know how it goes, church on Good Friday, church on Easter Sunday, watching television and, of course, that stupid project about clouds that Mrs. Banner wants us to do."

"How about you, Rosie?"

She wanted so much to share the exciting news of visits from alien beings but knew it could put her in danger.

"Same thing for me. Easter was nice. I worked on my project, too."

They went to Denise's house where Mrs. Perry made egg salad sandwiches for lunch.

"She said she has to do something with all those hard-boiled eggs," Denise said.

On Wednesday, Rosalie went to the library. She told the librarian she wanted to look up books related to aliens.

"Aliens? Like UFO's?" she asked.

She was a tall, thin woman with a pointed chin and beady eyes, short brown hair and large glasses.

"Yes, please."

"Well, you know they're not real, don't you? All that nonsense in 1947 about a UFO crash at Roswell was nothing but a weather balloon. They're nothing but stories from people who need to find better things to do with their time."

"Can you tell me where the books are anyway? I think it's pretty interesting."

The woman rolled her eyes and waved her hand. She seemed annoyed.

"This way."

Rosalie followed her to a bank of small drawers with little cards containing letters slipped into brackets on the front.

"Aliens," the woman said. "A to Am. You'll find numbers that represent the section, followed by more numbers that represent the shelf location of the book itself. Good luck."

When she walked away, Rosalie had the strong urge to call her back and tell her about the visitors in Sigmund's office, especially the part about the invisible woman.

"Oh, the heck with you," she whispered to herself and proceeded to find what she sought.

She found several books about alien visits, but none made reference to other-dimensional beings. They all seemed to discuss flying saucers and creatures from the sky. Nevertheless, she thought, it seemed a lot of people had had encounters. She closed the last of the books she had taken from the bookshelves, pushed them into the center of the table, and rose.

"Wait a minute," a soft voice said.

Rosalie turned and found the librarian behind her. She wondered how the woman could move about so quietly.

"What? Have I done something wrong?"

"No. I wanted to share something important with you. Look in your Bible. Read about Sodom and Gomorrah. Read about Ezekiel. These are some of the first recorded accounts of extraterrestrials. Ask yourself one question, child. Did they come from the sky or a parallel universe? Maybe angels and spirits are actually inter-dimensional travelers. Just think about it."

The librarian then turned and walked toward the high bookshelves, stopped and gazed at Rosalie for a few seconds. She disappeared around the corner of the last one.

"Wait! I have a question," Rosalie said, moving in the librarian's direction. "Wait, one thing."

"Shhh," came a warning.

When Rosalie turned, she found the librarian standing on the opposite side of her desk.

"Weren't you just here?"

The woman frowned.

"Be quiet. This is a library."

Rosalie stared at her for a long time.

This lady's crazy.

"You just told me to read the Bible. I just wanted to know why."

The librarian shook her head.

"I told you no such thing. However, it wouldn't hurt for you youngsters to spend time with the Good Book instead of that trash with which you seem to be taken."

She turned and walked away, not once looking back.

Rosalie looked toward the area where she was sure she saw the librarian disappear. She walked to the edge of the row of bookshelves and scanned the area behind the last one. There was nothing but a bare wall.

She walked toward the door, passing the desk where the librarian glared at her. She approached the woman.

"Did you tell me to read Ezekiel in my Bible?"

"Of course not," she said, frowning. "Why would I suggest such a thing? I said it wouldn't hurt for youngsters to read the Bible. Why? Are you interested in seeing one? We have several."

"No, I have one. I thought you said I should read Ezekiel."

The woman shook her head.

"Ezekiel? Really? Why for Heaven's sake; because some so-called scholars think what he experienced was a visitation from extraterrestrial beings?"

"I don't know," Rosalie said. "All I know is that someone, I thought it was you, told me to read that and the story of Sodom and Gomorrah."

"Sodom and Gomorrah?"

"Yes. She said I should ask myself where the angels came from."

"Are you a Christian?"

Rosalie nodded.

"Then I'd suggest you talk to your priest or pastor about such things. Never, ever listen to a scientist. They're all nothing but a bunch of atheists. They don't believe in anything they can't see, touch, taste, smell or feel."

"I believe in things I can't see," Rosalie said and added, "Like air and sound."

The librarian tilted her head, squinting her beady eyes as she spoke.

"And God, I hope."

"Yes, God. I believe in God."

"Then, I suggest you stop all this nonsense about angels being aliens and practice your faith."

She appeared finished with the conversation as she lowered her head and began stamping dates inside a stack of books on her desk. Except for the soft tap of her stamp on the ink pad and then on the book, it seemed eerily quiet.

"Thanks," Rosalie said.

The woman stopped and raised her head.

"For what?"

"For trying to help me. Can I ask you one question?"

The woman appeared annoyed as she dropped the stamp and leaned forward as if anticipating yet another annoying question from her young visitor.

"Yes, what now?"

"Isn't it possible that if God created the Universe, he could create people on all of the planets? Maybe, just like there are different kinds of people on Earth, there are different kinds of people throughout the Universe. Isn't that possible?"

The librarian sat taller, her chin set in an indignant pose. She seemed to contemplate the question. Just when Rosalie was sure she was about to be asked to leave, the woman allowed a smile to touch her lips.

"Well, I suppose so," she said. "Is that all?"

Rosalie smiled back, happy to know she could persuade an adult to see something from a different perspective.

"Yes, that's all. Thanks again."

She nearly ran all the way home, a triumphant smile on her face.

Carlotta was on the front patio with Catherine. Stanley was sitting on the step watching a ladybug crawl over his hand. Mr. Johnson was planting daffodils along the front porch. He nodded to Rosalie when she neared.

"Hi, Mr. Johnson."

"Miss Rosie."

"Where have you been all day?" Carlotta asked. "You're all flushed."

"I was at the library. Hey, Carlotta, can I borrow your Bible? There's something I want to read up on."

Now, Mr. Johnson stood and appeared to place his attention on Rosalie. She could tell he was listening to their conversation.

Carlotta, however, appeared pleased and smiled at her request.

"Sure. It's in the drawer next to my bed. If you have any questions, bring it out here and we can read it together."

"Okay," Rosalie said and hurried inside the house.

She retrieved it and went to her room, closing the door. By dinnertime, she'd read the Biblical accounts of Ezekiel, with its fiery chariot that descended from the sky.

"And I looked, and, behold, a whirlwind came out of the north, a great cloud, and a fire engulfing itself, and a brightness was about it, and out of its midst as the color of amber, out of the midst of the fire.

"Also out of its midst came the likeness of four living creatures. And this was their appearance; they had the likeness of a man.

"And each one had four faces, and each one had four wings.

"And their feet were straight feet; and the sole of their feet was like the sole of a calf's foot: and they sparkled like the color of burnished bronze.

"And they had the hands of a man under their wings on their four sides; and the four had their faces and their wings.

"Their wings were joined one to another; they turned not when they went; they went each one straight forward.

"As for the likeness of their faces, the four had the face of a man, and the face of a lion, on the right side: and the four had the face of an ox on the left side; the four also had the face of an eagle."

She rested the book on her lap.

"Wow," she whispered.

She found the story of Sodom and Gomorrah, where angels warned the people that they were in danger. She couldn't understand why Lot would offer up his daughters to save strangers. Yet, the strangers had spared him and his family.

"Except for Lot's wife," she whispered. "She should have just kept going. That's a strange story."

The destruction of the two cities, she thought, sounded an awful lot like the blast that destroyed the two cities in Japan at the end of the war, a sad memory from her history lesson. She recalled feeling badly that so many innocent people had died.

She refocused her attention to the task at hand, closed the Bible and stared into space, her mind reeling.

She knew there had to be more books about this new way of looking at history. She decided to ask Sigmund. She wondered if he'd ever discussed such theories with his parents, especially since his father was a pastor.

Once again, she found that she could barely wait for his return.

Chapter 15

Armand Bennett closed the file folder. He removed his glasses and ran his hand over the top of his bald head as if smoothing back his long-departed hair. He'd given up on the obvious "comb-over" the year before.

"Fucking Lowe," he seethed. "The Lion? The liar is more like it."

He opened the folder again and perused the first page. A series of numbers ran across it, a formula that he'd never seen before. What, he wondered, was its meaning? And from where did it really come?

He recognized the first three steps. They were the ones that were programmed into the vibrational accelerator. The sequence, in theory, had the capability to send an object into the future. But how?

He glanced at the calendar on his desk. The tenth was circled in red. That was the day they were going to make their next attempt to send a timepiece forward. It would be the first time using the new formula.

Sigmund had assured him their new trials could bring success. He said they were closer to stabilizing the material to be sent forward.

"We're close," Sigmund promised. "A minor adjustment could make all the difference. I'm working on the last section of the formula."

Dr. Bennett shook his head. His thoughts focused on the war.

Had it not been for the end of the war and the death of Hitler, Sigmund Lowe might have had the opportunity to take the research further. If only the war could have lasted another year, he knew, they would have been more advanced in their research.

He sat back and let his head fall to the back of his chair so that he was staring at the ceiling. He mentally chastised himself for such thoughts.

We can go forward, but not return. We can go forward, but what awaits us? If it's trouble, we're doomed. What is the point of this experiment if it solves nothing? Think Armand, think.

He had asked the same questions of the Germans, his top two scientists, but they had no answers.

"I don't know the purpose of traveling forward in time," Sigmund said. "I only know we were given top priority on this experiment."

"What, do you think, did your fuhrer have in mind?"

Otto seemed to want to offer an answer, then settled back into his chair. Sigmund had shook his head.

"I don't know. We didn't ask such questions. We did as we were told." At that, Otto had nodded.

"We did. That is certain."

Now, seated at his desk, Bennett lowered his head and stared at the formula again. He separated the numbers into groups. He knew the first section was dedicated to forward movement. He made a heavy red mark between the first and second group.

He stared at the second group of numbers. His mind was blank. He picked up the telephone and dialed a number. A man answered.

"We have a problem. We have the formula, but no one here knows how to move past the first part. We're stuck on the second step. I was thinking, there might be another part of this formula that Dr. Lowe isn't sharing."

"And what do you want me to do with this information?" the man asked.

"Find out if there are any other steps."

There was a long silence.

"Bring me the formula. I'll try to find out if there's more to it."

The telephone line went dead.

"Try? You'll try? You better do more than try, my friend," he said into the silent receiver.

Otto Kramer had returned from Washington with a renewed hope. The new formula and a host of new scientists could be the answer. It had been fourteen years since he arrived in the United States; fourteen years of little progress.

He wondered from where the new formula had come.

"Lion, have you been holding out on us?" he asked the empty room.

He wished he had the courage to confront Sigmund about the origin of the formula. He recognized part of it. Obviously, it was included so that they would realize it led to the next step.

"The next step. What in God's name is the next step?"

He had been writing and re-writing the formula over and over again hoping something would make sense.

The telephone rang and he absent-mindedly picked up the receiver.

"Hello."

"Otto, it's Sigmund. I think I know what this means."

"What, the formula?"

"Yes. I think it is coordinates. Do you have it in front of you?"

"Yes, I'm looking at it right now."

"Look at the first section. We've seen this part before, yes?"

"Yes."

"Look at the next six equations, break them into two sets of three. Do you see it?"

Otto scribbled on a separate sheet of paper.

"Lion, what am I looking at?"

"Latitude and longitude, maybe?"

He placed a thick backslash in what he assumed was the appropriate spot. His eyes grew wide.

"Germany. The laboratory, yes?"

"I believe so. The first part, as we know, were the coordinates we set into the vibrational accelerator that sent the timepiece into the future. They're the time coordinates. The second set of numbers, the numbers that Dr. Auman had programmed in, is most likely the space coordinates. You see the infinite numbers aren't really infinite. While they looked like a loop, they actually stop somewhere in the future, at a time and location.

"With the third part of this sequence, we can investigate and perhaps navigate. We can change the course of any given object that we send forward. Otto, with these equations, we can most likely determine when and where our precious bell will show up. If we do not like its trajectory, and if this is what I think it is, we can redirect it."

Otto allowed a knowing smile to cross his face.

"Lion, you are brilliant. I'd forgotten how the old ways were. No one person had all of the information. Each of us had a small piece of it. You and I worked on the first part, the starting point in space and time. Dr. Auman had the second part, the future space and time coordinates. Most likely, someone at the laboratory would have been given the third part, a way to manipulate the item as it moves through the space and time continuum."

"Yes, I think that is it. What we have here, I believe, are the two sets of coordinates. It should not take us long to build the next part now that we know what it is we need. Imagine stepping out of this time and space and into another dimension. It boggles the mind, yes?"

"It does, indeed. So, tell me, my friend, where did you get this information? You can trust me. Have you had this the whole time you were here in this country?"

"No, I swear. When I returned home the other night, just as I told you, they were in my office."

Otto frowned. He didn't believe that for a second. How could anything simply end up in one's possession unless someone delivered it?

Sigmund, Lion, you are holding back information. I'll find out how you received it, make no mistake.

"I think we should call Dr. Bennett right away," Otto said.

Sigmund seemed to hesitate.

"Yes, yes, of course."

"What is wrong?"

"Nothing. We'll bring it to him first thing in the morning. Right now, I have to get some sleep. I'm exhausted."

"Good night, Lion."

Otto heard Sigmund laugh.

"What's so funny?"

"That name seems to have followed me here. I am surely nothing as noble as a lion."

"Maybe not, but you are one brilliant son of a bitch. No insult to your mother, of course. It's just a saying. The Americans, huh?"

"Good night, Otto."

"Good night, my friend."

He hung up the telephone.

"Lion, my good friend, what the Hell are you keeping from me?"

Sigmund replaced the receiver in its cradle.

"Lion. Really."

A light rap on his door caught his attention.

"Yes."

"Sig, can I talk to you a minute?"

"Come in, Rosie."

When she entered, he saw she was wearing pajamas and pink fuzzy slippers. She looked almost comical. In his country, when he was a child, no one wore such things.

"I know it's late, but I've been dying to talk to you all day."

"I could tell. You looked as though you would jump out of your skin all evening. I knew you had something on your mind. What is it? Have you had another visit?"

He was half teasing and, therefore, shocked when she nodded. He motioned for her to take the seat in front of his desk.

"Really?"

"I think so. I was at the library today and," she said, relaying the unusual event that had occurred.

When she was finished speaking, he sat back.

"So, did you read the Bible?" he asked.

She nodded, a huge smile on her face.

"It's amazing," she said. "Both of those stories sound like visits from aliens from outer space, don't they?"

"Rosie, there are many stories throughout history such as those and they are all subject to interpretation. Many are in the Bible, many are sewn into the fabric of different cultures."

He rose, walked around his desk and went to the bookshelf to the right. He pulled out a book and opening it, took the chair next to Rosie.

"Here, look at this. It's a picture by Domenico Ghirlandaio called "The Madonna with Saint Giovannino" that he painted in the fifteenth century. Interesting, yes?"

She nodded.

"Do you see that?" he asked pointing to a disk-shaped object in the sky. "What do you think that could be?"

While her eyes grew wide, she remained speechless. He continued speaking, his voice soft.

"It appears that throughout the centuries of recorded history mankind has been visited by other-worldly beings. Do they come from the sky? We do not know. Do they materialize from another dimension? We do not know that either. But there they are, in drawings, paintings, writings, and in stories passed down verbally. Every culture has some kind of story about people from the stars or the heavens. And, Rosie, even people from the United States have such stories."

"Well, I don't know how they got here, but they were here, right in this very room, right in this very spot," she said, placing her foot on the spot where the man had stood. "I saw and heard him. And the lady. I heard her. I wrote down what the man told me to write and I made a journal to remember what the lady said. I know they're real."

"Yes, they are real. I know a part of you most likely wants to go out and tell everyone, yes?"

She nodded, a sheepish grin on her face.

"But you know you cannot, yes?"

"Yes, I know. But what should I do? This is the third time they spoke to me. I know that the woman who visited me here was the same one who was at the library today. I don't know how she did it, but she looked exactly like the librarian and then she disappeared into a corner."

Sigmund shook his head. He had no idea how these beings were able to communicate through other people or how they were able to materialize and dematerialize. All he did know was that he believed Rosalie. She had proven herself with the intricate equations she'd provided. He knew there was no way she could have known the formula on her own.

"For now, try not to let this upset you. I'm afraid I've pulled you into the thick of things. But, Rosie, I will protect you with every fiber of my being. I won't let anything bad happen to you. I promise you that. But you have to do your part. Tell no one. I don't want to frighten you, but your life could be in danger if anyone knew what you witnessed. Do you understand?"

"Yes, I understand. But I'm telling you, the next time that lady comes to me, I'm going to turn around as quick as I can and look her straight in the eye."

"She'll most likely be wearing dark glasses."

"Then, I'll look her straight in the nose."

He laughed at her answer, a child's reply.

"You had better get to bed. I don't want your sister to blame me when you fall asleep at the breakfast table."

Rosalie smiled at his remark.

"Can I ask you a question?"

Sigmund could almost sense what she was about to ask. She wanted to know if he was a Nazi and, he thought, she was about to ask him point blank. He nodded.

"Ask me anything."

"Are you an atheist? I mean, the librarian said all scientists are atheists."

"No, I'm a Lutheran. I believe in God. I believe God created the Universe and every living creature in it."

"That's about what I told the librarian. Well, I'm glad. Now that we're in this together, I'd hate to think I'm in cahoots with someone who doesn't believe in God."

"Cahoots? What is cahoots?"

"It means you and I are in this mystery together. We share secrets and information. You will share stuff with me, won't you?"

Sigmund took a deep breath. She made quite the request. How could he promise to share the top secret information for which he has been entrusted with a teenager? He knew there was no way he could share *everything*. For one, it could put him in jeopardy of losing his citizenship and, more importantly, it could put her in danger.

He looked into her innocent eyes, eyes so much like those of his wife, another person he'd protect with his life, and smiled.

"Of course," he said. "After all, we're in cahoots. Now, go get some sleep."

She stood and leaned forward to place a light kiss on his cheek.

"Good night, Sig."

"Good night, Rosie."

Rosalie felt good about her meeting with Sigmund. She felt a connection she never thought possible.

She climbed into bed, her mind racing with thoughts about him and the strange beings who seemed intent on scaring her to death. She settled down after fifteen minutes and allowed the events of the past week to drift in and out of her thoughts. She decided not to feel frightened. She was safe in her bed with Sigmund right next door.

"Oh, crap," she whispered.

She wondered why she had to think of that. The people who were able to materialize stepped out of nowhere, yet somewhere in the direction of her bedroom. She turned on the small lamp by her bed and looked toward the wall that separated her room from Sigmund's office.

On the wall, Einstein looked back.

"You'll protect me while I sleep, won't you?" she asked the picture.

His gentle black eyes seemed to comfort her. She shut off the lamp and pulled the light blanket over her head. She was as still as possible, waiting to hear the crackling sound. When an hour passed and there was no sound, she drifted off to sleep.

Chapter 16

Denise and Joseph were finding it almost impossible to spend any time with Rosalie. On Friday, sitting in the Perry kitchen, they decided to call her on the telephone. The Perry's owned the second house from the entrance in the Silver Peach Acres development.

"Let's meet at the park," Denise suggested. "We only saw you one day during this whole spring break. I thought we were going to hang out all week."

"I know. I'm sorry, but I can't. I have to finish my cloud project. Actually, I'm heading to the library now."

Denise hung up the telephone and shook her head.

"What's that girl up to?" Joseph asked.

"Don't know, but she's allowed to have secrets. Anyway, she's going to the library this morning."

"Yeah, but this is too weird. It's not like her to spend so much time at the library. Let's follow her."

As much as Denise wanted to refuse, she was curious as to what her best friend was up to. She thought about his suggestion for a few minutes, then nodded.

"Okay, but just this once. We don't want to make a habit out of spying on our friends."

Joseph smiled broadly, his eyes appearing almost mischievous to Denise. She shook her head and lightly punched his arm.

"Just this once," she repeated. "Promise me, Joey."

Joseph laughed and said, "Sure, I promise."

Not more than ten minutes passed and they noticed Rosalie rushing along the sidewalk past the Perry house, books piled in her arms. Joseph sprinted out the side door and peered from behind a bush. Denise was directly behind him.

"Let's go," Joseph said.

"Jeez, Joey, don't you know how to follow someone? You're supposed to let them get far enough away that they don't realize you're behind them. Wait until she turns the corner. Golly, and you want to become a spy someday."

Joseph waited patiently until Denise gave him the okay. When Rosalie passed the Silver Peach Acres sign and turned to walk along Main Street, she tapped his arm.

"Let's go."

Joseph followed Denise to the corner where she stopped behind a truck parked in front of the dry cleaners and peered around it. She lifted her right hand and waved him on without looking back. Joseph stayed close behind.

The library was three streets before their school, a two-story building with long windows on both floors. They waited until she went inside and ran up the stairs.

Looking through the glass doors, Denise said, "She went to the second floor. Come on."

Again, Joseph obediently followed.

Their footfalls seemed to echo off the walls of the quiet stairway.

"Darn," Denise said and gently set her foot on the stairs, making sure her shoes made no sound.

"See, that's why I wear sneakers," Joseph said. "I can sneak around without being discovered."

Denise ignored him. They waited several minutes, hidden behind a partition. Every now and they, they'd peer around it.

"There she is," Denise whispered.

Rosalie was seated at the last table on the right. Her head was down as she flipped through the pages of a thick book.

"Let's go behind that shelving unit and watch her. We'll be able to see her over the books," Denise said.

Once again, Joseph obeyed, quietly following her along the back edge of the high shelving units that stood in front of the large windows.

They found a spot a few feet from Rosalie. She seemed unaware that she was being watched. After a few minutes, she rose and headed to the last unit where she reached for a book on the fifth shelf. They had a clear shot.

"What's she looking at?" Joseph asked.

Denise shrugged.

"I don't know. I think she's talking to someone in the corner."

Joseph backed up and aligned himself with the edge of the bookcase. He had a clear view of the corner.

"There isn't anyone back there," he whispered.

"Well, she's talking to someone. Come on, let's get closer so we can hear what she's saying," Denise said.

They made their way to the next to the last bookcase. Denise frowned as she watched Rosalie. It appeared she was talking to someone but for the life of her, she couldn't see to whom.

"I think she's talking to the wall," Joseph said, his voice so low Denise could barely hear him.

"Shh," she responded.

Rosalie then did a strange thing. She opened the book she had in her hand, turned it around and appeared to show its contents to someone. She smiled and closed the book. She remained in her spot for a few seconds, as though listening to someone.

"I can't stand this anymore. I'm gonna sneak over there and see who she's talking to," Joseph said. "Wait here."

Before Denise could stop him, he disappeared around the bookcase. A few seconds later, Denise heard Rosalie scream. She rushed up to the girl.

"What's the matter?"

Rosalie pointed. When Denise turned, she discovered Joseph lying on the floor.

"What happened?"

"She zapped him," Rosalie said. "She actually zapped him."

"Who? There's no one here."

Denise got on her knees and leaned over Joseph.

"He's not breathing," she said, her voice cracking. "Oh, my God, Rosie, he's not breathing. He's dead."

Rosalie joined her on the floor. She put her ear against his chest. It was still.

"What do we do now?" Denise asked. Then, turning to look into Rosalie's eyes, added, "Who did this?"

"It's them; the aliens."

Denise frowned.

"Aliens? Do you mean space people? Martians? There's no such thing."

"Yes, there is and I'm not sure where they're from."

"We have to call someone. This is horrible; just horrible."

"Are you sure he's dead? Maybe he just stopped breathing, like when you fall real hard."

Denise grabbed her hand and put it on Joseph's wrist.

"No pulse," Rosalie whispered. "Denise, what have I done?"

Denise realized that Rosalie was beginning to panic. Being the true pillar of strength she believed herself to be, she consoled her friend. Yet, even she was shaking, tears burning her eyes.

"C'mon, let's ask the librarian to call the cops," she said.

Denise leaned on Rosalie's shoulder to stand, then helped her to her feet. Just as they were about to call for help, Joseph began to stir.

"What happened?" he mumbled, barely audible.

Both girls began laughing at the same time. Denise knelt beside him again, holding his hand and grinning.

"I just asked Rosie the same thing. She said someone zapped you. Did you see anyone?"

Joseph got to his knees, shaking his head, then stood on wobbly legs.

Rosalie hugged him and patted his shoulder.

"What's with you two?" he asked, weakly.

"We thought you were dead," Rosalie said.

Denise nodded and repeated her question.

"Did you see anyone?"

"Uh-uh, I didn't see anybody. I came around the corner of the bookshelf and I saw a bright light and the next thing I knew, I woke up and saw you two."

With no satisfaction from Joseph's account, Denise turned to Rosalie.

"You said aliens zapped him. Who did you mean?"

Rosalie didn't answer. Instead, she turned around, gathered her books and hurried away, not looking back even as they called her name. She passed the librarian who was moving in the direction of Denise and Joseph, her finger held to her mouth to indicate they were making too much noise.

With her heart beating wildly, Rosalie headed home. Joseph and Denise were fast on her heels, calling her name.

After two streets, she finally stopped, leaned forward and gasped for breath. What, she wondered, was she going to say to them? She knew explanations were in order.

For some reason, the lady, who now appeared as an angelic figure with strange blue eyes, found it necessary to send a bolt of electricity in Joseph's direction.

Although, by the time it was over, he seemed no worse for the attack. It didn't matter. Rosalie knew she was responsible for what had happened.

"What are you up to, Rosie?" demanded Denise in between gasps of breath. "You better tell us right now or we're not going to be friends with you anymore. Joey was almost killed."

Joseph looked startled.

"Killed?"

"Yes, you had no pulse," Denise said. "You have some explaining to do, Rosie."

Rosalie looked at Joseph. She thought he looked as though he was still in a daze. She held out her hand and touched his shoulder.

"Are you okay, Joey?"

He nodded, a small smile trying to widen his lips.

She turned to Denise.

"Look, I'm involved in something. It's big, really, really big. It's so big that I think you guys would be better off if you *weren't* friends with me."

She could tell by Denise's reaction that wasn't the answer for which she sought.

"Joey, I'm real sorry. I wish I could explain what happened to you, but I don't know."

"You were there," Denise insisted. "You must know."

"Now that I think about it," Joseph began, scratching his head, "I might have seen something in the light. It looked like the shape of a lady. It all happened so fast."

"That's impossible. I was right behind you and no one was there," Denise said.

Rosalie looked from one face to the other and knew she had to share her secret.

"Look here, guys. If I tell you, you have to swear not to tell anybody. I mean a real swear, a pinky swear."

Without hesitation, Denise and Joseph offered their right hands, an arched pinky ready to seal the deal. Rosalie hesitated. She wondered if she was doing the right thing. After a few seconds, and realizing that Joseph had, in fact, seen something and wasn't likely to let it go, she put out her hand.

Three pinkies locked together, held for a full fifteen seconds, made a final shake and released.

"That lady you saw was real. She pops in and out whenever she wants. I'm not sure why, but she does."

"Okay, so I'm not crazy. I knew I saw a lady."

Denise appeared confused.

"I didn't see her."

"That's because, like I said, she can appear and disappear in a matter of seconds. It's crazy. This is the third time she came to me."

"What does she want?"

"I'm not sure."

"When was the first time?"

Rosalie explained the string of circumstances that led to the library encounter. The visit by the strange man and the three visits by the tricky woman.

"First, she was invisible. Then, she looked like that librarian and this time she looked all luminous with freaky blue eyes."

Rosalie decided to leave out all information regarding Sigmund and the secret formula.

"It must have something to do with your brother-in-law's research," Joseph said. "The first time was when you were in his office, right?"

Rosalie nodded.

"I didn't even think you were still spying on him," Joseph said. "Didn't you tell us that you trusted him now?"

"Yes, I do. But this is definitely connected to his work."

"Yes, otherwise why would they bother you?"

"I'm not sure," Rosalie said. "I do know this, though; every time one of them pops in and out, my heart beats a million times a minute."

Joseph and Denise laughed at that.

"Okay, guys, remember our pinky swear. Tell no one. I don't want to end up in a looney bin."

"You have to find out what they want," Denise said.

"Oh, so now you believe us that we saw a lady, huh?"

"Well, it's either that or the two of you are hallucinating."

"I know what I saw," Joseph said. "And I believe every word Rosie just said."

"I believe her, too, Joey. But it's just a hard thing to explain."

"Oh, I'll get an explanation," Rosalie said. "I'm going to talk to Sig the minute he gets home."

She laughed at her own words.

"What's so funny?" Joseph asked.

"Every time Sigmund walks in the door anymore, I'm there waiting for him with some fantastic tale. He's not going to want to come home anymore."

"Either that, or he's gonna tell your sister to send you back to Brooklyn," Joseph said.

"Oh, he'd never do that, would he?" Denise asked, a note of concern in her tone.

"No, he wouldn't do that. He and I have grown pretty close and, now, we have something in common. We have a secret. But, like I said, you can't tell anyone else."

"We promise," Joseph and Denise said at the exact moment.

Rosalie felt certain they were as good as their word.

"Was I really dead?"

"I think so," said Rosalie. "Did you see a light or God or angels?"

"No," he said.

"Well, it was only for a few seconds," Denise said. "If you stayed dead, your guardian angel would have escorted you to Heaven."

"Well, you're not dead," Rosalie said, hugging him again. "And I don't have to explain anything to the cops."

"Or Joey's mother," Denise added.

That thought caused Rosalie to shiver.

"I have to get home. Carlotta will be worried."

"I think we should keep this between ourselves," Joseph said. "I don't want the other kids at school asking me what it was like being dead."

"Joey, don't talk like that. We won't tell anyone, especially our parents. We'll get to the bottom of this," Denise said. "Right, Rosie?"

Rosalie nodded.

"Yes, we will. Well, I'm sorry again, Joey. Really, I am."

"It's okay," he muttered meekly.

Rosalie left her friends at the front door of the Perry house and waved goodbye. For the first time in a long time, she felt a sense of relief.

For one, she was glad her friend was alive. And, she had to admit, it felt good to be able to talk to another human about the strange beings who'd decided to visit her.

She felt secure in their kinship. It was a secret she knew was safe … for now, anyway.

Chapter 17

When Rosalie arrived home, she was glad to see the Cadillac in the driveway.

Carlotta and Mr. Johnson were standing out front. She was showing him where she wanted the new shrubbery placed along the driveway.

Rosalie tried to slip past them as she was still in turmoil from the library incident.

Mr. Johnson was the first to notice her and appeared taken aback.

"Are you okay, Miss Rosie? Maybe you oughta sit down a bit," he said.

"I'm fine."

Carlotta reached out and grabbed her hand.

"Rosie, are you sure you're okay? You're as white as a sheet. Mr. Johnson's right; you look like you need to sit a while."

"I'm fine. I just have a lot of work to do."

"Well, I sure hope you're not coming down with a cold."

"Really, I'm okay," she said and went inside the house.

Without putting down her books, she went to the partially opened door.

"Sig, can I talk to you?"

He nodded and waved her to the chair that faced his desk.

"I have to leave for the laboratory in a few minutes, but sit, tell me what is on your mind. You look as though you saw a ghost."

"Well, you're close," she said and related the most recent experience at the library.

"Oh, my God, is the boy all right?"

"Yes, he seemed okay. I just left him and he seemed normal. Well, normal for Joey."

Sigmund smiled at that. Joseph was, indeed, a funny one.

"Good. Good. But, are you sure he had no pulse?"

"Yes, I'm sure, and he wasn't breathing. Then, all of a sudden, he was awake and asking us what happened. It was crazy."

"This is insane. What was your explanation to your friends?"

"I just said I didn't know what happened and that I was as confused as they were."

"And they were satisfied with that?"

She nodded.

"Well, Rosie, you will let me know if she, or the man, come to you again, yes?"

She had grown so comfortable with his manner of speaking, she now enjoyed it.

"Yes," she agreed.

Before standing, she considered telling him that Joseph and Denise knew the whole story, then decided against it. She recalled Sigmund's warning. No one, he'd insisted, could know. No one.

The weekend passed without a word from her friends. She found that odd. Surely, she thought, they'd be drilling her about the aliens.

On Monday, when she arrived at school, she discovered they were behaving even more oddly. Why, she wondered, weren't they asking for more information?

At lunch, when she could no longer stand the suspense, she blurted out, "What's with you two? Don't you want to know what Sig said?"

Almost simultaneously, their eyes shifted toward each other and back to her. Denise spoke.

"What Sig said about what?"

"About the lady at the library?"

"What lady?" Joseph asked.

"The librarian?" added Denise, a slight frown.

"No, the other lady. The one in the light."

Again, uneasy expressions crossed their faces.

"What in Heaven's name are you talking about, Rosie?" Denise asked.

"The lady Joey saw."

"I didn't see a lady."

Rosalie put her milk carton on the table so hard, milk squirted through the folded opening at the top.

"Friday, at the library. Don't you guys remember?"

"Yeah, we were at the library and we saw you there," Joseph said. "Actually, we followed you. We were wondering what you were up to."

"Right," Rosalie agreed, nodding. "And you saw me talking to someone and you snuck up behind the shelf to see who it was. Remember?"

Joseph shifted his gaze to Denise.

"I do remember following you and sneaking around the book shelf, but there was nobody there. Isn't that right, Den?"

"Yes, that's right. Golly, Rosie, what's the big deal? You said you weren't mad at us for following you. We were just curious. You said it was okay with you."

Rosalie felt a cold shiver climb up her spine. The back of her head felt funny, as though a million bees were crawling on her scalp.

"You guys don't remember seeing me talking to a lady?"

"No," Joseph said.

Denise shook her head slowly and said, "Hey, are you okay? You've been acting very strange lately."

"That's why we followed you," Joseph added. "And what did you mean about Sigmund?"

Rosalie realized the strange visitor had done something to her friends. And, she thought, the woman could be more dangerous than she'd anticipated.

"Rosie, you look funny. Are you okay? Joey, let's take her to the nurse."

"No," Rosalie replied. "No, I'm fine. I'm just a little confused. I'll be okay."

They shrugged their indifference and Denise changed the subject to the upcoming spring festival, which was a little more than two weeks away.

Rosalie listened as they planned their float for the parade. It was as if the whole matter of strange visitors from another dimension didn't exist. For a moment, she wondered if she had *dreamed* the whole thing.

When Sigmund returned home that evening, she reported the day's events, calling her discovery a "mind sweep" to Sigmund.

"They didn't remember anything except that they saw me at the library."

Sigmund, she noticed, didn't seem shocked. She asked him why.

"If they have the ability to time travel, perhaps they simply went back and changed the outcome of that afternoon. It is probably for the best."

Rosalie realized it *was* for the best. She could erase the feelings of guilt and betrayal from her mind. In the future, she promised herself, she'd keep her secret. After seeing Joseph lying lifeless on the library floor, she knew she was dealing with powerful beings.

The days seemed to fly for Rosalie. With the festival getting close, she was busier than ever preparing her costume. She would be a fairy and sit atop a giant mushroom surrounded by hundreds of plants, many of which came from Denise's father's florist shop. Joseph and Denise had similar costumes. Their jobs were to toss rose petals to the onlookers.

She was glad she hadn't had any more visits.

She glued the last strip of daisies to the hem of her dress and placed it on a hook. It was long and white and much too fluffy for her taste. Tonight, she would only entertain visions of beautiful floats and the party that would follow.

As she climbed into bed, she heard the telephone in Sigmund's office. She could hear the deep murmur of his voice. When her curiosity got the best of her, she climbed out of bed and went to her desk. The hole behind Einstein's picture hadn't been filled in yet so she seized the opportunity.

"No, I cannot do that," Sigmund said. "Why?"

There was a short silence and he said, "Okay, let me see what I can do."

He slammed the receiver into the telephone body. He looked distressed.

She couldn't help but wonder what that was about. She slipped the picture back onto its hook. She was still seated on her desk when she heard a light knock on her door.

"Rosie, are you still awake?"

She jumped off the desk and scurried to her bed. She sat up and turned on the lamp.

"Yes, come in."

He entered. His face was ashen, his mouth pulled down at both sides.

"What's wrong? Are the kids okay?" she asked, hoping to eliminate any suspicions he may have.

"Yes, everyone is fine. They're all sleeping. Carlotta had a headache and went to bed early."

He went to the desk and sat in her chair, turning it to face her.

"Rosie, we have a problem."

Rosalie's heart began to pound.

"You might as well blurt it out, Sig. I'm already scared to death."

She had hoped he'd smile and reassure her there was nothing for which to be frightened. When he didn't, she felt sick to the stomach.

"Dr. Bennett wants to know from where the formula has come. He thinks I'm working with the Russians. Well, he hinted at that, at least."

Rosalie shifted uncomfortably in her bed.

"The Russians? The Communists?"

He nodded.

"Rosie, I think we will have to inform Dr. Bennett of your visitors. I didn't want to involve you in all this but, it appears, you are the key."

"Me?"

He nodded again.

"They only visit you. I don't know why that it, but I promise to protect you."

Rosalie didn't know if she was comfortable with that remark. From what, she wondered, did she need protection?

"Will he want to stick probes in my brain?"

Sigmund laughed.

"No, I don't think they do that."

"You don't think or you know?"

"I know," he said, still smiling.

"And who are they? I thought I only had to talk to Dr. Bennett."

"It's just an expression, Rosie. You will speak directly to him. No one else will be present."

"What about Dr. Kramer?"

Sigmund hesitated.

"Yes, Otto. It's possible he might be present. That wouldn't bother you, would it? After all, you know Dr. Kramer."

She wondered if she should admit that she still had suspicions about Otto Kramer. She decided to trust Sigmund. He said he'd protect her and she felt sure he would.

"I guess that will be okay. So, what will they do?"

"Ask questions, I suppose. They'll want to know when the visits occurred, what the visitors looked like, and what they said. Just tell them what you told me."

"Okay. You'll be there, too, won't you?"

"Yes, of course."

When Sigmund returned to his office, Rosalie could hear the low murmur of his voice. She assumed he was calling Dr. Bennett, explaining why he held back information about her.

"He's not gonna be happy," she said and climbed into bed.

She pulled her blanket to her chin and placed her hands at her sides, remaining as still as possible. She wanted to sleep, to drift into her favorite dream, the one where she can fly over the Pacific Ocean like a seagull.

When sleep wouldn't come, she rolled on her side, turned on the lamp and pulled out one of the books she'd previously borrowed from the library. She flipped the pages, coming to a picture of people flying around in something called a "virmana."

As her eyes grew heavy from reading, she allowed them to shut. Her head slowly sunk into her pillow as the book fell to the carpeted floor.

She was flying, swooping toward the ocean, her fingers skimming the salty waves. She felt as though she wasn't alone. When she turned her head, she discovered a lady flew alongside her.

"Hello, Rosalie."

Rosalie looked into her eyes of deep blue, almost black. Her hair was white and as long as her body, willowing past her feet.

"Are you the lady from the library?"

"Yes."

"Is this how you really look?"

"Sometimes."

"You made Joey and Denise forget what happened, didn't you?"

"Yes. It was for their own good. You understand that, don't you?"

"Yes, I do. In a way, I'm glad."

"Good. I want you to feel good about helping me."

Rosalie felt a warm feeling settle in her chest.

"I do feel good. I want to help."

"How do you like flying?"

"I love it. I see you can fly, too. Can you always fly?"

"Oh, yes, I can fly to the ends of the universe if I want," she said.

Rosalie smiled, feeling comfortable with the being.

"Can I? I'd like to fly to the ends of the universe, too."

"Not yet. There will come a day when you can, but not now; not in this incarnation."

A dolphin emerged from the ocean and Rosalie gently stroked its back before it disappeared beneath the water.

"Wow, did you see that?"

135

"Yes. I summoned him so that you could pet him. He's lovely, isn't he?"

"Yes, he is. I always loved dolphins."

They flew together for a few minutes. Rosalie enjoyed the soft breeze that seemed to reach out and embrace her.

"Rosalie, dear, I have a request. When you tell Dr. Bennett about the visits, don't mention me. Can you do that for me?"

Her voice was as soft as velvet, soothing.

"Yes, I can. But, why?"

"One day, I will explain. For now, my dear, it's best if they know only about the man."

"But I'm not sure what Sigmund told him. What if he already told him about you?"

"No, Sigmund has told them nothing about the visits. All he said was that someone close to him was a key element in the discovery of the formula."

"Should I tell *him*?"

"Yes, of course. Tell him of this visit."

Rosalie lowered her head and suddenly she was heading into an enormous wave. She couldn't stop herself as she slammed into the wall of water. She felt the cold ocean engulf her and, in an instant, she was awake. It was morning.

"It was a dream," she whispered, her heart pounding. "It was only a dream."

Dr. Bennett arrived at his office shortly after daybreak. What, he wondered, was up Dr. Lowe's sleeve? What nonsense was he going to come up with to cover his tracks?

First he brings in a string of computations that were way beyond his scope of knowledge. These formulas, he claimed, simply appeared on his desk. Now he says he can elaborate on how they came into his possession.

"What game are you playing, Dr. Lowe?"

He'd made a call to his agent who assured him that the good doctor had been just that – good.

"I've followed him. I've tapped his telephone. I've even read every piece of mail before it reached his home. Whatever Dr. Lowe is up to, he's very clever about it. I haven't been able to implicate him in anything unusual. In fact, Armand, it's almost too good to be real."

"Well, keep on him and report back to me."

It had been days since his last contact with the agent and frustration was settling in. Somehow he had to get to the bottom of the mystery.

How could Sigmund Lowe have obtained that formula? How?

As a last-ditch effort, he called him at home and informed him that the government was about to do a full investigation on him and everyone working on the project.

"They'll investigate your family, too," he warned.

To that, Sigmund had reacted and Dr. Bennett instantly knew the good doctor was protecting someone, and likely someone in his family.

"I'll call you back," he'd said.

Armand Bennett had waited the scant minutes it took for Sigmund to return his call.

"I'll be in your office Friday with the answers you seek. However, you must promise that no harm will come to the person I will bring with me."

"Of course not," Dr. Bennett agreed. "This is all top secret. Whatever you reveal will stay within this office. Trust me, son, I'm on your side."

As he waited for Sigmund to arrive, he pondered what could have occurred to cause the man to finally cooperate.

He thought about his inner circle.

The only person who wasn't on the list of conspirators was the gardener, Mr. Johnson. He had already been cleared. Armand Bennett smiled. Yes, he knew all about the former Tuskegee Airman who resided in the small apartment above the Lowe's garage. He recalled how Mrs. Lowe brought attention to him when she fought the homeowners' association people about allowing him to reside inside the gates of the prestigious community.

No, it was one of the others, but who? Who was Dr. Lowe protecting?

His wife? She was active in the African-American Civil Rights Movement. There was still questions about their goals in America.

His father? The good pastor knew a lot of people from all over the world. Anyone could be offering information for a favor.

The Reverend's wife? Even Herta Lowe's name was on his list.

Otto Kramer? They had been friends since childhood.

The anticipation was overwhelming, like waiting for the taste of a fine wine on a cleansed tongue.

Chapter 18

Rosalie awoke to the sound of chirping birds and a brilliant ray of sunlight that found its way into her room, spilling like a silver stream onto her bed.

She sat up and gently rubbed her eyes. There came a light knock on her bedroom door. Before she could speak, the door opened slightly and Stanley stuck his head between the door and the jamb.

"You awake, Rosie?"

She found her nephew looking at her as though he had important news.

"Yeah," she said, patting her bed. "Come over here and give me a hug."

Stanley pushed open the door and bounced onto her bed, throwing his arms around her neck and placing a kiss on her cheek.

"Guess what? Today is spring," he said.

Rosalie chuckled.

"Well, yes, it's the first day."

"Mama said it's not gonna snow anymore."

"You better not let your daddy hear you saying gonna," she scolded, gently pinching his cheek.

He smiled sheepishly.

"Oops, sorry. I mean going to. Anyway, Papa said you're going to work with him today. Can I go, too?"

Rosalie heart suddenly became heavy, feeling as though it was sinking to the pit of her stomach.

"Oh, that's right. I almost forgot about that."

"What's the matter? Don't you want to go with Papa?"

Rosalie had been dreading this day all week. Although she and Sigmund had gone over what she would report, she still hadn't told him about her dream. She was afraid he'd think she was being foolish. She realized she had waited long enough.

"Is your Papa in the kitchen?"

"Yes, he's eating pancakes. He said to wake you up so you can get ready."

Rosalie hugged Stanley and returned him to the floor. She patted him on the bottom as she spoke.

"Scoot out of here and tell daddy I'll be ready in five minutes."

Stanley giggled and left the room. She dressed, ran a comb through her hair, now only shoulder length and easy to manage, and went to the kitchen. Carlotta placed an empty plate in front of her.

"Good morning, Rosie. Would you like pancakes or eggs?"

The thought of food caused her stomach to become queasy.

"I'm not hungry," she said.

"You have to eat. I'll make you toast."

Rosalie nodded her agreement and turned toward Sigmund whose face was hidden behind an open newspaper. There was more front-page news about a recent march and sit-in. She placed her hand in the air above the centerfold and he lowered the paper a few inches so their eyes met.

"Don't be nervous," he said, sounding as though he read her mind.

"But I am, Sig. I have to tell you something."

He folded the newspaper and placed it on the table.

"What?"

Rosalie looked toward Carlotta, wondering if she could talk about the visitors. Again, as though reading her mind, he patted her hand and whispered, "We can talk in the car. Eat something. I don't want you to have to talk over a loud grumbling tummy."

At that, Rosalie laughed and it was as though her heavy stomach became light. If he could still crack jokes, the situation couldn't be all that dire. She decided she was hungry after all. Besides, she thought, Carlotta might become suspicious if she realized how nervous she felt. As far as she knew, Rosalie was merely invited to do a follow-up visit.

After a hearty breakfast and a round of goodbye kisses, Rosalie and Sigmund left. He started the engine and, as it warmed up, asked, "So what's wrong, honey? You know there is nothing of which to be afraid."

"I had a dream," she said.

"A dream?"

"Yes. A few nights ago, the night you said I'd have to tell Dr. Bennett about the visitors, I had a dream about the lady. She said I wasn't to tell him about her. She said I could tell him about the man, but not her."

"It was just a dream, Rosie. If she really didn't want him to know about her, she'd visit you while you were awake. Anyway, I would think so."

"No, Sig, it wasn't an ordinary dream. It was so real. When I woke up the next day, I felt like she had actually visited me."

Sigmund looked as though he didn't know what to make of this new revelation. Rosalie offered what she considered a possible explanation.

"Maybe she didn't visit me because I was never in the right spot. She only came to me in your office and at the library. And I haven't been in either place all week."

Sigmund put the car in gear and moved the Cadillac into the street. As they headed along the tree-lined streets of the quiet suburban neighborhood, each house boasting a unique grandeur, he seemed deep in thought.

Rosalie appreciated the irony of their surroundings and the subject matter. She smiled to herself. Somehow, it didn't seem like the proper discussion in the midst of everyday mediocrity.

"I tell you what we'll do," Sigmund finally said. "Tell them about the man. After all, it's the formula Dr. Bennett is interested in. Later, if you receive any further instructions from the woman, we'll decide if Dr. Bennett needs to know. Yes, we'll keep him on a need-to-know basis. He does that to me all the time."

Rosalie had no idea what a need-to-know basis actually meant or its relevance to their situation, but she liked the sound of it. It solved her problem and shortened her report to Dr. Bennett.

They arrived at the office just as Otto was getting out of his car. He walked to the driver's side and tapped on the window. Sigmund rolled it down.

"Good morning," Otto said.

He bent his lanky form lower and looked into the car.

"Is that Miss Rosie I see?"

Rosalie had decided a long time ago that, for some reason she couldn't explain, she didn't care for Otto Kramer. However, under the circumstances, she forced a smile.

"Good morning, Dr. Kramer."

She had hoped it wouldn't be necessary for him to be present.

"So, Miss Rosie, am I to understand that it is *you* who can shed some light on some interesting and important matters?"

Rosalie looked to Sigmund. He smiled slightly and nodded.

"Yes, I think I can."

Otto straightened and backed away from the car. He hurried around to the passenger side and opened the door for Rosalie. Sigmund got out and joined them. They walked toward the building, three abreast. The whole time, Otto seemed to want the information without waiting for Dr. Bennett.

"Is it about the formula? Do you know something about that? Did you see or hear something?"

Rosalie allowed an uneasy look to cross her face as she looked up at Sigmund. She was amazed how he always seemed to know what was on her mind.

"Otto, for God's sake, give the girl a break. You will find out what she has to report when we reach Dr. Bennett's office. You're going to give her an ulcer."

Although there was a hint of laughter in his voice, his tone had that of a reprimand. Rosalie was beginning to believe she would be able to depend on Sigmund to protect her.

They passed the security guard who checked their identification badges, went through the glass doors and turned down the corridor. When they reached Dr. Bennett's office, his secretary, Judy Mason, ushered them inside. He was already at his desk.

"Rosalie," he said. "What a nice surprise!"

Rosalie thought he looked more confused than surprised.

"Hello, Dr. Bennett."

He stared at her for a few seconds, his mouth slightly agape.

"My goodness," he finally said and shifted his gaze toward Sigmund.

Sigmund smiled, a slight shrug moving his shoulders.

"Yes, Dr. Bennett, it's Rosalie."

Dr. Bennett turned toward her, still sporting a look of astonishment.

"Well, dear, would you like hot chocolate or, perhaps, tea?"

Judy Mason waited for her reply.

"Nothing, thank you," she said, her stomach once again feeling like a ball of lead.

"Just coffee," he said and the woman left.

Rosalie listened as they discussed the weather. Who, she wondered, cared if it was the first day of spring? She was here to talk about alien visitors.

Judy Mason returned a few minutes later with a tray. When they were settled and the coffee served, she left.

Dr. Bennett stood, shut the door and turned his attention to Rosalie.

"So, dear girl, since your brother-in-law has brought you here, I assume you have information to share. Again, I must admit, I would've never guessed it was you."

"Yes, I had a visit from a stranger."

"A stranger? Hmm, tell me about this visit."

"He was a man or, at least, I think it was a man."

"What did he look like?"

"He wore black clothes and sunglasses."

She continued to describe the incident in Sigmund's office. She didn't mention the camera; just that he asked her to write down the numbers and formulas on a certain page. She didn't mention the woman, either.

Otto had been so quiet, Rosalie had almost forgotten he was in the room. When he did speak, his voice sounded almost shrill.

"That's impossible," he said. "People can't just pop in and out like ghosts. The girl has an overactive imagination."

"Quiet!"

Rosalie was shocked to hear Sigmund use such a stern tone. They both stood, facing each other, their expressions angry.

"I will not be quiet. This is impossible and you are idiots if you believe a single word."

Otto turned to Rosalie, moving close enough to tower over her.

"Tell us the truth, girl. Where did that information come from? Explain how you knew how to write the mathematical formulas. How do you know what an integral number is? Surely they do not teach that in grammar school.

Be truthful. Was there someone in Sigmund's office who actually came to see him? A person?"

"Stop badgering her," Sigmund demanded, drawing his attention.

Rosalie wanted to stand and run away. She noticed Dr. Bennett didn't speak while the two men argued. When she looked at him, she saw he was looking back. He winked and nodded as if to indicate that this behavior was normal. Finally, after a few more angry words passed between Sigmund and Otto, he stood and pounded his fist on the desk. They immediately stopped.

"Sit down, both of you. You're acting like fools. Sit. Now."

Like obedient schoolboys, they returned to their chairs. Rosalie looked at Sigmund who was now focused on Dr. Bennett.

"Gentlemen," Dr. Bennett began, "what the girl says is not only possible, I believe it has happened before."

The room grew deathly silent. Rosalie was sure she could hear the pounding of her heart. She stared at her hands that were now clasped tightly on her lap, her knuckles almost white with stress.

As if from nowhere, Sigmund's large hand rested on top of her hands and he gave them a small reassuring squeeze. She lifted her gaze to meet his.

"Everything is okay, Rosie. Do not fret. Do not be afraid."

"What do you mean it's happened before?" Otto asked. "When? Where?"

Dr. Bennett sat down and looked from one face to the other as he spoke.

"It was during the war, close to the end. One of my men was working on a project to decipher a message we'd intercepted. He reported that a man appeared out of thin air, right before his eyes, exactly as Rosalie described it. The fellow then gave me the key to decipher the message.

"Of course, I didn't believe a word he said. I assumed someone, somehow figured it out. Before I could question him further, he was killed when bombs decimated his post."

"Did you report the incident?" Sigmund asked.

"Yes, I did. My superiors instructed me to never speak of it again. I'm now wondering if our government has been aware of these visitors all along. They had made reference to them contacting the Germans. I now see how foolish I've been as I believed it was nothing but misinformation."

"No, Dr. Bennett, it's real," Rosalie said.

He leaned back in his chair and said, "Needless to say, but I will anyway, this conversation does not leave this room. Understood?"

There was a long silence. Rosalie wondered if the men were trying to make sense of the visitations. Otto turned to Rosalie.

"I'm sorry if I frightened you," he said. "You see, I was sure something else had happened."

"What did you think happened?" Sigmund asked.

Otto became uncomfortable. Rosalie watched as he shifted in his chair.

"Well, Dr. Kramer, what did you think happened? Answer the man," Dr. Bennett said.

"I'm ashamed to say it aloud."

He looked toward Sigmund when he spoke.

"Ashamed?" Sigmund asked.

"Yes. I thought, perhaps, you had help from the other side."

"The Russians?"

"Yes, I thought you sold out to them."

Rosalie almost burst out laughing. All the time she was thinking Sigmund was a Communist, Otto was thinking the same thing.

"Otto, I thought you knew me better. I thought you trusted me. How could you think such a thing?"

"Okay, now, gentlemen, let's not get into another shouting match," Dr. Bennett said. "Let's move our attention to the matters at hand."

He focused his attention on Rosalie.

"Why do you think they came to the girl? Why not Dr. Lowe or you, Dr. Kramer? Why not me?"

Rosalie realized the three men were looking directly at her. She wondered if she should expose her own suspicions and tell them about taking the pictures and the warning she'd received from the visitors.

Before she could make up her mind, Sigmund spoke up.

"I think I know why things transpired as they did. Perhaps they had planned to visit me that night and the visitation had already been set in motion. I recall that I was called away. My son had become sick and my wife and I took him to the hospital. We had left Rosalie in charge. When they arrived, instead of finding me there to greet them, they found Rosalie."

"But what was she doing in your office? I thought you said your office was off limits to everyone in your household, including your own wife. Why was the girl in your office?" Otto asked.

All eyes were on Rosalie. She focused on Sigmund, who looked as though he would burst from stress. She said the first thing that came to mind.

"I heard a noise, so I went in."

Chapter 19

When the family had all gone to bed, Sigmund retreated to his office. He dimmed the lights and pulled the shades down tight. He went to his desk and turned on the lamp. The light showered onto the pages containing the formulas.

The meeting earlier in the day had gone well. Dr. Bennett accepted the fact that the visitors delivered the formulas to Rosalie. He went as far as to share a similar incident from his past and asked them to keep the entire incident, from the visits to the meeting, a secret.

"And if they visit you again, Rosalie, you'll let Sigmund know immediately."

"Yes, sir," she'd said.

A smile touched his lips at the thought of his young sister-in-law. Rosalie had maintained her demeanor, not once showing how frightened she was to be pulled into the drama.

He focused his attention on the computations, going over each line, separating the ones he understood.

The answers were right in front of him. The equations for time and space were understandable. A minor adjustment and he could change the coordinates of the bell's trajectory. The bell, he thought. He had been filed with fear ever since the day he pressed the button that sent it into the future. After more than a decade, the damn thing still hadn't shown up.

"Where the hell is that bell?" he whispered. "I have to fix my mistake."

He knew if he could somehow locate it in a parallel dimension, the one in which it was now moving, he could take control. But how? How?

The solution, he believed, existed in space and time continuum. He went over the final phase. What did all this mean? Was he to build a transporter? He scratched his chin. Perhaps, a star gate? Was he to build a bridge? And, if it was the latter, what would be on the other side? Would he be able to move in and out of a parallel dimension? And, if so, would he be capable of traveling to another time period?

His mind reeled. He knew what he had to do. Just as he began to draw a schematic for the final piece of the puzzle, his private telephone rang.

"Shit!"

He didn't want to pick up the receiver. After several rings, it stopped. He returned his attention to his drawing. His engineering skills would be needed for this part. He knew many of the scientists who came to America with him were involved in building rockets, but those were for space travel in this dimension.

What he was building was a device to take him *out* of this dimension.

The telephone rang again. Obviously, he thought, whoever was calling wasn't going to stop until he answered. He snatched the receiver from its cradle.

"Hello," he said, his tone reflecting his annoyance.

"Sigmund, it's Otto. I'm in trouble."

Sigmund sat tall as though by drawing away from the sketch he could concentrate more clearly on Otto's call.

"Trouble? What kind of trouble?"

"Can I come to your home? I'd like to discuss it in person."

Sigmund agreed and within thirty minutes Otto was at his door. Sigmund led him to his office.

"Why is it so dark in here?"

"I was working," Sigmund said and closed the door.

He motioned for Otto to take the chair directly in front of his desk.

"What has happened?"

"I received a call from Bennett. He says there are men from the DOD here to speak to me. It seems several of my memos have fallen into the wrong hands and they are questioning my loyalty."

Sigmund frowned. If the Department of Defense was involved, it could get ugly. This, he knew, was their worst nightmare. If, somehow, they were involved in any nefarious activity, no matter how minor, they could be deported or imprisoned.

"What can I do?"

"I have an idea. I don't know who would have gone into my personal folder and sent them out and, to be honest, I'm not sure who was to receive them. Obviously, it is not someone the government wants to have such information."

"I see, but how can I help?"

"They know when the information in the memos was transmitted. I was at home, sleeping. I remember I had a cold and had stayed home to rest. But, of course, I was alone and cannot prove it. They are saying I could have sent the information from one of many locations.

"Sigmund, I need you to vouch for me. Say I was with you."

"What day was it?"

"It was the Monday after Easter."

Sigmund nodded, recalling that he had been working from home that day. While it would be easy enough for him to back up Otto's story, he wondered if it was safe to do so.

"You say you were home alone?"

"Yes. I slept all morning. They're saying the information was passed along in Atlanta. I was nowhere near there."

Sigmund hesitated.

"I want to help, but --."

Otto interrupted.

"But what? Sigmund, I know you sent the bell away. I didn't blame you. I never told anyone, not even Dr. Bennett. Because of your actions, we live under the threat of it crashing into our world. We don't know when or where? And what would Dr. Bennett say if he knew you were only focused on fixing your fuck-up?"

"You knew it was me?"

"Yes. Why do you think you weren't followed on that terrible morning at the complex? It was I who protected you, Sigmund. I was there that day when the others were killed."

Sigmund could feel his throat become restricted, a hard knot burying itself, choking him, blocking his breath.

"What? You were there? I did not see you."

"I was in one of the jeeps; the one with the canvas top."

The realization dawned on Sigmund, the horror that his closest friend was responsible for the deaths of his colleagues.

"But, why? They were our friends, Dr. Auman, the others."

"I didn't have a choice. I was summoned to Berlin. I was ordered to lead the assassins to the complex. I picked that day because I knew you were not supposed to be there. You were supposed to be at your parents' home. You were permitted to remain there until the next day because we thought they had died."

Sigmund recalled that he had returned a day early.

"How did you protect me?"

Otto grinned, lifting his light eyebrows, his pale eyes wide.

"I told them the coordinates had previously been set. I pretended to find an error. I told them a mistake had been made, or perhaps Dr. Auman had anticipated their arrival and set the experiment time an hour earlier than planned."

"Dr. Auman, yes," Sigmund said, almost to himself. The sight of the soldier shooting him caused him to recoil.

"Sigmund, let me tell you, it was horrible. He was still alive, writhing in pain, and the lieutenant asked him if anyone else was there. He told him to go fuck himself and the lieutenant killed him."

Sigmund shook his head.

"Yes, I saw it."

"The lieutenant then came to the jeep and asked me if anyone was unaccounted for. I told him you had been called away for a personal matter and that you posed no threat.

"Then they heard the sound coming from the location of the bell and rushed to the laboratory. I was close behind them. Since there was no one else

146

there, I knew immediately it was you who pressed the button. But I didn't tell them. I lied, endangering my own life. Luckily, they believed me and you were able to get away."

Sigmund stared in shock.

"Now that I think of it, it did seem too easy. I thought surely they'd follow me."

"So, what do we do now? I saved your life. Don't you think you owe me the same kindness?"

Sigmund pondered the circumstance in which he found himself. Otto had indeed saved his life, but he was also responsible for the deaths of the others. And now, now he wanted him to tell a lie to the government.

"Why do you need me to lie for you, Otto? Are you innocent or have you given information to the enemy? I find it rather odd that you accused me of the same thing just this morning."

Otto's tone became indignant.

"I *am* innocent. Of that, you can be sure. However, I cannot prove my whereabouts. I cannot prove I was not in Atlanta. They were my memos. The information came from my office. It is bad, my friend, very bad. Without your cooperation, I am a dead man. They will not deport me; they will hang me for treason. I need your help. What is your answer?"

Sigmund knew the consequences of his actions. If caught covering for Otto, he could suffer the same fate. Yet, if Otto was innocent and wrongly convicted, he would never be able to live with the guilt.

After a few moments, he looked across the desk, square in the face of his friend and colleague.

"Tell me, Otto, if you had anything to do with this information leak. Are you responsible in any way, whether intentionally or unintentionally?"

Otto shook his head vigorously.

"I swear, Lion, I am innocent. I am completely innocent."

"I will tell them you spent the morning with me going over our progress. I will say you arrived shortly after nine and left after lunch. It's easy enough to remember. We will keep it simple."

Otto nodded his agreement, a sense of relief on his face.

"The timing is perfect. That is, of course, as long as you were home alone."

Sigmund instantly recalled the short conversation with Rosalie. If this lie ever became public, surely the girl would have enough information to get them both hanged. How, he wondered, did Rosalie always seem to become embroiled in his life?

Otto cleared his throat.

"Well?"

"No, I was alone."

Chapter 20

When Rosalie visited Dr. Bennett on Friday, she discovered, much to her own surprise, she wasn't intimidated by the scientists and their seemingly endless questions.

After a few uneasy minutes, she'd found herself liking the fact that she knew something they didn't. When it was over, she seemed to stand a little taller with an air of self-confidence she'd never experienced.

"I'm proud of you, Rosie," Sigmund had said, as he patted her back. "Very proud, indeed."

That acknowledgement made her feel even better about herself. For the fourteen-year-old, the experience served as a stepping stone to maturity.

On Wednesday of the following week, Rosalie was seated at the desk in her room, under the watchful eye of her hero, Albert Einstein, when she heard a sound by her window.

The familiar crackle lasted only a few seconds, but she knew what caused it. She turned quickly to find the man standing on the other side of her bed.

"What do you want from me? I gave Sigmund the information. I'm busy right now. I'm studying for a vocabulary test."

When he spoke, his words didn't drift across the room on sound waves that could be picked up by the vibrations of her eardrums. Instead, they seemed to come from somewhere inside her head.

"Why didn't you tell them about your other visitor?"

"Other visitor?"

"Oh, Rosalie, you are such a horrible liar. You have an obvious 'tell'. It's an unconscious action brought on when one attempts to deceive another. In your case, your eyelids flutter ever so slightly when you tell a lie."

"They do?"

He made what sounded like a low chuckle. To Rosalie, it felt as though it was she who laughed.

"Yes, they do. Surely, if Dr. Bennett was aware of yours, he would have realized you didn't tell him the truth."

"But I did tell him the truth."

"Not the whole truth. You never told him about the woman, the very one you are trying to deny to me."

Rosalie wanted to get up and run out of her room. Her eyes shifted toward the door.

"It's no use trying to leave. Surely you realize you cannot stand."

She tried to plant her feet on the floor but discovered she had no motor control of her lower extremities.

"Hey, what have you done to me?"

"I've done nothing to you, physically. However I've convinced your mind that you do not have the ability to move your feet."

She tried to stand.

"It's hopeless, girl. Stop trying. You'll only frustrate yourself. Now, explain why you didn't tell Dr. Bennett about the visits from the woman."

"Okay, Mr. Smart Alec from another planet, I'll tell you. Yes, a woman did visit me. She said I shouldn't tell anyone she was here. If you're so smart, why didn't you know that?"

"I knew she visited you. We have ways of knowing such things. However, just as she cannot hear what we discuss, I cannot hear what she tells you."

He paused and, as he did, she sensed he was anticipating how to handle her. She wondered how she could feel so connected to his thoughts. Before she could ask, he spoke.

"Rosalie, did she explain *why* you shouldn't tell anyone about her?"

"No. She just came to me in a dream and told me."

"Hmm, in a dream; very interesting. And you believed your dream was reality?"

"It felt real."

"Tell me, Rosalie, how many times has she visited you?"

"Oh, so maybe you're not so smart after all. Why should I even tell you?"

"For one, if you ever want to stand on your own two feet again you should and, two, because if you don't tell me, I will erase your entire memory of my visits."

Rosalie pursed her lips. She felt the same animosity toward the visitor that she had felt toward Sigmund before she got to know him.

"She visited me once here and twice at the library."

"Really?"

"Yes, really. Why would I lie? Besides, look at my eyelids, not fluttering one bit," she said in her most sarcastic tone.

The man stepped closer and touched her temple. Once again, she could feel the light flutter. She could see the incident at the library and what followed. She shivered at the mental sight of Joseph lying on the library floor.

"Your friends. Most unfortunate. Aha, so she has erased their memories? Clever."

"How do you know all that?"

"She would never allow anyone else to know about her visits, especially your friends. It seems you and Sigmund are the only people she wants to know of her existence."

"Why?"

"Yes, why? I ask myself the same question."

"Maybe she's smarter than you."

"Oh, she is definitely smarter than I. She is also more diabolical. I come to you and give you important information and I allow you to share it with the world. I give you information that will move mankind forward. I know you didn't understand what I had you write, but surely you realize it is of utmost importance to Sigmund and his colleagues.

"Tell me, Rosalie, what has she given you? Nothing. She comes to you unseen and again disguised as a human being you recognized."

"The librarian?"

"Yes, indeed. The next time she comes to you, ask her who she is and from where she came. Go ahead, ask her. She will give you no information; only speculation."

"She told me to look up information about alien visits and stuff like that. She said I should read parts of the Bible."

"Ah, yes, the Bible. And, of course, you relate her instructions to what you call the good book."

Rosalie had to agree that reading about such things in the Bible did lend a certain amount of credibility.

"And did your brother-in-law show you religious pictures that seem to back up her credibility?"

"Yes, he showed me a picture of the Blessed Mother."

The man backed away, moving again to the spot where he had appeared.

"You are on the brink of womanhood. It is time you stopped thinking and seeing the world as a child. It's time you open your eyes and see the world as a young adult. You are no longer a child. Don't let anyone manipulate you; anyone from this world or any other world. Do you understand me?"

Rosalie wasn't sure what was being implied.

"Are you telling me not to trust her?"

"I am telling you not to trust anyone who tries to manipulate how you view the world. You have been given a great gift, Rosalie. You are among the scant few who have seen that there is more to life than what happens on this planet."

"Are you from another planet? Another dimension? What?"

He smiled and allowed the crackling sound to absorb him into invisibility.

She stared at the empty space by her window for several minutes without moving. Her mind reeled with his words. When she finally stood, she found that her legs were alive with what could only be described as pins and needles.

"Crap! I don't know who to believe. It's Mama and Mr. Pinella and Sigmund all over again. I hate this."

She sat down again and tried to study, but her mind was too chaotic to comprehend the simple words on the page. She needed to find the meaning and implications of new words; words not found in her every-day vernacular.

It's time I stopped thinking and seeing the world as a child, huh? Well, maybe if all of you would stop telling me what to believe, I'd be able to think like an adult.

After dinner and the nightly ritual Sigmund and Carlotta shared with their children that included play time, bath time, story time and bed time, Rosalie sought her own private time with her brother-in-law.

Carlotta had a meeting at the church. They were planning to hold what she called a "sit-in" at the local public school because a little girl with brown skin was not allowed to attend classes.

Rosalie wasn't sure why it was such a big issue. Where she came from in Brooklyn, she had many friends of many races and religions. Why, she wondered, did these people in Georgia make such a deal of it?

Carlotta, who seemed excited about the pending event, talked of little else. When it was time to leave, she kissed her husband and left the house. With the children already in dreamland, Rosalie took her opportunity.

"Sigmund, before you lock yourself in your office for the night, I have news. I had another visit today."

Sigmund nodded as though he'd expected as much.

"You know?" she asked.

"Dr. Bennett has brought Dr. Kramer and me up to date on surveillance notifications. So, yes, we knew there was another contact here today. I assumed the visit was to you, as they don't seem the least bit interested in Carlotta."

Rosalie thought about her sister. She stiffened.

"They better leave her alone, and the kids."

Sigmund smiled.

"Yes, I agree. However, they seem to be drawn to you. At first, I thought it could be possible because I was not at home when the first visit was made. But, they have had ample opportunities to visit me and, yet, they do not. It is you, Rosalie, only you."

"But why? I don't know anything about anything. I'm fourteen."

"So, who came to see you today?"

"It was the man. He knows about the woman and said he keeps asking himself the same thing about the woman's visits. Anyway, he also said I shouldn't trust her."

"Why?"

"He said it's because she doesn't give us any information. Is he right?"

Sigmund scratched his chin, his sign for deep thoughts.

"He could be right, I guess. What he has given has helped us make giant leaps in progress. The woman, it appears, is trying to - -,"

When he paused, she said, "Manipulate me?"

151

"Perhaps. I was going to say educate you. But she could be trying to manipulate you."

"That's sort of what the man said."

Sigmund raised his eyebrows.

"Really?"

She nodded.

"The only thing, though, is that when she comes to me, I feel good after she's gone. Every time he visits me, he touches my head and reads my thoughts and makes it so that I can't move. I hate that."

"They are mind games, Rosie. They are ethereal creatures who have no physical properties in this dimension. Neither can touch you. They can only transfer their thought patterns into your thought patterns. In other words, you only think you cannot stand. It seems to me he's every bit as manipulative as she."

"Like when she appeared as the librarian?"

"Exactly. You actually saw no one, but in your mind she was standing there right in front of you and she cleverly used the form of a woman you recognized."

"What about the man? I never saw anyone who looks like him."

"He creates an image in your mind of a man in black with dark glasses. It is a simple image. If he were to remove the glasses, even in your mind, you would see what he really looks like."

"And what is that?"

"Light, most likely. They are creatures of energy, pure potentiality as far as we are concerned."

"Potentiality?"

"Yes. It means they have the potential, the ability to create just about any image they want. It was dark in my office, so the man chose to appear as a human man in dark clothing. The woman, if you recall on her first visit, chose not to reveal any image. Then, when she did, it was of someone with whom you were comfortable."

"What if they appear as someone I know, like Carlotta or you?"

"You would instinctively know it was not us. We have a real connection. We could find each other even if we were blindfolded."

"I'm not sure about that."

"Rosalie, trust me on this. I remember once, a while ago, Carlotta and I attended a party. The host decided to play a game where the women were blindfolded and the men were told to line up. Without actually touching their husbands, the women were able to choose their spouses from the line-up. It was very interesting. When I asked Carlotta how she knew she had found me, she said 'I don't know. I just knew in my heart that it was you. It was like I could sense your energy.' And that was a very eye-opening experience."

Rosalie shook her head.

"Wow, that's amazing."

"Yes, indeed. So, my dear sister, do not worry for they cannot fool you."

Rosalie felt a sense of relief.

"What else did the man say?"

"He said I should not trust anyone and that I've been given a great gift. I know something most people don't."

"And what is that?"

"That there is more to life than what we see right before our eyes. In a way, he's right. As a matter of fact," she added with a chuckle, "I couldn't concentrate on anything all afternoon. It was like I was starving for more important stuff. It was like my homework was for little kids and I was too grown up for such simple vocabulary words. After that, I found my homework boring. Does that sound strange?"

He shook his head.

"That sounds like someone who is on the brink of a new discovery."

"He said something like that, too. He said I should stop thinking like a child or something like that."

"Yes, I see what he means. I believe he was saying that you are on the brink of womanhood."

"Womanhood?"

Sigmund smiled and nodded.

"And, I think he is correct."

Chapter 21

Rosalie had entered a transitional period in her life; of that, she was sure. If dealing with other-worldly beings was part of being on the brink of womanhood, she wished for childhood, that uncomplicated time when trust came easily and mysteries had not begun to present themselves.

Thankfully, the turmoil settled down and she found life quiet for a few days. However, while she focused on her mundane, peaceful life, she also found that reading grade-level books, simple mathematics and rudimentary science bored her.

She was, in fact, starved for more knowledge, a higher level of learning than her eighth-grade teachers could offer. She could barely wait to begin high school in September. Surely, she thought, school would become more of a challenge.

Homework came easy; too easy. Whatever the visitors had done to her mind, she discovered, everything she was taught seemed to sink in the first time. She no longer found it necessary to study for a test.

She discussed it at length with Sigmund on Friday evening.

"Before the man came the last time, I remember going over my vocabulary words so many times and I still missed some of them. But now, I read them and their meaning and, instantly, it's imbedded in my mind and easy to recall. How is this possible?"

Sigmund seemed to ponder her question.

"Do you remember the sequence of the formula?" he asked.

"Yes, I do, every part of it. I could write it out again right here and now. And, Sig," she added, eyes wide and filled with a certain satisfaction, "everything Miss Nettleson, my math teacher, shows me, I absorb as though I knew it all along. Does that make sense?"

"Some believe we have known all there is but have forgotten when we were born, forced to learn it all over again."

Rosalie nodded her agreement.

"Yes, that's how I feel; like I already know it and she's just helping me remember it or reminding me."

Sigmund scratched his chin. Rosalie could almost predict what was about to be suggested.

"You want to run tests on me, right?" she asked.

"So now you read minds, too?" he said, laughing.

She laughed, too.

"It feels like that. Actually, I love it. Sig, do you think the man made me smarter?"

"It appears he did something to you."

The man, indeed, changed the way she approached her lessons. This new way of learning had also opened up free time allowing her to do more research, an endeavor she sought at the local library.

Early Saturday morning, Rosalie helped decorate the float she and her friends were displaying in the Spring Festival Parade later that day.

She had spent little time on the project, something that caused her friends to complain. She did, in fact, feel guilty that Joseph and Denise did most of the work.

As she stapled the last flower in place, she announced to her friends that she was in a hurry to get to the library.

"How come you're always too busy to hang out with us?" Joseph asked. "And what about the parade?"

"I can't help it," she said. "I have things to do."

"What kind of things?"

"I don't know; things. Mostly, I'm kind of bored with school."

"Why?"

Rosalie wanted to tell them about her new-found intelligence but realized one question would lead to another and, in the end, one of the visitors would only come back and erase their memory.

She looked at their innocent faces, faces she loved. At that moment, she decided to break off her friendship in order to keep them out of harm's way.

"Look, I have to go. I met some kids and we're going to meet up at the library. We're working on a science project."

"What kind of science project?" Joseph asked.

Denise squinted her eyes and moved close to Rosalie.

"Are you saying you don't want to hang out with us anymore? What's the matter, are you too smart for us all of a sudden?"

As much as Rosalie wanted to apologize, she knew she had only one course of action. She lied.

"Do you guys know anything about quantum mechanics?"

Rosalie had no real idea what that meant. She wasn't even sure from where it came.

"Maybe not," Denise said, her eyes showing her hurt feelings, "but I do know about friendship and it seems to me you forgot how to be a friend."

She turned to Joseph.

"Come on, Joey, let's leave Miss Brilliant Mind to her new friends."

155

Rosalie wanted to cry, to hold them back and tell them how much she loved being friends with them. Inside, though, she knew cutting them loose was the highest form of friendship.

"Whatever," she said, turned and walked away.

She couldn't look back. Instead, she ran to the library and immersed herself in books about quantum mechanics, a subject that, that morning, she hadn't even known existed.

She sat at a long table reading about the double-slit experiment where it was demonstrated that light and matter can display characteristics of both waves and particles. Somehow, somewhere in the recesses of her mind, she understood the process. Without knowing from where her thoughts came, she found herself looking up people like Thomas Young and Isaac Newton.

Rosalie looked at her wristwatch. It was a quarter to twelve. The Spring Festival Parade was set to begin at one o'clock. She wondered if Joseph and Denise would still allow her on the float.

She put the books back in their spots, knowing instinctively where each belonged, and packed up her belongings.

It was then that she heard a crackling noise. She turned to find a woman standing at the end of the long table. She had never seen this visitor before, yet there was something familiar about her.

"Are you the lady who came to me before?"

The woman's mouth didn't move, yet Rosalie could hear her soft voice fill her mind.

"Yes. How are your studies coming along?"

"It's easy," she said. "I think the man did something to my brain."

She heard the soft laughter of the woman.

"He did nothing to your brain, child. I've given you the gift of understanding. Once you understand a thing, you've learned it and it will never be forgotten."

Rosalie felt confused. Her change came about after the meeting with the man. As though reading her mind, the woman spoke again.

"Trust me, Rosalie, I gave you this gift. He would have you believe otherwise."

"Let me ask you something? Are you aliens?"

"Well, yes, in a way."

"In a way? How can you be aliens in a way? You either are or you aren't, right?"

The woman laughed.

"Oh, child, you have so much to learn. In the sense that we do not come from another planet, we are not what your society would call aliens. However, we are alien to your world."

"Then, you are aliens."

Again, the woman allowed a soft chuckle to fill Rosalie's thoughts.

"We are from another dimension. Your scientists pretend to know from where we come. They say it is outer space. We are not as far away as that. We are right next door, like a neighbor, watching, waiting for you to let down your guard.

"We can appear physically and mentally. We can fly our airships through the curtain that separates our worlds. We choose the sky because it's the safest way. And, when we do, you all look up and say we came from outer space."

She laughed and added, almost sarcastically, "Why are you people so smug, so all-knowing?"

"Could you live here if you wanted to?"

"We could."

"I don't understand. Is there a choice/"

"Yes, there's always a choice. I, for instance, don't want to be born into a tiny body, have to grow up under the tutelage of ignorant people and face the trials and tribulations human beings face on a daily basis. It sounds horribly uncomfortable and burdensome. Therefore, I remain in my own dimension of spirit and light."

Rosalie allowed the concept of birth to settle in her mind. She'd never thought about life in such a way. She had never thought about existence before. She merely woke up each day, did what was expected and rested each night. Never would she have imagined that she'd be contemplating the prospect of choosing to be or not to be born. After a few moments, she formed an opinion.

"I don't mind being a human."

"Well, that's rather odd after all the grief you've been through."

Rosalie thought for a moment.

"Maybe so, but look at all the good stuff that's happened. I have my sister and Catherine and, my sweet little nephew, Stanley. I love him so much."

"Oh, yes, Stanley. He reincarnated with a purpose, to help his father. But, let me tell you something. While he came to Earth with the best of intentions, once he got here, once he became embroiled in the human experience, the dear boy has totally forgotten his mission. It's happened over and over again. Very few who incarnate into human beings follow through on their mission."

"Yes, but look at all the souls who have."

"A handful, my dear, a child's handful."

Rosalie understood the implication of such a minute amount of people. She had no response so she changed the topic.

"Why do you come to me?"

"Because you are open to it. You have a wild imagination and you have more courage than you realize. The night the man appeared to you, he was trying to stop you from getting involved in Sigmund's business. He and his kind tried to reach you in your dreams, but you wouldn't let them in. They waited for the right moment, the night you were there, alone in his office and spying, for lack of a better word, on Sigmund.

"The visitor warned you to back off. I watched and almost laughed aloud when you wrote more notes in your little marble notebook and stuffed it under your mattress."

"You heard him?"

"Yes, of course. I can see and hear everything."

Rosalie pondered her statement. Somewhere, deep inside, she had a feeling the woman wasn't being completely honest.

"You know what you have to do, and that man is trying to stop you. He'll use whatever measures he can."

"He did frighten me."

"He is nothing but a mere figment of your imagination, just like me. I am not here, exactly. Our realm is in another dimension. I exist only in your mind while on this planet."

"That's what Sigmund said."

"He's correct. His former statesmen had several communications with the other-worldly visitors."

"How can you do that?"

"We can manifest ourselves better when you are sleeping. Unfortunately, when we do, you assume it was a dream."

"Like when I was dreaming that I was flying over the ocean?"

"Exactly. And, by the way, that isn't really a dream. We have the ability to soar and you held onto the memory of that experience. Good for you."

Rosalie smiled and stood taller. Compliments from a superior being was something to relish. The woman continued to speak.

"Nevertheless, the visitor you had is part of a network of beings who want to accelerate the demise of mankind through technology. They've done it before, many times, in fact, and they plan to do it again.

"My mission is to stop them. I believe in mankind. I believe humans are good, albeit somewhat misguided."

"How are they trying to destroy us?"

"Time travel. Time travel upsets the natural order of things here on Earth. Where I come from, there is no such thing as time; there is only the present moment and each present moment unfolds into new opportunities.

"Humans, on the other hand, see themselves on a limited time schedule and, therefore, wish to control it, manipulate it.

"The Nazis were trying to undermine the laws of physics. They weren't interested in sending people and things into the future, they wanted to send weapons into the past, to the places where the allied forces had advanced.

"Could you imagine if they had lined the beaches of Normandy with enough mines to decimate the entire area? Everyone would have died. Go back to your history books and study the allied maneuvers. Could you imagine if the Nazis had that information beforehand?"

Rosalie felt a cold chill surround her.

"They would have won the war."

"Yes, they would have won the war. And that was Hitler's goal. He cared nothing about science and research for the good of mankind, he only wanted to become the leader of the world."

"The whole world?"

"Yes."

Rosalie looked away as a feeling of bewilderment crept in.

"What has all this to do with me?"

"It's not you. It's Sigmund. You see, in trying to stop the Nazis from using time travel to harm mankind, he sent an object into the future. No one, not even us, knows when and where it will reappear."

Rosalie quickly lifted her hand to her mouth as though trying to contain the sound of shock that escaped her lips.

"That sounds really scary," she said.

"It should. Could you imagine something suddenly appearing out of nowhere? I am trying to help him fix the coordinates so that he can intercept the object."

"What did he send into the future?"

"A device capable of causing much destruction. It's a bell-shaped object."

"I saw it in his notes. It had a swastika painted on it."

"Yes, that's it."

"What can I do about this? I'm just a kid. And what can Sigmund do?"

"At this point, nothing, but I'm working on it."

"Please, lady, tell me why you beings are coming to me? I can understand Sigmund. He's a scientist and he's responsible for all this, but why me?"

"You are my agent, Rosie. I sent you here to do two things. You are to stop all future research on time travel and, secondly, you are to help Sigmund intercept the bell."

"I don't understand. Why did the *man* give me the formula?"

"He wanted you to give it to Sigmund and, indeed, you did. He is chaos. He enjoys creating conditions for catastrophe."

"Chaos? And who are you?"

"I am peace."

Rosalie suddenly felt light-headed. She closed her eyes to stop what she perceived as a spinning room. After a few minutes, she finally composed herself enough to open her eyes. When she did, she realized she was alone.

"Peace," she whispered. "She's peace."

As she headed for the door, she checked her wristwatch and noticed that no time had passed.

How'd she do that? I'm just not so sure about her. Peace? I guess we'll have to see about that.

Chapter 22

Rosalie left the library and ran home. She was out of breath by the time she reached the front door. She wanted to tell Sigmund of her newest experience and how the lady was able to stop time.

She grabbed the doorknob and turned it. Just as she was about to rush into the house, she heard muffled voices coming from inside. She eased the door open and discovered it was coming from Sigmund's office. She crept closer, putting her ear to the place where the doors met.

"Goddamn it, Lion, if you know anything else, you have to share it. Both of us could end up in Argentina for the rest of our lives."

She recognized the voice. It was Otto Kramer.

She checked the house to make sure no one else was at home. When she was sure, she hurried to her room and climbed upon her desk. She watched and listened intently as the men argued. She tried to remain as quiet as possible. It sounded as though everything the woman told her was true.

"We must find a way to protect them," she heard Sigmund say.

Who, she wondered? Who needed protection?

"How? How do you convince millions that an unidentified flying object is about to crash land in the middle of New York City? What do you think they will do, evacuate the city? No, my friend, they will tell you that you have lost your mind."

"We have to try, Otto. We have to try."

"I don't have to try at all. As a matter of fact, I don't want to try. You are such a fool, Sigmund. You are trying to stop something that you put in motion almost fifteen years ago."

That's what the lady said. She said he's responsible. He did it.

"I didn't know. I believed the bell would show up at our sister laboratory at a pre-determined time. I had no idea other time and space coordinates had been set. I don't know how that happened."

"I'll tell you how it happened. Dr. Auman and I set the coordinates the night before. We'd talked for many hours about the war. Germany was about to fall to its knees. The United States was about to rise triumphant and take over all of the work we had accomplished. We decided, then and there, we wanted Russia to have the technology, not the Americans.

"We set the coordinates for New York City, 1965. It will bring the United States to its knees, justice for their defeat over Germany. It will destroy the financial center of the free world. Russia will then be in a position to take the lead and become the most powerful country in the world."

"Have you been feeding information to the Russians all this time?"

"Yes, with your help."

Sigmund seemed to freeze in the conversation. Surely, she thought, if he knew what was happening, he would have recoiled at his part in Otto's scheme. Yes, she thought, he had protected him and by doing so, put himself in harm's way.

"What will you do, Lion? Will you explain how you lied for me? You told them I was with you the day after Easter. That was my one slip and you rescued me. If you tell them you didn't know, they will laugh in your face."

"Yes, and then throw me in prison," he agreed.

"Not to mention that it was you who sent the bell straight into the heart of New York City."

"You set me up?"

"I did no such thing. Actually, I was going to send the bell away. You were not supposed to be there. You came back earlier than I had anticipated. Why were you in such a hurry to return, especially after losing your parents? I tried to spare you. Then, I looked to the laboratory and noticed you by the window. I went inside to do my part, but you, my friend, did it for me. I remember thinking that when all was said and done, I'd need you to help me retrieve it."

"What would you have done if I had not sent the bell into the future?"

"I would have done it."

"So, you let me go, yes?"

"Yes. Was it not for me, you would have been hunted down and killed within hours. But you did push the button, Lion. You let your ego push you to be the hero and by doing so set your fate; a fate that has been and will forever be linked to mine."

"Otto, how could you be involved in this?"

"Money," he said, adding no explanation.

"Money? That's it. Surely it is because you have loyalties to Germany, your own country."

"Oh, I wish I had your integrity. I could hold my head high and say that I wished to avenge my country, my fuhrer. But, alas, I have none. I have been playing one side against the other all along. And why, you ask? I tell you because it is profitable. But the high and mighty, well brought up son of a pastor, you look for something more, something deeper. Well, my friend, there is no well of anguish from which I produce my retaliation. I will give whatever I am capable of giving to the highest bidder and, in this case, Russia."

"I am ashamed to have called you my friend."

Otto's German accent seemed to become coarser than usual as he spoke.

"Oh, boo hoo, my heart is breaking. We are not friends, *Sigmund*. We have not been friends for a long time. Our philosophies are too different. And, know this, had I known about your parents' plan to help those Jews escape, I would have had the soldiers at their door. I would have used it to gain even more trust from the fuhrer."

"Fuck the fuhrer."

Rosalie couldn't stop the smile that touched her lips at the sound of Sigmund's harsh words against the diabolical leader.

She cringed, however, when Otto laughed aloud.

"Yes, fuck the fuhrer, and the President of the United States and everyone else who thinks they know how to rule the masses. I say fuck them all. The only thing that matters to me is who will give me the most value for my knowledge."

"So what do we do now?"

"Join me, Lion."

Rosalie noticed he switched back to calling Sigmund by his nickname. Although young, she was able to appreciate how he used it to coerce Sigmund.

"We could both manipulate another country's future, just as we have the United States. We can send Russia in the direction we wish and, all the time, enjoy the vast riches they will bestow upon us."

"Get out of this house, immediately!"

Otto stood so quickly, his chair fell backward. He yanked open the doors, sending them deep into their pockets. As Rosalie hung the photo on the hook, she heard the slam of the front door.

Sigmund's not a Communist. Thank goodness, he's not a Communist.

Rosalie waited until she heard Sigmund leave the house and drive off. She went to the foyer and checked the time on the grandfather clock. In a few minutes, she'd have to get to her school in time to participate in the Spring Festival Parade on Main Street.

She wondered if they would even allow her to ride with them.

The doors to Sigmund's office were closed. She pulled them apart and went inside. Looking around, she realized there was nothing to commemorate the conversation she'd just witnessed.

Wow, I was right. Dr. Kramer is a Communist. But what do I do about it? Jeez, this is hard.

Just as she was about to leave, she heard the crackling sound. She turned to find the man standing in the shadows.

"She said you are chaos. Are you?"

"I am not chaos."

"Then take off your glasses and let me see the light that Sigmund says will come from your eyes."

The stranger lifted his dark glasses. Instead of streams of brilliant light, the room became engulfed in darkness. Rosalie felt the burdensome weight of

162

it. It was like the ring of a black hole, the interior pulling her over the event horizon and into its darkness.

"Hey, mister, where did you go?

She felt as though she were flying, however, it wasn't similar to the times she soared in her dreams with the woman entity. It wasn't the light, drifting flight like a leaf on the wind. Instead, she felt heavy, as though being pulled down and being forced to use every muscle in her body to stay airborne.

The darkness stretched out, beyond the walls of Sigmund's office, beyond the hallway, and beyond the walls of the entire house.

Frantically, she looked around. There was nothing but darkness in every direction. She lifted her hand but could not see her fingers in front of her eyes. She could feel her heart pounding as she flew around in what felt like large circles.

"Hey, mister," she called. "Is it the end of the world?"

There was nothing but deadly silence matching the deathly darkness.

"I want to go home," she demanded. "Hey, mister, I want go to home."

When she said that, she noticed a tiny light far, far away; almost invisible. But it was there, like a grain of sand. She turned toward it and felt herself moving in that direction. She flew for what seemed like hours, yet she wasn't tired.

Why, she wondered, didn't the speck of light get closer? It seemed to actually move farther out of reach.

She concentrated on her movement, soaring even faster toward the light. There was no wind resistance, no movement around her. Yet, somehow, she knew she was moving in the right direction.

"Rosie!"

She stopped. It sounded like Stanley's voice. He was calling her from somewhere beyond the speck of light, far, far away.

"Rosie!"

She concentrated on his voice and began to move toward the light until it appeared a bit larger. Now the size of a dime, she rushed forward.

"Rosie!"

She moved closer and closer, the minutes turning into hours. Her slow progress caused her to feel an overwhelming frustration.

"I'm coming, Stanley," she called, her voice being absorbed into the void around her.

She tried again.

"Stanley! Stanley!" she called in her highest voice.

Her words disappeared into the ether like soundproof tiles in a music studio.

"He can't hear me," she said.

"Rosie!"

She kept her thoughts locked on the small light and the sound of Stanley's voice.

"I'm coming, kiddo, I'm coming."

Finally after what felt like a full day, she began to notice that the light appeared larger, perhaps the size of a light bulb. She believed that meant she was making progress. She moved forward, relentlessly focused on her nephew's voice.

"Rosie!"

Hours turned into days, but still she kept moving.

"Rosie! Answer me."

It seemed to take a long, long time, but finally the light grew as big as a spotlight. Still, the boy's voice called her name.

"Rosie!"

After what felt like a week in the darkness, the light began to grow in noticeable increments. It appeared as the moon at night, large and bright. She knew she was close.

"What is that light, mister? Is it Heaven? Am I dead? Or, is it the doorway back home?"

The man didn't answer.

"Hey, lady, are you here?"

Still, no reply.

"Damn it, you creepy aliens. I'm tired of this shit. I want to go home."

The silence remained, except for the sound of Stanley's voice.

"Rosie, you better answer me."

If the light was a portal that led back home, she assumed, the closer she got to it, the better. She hoped by moving in that direction, it would become large enough and close enough for her to step through.

Time wore on. After what felt like weeks to Rosalie, she approached the light. Oddly, she wasn't tired. It stood before her like a silvery curtain.

She stopped. It had the same feeling as the black hole she had entered, the same pull. She didn't know what to do.

"Does this lead home? Should I walk through it?"

Again, silence.

At this point, she knew she was on her own. She reached out her hand and pushed it into the light. She could feel something hard and flat. It felt like the door in Sigmund's office as it had two handles. She grabbed them and pulled them apart. Just as they separated, the light from the foyer filled the room.

There, in the hallway, stood Stanley holding a string with a bright red balloon attached.

"Look what I got," he said. "Hey, how come you didn't answer me? I called you ten times."

Rosalie stared at the boy. His face was aglow, his skin like translucent alabaster. She turned back to Sigmund's office. She could see the black hole closing, getting smaller and smaller until it nearly disappeared into the recess from where the man had entered. Yet, she could still see it as a black dot.

"Rosie, look what I have, balloons. Aren't they pretty. Neecie gave them to me. I'm taking them to the Spring Festival."

Rosalie turned back to the boy. His features appeared normal.

"Yes, they're nice, Stanley," she said, almost absent-mindedly.

She felt as though she had been away for a long time. The experience had been so traumatic, she found herself unable to focus on her surroundings.

She took several deep breaths. As she calmed down and her heart began to beat normally, the feeling of dread lifted. The experience now felt like a strange dream. Still somewhat confused, she asked, "Did I miss the festival?"

"No. It's today. C'mon, Neecie and Joey are waiting for you outside. Wait till you see the float. Mr. Johnson put a real palm tree on it. It's cool."

Rosalie went to the front door. Outside, her friends waited by the large decorated flatbed that was attached to Mr. Perry's station wagon.

"April Love," she muttered, reading the sign that was stretched across the side of the base.

"It can symbolize how much we love spring and Pat Boone," Denise had said when they decided on its theme.

She recalled that Joseph had shook his head and rolled his eyes.

"All the girls love Pat Goon," he had teased.

Denise waved to her as she stepped outside. She was fussing with the sod floor of the float. Joseph was attaching a ribbon that had come loose. Mr. Johnson was securing the palm tree behind the throne.

"Are you okay, Miss Rosie? You don't look right. What's happened?" Mr. Johnson asked. "Carlotta's in the kitchen. I can get her."

"No, I'm okay."

"Come on, Rosie. The parade starts in twenty minutes," Joseph said.

A rush of memories overcame her. She saw herself working alongside them stapling hundreds of flowers to the float. She recalled holding one end of a long yellow and white striped ribbon while Joseph tied the other end to a pole. When was that? Last week? Last month? And why are they here? Didn't she tell them their friendship was over?

She approached the float and ran her hand across the fluffy green floor.

"I remember decorating this."

"Well, I hope so," Denise said. "It was just this morning."

She patted down a lump of sod behind the throne where Mr. Johnson had placed the tree.

"There," Denise said. "All done."

"That was this morning?"

Denise looked at her and then to Joseph. He shrugged.

"She getting batty again," he said with a laugh.

To Rosalie, the memories of decorating the float seemed to have come from many weeks, perhaps a month ago.

"That was only this morning?" she asked a second time in bewilderment.

"Rosie, what's wrong with you?" Denise asked. "You're acting like a crazy person. Are you okay?"

Rosalie recalled the confrontation they had before she went to the library. It seemed as though it happened a long time ago, too. It was their last conversation.

"Aren't you guys mad at me?"

"For what?"

"Going to the library. Making new friends."

"Oh, yeah," Joseph said, laughing. "I hate it when you go to the library. And you're only allowed to be friends with us. Get real."

"So, we're friends, right?" she asked.

Joseph and Denise shrugged and nodded at the same time.

"Okay, kids, let's get this thing to the school before the world ends," Mr. Perry said.

Rosalie suddenly was overcome with the feeling of darkness, the way it seemed to envelope her, the feeling that the world as she knew it had ended and she was left to find her way through the abyss. She shivered.

"What's the matter, Rosie, are you ill?" he asked.

"No, Daddy, she gets like this every once in a while. She's okay. Isn't that right, Rosie? You're okay, right?" Denise said, patting her arm.

Rosalie shook off the feeling of dread that seemed to want to surround her. She forced herself to smile.

"I'm okay. I had a weird dream about the end of the world and - -,"

"It was just a dream," Mr. Perry said. "Come along now and let's get this beautiful float to the school. We're in second position in the parade."

Rosalie obeyed and climbed in the back seat with Joseph. He looked at her with a strange expression. She could see Mr. Johnson by the float with the same look on his face. Denise joined her father in the front seat. Every now and then, during the five minute drive to the school, she'd turn around and smile at Rosalie.

They think I'm crazy. I think I'm crazy. I know what I experienced and that man may not be chaos, but he sure as heck isn't peace. I think he's death. And I think the lady is right. He wants to destroy the world; end humankind. And, I wonder, did I actually have that conversation with Denise and Joey or was it just my imagination? Did I even go to the library today? Did I see the lady again? Did Sig and Dr. Kramer really get into an argument? I don't know if I'm just hallucinating or if these aliens are playing with my head. I wish they'd pick on someone else.

"A penny for your thoughts," Joseph said, interrupting her disturbing mental rant and bringing her back to the present.

"You don't want to hear my thoughts, Joey. They'd scare the heck out of you."

He shrugged.

"Whatever."

Yes, whatever. If you only knew. If you only knew.

Chapter 23

It was Monday morning and Sigmund paced his office floor. Every now and then he'd stop, look out the window and pace again.

On Saturday, Otto Kramer, his lifelong friend, had put him in a precarious situation. After Otto left, Sigmund headed to his father's church where he sought his father's advice.

"Papa," he'd said, "Otto asked a favor of me and I agreed to help him. But, I'm afraid, things have changed and now I am facing a dangerous situation. I need your help."

"What has Otto done?"

Sigmund couldn't find a way to explain what had transpired without giving away government secrets. Although he tried to skirt the real issue, he left his father bewildered.

"Son, I understand your predicament so I will not insist you reveal anything that could make matters worse. What I will do, however, is offer this advice. Follow your heart. Who are the people who mean the most to you? They are the ones you must protect. Do whatever you have to do to protect them. A real friend does not put anyone in such a situation. I have total faith in you and I know you will do the right thing."

Sigmund left the church and headed downtown to meet Carlotta and the children for the parade and spring festivities. Afterward, they went to a local restaurant for dinner. Rosalie, he noticed, was in a strange mood.

"What's the matter with you, little one?" he'd asked.

She merely shook her head and looked away.

"I don't want to talk about it," she'd said.

He wondered of what it was she didn't wish to speak. He had the feeling something happened so he pressed the matter. It was the first time she had almost became curt.

"Sig, I don't want to talk about it, I said. Just let it go."

She seemed to avoid him for the remainder of the weekend. He also knew he had other, more important, matters with which to deal. He had to find a way to fix the problem created by Otto Kramer and still maintain his citizenship in the United States. His father was correct, he knew. He had to do whatever it took to protect Carlotta and the children.

He caught sight of Dr. Bennett arriving. He wondered if it was wise to involve him or would that only make matters worse.

"Damn you, Otto!" he said, slamming his fist against the window sash.

At that moment, the telephone rang. He went to his desk and picked up the receiver.

"Sig, it's Rosie."

He hesitated, then let out a long breath.

"What is it, Rosie? I am very busy."

"I have to speak to you."

Again, he paused.

"Does this have anything to do with the mood you've been in all weekend?"

"No. I wasn't in a bad mood, was I? Anyway, I don't want to talk about it on the phone."

"I will be home by seven. We can talk then."

"No, not at home either. Can we meet at the park?"

"What park?"

"You know the park. Stanley's favorite spot."

Sigmund wondered why the girl was being cryptic. The place she proposed to meet was behind the playground at his father's church. It was a small and private spot where the woods met a creek. Stanley liked to watch the water dance over the rounded rocks that lined the creek bed.

"Rosie, what is this about?"

"It's a surprise for Carlotta's birthday. I have a great idea."

Sigmund frowned. Carlotta wasn't having a birthday for six months. Why, he wondered, would she want to discuss that?

"I have to work today."

"Work, schmerk," she said. "C'mon, meet me."

He knew Rosalie hated expressions like that, often complaining when anyone stuck two words together to make a rhyme, especially when they made no sense.

"Work, schmerk? Hmm, you must really have something expensive planned for your sister to use such a silly expression. How much is this going to cost me?"

"Not much. Besides, I still have the money my mother left me, so I can pay for half of it. Will you meet me? I have to tell the guy who sets things up today."

"Today? Rosie, I should be angry with you. Why do you wait until the last minute?"

"I'm sorry, Sig. Will you help me?"

"Sure. I'll meet you in thirty minutes."

Even though his mind weighed heavy with Otto's proposal, he knew something must have happened that was significant enough for Rosalie to call him from work and especially request they meet in such a clandestine location.

Rosalie hung up the telephone and rushed outside. It was a bright spring morning and she was glad to have the day off from school. The teachers were meeting with parents to discuss report cards.

She headed straight to St. John's Lutheran Church. She took the shortcut through the courtyard in the back, past the playground, and emerged onto the overgrown path that led to the creek.

While she was anxious to speak to Sigmund all weekend, she couldn't bring herself to relive the horror of her experience. Everything around her seemed out of place, strange.

When she had awakened on Monday, however, she discovered that the world felt normal again. She dressed, ate breakfast, helped Carlotta with the children, and asked permission to go to the library. Although she felt the sting of guilt for lying, she knew it was best to keep her sister out of it.

Sigmund sounded annoyed when she called. Surely, when he heard what she had to say, his attitude would change.

After more than a half hour, she heard the sound of footsteps heading toward the clearing. She turned to find him walking toward her. The sun reflected off his light hair and, she thought, he looked like an angel. All he needed was a set of large silver wings. She was glad he had a smile on his face.

"Work, schmerk? Really, was that the best you could do?"

He sat on a large rock next to the creek.

"So, what is so important that you pulled me from my office in the middle of the morning? Thankfully, the traffic is light at this time of the day."

She sat on her sweater that she'd spread on a patch of clover.

"A couple things," she said.

Sigmund leaned forward, resting his forearms on his thighs and clasping his hands. Their eyes met.

"What has happened?"

Rosalie lifted her bottle of Pepsi Cola and swallowed a mouthful. She hoped its sweetness would help counter her sour words.

"I heard you and Dr. Kramer talking. I know he's a commie."

Sigmund didn't speak. He merely nodded, his features expressionless.

"And, I had a visit from the man again."

"Hmm, I suppose he's the guy who *sets things up*. When you said that, I knew that was what you meant. What did he say?"

"It was horrible," she said, her eyes filling with tears.

Her throat felt constricted and she tried to swallow. It hurt, so she took another swig of soda, trying to ease the discomfort. She then described her experience, making sure to emphasize how long it seemed to take.

"It felt like a month passed. And then I had to go to the Spring Festival and act like nothing happened. It was so hard. All I wanted to do was cry. And, yes, that's why I was in a bad mood all weekend."

He leaned forward and stroked her hair.

"Shh, shh, little one. It's all just a mind trick. Why would he do this to you? You are a child."

"That's not all. I had another visit from the woman, too."

"Again? Oh, my God, Rosie. I am so sorry."

"Yes, actually, I saw her first on Saturday. She came to me at the library. I rushed home to tell you about it and, Sig, she actually made time stand still. Anyway, that's when I heard you and Dr. Kramer. After you both left, I went into your office and that's when the man appeared and made me have that horrible experience. I really hate that guy."

"I don't blame you. I wish there was some way I could be with you when they appear."

"Me, too. What should we do?"

"Well, as you are aware, I have enough problems with Dr. Kramer. He's a bad man, Rosie. I'm glad you had the good sense to bring me here to tell me about your discovery. Who knows if he had listening devices planted in my home. My first concern it to keep my family safe."

"And me, too, I hope."

"When I say my family, Rosie, you are automatically included. You do believe that, yes?"

"Yes, I know. But, what do we do next?"

"Somehow, I have to figure out how to detour the bell. You heard where it will land. I'd like to tell you how it happened."

When he finished, she smiled, glad to finally hear the whole story.

"So, that's how you got the name of Lion, huh? Wow, that's an amazing story. But, I know you did what you thought was right. And I'm going to do whatever you want me to do to fix things. You can count on me, Sig."

"Thank you, Rosie. Now, I have to concentrate and, it appears, all of these visits, not to mention Otto's acts of treason, are getting in my way."

"You can do it. I know you can," she said.

He continued to stroke her hair. To Rosalie, it felt as though he were petting her as one does a Cocker Spaniel.

"I am so sorry that you have been drawn into the middle of this drama, Rosie. Believe me, if I could summon the woman and ask her to clear your mind, I would. You are just a child. You don't need to know of such matters."

"Well, it's too late for that. I'm in the middle of it and I don't think there's anything we can do about it. Just tell me what you want me to do and I'll do it. Do you want me to try to get the lady to come to me? Maybe I can try to dream about her and that will make her come."

Sigmund pulled back his hand and stood, facing the creek. He seemed to be concentrating on the water as it cascaded over the rocks. After a few minutes, he turned to Rosalie.

"Yes," he finally said. "Yes, try to summon the woman and ask her advice. She says she is peace. Well, we could use some of that. As far as the man is concerned, I'm not sure what he wants. I don't understand why he would give us the information we need if he was trying to hurt us. We are now in a position to complete an experiment, something we could not achieve without his help. I believe the key here is the woman. I guess we will have to trust her for now."

Rosalie agreed. The discussion ended. Sigmund was the first to leave the creek. He went through the church courtyard and disappeared around a wide hydrangea bush.

In the quiet afternoon air, the sound of his car's engine drifted gently into the opening. After a few seconds, it faded away.

"Lady," Rosalie called, "come to me. Tell me what to do."

She waited. The only sound came from the creek. She looked down at the stones, smooth from years of the water's work.

"Mr. Creek, how do I smooth out this mess?"

"Are you talking to inanimate objects?"

Rosalie jumped and turned quickly. A light emanated from behind a bush. In a second, it transformed itself into a woman.

"Mama," she whispered.

"No, I am not your mother. It's just that, out here in the wild, I thought you'd prefer to see an image you recognize."

The woman's soft voice whispered inside her head as the image of her mother merely stood completely still.

"How do you do that?"

"It's a learned skill."

"I was hoping I could get you to come to me in a dream, but this is much better. Sigmund and I have a problem."

"Yes, I know. I've heard everything. Your brother-in-law thinks I should clear your memory of all this drama. How noble of him."

"He *is* noble," Rosalie said.

She wasn't sure she appreciated the woman's tone. Then again, she thought, the woman had chosen to use her mother's image, a woman with a distinct hatred for Germans. Maybe the tone was normal, but her perception of it reeked with sarcasm.

"Would you want me to clear your memory? I can, you know."

"No, I just want you to help me help Sigmund. Can you do that?" Rosalie said.

"I could," she replied. "I absolutely could."

There was a long silence.

"Well?"

"In good time, Rosie, in good time. For now, I would suggest you go home and act as though nothing has happened. Don't speak to anyone about Sigmund or Dr. Kramer. Don't share my visit with anyone, especially Dr. Bennett."

"What about Sigmund?"

"Yes, of course, you can tell him, but no one else. In the meantime, let me see what I can do to help you. Somehow, you need to expose Dr. Kramer without involving Sigmund."

"Yes, exactly. How can I do that?"

"Child, child, it is not for you to worry about such things. You must put your complete trust in me. I will see you through this drama, as your brother-in-law calls it."

Rosalie had a flashback of the many people in her life who told her to trust no one. She thought about how the woman, this woman, had killed Joseph and then brought him back to life. She could see how the woman had the ability to appear to her at will and in familiar forms. She knew she had to trust someone. It appeared this was someone deserving of her confidence.

"Okay, I will trust you. Just tell me what to do."

"For now, as I said, do nothing. I will be in touch with you within the week. In the meantime, go spend time with your friends. You had hurt them deeply and, in doing so, have brought attention to yourself. That is why I erased their memory of the discussion you had on Saturday. You mustn't do things like that. Believe me, you are being watched. The best thing is for you to resume your normal life."

Rosalie agreed. The woman allowed a smile to cross her borrowed face. Rosalie immediately felt the warmth and love for her mother. As she faded out of sight, Rosalie stared at the bush with its new buds trying to enter the world. She touched a cluster of newly formed leaves, small and huddled, waiting for rebirth. When she did, the cluster seemed to fall apart in her hand like an over-watered begonia. It caused her to shiver.

"Wow! That was weird."

She decided it best to take the back road home. She ran along the creek to a place where it led to an old wooden bridge, wide enough for a wagon. When she arrived home, the first thing she did was enter Sigmund's office.

She looked around, her eyes scanning until she saw the black dot that she now realized was the link between the material world and the ethereal.

"I'm not going there," she said aloud to herself.

"Hey, mister, are you there?"

After a few minutes, she heard Carlotta enter the house.

"Rosie," she called.

"I'm right here," she said, stepping into the lighted foyer.

"Rosie, I have news for you, good news. You've been accepted by a local university, a private school. Isn't that wonderful? They are accepting students who excel in science. Sigmund had me apply for you and they looked over your grades and they want you."

Rosalie didn't know what to make of the news. She knew nothing of any programs for budding scientists. And, she thought, it was strange that Sigmund hadn't mentioned it.

"It was Sigmund's idea?"

"No, not really. He didn't know about the program until Otto mentioned it. Actually, it was Otto's idea. He encouraged Sigmund to approach them on your behalf."

For the second time that day, a cold chill assaulted her senses. Why, she wondered, would Otto suggest such an idea?

"What do I have to do? I mean, when would I go?"

"You don't have to do anything except say you want to go. The program starts in July and runs throughout the summer until the second week in August."

"So, I wouldn't be here most of the summer, right?"

"Yes, but it's such a great opportunity. You still want to be a scientist, don't you? I mean, if you don't want to go, just say so."

Carlotta appeared agitated.

"Can I think about it?"

"Yes, of course. Think about it and when Sig comes home, we'll talk it over. How does that sound?"

"It sounds okay. It's not that I'm ungrateful or anything."

Again, Carlotta seemed to react. Rosalie realized her sister was anticipating how it would look for Sigmund if he nominated her to attend the program and she refused. She decided it was a normal reaction for a wife, especially the wife of a German scientist.

"I'll probably go," she offered, hoping to calm her sister's worries.

It seemed to work as Carlotta allowed her usual smile to soften her features.

"Listen, I have to go pick up the kids. They're at the Lowe's house. I just wanted to give you the good news. Anyway, I hope you think it's good news."

Rosalie smiled and nodded. She wasn't sure what Otto Kramer was up to, but if he thought he could just ship her off to some school while he got Sigmund deeper in trouble, he was dead wrong.

"Okay, sweetie, I'll see you later. Here," she said, handing her a small bag. "It's ice cream. Can you put it in the freezer?"

Rosalie took the bag and Carlotta left. She went to the kitchen and opened the freezer door, removed the ice cream from the bag and placed it on a shelf. She took a Popsicle from a box and stood by the sink to eat it.

She was glad to be home alone. It gave her the opportunity to think about all that had happened over the course of the last few days. And now, she had to consider what Otto Kramer had on *his* mind.

While she wanted to remain in the kitchen, she knew her answers lived in another part of the house. She headed back into Sigmund's office and sat at his desk. When she turned on the lamp, she noticed movement in the corner.

"Oh, so it's you, huh?"

The man stepped forward. He reached across the desk and touched her temple. Again, the butterfly flapped its wings and Rosalie relived the entire conversation with Sigmund. The man pulled his hand away.

"The woman has returned?"

Since she didn't recall that when he touched her temple, she decided to keep it a secret.

"You seem to know everything," she said in her most sarcastic tone. "You tell me. Did the woman return?"

"She has great abilities. She can hide from me even in your thoughts. She finds something inside of you, something that you hold onto, like a memory or anger, and she keeps her presence behind the mental walls you construct."

"Mental walls? What are you talking about?"

The man stepped back. She had a full view of him. He was tall and slender. His clothes were black and covered most of his body. His hands had a strangeness about them, as if they were nothing more than flutters of light, a dark, menacing light, yellowish; not clear and bright like the woman.

"What do you want?" he asked.

Rosalie was taken aback.

"What do I want? What do you want? And don't even think about sending me into the dark place again. That was the most horrible experience I ever had."

"That place, that dark place as you call it, is where the woman wants all of humankind to dwell. She is pure evil. And that place, that endless darkness, is what we are working to stop. This is what we are up against."

Rosalie didn't believe him.

"Well, don't ever send me there again."

She sensed that the man was annoyed.

"I didn't send you there. She did. You simply won't accept that. Nevertheless, you called me here. I heard you. What is it you want from me?"

Rosalie realized she had, in fact, summoned the man.

"Yes, I needed to ask you something about Otto Kramer. You know him, don't you?"

"Yes, we know him."

"Well, he's trying to get Sigmund in trouble. And he wants to send me off to a college somewhere. I think he's on to me and he wants me out of the way while he does his evil deeds."

"Evil deeds? Hmm, interesting choice of words."

"He's a commie," she said.

"He is not a commie, as you say. He doesn't believe in their form of government or their way of life. He doesn't care about the Russians at all. He is what is known as a mercenary. He'll sell out to whoever will give him the most money. Right now, as a matter of business, he does have allegiances with the Russian government. And when he has drained them, he will sell himself out to the next highest bidder. He is not only doing evil deeds, he is an evil man."

"Is he the devil?"

The man didn't answer right away. It was as though he wanted to think about his answer. Rosalie waited with a most impatient look on her young face.

174

"No, he's just evil. Get out a piece of paper and a pen and write down what I say."

Rosalie opened the top drawer and withdrew a small notebook and a pen. She sat poised to write.

"Go ahead."

The man rattled off numbers and equations. Without hesitation, Rosalie knew exactly how to document it all. A few times, she shook her head as she jotted down ribbons of formulations, equations that included words like "wavelength" and "photoelectric equation." She drew triangles and funny little brackets to distinguish one set of numbers from other.

"Give that to Dr. Lowe and only Dr. Lowe. Understand?"

She looked at the pages filled with information.

"Is that it?"

"No. I have more information. You will need a fresh sheet of paper. Tear one out of the book and close it. Write what I tell you."

Once again, she kept pace as he rattled off formulas and strings of long equations. When he finished, he stepped back into the darkness.

"Hey, mister, wait. What do I do with this?"

"Give it to Dr. Kramer. Tell him that you were told to give it to Dr. Bennett but that you don't trust him."

"He's not going to believe that. He'll just ask why I didn't give it to Sigmund."

After a few moments silence, he said, "Figure it out, Rosalie. You will find a way. You are a clever girl. I have to go."

She watched as he seemed to melt into the bookcase, leaving nothing behind but the familiar crackling sound and the scary black dot.

She remained at Sigmund's desk and perused both sets of notes. She wondered how she was capable of comprehending what the man had dictated.

"I can't believe I wrote this stuff down," she murmured to herself.

Somehow, she knew, she had to deliver them to their prospective targets. She wondered if the man was working for or against her. She wondered if the notes for Sigmund were a trap.

As though a light flashed across her overactive mind, she smiled.

"I'll give them both to Sigmund," she said to the empty spot where the man had stood. "He'll know what to do with them."

She felt good about her decision. The man had said to figure it out and, with that in mind, she knew exactly what needed to be done.

A loud knock on the front door shook her from her comfort zone. The front door opened and Otto entered.

"Lion, Lion, are you home?"

Rosalie wished she had locked the door after Carlotta left.

She tried to slide beneath Sigmund's desk, but her movement caught his eye.

"Lion, is that you?"

He stepped into the office and stopped.

175

"Oh, Rosie, hello. Did you hear the good news?"

"Y-yes, thanks. Wow, college at fourteen. That's so cool."

Otto took the seat across the desk so they were face to face. He seemed pleased with himself, she thought. Or, she further thought, was he playing her for a fool.

"So, you'll go, yes?"

When Sigmund spoke that way, she liked it. When Otto did it, she wanted to spit at him. Instead, she smiled and nodded.

"So, what do you have there?" he asked.

Rosalie suddenly realized why he was there. She knew the house was being monitored for anomalies. Surely, he knew a visitor had just left.

"It's notes from one of them," she said.

He seemed pleased with himself. She noticed how smug the expression on his face became. Yes, she thought, he knew and he was sent in to confiscate the notes.

Oh, this spy thinks he's so clever.

"Is that for Dr. Bennett?"

She could hear the visitor's instructions in her mind.

"Yes, it is."

The next words that escaped her mouth seemed to do so on their own volition.

"I'm not sure if I trust Dr. Bennett. Would you like to see them first?"

Otto nearly spring from his chair, his long wiry body appearing like a praying mantis about to jump on the desk. He had a wide smile on his face. He took the paper she offered. His eyes scanned the information.

"If you were a puppy, Dr. Kramer, I think your tail would be wagging now," she said. "I did good, yes?"

She almost laughed at her own words.

"Yes, you did real good, Rosie, real good."

She folded her hands on the closed notebook that contained the formulas intended for Sigmund.

"Is there anything else, Dr. Kramer? I really have a lot of homework to do."

Otto kept reading, nodding his head and, every now and then, lifting his eyes to meet hers.

"I understand, homework. Okay, Rosie, I'll go now."

"Okay, I'll tell Sigmund you stopped by."

"No need," he said. "I'll stop by his office now and see him in person. Take care, Rosie."

He was nearly in a full run when he reached his car. She stood and watched him through the office window.

"Idiot," she mumbled.

She wasn't sure, but could've sworn she heard a low rumble of laughter from the dark corner of the room.

Chapter 24

Otto Kramer rushed back to the government facility, told his assistant that he wasn't to be disturbed and retreated to his private office, locking the door. There, he opened the folded sheet of paper and placed it on his desk.

"Let me see," he mumbled as he perused the equations.

He viewed the theories laid out before him. As he went through the sequences, he unconsciously nodded his head.

Now, to actually put the theory into practice.

He grinned when he realized he could use the new IBM 7000 mainframe computer that had been installed, compliments of the DOD. It would give him the power he needed. He let a shrewd smile cross his face.

As the afternoon turned to evening, the laboratories and offices were darkened and the parking lot emptied. He left his office and headed for his assigned laboratory.

He worked through the night, his slim form bent over a table where he used the schematic he'd drawn up from Rosalie's notes to create a small device, a black box, capable of producing enough power to access the invisible curtain that stood between the material and ethereal worlds to such a degree that he could literally walk out of this dimension and into the next.

His heart beat wildly with anticipation as he flipped the switch that exposed the barriers of his world.

When he did, a shimmering wall of what could only be described as liquid crystal appeared before him. Millions, if not trillions, of zeroes and ones created the fabric that emanated from the two pillars he'd constructed of coiled wire that stood six feet apart.

He approached and put forward his hand. It slipped through the veil and disappeared from sight. He smiled and snatched it back, wondering if he should be so bold as to stick his entire head though the shimmering curtain. What, he wondered, would he see?

"I'm a scientist," he mumbled to himself. "We take chances. Go ahead, Otto, do it."

He hesitated, then stuck his hand through the curtain again and waited a few moments. He tried to wiggle his fingers enough to disturb the flow of the curtain. It didn't move. He pulled his hand back and examined it. It had a strange glow that lasted a few seconds before returning to normal.

Hmm, I wonder if I will glow like that if I step into it.

He moved closer to the curtain and leaned forward, his head piercing the veil. At first, everything was black, a void with no sound. Then, as his eyes became used to his surroundings, he began to see specks of light to the left and right. He lifted his head and saw something so beautiful, it caught his breath.

"Oh, my God," he muttered, his words drifting into the strange new land. "It's magnificent."

He pulled his head back, returning to his familiar world. He caught sight of his own reflection in the glass door of a supply cabinet. His face was aglow for a few seconds and, like his hand, it returned to normal. He felt somewhat lightheaded and shook his head a few times in order to adjust to the material world. The feeling faded.

This is wonderful.

Something inside stirred. He wanted to call Sigmund and tell him of his amazing experience. He turned back to the curtain that, by now, looked as though it was ready to disappear.

"No," he said and rushed to the device on the table.

Before he could reach it, he heard a crackling sound and the curtain disappeared. He rushed to the spot where it stood and felt the air. It was crisp, as though someone left a window open in January.

"It's gone," he said to himself.

He turned off the device and waited a few seconds. When he switched it on again, nothing happened. He examined the device for the next two hours. He couldn't determine why it didn't work.

"If I get you running again," he said to the inanimate box, "I will not hesitate to jump into the next world."

He looked at his watch. It was almost three o'clock. While his first attempt was a success, he felt a slight disappointment that he couldn't get his device working a second time. He packed up his equipment and his papers, returned to his office where he left his jacket and left the facility. He went straight home and laid across his bed hoping to get a few hours of sleep.

As he drifted off, he saw the amazing images in his mind. There was a white bridge that crossed a small lake. The water in the lake was unlike anything he'd ever seen. It wasn't clear, yet it seemed to be made up of every color that ever existed. It flowed under the bridge like a million tiny crystal waves, sparkling against an amazing azure sky.

He had been so taken aback by the beauty of the bridge and water, he hadn't taken a moment to see what lay beyond it.

"The next time," he muttered in his half-sleep state. "Next time."

Rosalie once more waited with great anticipation as Sigmund walked through the front door. As soon as he closed it, she burst into speech, talking quickly and quietly, almost in a whisper.

"After you left, the woman visited me at the creek. Isn't that strange that she was there?"

He removed his jacket and hung it on the coatrack.

She didn't give him the opportunity to respond before she added, "And the man was *here* today."

He nodded and patted her shoulder.

"Rosie, calm down. You're going to give yourself an ulcer. Trust me, everything will work out. We will talk after dinner."

He disappeared into the kitchen where she could hear him interacting with his family. She shook her head and wondered how he was able to act so casually when his world was on the brink of destruction.

She followed him into the kitchen where Carlotta was standing by the counter rolling dough.

"We're having chicken pot pies tonight, Rosie; your favorite."

"Rosie, hey Rosie," Stanley said from his spot at the table. "Look at what I drew. It's an angel."

Rosalie glanced at the picture Stanley had drawn. It was a woman with giant wings that appeared to be more of a starburst than actual wings.

"That's nice. How do you know how to draw angels?" she asked, playfully.

"Cause I saw one in your room. She said she was your guardian angel."

At that, Rosalie and Sigmund locked gazes and simultaneously turned toward the boy.

"Angel," Catherine repeated and giggled. "Mommy, angel."

Carlotta was engrossed in forming small balls of dough, flattening them and placing them into a large muffin tin.

"Very good, Catherine," she said, absentmindedly as she formed the base for the pot pies. "Good girl."

Rosalie silently mouthed, "Angels?"

Sigmund shrugged and bent down to kiss his son.

"So, you talk to angels, yes?"

"Yes, Papa. But just one angel, Rosie's angel."

Rosalie's eyes widened.

"I have to get something from my room," she said.

Sigmund nodded and distracted the boy as she rushed past him and down the hall that led to her bedroom.

She entered and looked around. It was empty. After a few moments, she heard the now-too-familiar crackling sound.

"Rosalie, I warned you not to trust anyone but me. Why did you allow the man to persuade you to help him? Why did you give the notes to Dr. Kramer? Do you have any idea what you've done?"

Rosalie's heart pounded so hard, she thought she'd faint.

"I-I didn't know. He said to give him the papers, so I did."

"But did I not warn you not to trust him? Why have you disobeyed me?"

"Oh, my goodness, what will happen now?"

Rosalie focused on the woman. She no longer appeared as the librarian or Anna Mary. Instead, she appeared just as Stanley drew her. She was long and elegant with enormous wings that looked like a bright star was glowing behind her, similar to how she appeared in her flying dream.

"You didn't hurt Stanley, did you?"

The woman laughed.

"Why would I hurt a child? No, I didn't hurt him. But I'm afraid you have; you've hurt everyone on this planet. Because Otto now has the ability to pierce the curtain and step into the space-time continuum, he has the power to destroy us all.

"Oh, dear girl, I warned you. That male entity is chaos. He represents all that is wrong with man. He's been manipulating you from the start. He puts thoughts in your head of which you aren't even aware."

"Really?"

"Yes. I saw how easily you turned your back on your mother's religion and joined the Lowe's church. That decision," she said and paused, "he did that, not you. Surely, your mother is watching from Heaven and she's crying. I'm afraid you've broken her heart.

"Has chaos not pulled you into the depths of Hell?

"And now this. He is evil and now Otto Kramer has the ability to go back in time and change the outcome of the war. He must be stopped."

"But how?"

"Sigmund must end his life."

Rosalie wasn't sure she heard the woman correctly.

"Sigmund has to do what?"

"He has to kill Otto Kramer before he completes the device that will allow him to step in and out of time. Tell Sigmund and don't hesitate. There is no time to lose."

The room seemed to brighten so much that she had to close her eyes. When she opened them, the light and the woman were gone.

She stood and stared at her reflection in the mirror on her dresser.

"Holy cow! I broke my mother's heart and now Sigmund has to kill someone; his friend. What have I done? What have I done?"

Her reflection revealed the pain that had seated itself deep in her soul. For that moment, Rosalie despised herself.

When she returned to the kitchen, Carlotta was setting the table as Sigmund drew pictures with Stanley.

"What did you need from your room?" Carlotta asked.

Rosalie, caught off guard, shrugged and said, "I don't know."

"You don't know? Rosie, you said - -,"

"I know," she snapped. "When I got to my room I forgot why I went there. Didn't you ever do that?"

Carlotta smiled and nodded.

"Sure, we all do that. Why are you so upset?"

"I'm not upset," she said and turned to Sigmund, her eyes stinging from her tears. "I really messed things up."

Sigmund stood and approached Rosalie.

"You messed nothing up, Rosie. Please, relax."

"What in all that's holy is going on?" Carlotta asked, her question more a demand for an answer.

"Because of me, the world's going to end."

At that, Carlotta stiffened and turned to her husband.

"What is this all about? You two have been up to something these last few weeks and it's obvious that whatever it, it's upsetting my sister."

As upset as she was, Rosalie almost laughed at the guilty expression on Sigmund's face. His flaxen hair looked white against his now crimson face. His blue eyes grew wide.

"Carlotta, my darling, I do not know why the girl is so upset. We are up to nothing."

He turned to Rosalie.

"Is it about the school? You want to go, yes?"

By now, Rosalie had composed herself enough to realize she was not in a position to share her knowledge with her sister. She looked from Carlotta's concerned face to Sigmund.

"Yes, that's it. I know it's a great opportunity but I don't want to leave this house."

Sigmund settled back into his chair.

"There you have it. The girl is upset about leaving home. Perhaps the university is not right for her at this time."

"Really? How is that the end of the world?" Carlotta asked.

"She is a teenager. Everything that does not go smoothly is like the end of the world. That is what you meant, Rosie, yes?"

Rosalie nodded.

"Dinner's almost ready," Carlotta said, shaking her head.

She put her hands on Rosalie's shoulders and looked into her eyes with a soft expression, one of love.

"Rosie, honey, we can talk this over later. Please, you've been through so much, don't let this make you so upset. I want you to be happy."

Rosalie took a deep breath and stepped forward, wrapping her arms around her sister.

I've been through so much, Carlotta? You don't know the half of it. I've been to Hell and back, and now I'm going to take everyone else with me.

Chapter 25

As the sun crept above the horizon behind the Lowe house, Rosalie lie awake. The long talk she had with Sigmund the night before did little to calm her nerves.

"I will handle Otto."

"Will you murder him?"

Sigmund had laughed.

"No, I won't have to kill him. I have an idea, but I will need your help."

Rosalie listened intently as Sigmund laid out his plans for Otto. While they appeared on the surface to make sense, there was something nagging at the back of her mind; something upon which she couldn't put her finger.

"So, you'll act like you're helping him, but you'll actually be setting a trap?"

"Yes, exactly. He has asked me to join him. I will tell him that I am afraid *not* to join him. I must gain his confidence so he will tell me everything."

When he put it that way, she decided, it seemed to make sense.

"So, what do you want me to do?"

"For now, nothing. There will come a day when I will ask you to lie for me. Will you do that, Rosie? Will you lie for me?"

"To who?"

"Whom," he said. "Whether it's the man or the woman asking, you must tell them you no longer trust me and you believe I've joined Dr. Kramer."

"They'll know. They read my mind or eavesdrop on me. They'll surely know if I'm fibbing."

"Not if you keep telling yourself that you don't trust me. Keep saying it over and over again. They are, in fact, reading your mind, but only if you allow them to do so.

"Build a wall in your mind with your thoughts and that is what they will read, a wall of lies. I am doing that right now. I've trained myself to keep my innermost thoughts and feelings in a locked compartment in my mind. That, Rosie, is why they come to you and not me."

"Really?"

"Really. I couldn't figure it out. Why Rosie? I kept asking myself the same question. This is why."

"Wow, that's amazing. I'll have to practice."

"Yes, indeed, do practice. It's all mind control. Do you understand? You have to be in control of your own thoughts."

"I can do it," she said.

"And, Rosie, if you are called in to speak to Dr. Bennett, you will tell him that you have no knowledge of my activities."

"Why?"

"We don't know who to trust."

"I trust you."

"Good. And I trust you. Let's keep it that way."

"What about Carlotta?"

Sigmund had allowed a worried look to cross his handsome features. He ran his fingers through his thick blond hair, then scratched his chin. Rosalie knew he was thinking up an answer.

"Tell her nothing. She doesn't have to be involved. Actually, the less she knows, the safer she will remain."

"Sig, will the world end because of me?"

"No, of course not. Now, just be still. As I said, I will handle Otto."

"If you have to kill him, will you tell me?"

"Would you want to know?"

Rosalie thought about it for a few long moments.

"I don't want to know, but if you don't tell me, somehow I think I'll wonder about it for the rest of my life."

Sigmund laughed.

"How about this? I will tell you the truth whenever you ask a question and, this way, you will have control of the information that comes your way. Will that work for you?"

"Yes, I think that will work. Anyway, here," she said, handing him the notebook with the new equations. "The man said I should give this to you and only you. Of course, the woman said I shouldn't give it to you. Damn, oops, I mean darn, this is so confusing."

He took the notebook and thanked her.

She left his office wondering if she had done the right thing. She decided to give the whole "thought control" thing a try. In order to *not* think about her decision to give Sigmund the new formulations, she played cards with Stanley and helped Carlotta get Catherine ready for bed. She kissed her sister and reminded her that she was grateful.

She took a long bath, read the next chapter of her history book, and headed to bed. She stared at the ceiling throughout the night. The light from the street filtered through the sparsely clad branches forming intricate patterns.

Over and over, she repeated her mantra of distrust for Sigmund. Yet, the fact that she trusted him enough to give him the notebook seemed to shove past the wall of mistrust and make itself visible.

"I'll never fool them, never."

As the sun rose, the forms on the ceiling disappeared.

Her fears, however, remained.

Sigmund left for work early. He'd hardly slept. He assumed Rosalie was feeling the same turmoil that stirred within him. The sun had barely offered enough light to turn the eastern horizon pink by the time he reached the laboratory.

The first thing he did was visit Otto's lab. He tried the combination on the touchpad and discovered that it had been changed.

"Secrets, my friend?" he mumbled.

He had expected as much. He went to his office and sat behind his desk in the dark. He thought about his discussion with Rosalie the night before. He wondered if she'd trust him enough to lie. He shook his head as he recalled her marble notebook. If those old suspicions surfaced, would she retreat to her original plan? Would she expose him as a traitor? Then again, she did give him the notebook that contained the new equations.

He heard a noise outside his door. Through the opaque glass, he saw the form of Otto Kramer. He stood outside the office, tried the door, discovered it was locked and, as though being caught up in an enlightening realization, ran toward his office.

Sigmund stood and unlocked the door. He followed Otto in the dimness of the night security lights. Otto went into his office and shut the door.

Sigmund walked up to the door and rapped lightly.

"Come in, Sigmund."

"You saw my car, yes?"

Otto nodded.

"You are in early. It's just six-thirty. Do you have a decision?"

"Yes. I will join you."

Otto smiled.

"I thought you'd see the light. Lion, I have the most astonishing news. Rosalie, as I'm sure you already know, has passed on the formula for time travel to me."

"Yes, I know. She has told me. Have you tried to translate it into a working prototype?"

Otto became excited and nodded. He went to a vault he'd placed in the corner of his office and opened it, shielding the combination. He removed a black box.

"I was able to use the same prototype of the vibrational accelerator as a base on which to build a new device; a device that can open a portal. Come, Lion, follow me."

Sigmund followed him along the corridor. When they came to the laboratory, Otto unlocked the door and went inside. When he turned on the light, Sigmund noticed two poles, six-feet high, and made of intertwined copper wire in the center of the room. They stood like two golden pillars.

"What are these?"

184

"You'll see," Otto said over his shoulder.

He knelt down and placed the revised vibrational accelerator, now with several silver levers and knobs on the floor near the pillars, forming a triangular configuration. He turned it on, moving the levers up and down.

"I'm setting a frequency," he said.

After a minute, there was a crackling sound as shards of glasslike sparkles rushed toward the center of the space between the pillars.

Electrical currents jumped from the innocuous black box. Seconds later, before Sigmund could catch his breath at its magnificence, a curtain appeared, a drape composed of a million tiny droplets of zeroes and ones formed from iridescent lights. Soon it formed a curtain.

"It's code, Lion, living code. It's a passageway to another dimension."

"Oh, my God," Sigmund whispered, his eyes wide. "Is this what I think it is?"

Otto seemed unable to contain his excitement as his head bobbed in reply.

"Yes, yes. It is. It's the entrance to the dimension that parallels this one. From my calculations, I believe I can traverse through time. Lion, do you see the possibilities?"

Sigmund stood motionless, taking in the full implications of Otto's discovery. His mind leaped to the possibility of changing the coordinates on the bell. Before he could voice his thoughts, Otto spoke.

"But, Lion, there is a problem. I cannot keep the box on for longer than a minute. However, I know you are dying to see what lies behind it. Go ahead, stick your head through and see infinity with your own eyes."

Sigmund approached the curtain and touched it with his finger. It sent outward ripples across the surface. He stuck his hand through and watched as it disappeared into the illuminated curtain. His hand tingled. He moved his face close, his nose piercing the veil. It, too, tingled.

"Go ahead. Don't be afraid. Go ahead and stick your head through the curtain."

Sigmund pierced the streaming shards of light. Every inch of his face felt as though it was alive, tingling. He moved his hand and saw that he left behind a stream of silver sparkles. He shook his head and more silver burst in front of his eyes. He laughed aloud.

"This is amazing!"

Something slightly to the left caught his attention. He became still. He could see a bridge adorned in flowers and each one glowing from within. The bridge crossed a small creek. It, too, held the same glow. On the other side of the creek, he saw the figure of a man; a man dressed in black. He wondered if it was the man who had visited Rosalie.

The man crossed the bridge and approached Sigmund. As he did, a steady stream of commands filled Sigmund's mind. He couldn't stop the influx. Then, as if in a trance, he nodded and stood straight and his head and hand returned to the material world.

"Lion, this is how I can travel back in time."

Sigmund turned to find Otto at his back. He had a folder in his hand, his wire-framed glasses tethered on the tip of his long nose.

"I brought this folder with me from Germany and, with the information I have here and what Rosie gave me yesterday, I can go back and disable the bell."

"You can do that?" Sigmund asked, sensing some relief.

"Yes, of course. We already had the location coordinates for the laboratory in Germany. Now we have the time coordinates for the day you sent the bell into the future."

"I don't understand. I thought you *wanted* it to land in the heart of New York. Otto, what are you up to?"

Otto laughed.

"What am I up to? Lion, with what I've discovered, I can manipulate the bell at will. And I can build many more.

"With this knowledge, I have the power to not only demand anything I wish from Russia, but I can do so with every country worldwide. What do you think the Egyptians will give me not to send a trajectory into their precious pyramids? What will the Roman Catholic Church give me not to destroy St. Peter's Square? With this ability, we can live like kings. Money is power, Lion."

Sigmund scratched his chin, his mind racing. His long-time friend wanted to manipulate the world powers.

"You have discovered the ability to manipulate the space-time continuum and with this ability it is your desire to do what, threaten to destroy anyone who will not pay you for protection from unidentified flying objects?"

"Yes, exactly. At first, I only wanted to offer myself to Russia. But now, now I can demand payment from all countries. Do not pay and find a UFO heading for your financial centers or your ancient structures or the White House."

"Otto, have you lost your mind? You cannot do this."

"Yes, I can and I will. But I need your help. I need someone to keep the curtain open."

Just as he said that, there was a crackling sound and the curtain disappeared. Otto turned abruptly.

"See, that is the problem. I need you to re-open the curtain. This is your insurance that I won't do anything to harm you or your family. I need you on this side. It takes two people."

Sigmund examined the box closer. The levers were aligned with rows of numbers. There were two small antennae jutting from the back corners, toward the golden pillars. He examined the connections and made a minor adjustment. When he turned the largest knob, the curtain re-appeared.

Otto was at his side in one step.

"You see how easy it is. You turn a knob and the world is at your feet. Lion, think of what you could accomplish with this ability. What do you want? You can have anything you desire."

Sigmund turned and looked into Otto's wild eyes.

"Well?" Otto asked. "Will you help me rule the world? So far, the people in charge have really fucked things up. We barely escaped annihilation with a second world war. A third world war will destroy mankind. It is our duty, our obligation, to rule."

There was a small part of Sigmund that knew some of what Otto said was true. Another war like the last one and, chances were, mankind would be wiped off the face of the Earth. He thought about what he witnessed as a result of the United States dropping the atomic bomb on Japan. The photos of Hiroshima and Nagasaki tugged at his heartstrings. The utter destruction caused him to shudder.

Otto interrupted his thoughts.

"We can control nuclear warfare, Lion."

"How, by threatening to destroy them if they don't make us rich? Do you think no one else will develop nuclear bombs?"

"They wouldn't dare."

Sigmund realized the truth in Otto's words. If a country developed nuclear bombs, it would be simple to go back in time and intercept them.

"We will become the guardians of peace."

"The guardians of peace, Otto? We will threaten to destroy any country who will not remain peaceful? Peace has to be achieved by people working together for the good of mankind."

Otto laughed.

"Yes, that's right. However, we tried to make peace happen like that and, guess what, it didn't work. After World War I, everyone decided to never face off on the battlefield. There was a short-lived peace and not more than a decade or two passed and the world was at war again.

"No, the only way to insure peace is through the threat of destruction."

Sigmund nodded. The curtain disappeared again. This, he realized, was a two-man operation and the only way to retrieve the bell.

"I'm afraid you are correct, my friend. Go into the past. Fix the coordinates on the bell and return. Have the bell arrive here, today. I will wait for it. And when you return, we will devise a plan to keep the world at peace. And," he added, with a deep laugh, "become filthy rich."

Otto seemed to shiver with delight. He switched on the knob that made the curtain appear and stepped forward.

"Now, remember, when it shuts off, turn it back on. Keep the curtain glowing, my friend, and we will change history."

Otto disappeared through the curtain. When he was fully immersed into the space-time continuum, Sigmund stretched out his hand and switched off the device. The room became quiet.

"Good-bye, Otto."

Armand Bennett slammed the telephone receiver into its cradle. His face had turned crimson, so much so that it reached across his bald head.

"Why did we ever get involved with these bastards in the first place?"

He stood and walked to the window. The parking lot was almost empty. The only two cars belongs to Sigmund Lowe and Otto Kramer.

What in God's name are these Nazis up to?

He'd received another call from his agent. There was yet another anomaly and still no call from Sigmund. He wondered what his top scientist was keeping to himself. Sigmund Lowe promised to call if they received another visit and now it appeared there were several more since the first.

He was glad he allowed his agent to drop him off this morning, long before the scientists arrived. They were up to something and, unbeknownst to them, he was in a position to catch them in the act.

He remained in his office, the lights off and the door locked, and waited. Sooner or later, he knew, he'd hear them. As though on cue, he heard their footfalls in the quiet corridor outside his office.

He went to his door and peeked between the half-open blinds. When they turned the far corner, he unlocked the door and, as quietly as he could manage, followed them.

They entered Otto Kramer's laboratory. He moved as close as possible without being discovered.

He could hear a conversation, the words muffled from behind the locked door. He cursed himself for not having their laboratories put on audible surveillance, too. He put his hand on the doorknob and tried to turn it. It didn't budge.

"Damn them."

He checked his pocket for the pass keys and he realized he'd left them on his desk. He wished he hadn't sent his agent home. He wondered if he should call security and have one of the guards open the door. Thinking that scenario might make matters worse, he made his way back to his office.

As quietly as he departed, he returned. He held the key, poised to insert it into the lock. At that moment, something strange happened. The interior of the laboratory seemed to radiate a shimmering light.

He pressed his ear to the door. Nothing but more muffled chatter.

He turned the key and pushed the door open no more than an inch. There was a strange crackling noise and the shimmering lights faded away.

He stepped inside and stood behind the row of filing cabinets that stood between the door and the work space.

"Good-bye, Otto," he heard Sigmund Lowe say.

He peered around the first cabinet and scanned the laboratory, a room no larger than twenty by twenty with no obstacles other than two odd-looking pillars in dead center. There was no sign of Otto Kramer.

He watched as Sigmund Lowe picked up a box, a black one with several silver knobs and levers. Armand Bennett's heart felt as though it would stop beating all together when Sigmund Lowe turned to face him.

"Where's Dr. Kramer?" he asked nervously.

Sigmund Lowe looked surprised.

"He's gone."

Armand Bennett backed up, his shoulder banging into the corner of the filing cabinet.

"I called security. They'll be here any second now."

"Really, Dr. Bennett? It's funny, I don't hear anyone running through the corridors to your rescue."

As Sigmund approached him, Armand Bennett grabbed his left arm and slid silently to the floor, a strange pale color on his face.

Sigmund bent down and checked his pulse. He shook his head in weary annoyance. He stood, shut out the light, closed the door and left.

In the quietness of the facility, the only sound came from the stealthy footsteps that led to the rear of the building.

Rosalie decided it was time to stop being afraid. Sigmund had assured her that he would handle Otto Kramer.

Even though she was warned to never trust a Nazi, she felt it was time she trusted someone. That someone, she decided, was her brother-in-law.

She dressed for school. It was time to focus on her own life. She still had to get out of eighth grade. All of the drama between Sigmund and Dr. Kramer was taking her mind off her schoolwork and her friends.

She went to the kitchen where Carlotta was placing a bowl of hot cereal in front of Stanley.

"Hi, Rosie," Carlotta said. "Did Sig say anything to you about going into work early today? It's strange because he usually wakes me before he leaves. When I woke up, he was already gone."

Rosalie thought about their conversation. Sigmund said he'd take care of Otto Kramer. She tried to act as nonchalant as possible.

"No, he didn't tell me."

Carlotta seemed unaffected.

"Well, he's a busy man. Maybe he didn't want to disturb me."

Or maybe he didn't have the guts to say he had to murder Otto Kramer before he went into the office today.

"Did you say something?" Carlotta asked.

Rosalie's eyes widened. She wondered if she had spoken her private thoughts out loud.

"Huh?"

"Oh, I thought you said something. It sounded like you mumbled."

"No, I didn't say anything," she said and poured chocolate milk into a glass.

Carlotta handed her a bowl of oatmeal. Rosalie ate and gulped the last of her milk.

"I gotta go," she said and sprinted out of the kitchen.

She went to her room, gathered her books, slipped her feet into her shoes and left the house. She wasn't more than a street away when she noticed Sigmund's car turning the corner. He pulled the car to the curb.

"Rosie, is everything all right at home?" he asked as he rolled down the window.

"Yes, I think so. Why?"

"Are Carlotta and the children still home?"

"Yes. Where else would they be. It's only quarter to eight. By the way, Sig, she was asking about you. She wanted to know why you went to work so early. Why did you?"

"Go to work early?"

"Yes. Jeez, Sig, what's the matter with you?"

"It's complicated."

"Oh, no, you didn't off Dr. Kramer did you?"

"Off? What do you mean? What is off?"

"You know. Do him in. Snuff him out."

Sigmund scowled and said, "Rosie, I think you have been watching too many police shows. And, no, I didn't *off* Dr. Kramer."

"Well, where did you go?"

"I had to go into the office."

"So, why didn't you stay there?"

"Rosie," Sigmund said, an exasperated hint in his tone, "I had to pick up something and now I'm taking it to my home, for safe-keeping in my office. And then, when I've done that, I will kiss my wife and children and go back to the office. Does that satisfy your many questions?"

Rosalie chuckled.

"Yes, I suppose so. Maybe I do watch too many detective shows on television."

He nodded and began to close the window.

"Sig."

He stopped the rise of the window at its half-point.

"Rosie, I did not kill Otto. Now, go to school and get good grades and make us proud."

At that, he closed the window. She noticed he had a strange looking black box on the passenger seat. Before she could what it was, he pulled away.

She stood at the curb watching as he turned into the driveway.

I wonder what that thing is.

All day long, she could think of little else.

Chapter 26

Armand Bennett stirred. He was overcome with confusion for a few seconds. Then, it hit him. He looked around the dark laboratory. Otto Kramer was gone. Sigmund Lowe was gone. And the black box was gone. The only thing of interest that remained were two cooper wire pillars, a reminder that something mysterious had occurred.

He stood on shaky legs, holding tight to the edge of the filing cabinet, the very cabinet that caught his arm and made a deep scratch in his skin. He rubbed the spot and realized it had bled, leaving a crimson stain.

"Damn it," he cursed.

He hurried to his office, moving steadily along the still quiet corridors. He went to his private bathroom and pulled out a small first aid kit he kept on a shelf. He removed his shirt and tossed it in the waste basket by the door. After wiping his cut with peroxide and placing a bandage on it, he put on a fresh shirt. Once at his desk, he sat back and tried to put his recent discoveries in order.

He made a list of events, starting at the very beginning. He spoke as he wrote.

"First, I overheard a conversation between Lowe and Kramer.

"Second, shortly afterward, there was an anomaly at the Lowe house.

"Third, I learned that anomaly came as a result of the girl, Rosalie DeLuca, having had a visit from a man, an 'other-worldly' man."

He stopped writing and stared into space, not focusing on anything in particular, and shook his head.

"Aliens? Possibly," he said.

He turned his attention back to his list.

"Fourth, we get a new mathematical equation that helps us move forward in our research. But not enough to allow us to reach our goal.

"Fifth, I get a call from my agent, who tells me that he picked up a conversation that places Otto Kramer under suspicion for espionage. It appears he's sharing state secrets.

"Sixth," he said and stopped again.

His mind filled in some events that didn't need to appear on the list; events like other calls of less significance from his agent. He returned his attention to his list.

"Okay, sixth, I discover that Kramer has received information that, for some reason, he will not share. I know this because my agent saw him leaving the Lowe home.

"Seventh, I follow his activity for two days. First, he goes to his laboratory and performs some sort of experiments. The next day, which is today, he does the same. This time, however, he has Lowe with him.

"Eighth, I follow the men to the laboratory and discover that Kramer has mysteriously disappeared and Lowe is in possession of a strange black box. I have no idea for what those damn pillars are used."

He perused the list, making other notations next to each entry. When he reached the final one, he shook his head.

Could the pillars be used to create a curtain between two worlds, like a star gate?

He turned his attention back to his list and, with a sense of embarrassment, recalled the frightening, no menacing, look on Sigmund Lowe's face. As the scientist had stepped toward him, Bennett anticipated a violent blow and was overcome with fear. The result was that he had passed out. When he awoke, all was quiet and Lowe was gone.

He sat back and shook his head again.

"Sigmund, my dear boy, what have you done?"

He picked up the receiver and dialed a number. When a man answered, he said, "Follow Lowe. I want to know where he goes, to whom he speaks, what he eats and drinks. Got that?"

"Yes, sir."

"And, for God's sake, keep an eye on the girl, too. Somehow, she's right smack-dab in the middle of this."

"Yes, sir. Is there anything else?"

"Just keep me informed."

He hung up and turned his chair around to face the window. He leaped out of his seat when he saw Sigmund Lowe pull his Cadillac into the parking lot. He stood and went to the window and watched as the man nonchalantly got out, locked the door and headed into the building.

His heart pounded in anticipation once more as he waited for the footfalls outside his door. A sense of relief overcame him as he heard other car doors shut as more workers reported to work.

He wouldn't dare harm me with everyone here. He wouldn't dare.

Sigmund walked through the double doors that led to the lobby of his building. He nodded to the receptionist who was already seated at her post. As he made his way to his office, he noticed movement behind the opaque glass of Dr. Bennett's office. That, he decided, had to be his first stop.

"Is he in yet?" he asked Bennett's secretary, Judy Mason.

"I'm not sure. I just got here. I didn't see his car in the lot."

As she spoke, she stood and went to the inner office door.

"Dr. Bennett, are you in?"

The door relented to her gentle push. Dr. Bennett was still standing by the window.

"Oh, so you are here. I wasn't sure. Dr. Lowe is here to see you."

Armand Bennett nodded.

"Show him in."

Sigmund could see his boss was more on edge than usual.

Judy Mason left, closing the door behind her.

"So, what in hell was that all about this morning?"

"What are you talking about?"

Dr. Bennett sat in his chair.

"Sit down, Dr. Lowe."

Sigmund took the seat opposite him. Before he could reply, the secretary entered with a tray containing two cups, a creamer and a sugar bowl, and two spoons.

"The coffee will be done in a minute. Do you need anything else?"

"No, damn it," barked Dr. Bennett. "And, Judy, knock before you enter with the coffee. Other than that, we don't want to be disturbed."

"Yes, sir," she said and quickly left them alone.

"Just because you fainted out of cowardice, you don't have to take it out on Miss Mason. She's done nothing wrong."

At that, Dr. Bennett bolted to his feet.

"How dare you speak to me in that tone?!"

"I'm not using a tone with you. I just think you are beside yourself with shame for fainting."

"I did not faint," Armand Bennett demanded.

Sigmund laughed.

"Really? Then, did you pass out from the loss of blood? That was a pretty nasty wound you received from the file cabinet."

Before he could retort, Judy Mason knocked on the door.

"Come in!"

She entered with a small coffee pot, her eyes shifting from Armand Bennett to Sigmund Lowe. She let a half smile touch her lips.

"He's in a mood today," she said as she poured the coffee.

She placed the pot on the tray and left, closing the door behind her.

"She has no respect, either," Armand Bennett said. "Both of you are insubordinates."

"Drink your coffee before it gets cold."

"This is ludicrous. How dare you speak to me in such a manner? What is happening around here? I feel like I'm losing control."

"Dr. Bennett, Armand, why don't you just settle down and drink your coffee. And, for God's sake, give your poor secretary a break."

Sigmund's voice was like silk, smooth and unencumbered.

193

Dr. Bennett, Sigmund noticed, seemed to calm down as he dropped into his chair. He picked up his cup and sipped the dark liquid. After a few moments, he lowered the cup to his desk and looked into Sigmund's blue eyes.

"What is going on?"

"You just needed to relax. You looked as though you'd have a heart attack. If you're calm, I'll be more than happy to explain what you witnessed."

"I know you and Otto were in that laboratory. When I entered, he was gone and you had that box. By the way, where is it?"

"You are right. We were both in the lab, but - - ,"

Sigmund explained the night's events. He referred to the black box as an "amplifier" used to generate the energy needed to open a pathway between two dimensions. When he finished, Armand Bennett seemed to take it in stride, believing every word.

"I took the box and hid it. I haven't decided what to do with it. This item could be very dangerous in the wrong hands."

"Yes, I agree," said Bennett. "I'll tell you what I think we should do. You should get this *amplifier* and bring it here. It should be under lock and key in a secure place. In the meantime, I'll visit Washington. They'll have the final word on what to do with it. It's not up to us. It's certainly not up to you. We're but small cogs clicking into a very large wheel."

Sigmund listened and, after a few seconds, shook his head.

"No, I'll tell you what I think we should do. I think we should tell no one about the amplifier.

"We will formulate theoretical calculations, leaving out a step or two, and present *them* to those in Washington. We will ask for what such a device *could* be used. If you and I are not satisfied with their plans for such a device, then I suggest we decide its fate."

Dr. Bennett seemed to think it over and nodded in agreement.

"Okay, Dr. Lowe, we'll do it your way, for now."

Sigmund drank the last of his coffee and left. He went to his office and pulled out the notebook with the equations the man had given Rosalie; the ones intended only for his eyes only.

He perused them, one at a time, step by step.

He scratched his chin.

He smiled.

Rosalie spent the day lost in the mystery of the black box. What, she wondered, could it be? And why did Sigmund bring it home?

Her school day seemed to last too long. As soon as the dismissal bell rang, she scooped up her books and ran to the door. From the corner of her eye, she saw Joseph and Denise looking her way. Instinctively, she waved, but never slowed down. The strange box was at the other end of her journey.

She was out of breath when she burst into the house. Carlotta was in the kitchen preparing dinner. Stanley was sitting on the living room floor watching cartoons. Catherine was next to him, playing with a Raggedy Ann doll.

She placed a kiss on both children. She went into the kitchen, poured a glass of water and gulped it down.

"Why are you so out of breath?" Carlotta asked.

"I ran home."

"Why?"

Rosalie had no answer so she merely shrugged.

Carlotta, displaying her normal complacency, asked, "So, how was school? Do you have any homework?"

Rosalie marveled at her sister's ability to change the subject and move on to other matters. She rattled on, not lifting her eyes.

"I always hated homework. I wanted to play outside after school, you know, being cooped up all day," she said as she peeled a potato and dropped it into a pot.

Rosalie felt the need to stop her bantering.

"Carlotta, school was fine. I have a new history teacher, Mr. Felcher. Mrs. Reynolds left to have a baby. The new guy seems nice."

Carlotta looked up and smiled.

"Oh, that's good," she said and turned her attention to her potatoes.

"Is Sigmund still at work?" Rosalie asked.

Even though she didn't see his car in the driveway, she decided to double-check on his whereabouts. She wanted to snoop around his office.

Carlotta nodded and said, "Yes. He called about an hour ago and said he'd be home at seven."

"Late, as usual. Anyway, I do have homework so I'm going to my room to do it. We're learning about Amsterdam. Oh, I need an encyclopedia from Sigmund's office. Would it be okay if I go in and get it?"

"Of course. You don't have to ask. He only wants Stanley to stay out of his office because he doesn't want to find drawings in crayon on his desk."

She let a lilting laugh accompany her words. Rosalie shook her head. Carlotta, she thought, lived in a dream.

"Okay. See you later," Rosalie said and headed to Sigmund's office.

Carlotta's behavior served to create a sense of contentment that, for Rosalie, felt good. Could life have returned to normal? Stanley didn't announce he had another visit from the angel. As usual, Sigmund was working late. And, as shown by Carlotta's behavior, there was nothing more pressing than the job of making mashed potatoes. Then again, she thought, there *was* still the mystery of the black box.

She went into Sigmund's office and, even though the drapes were open slightly, she still needed to turn on the light. She looked around the room, in every nook and cranny. There was no sign of the black box. Also, thankfully, the small black hole that tormented her was not visible, either.

She went to the bookshelf and pulled down the encyclopedia indicating topics in the "A to As" category. She placed it on top of her loose leaf book and turned to leave. As she did, she gave the room another going-over.

"Normal, Rosie, normal," she whispered to herself.

She was just about to shut off the light when the crackling sound stopped her dead. She shook her head and close her eyes.

"Okay, what now?" she said as she turned.

The man was situated in the dark corner by the bookshelf.

"Close the door and sit down," he said.

There was a part of her that wanted to run away, but a greater part found the courage to shut the door and sit at Sigmund's desk.

"You know, my sister is right there in the kitchen. And the kids are just across the hall. Aren't you afraid they'll see you?"

"Only you can see me," he said.

"Really?"

"Yes, I'm standing right smack in the middle of your mind."

Rosalie, not convinced, jumped up and opened the door.

"Stanley, come here a sec."

The boy stood and crossed the hall.

"What? Popeye's on."

"Look in there," she said pointing to the man by the bookshelf. "Do you see anything?"

Stanley looked into the office and nodded.

"Yes, I see Papa's books."

She patted his head.

"Go ahead, watch Popeye."

She closed the door and turned to the man. He smiled and waved her closer, inviting her to stand beside him. She took a step in his direction and, before she realized what was happening, a silvery curtain appeared before her.

"Come, visit my world."

Her heart began to pound. Visions of the black abyss filled her mind. She tried to clear her thoughts.

"Don't be afraid. I promise I won't send you there."

"Where?" she asked.

He smiled.

"Rosalie, you are amusing."

She immediately remembered what Sigmund had said. She tried to compartmentalize her thoughts.

I don't trust Sigmund. I don't trust Sigmund.

"Rosalie, this isn't about your brother-in-law. And it's not about his work. And, mostly, it's not about mind games. This is something for you; a gift."

Rosalie's mind raced. Was the stranger, the alien, actually going to invite her into another dimension?

"Mister, what do you want?"

196

"Today, child, I don't want anything from you. You don't have to deliver any messages. Instead, I want to give you something. Come, come with me. Trust me. It really is a gift."

"Why?"

"Because, you have done well. I want to share information intended for you."

"Oh, yeah, like what?"

"Questions. I know you are brimming with them. You deserve to have your questions answered."

Rosalie agreed with him on that. Her curiosity reached its peak and, no matter how hard she tried to refuse, she couldn't stop herself. She allowed him to take her hand in his.

At first, it felt like a thousand butterfly wings tapping her skin. Together, they stepped through the curtain and, much to her surprise, his hand felt solid.

She looked around and noticed that she was standing on the bank of a creek. She recognized it immediately. It was her favorite spot behind Reverend Lowe's church.

"I love it here."

"I know. Sit," he said, pointing to a marble bench surrounded by flowers.

She did as she was told and, for the first time, noticed a beautiful bridge crossing the creek.

"It's nice here," she said, feeling more relaxed than ever. "I suppose this isn't really the creek, is it? I mean, there's no bench or bridge behind Reverend Lowe's church."

"I created this scene to make you feel more comfortable. I merely made some improvements," he said.

Rosalie smiled and ran her hand over the smooth white marble.

"It really looks nice."

"So, tell me, Rosalie, what do you want to know?"

"Okay, where's the black box?"

"I have it. Dr. Lowe has given it to me."

"When?"

"This morning."

"But I thought you didn't visit him."

"We had a break-through. I was able to communicate with him and I requested the box. With it, we are capable of physically moving from one dimension to another. The woman who visits you wants that ability."

"Is the lady evil, like Dr. Kramer?"

He nodded.

"Well, she never sent me into that dark place like you did."

"I've already explained that to you. I know this will be difficult for you to believe, but I didn't send you into the abyss. She did. This is what she has in mind for all humankind. I am not chaos, she is chaos."

197

"Well, she seems friendly."

"Why? Because she appears as your mother? Rosalie, I heard what she said to you about following a new religion. She is using it to tear your family apart. When religion is used to segregate people, it becomes a tool for evil. We are all brothers and sisters in spirit."

"I know. Mama always said there is only one God. Have you met God?"

"Child, just because I live in a dimension that's different from the one in which you live and just because I can traverse time and space with unlimited barriers, that doesn't mean I've seen God."

"Does God exist?"

"Like yourself, I have my beliefs. Every religion in your world and mine tells of a Creator. All I can say to you on this matter of most importance is that I believe in a Creator. I am a being of faith."

Rosalie, although dissatisfied with his lack of proof, understood. Perhaps, she thought, when people go through a lifetime, it's up to the individual to believe or not.

It was as though the man understood and knew what she was thinking because he placed his hand on her shoulder. She could actually feel the weight and substance of the hand.

"Would you like to fly over the gardens?"

She jumped to her feet and, in a second, she was lifting off the ground. She soared high over the land. It was similar to the community where she resided with Carlotta and her family.

"There's our church and our house," she said. "Is that my school?"

"Yes," the man said.

She flew above the trees a little longer, taking in the beauty of the landscape below.

After a while, he said, "Let's descend and talk."

She settled on the bridge that crossed the creek. Streaks of sunlight filtered through the canopy of trees and danced on the bubbling water.

The air offered a calmness that was penetrating into her core, causing her to feel a peace she'd never known existed.

"What is this place? It's like home, but not really."

"It's what you call a parallel dimension."

"It looks like my town."

"Yes, it does. It is your town, just in another dimension. It's like when you look in the mirror and see your face and then out of the corner of your eye, you see yourself from the side. It's the same, but at another angle. That's the simplest explanation I can come up with."

At some level, she actually understood. She asked as many questions as she could think of and, after what felt like hours, there didn't seem to be anything else to discuss.

"I guess I have to go back to my own dimension now, huh?"

While she loved her life with Carlotta, something urged her to remain with the stranger. She looked into his eyes, now light and ethereal. He smiled and touched her cheek.

"Yes, I'm afraid so. It's time for you to return home."

Rosalie felt confused. This *felt* like home.

"Why? I really like it here," she said. "It's so peaceful and quiet. Nobody is telling me what to do or who I should trust. I feel safe here. And I like that I can fly and look in on my friends without them knowing. I like that I can check up on Stanley when he's in school, you know, watch over him. Why can't I stay here with you?"

The man looked long and hard at the girl. Rosalie could tell he was trying to make up a good answer.

When he didn't, she asked, "You don't know why, do you?"

"If I told you why, you wouldn't understand. Come. This is something you have to experience for yourself."

He took her hand in his and in a second they were flying high above the brilliant fields of green once more. The sky that looked so blue from below had turned to white. After a few minutes, they were standing at a different bridge, one twice the length as the one by the creek. It was adorned from one end to the other in flowers. The water flowed rapidly beneath her feet.

"Look there," he said in a gentle voice.

Rosalie focused on a new silvery curtain. As it cleared, she saw Sigmund and Carlotta and the children. Stanley stood almost as tall as his father. Catherine looked to be approaching womanhood.

"Wow, they've grown up so fast. I missed it," she said.

"And they missed you. Your sister missed seeing you mature to a fine and successful woman. Sigmund missed walking you down the aisle or dancing with you at your wedding. Your nephew and niece barely remember you.

"Rosalie, if you stay here, it will leave a hole in their lives. They will miss out on sharing a life with you just as you will miss out on sharing a life with them. Do you understand?"

She nodded.

"So, this hasn't happened yet?"

"No. I was merely offering you a glance at a possible future."

"That's not the future I want. Even though I really like it here, I would miss seeing them every day."

"Then, I suggest you go home and enjoy the rest of your life. Your job here is done. We appreciate your help. Now, you have so many wonderful things for which to look forward. You are surrounded by love."

She didn't know why she did it, but she wrapped her arms around the man's neck and hugged him tightly.

"It seems strange that I can touch you here."

"Yes, I'm sure it does. I was nothing but a series of electrical impulses in your brain for the longest time and now you know I'm real. Go ahead, child. Go home. Enjoy your life."

Rosalie lifted herself onto her toes so that her mouth was inches from the man's face. She gently placed a kiss on his cheek.

"Thank you, mister."

"Thank you, Rosalie."

She was by the small creek again. She crossed the marble bridge and stopped at the illuminated curtain. She turned and waved to the man. He returned the gesture.

She stepped through the curtain. As she did, she felt the gentle tingling sensation again and she was once more in Sigmund's office. Her legs felt heavy and she fell to her knees. Her body was aglow. She could see herself shimmer.

Her mind raced. So much time had passed, hours, she thought. Surely, the family wondered where she'd gone.

She climbed to her feet and looked around the office. Her books were still on Sigmund's desk where she'd laid them. She could smell the aroma of Carlotta's cooking. She heard Popeye singing about spinach in the living room, followed by Stanley's laughter.

"No time has passed. Darn, how do they do that?!"

Armand Bennett's agent knelt outside Sigmund's office window. He had a clear shot of Rosalie DeLuca. She turned on the lamp, took a book from the shelf and, for some reason, began speaking to the empty room. Then, she called in her nephew, pointed to the bookshelf. He shook his head and she allowed him to leave, shutting the doors.

"What's that girl up to now?" he mumbled.

His eyes grew wide when a silvery curtain appeared and the girl stepped through. A lump formed in his throat when she disappeared. He opened the window and climbed through, walked around the desk and surveyed the area.

"Damn! Nothing."

He waited a few minutes. A strange crackling sound began to emanate from the space where the girl had disappeared. He quickly rushed to the window and climbed out, kneeling again so he could view what was about to happen.

The curtain appeared and the girl stepped through. She fell to her knees. She looked as though someone had shoved a golden light down her throat as her entire body was illuminated. After a minute or so, she stood, picked up her books and left.

The agent stared in disbelief.

"What the hell!"

Chapter 27

Rosalie waited until the children were tucked in their beds before she told Sigmund about her journey into a parallel dimension. He smiled and nodded as she talked about the bridge and the man's kindness.

"I saw him there, too, when I peered through the portal Otto had opened. You see, I was given distinct instructions to deliver Otto to him. I had to follow them in order to move to the next step."

Rosalie's eyes grew wide.

"Dr. Kramer is on the other side?"

"Sort of. He's in that dimension now."

"Sig, you left him there?"

"I hope you don't judge me too harshly. Otto has been my closest friend since childhood. Needless to say, stranding him there was the most difficult thing I've ever had to do."

Rosalie gulped.

"Will he ever be allowed to come back?"

"I don't know. It's up to them."

"I don't understand. The man gave me the formula and said it was okay to give it to him."

"Yes, and Dr. Kramer used it to open the portal between our two worlds. You see, he thought he had discovered a way to travel in time."

Rosalie pondered Sigmund's words.

"Was it a trap?"

Sigmund nodded.

"I was the one who gave him the paper. The man knew I'd give it to him, didn't he?"

Again, he nodded.

"I'm not so sure I like being tricked."

"Rosie, what you've done has opened a way for us to discover how to traverse time and space. We have to do this. If we don't, there is a large bell-shaped object heading straight into the middle of New York City. Millions will die. The chaos will be overwhelming. No, Rosie, don't fret. You've done a great thing."

She couldn't shake the feeling that she'd been used, fooled by a stranger from another world. All of the good feelings she had for him vanished as quickly as they appeared.

She said goodnight to Sigmund and Carlotta, and went to bed.

She had a difficult time falling asleep. She finally drifted off around three and, almost instantly, the woman was at her side.

"Finally," she said. "I thought you were going to stay awake all night."

"Leave me alone."

"Now, Rosie darling, is that any way to treat a friend. And I am your friend, you know. You do believe me, don't you?"

"I don't know what to believe. I thought the man was my friend and it seems he was only using me to get Otto Kramer."

The woman seemed shaken.

"They have Dr. Kramer? How? When?"

Rosalie wished she hadn't said so much. She didn't know who to trust.

The woman placed her hand on Rosalie's arm and suddenly they were flying above the Pacific Ocean. Although she had never been to the west coast, she felt comfortable there.

"Look at the bridge," the woman said.

Rosalie set her gaze on the Golden Gate Bridge, its lights casting sparkling ribbons on the water.

"I do love it here," she said.

She was so relaxed, she felt she was floating more than flying. The woman remained at her side, her hand on her wrist.

"I'm sorry, child. Those men are cruel. They'll use whoever they can to get their way. Yes, I'm afraid they've fooled you. Tell me everything you know about the situation."

At that, Rosalie spoke about the visit to the other dimension, the black box and the other set of equations she'd given to Sigmund. She felt little relief when the woman assured her that she would take care of everything and Rosalie could enjoy a full night's sleep.

When the sun rose the next day, Rosalie awoke with a startle after nothing more than a short nap. Instead of the feeling of peace with what the woman had promised, she was tied up inside, torn, and wondering if she'd done the right thing. Then again, she thought, she wasn't responsible for what she said or did in a dream. After all, she wasn't even sure it was real.

Unfortunately, the days ahead proved that she was but a pawn in a dangerous game of chess, a game designed to bring ruin to humankind. But, she wondered, at whose hands?

Sigmund worked out the formulas the man had left for him. He produced what looked like a replica of Otto's black box. The only difference was that his device *would* actually transport a person into the stream of time and space.

For Sigmund, his daily schedule had begun with a shower in the bathroom attached to his office. He'd put on clean clothes and head to his laboratory. He spent the entire day working. He'd take a break and go to the cafeteria for a quick meal, usually a sandwich and coffee. He'd go to his office, make a short telephone call to Carlotta and head back to his laboratory. He'd work until he could no longer stay awake. He slept on a small cot in the back corner of his laboratory. He continued to work alone.

He'd put his staff on another aspect of the project, constructing the vehicle that could one day be used to travel in other dimensions.

Day after day, he followed his routine and each day he moved closer to unraveling the great mystery of the Universe – the ability to travel *back* in time.

Finally, it was time to test his creation. He checked the lock on his laboratory door. He wasn't ready to share his findings just yet. He closed the blinds tightly until the room became eerily dark.

He placed the box on the floor in the middle of the room. He confiscated the pillars from Otto's laboratory.

Now, with the pillars in place, he sat the box in a similar position as Otto had done. He held the silver handle on top of the box, pushing it forward. The harder he pressed, the more streams of what looked like lightening shot outward toward the pillars. When they reached the pillars, they bounced to the opposite side until the space between the columns was nothing but a series of active electrical streams.

Sigmund stood and faced the living wall before him. It was different from the silvery curtain that separated his dimension from that of the visitor. This was alive, crackling, spewing electricity as though it was liquid.

After several minutes, the current settled into luminous waves, flowing back and forth in a steady rhythm. He approached and put his hand near the flow of energy.

He wasn't sure what would happen if he stuck his hand through the glowing curtain. Would he be electrocuted? Would the energy pull him to the other side? And, if it did, would he be able to return? Perhaps, he thought, he was faced with the same dilemma Otto had faced with his device.

He backed away and perused his notes. The calculations he reached as a result of the formulas he'd received from the man, via Rosalie, seemed to suggest that he would create a portal that could be traversed in both directions.

He removed his glasses and rubbed his eyes. He put them on again and looked toward the door.

Did I lock it?

The last thing he needed was for someone to enter, turn off the machine and leave him somewhere out there, wherever that was. He double-checked the door. Yes, it was locked.

He made a call to Carlotta, informing her that he had finished his project and would be home soon. He asked to speak to the children, reminding them of how much he loved them.

"I love you, darling," he told Carlotta.

If these were the last words she'd ever hear him speak, he thought, at least she'd know how much she and the children were loved.

203

"Is Rosie home?"

"No, she's still at school. She's been itching to speak to you all week."

He wished he could have spoken to her, too.

He hung up the telephone and approached the portal.

"Here goes," he said.

He stepped through and immediately found himself in a dark space. He lifted his hand. While he couldn't see past it, he did see the reflection of light from behind him. He turned and realized he was just on the other side of the opening. He stepped back through it and was instantly back in his laboratory.

"Okay, okay, this thing works. Now, how do I move about on the other side?"

He passed through the portal a second time. He waited a few minutes wondering if a light would appear. His heart began to beat a little faster when off to the right, he saw what appeared as a beam of light. At first it was small, but as the minutes passed, it grew. It became larger and larger until the entire area was white. While he could see, he realized, there was nothing there. He waited a little longer.

"What are you doing here?" a voice asked.

He thought surely it was the voice of God. He had crossed into the spiritual realm and was being interrogated by the Creator. Having been brought up in a religious environment, he asked, "Are you God?"

The voice remained quiet. Then after a minute, it sounded like the being said, "No, I'm Timmy."

Sigmund wanted to laugh. His mind raced.

Are you God? No, I'm Timmy. Timmy?

He thought about a television program about a boy and his collie.

"Timmy?" he asked, verbalizing his thoughts. Of course, he didn't use the incredulous tone from his thoughts. It was more of a question.

The form began to take shape. It became a being who stood about ten feet tall with wide shoulders and an odd-shaped head. It was almost square with small antennae-like objects protruding from the top on both sides.

"What are you?" Sigmund asked as the being came closer.

"I am the time integral manager executive engineer. What are you?"

Sigmund frowned.

"I'm a human being, of course."

"From where?"

"Earth."

"But how did you pierce the barrier into this realm?"

"I got help."

"From whom?"

Sigmund wasn't sure how to explain the strange visitor with the extensive knowledge of dimensional travel.

"A man," he said, hoping that would suffice.

"A man? A human?"

"Hardly. He came into my world from a parallel dimension."

"Why?"

Sigmund explained the series of events that led to his arrival in the being's realm. By now, the being was no more than five feet away.

"Where, exactly, am I?" Sigmund asked.

"You are in the space and time corridor."

Sigmund responded with a shiver. He'd made it. He was exactly where he needed to be.

"Can you help me divert a bell? I need to change its direction."

The being, who on closer view appeared almost solid, stopped. He seemed to be considering what to do with the intruder. At that, Sigmund decided a better explanation was in order.

"You realize I'm only here because I want to help my fellow man. I want to stop a catastrophe. I don't mean to trespass where I do not belong."

"That is right. You do not belong here. The material world should not enter this realm. It's very dangerous. Have you any idea what greater catastrophe you could cause if you change something in this realm? One wrong move and the dinosaurs would still roam the Earth and mankind not exist. One mistake and chaos would reign over your planet."

"I'm afraid chaos already reigns over our planet. And that's exactly what I'm trying to avoid, worse chaos. Can you help me or not?"

His tone changed from frightened to demanding. The being seemed to respond, stepping back. Sigmund felt he was losing credibility.

"Listen, Timmy, my friend, I only need to divert a flying bell and I'll head right back to my dimension and destroy the device I created that brought me here in the first place."

"My name is not Timmy. I am the TIMEE. The time integral manager executive engineer, TIMEE. I keep the flow of time whole, unbroken, connected from one second to the next. Understand?"

"Oh, I thought it was your name."

"Why would I need a name? There is no one here but me."

Sigmund tried to wrap his mind around the situation.

"So, you are a being who sits alone and keeps time moving forward?"

"In a sense. This is my duty."

"But you are a conscious entity."

"Yes, I am. I am the time integral manager executive engineer. I am time. You see, certain dimensions exist in what can only be described as corridors. They align with a dimension. Some dimensions only need a time corridor, some only need a space corridor. Your universe requires a time and a space corridor."

"You're time? Are you space, too?"

"No, time is time and space is space. Together, our energy flows into many dimensions and moves along, giving, for instance in your case, humans the ability to experience a limited time in a limited space."

"Where's space?"

"You're standing in it."

Sigmund shook his head. He knew there was no way this being could explain time and space well enough for any human being to understand, no matter how intelligent they were. At that point and realization, he decided, it didn't matter. He had a purpose and this was the way to achieve it.

"Can you help me?"

"Yes. First, I must set the location coordinates. Do you require to be in the place from where you entered this realm?"

"No. I have the location coordinates," Sigmund said, and rattled off the space coordinates from memory.

"Ah, that would be Germany, a country on the other side of your planet."

"Yes, Germany."

TIMEE appeared to type data into an invisible keyboard. Sigmund assumed he was accessing the space corridor dimension.

The ambient air seemed to change several degrees. Immediately, Sigmund looked toward the portal. He could no longer see his laboratory. He was relieved that, at least, the curtain remained alight.

"We can move through the time corridor along this route."

"If I stepped through the portal, would I be in Germany?"

"Yes."

"When?"

"Now."

Sigmund shook his head in amazement.

TIMEE lifted what appeared as an arm and waved him on. Sigmund followed. Every now and then, he'd look back over his shoulder to make certain the portal remained open.

"I will now escort you to the place *and* time where the action you need to correct exists."

Sigmund felt as though he were walking on air as his footsteps barely touched down on anything solid. He seemed to be moving in a distinct direction, yet the portal remained to his right.

"Where, exactly are we going?"

"We are going backward. Isn't that when you need to return, in the past?"

"Yes," he said. "To move forward, I suppose I have to go backward."

"Exactly," TIMEE said. "Exactly."

Chapter 28

Rosalie found the following week to be the most stressful of her life. Sigmund was never home. Day after day she'd drill Carlotta about his behavior. Night after night, the woman would appear in her dreams and warn her that Sigmund was about to destroy humankind.

Torn, she didn't want to act until she spoke to Sigmund.

"Can I call him?" she asked.

Carlotta smiled and shook her head.

"Not when he's in his lab. Rosie, what's so important that you must speak to him this very second?"

"Oh, you wouldn't understand."

When more than ten days passed, Rosalie was convinced she had to act. Early the next day, she slipped into Sigmund's office to use his private telephone. She called Dr. Bennett and asked if she could visit him at his office.

"Sure," he said. "I've only seem glimpses of your brother–in–law here and there. Most of the time he's locked in his laboratory. I never like to disturb a genius when he's in creative mode. What is this about?"

"I have to speak to you in person. It's about the visitors."

"I'll have someone pick you up at your home after school."

Rosalie hung up the telephone and covered her face with her hands.

Am I doing the right thing? The man used me to get his way. The lady said I should trust only her. And where is the man? I haven't seen him since that day in Sigmund's office. He got what he wanted. He was just using me. I'm afraid the lady is right and I have to destroy the time travel machine that Sigmund built. I have to get into his laboratory.

She wiped her tears and searched Sigmund's office for her marble notebook. It was behind all of the folders in the bottom desk drawer. She perused her original notes. When she was satisfied that she was on the right path, she took the book, stood, shut off the light and left to get ready for school. Soon, she thought, she'd get her chance to right her wrongs.

Armand Bennett placed the receiver in its cradle. It was about time. He'd received a call from his agent, a strange call that involved Rosalie.

"She actually stepped out of this reality and back in?" Dr. Bennett asked.

"That's what it looked like, sir."

"Keep an eye on her and let me know if she disappears again."

That was more than a week ago. He was anxious to hear what the girl had to say. Perhaps, he thought, she could explain her disappearance and reappearance.

Dr. Bennett hoped she would bring up the incident so he could question her as to where she'd disappeared without revealing that she was being watched.

After school that day, Rosalie rushed home. She'd worn her best outfit, a white blouse and a poodle skirt with tiny pocket behind the furry body of the dog. Dr. Bennett promised he would have his agent drive her to the laboratory. She wanted to look her best for the meeting.

When she arrived home, she discovered Mr. Johnson leaning against his car, a black Ford with tinted windows. He wore a dark suit with a white shirt and a tie.

"Hi, Mr. Johnson," she said as she approached. "Wow, you look nice. Are you getting married today or something?"

"I'm here to drive you to Dr. Bennett's office, Miss Rosie."

"Really? He said he was sending his agent."

Mr. Johnson smiled and opened the back door. Rosalie stepped forward, then stopped.

"Are you Dr. Bennett's agent?"

"Yes. Please get in."

"No, wait a minute; you're our gardener."

"Miss Rosie, please. Dr. Bennett is waiting."

"Does Sig know you're a spy?"

"I'm not a spy; I'm a federal agent. I cannot tell you anything else. All I can do is ask you to trust me. I know you've been through a lot. Let me get you to safety."

"Safety? I'm not in any danger."

"Yes, Miss Rosie, you are. Please, come along quietly."

Rosalie wanted to bolt, but suddenly her forearm was seized by the agent's large hand. He guided her into the back seat. When he shut the door, the locks automatically clicked.

Several times during the trip to Dr. Bennett's office, Rosalie focused on the rear view mirror, trying to get the man to make eye contact. Every time Mr. Johnson's eyes met hers, she allowed an angry frown to furrow her brow. He merely shook his head and turned his eyes to the road ahead.

"Hey, Mr. Johnson, can I ask you another question?"

He nodded.

"You're not really a gardener, right?"

"It's my hobby and it's what suited me for this assignment."

"Did you fight in the war? Carlotta said you did. She said you were a veteran."

At first, Mr. Johnson didn't respond.

"Well, did you?"

"Yes, Miss Rosie. I fought in the war. I flew airplanes."

"Did you ever kill a Nazi?"

Again, Mr. Johnson hesitated.

"I promise I won't tell anybody. I just have to know. I have a problem with a couple of Nazis and I have to make a decision, a grown-up decision."

"I realize that. This is something a child shouldn't have to deal with."

"I'm not a child."

"Oh, I'm sorry, make that a young lady. But, as far as I'm concerned, you shouldn't be in the middle of this mess."

"Exactly! That's what I'm saying. But, I am and I have to do the right thing."

"The right thing for who?"

"Humankind."

Mr. Johnson slowed the car and pulled to the curb. Rosalie looked out the window and noticed they were at the entrance to a small park.

"Are we here?"

"No," he said and shut off the car.

He turned and faced her.

"Miss Rosie, I just want to say one thing. You are not a child; you are right about that. But you are not an adult, either. I don't know what's going on inside your mind. All I do know is that, as we mature, we realize that the whole world is not black and white, decisions are not that clear. There are gray areas where one is often called upon to make grave decisions. It is in those circumstances that we make choices that have the capability to change a life, perhaps the whole world. Do you understand what I'm saying?"

"I think so."

"You asked me if I ever killed a Nazi. I assume you asked that because you have a decision to make involving Dr. Lowe. Is that correct?"

She nodded, tears burning her eyes.

"Well, let me tell you my story. Perhaps it can help you see through the murky gray area that you are now in. Yes, I killed Nazis, many of them. But that was war. They were men who, if given the chance, would've killed me. You understand that, don't you?"

Again, she nodded.

"But now you work for a Nazi."

"No, I work for the government of the United States. My assignment was to observe Dr. Lowe and, if necessary, protect him. To protect all of you, in fact. However, I will say this. In my time here, I've learned that people are people and we need to evaluate them on how they live, how they treat others and not on their heritage, color, or religious beliefs. Do you understand?"

"Yes, I do."

"You see Dr. Lowe and Dr. Kramer as Nazis. I see them as men who were chosen because of their intelligence to work under a government that forced them to make choices. I'm afraid Dr. Kramer has made some bad choices, but Dr. Lowe has been nothing short of decent. So, if your plans include doing something drastic, I would ask you to evaluate him and how he's treated you."

"He's been kind to me, that's for sure. I actually like him. But, Mr. Johnson, I have information about him that nobody knows. That's why I have to speak to Dr. Bennett."

"Well, then, let's get you to his office. I've worked with the man for many years and, surely, he's bursting with curiosity about your news."

He turned and started the car. For the remainder of the trip, he didn't speak. Rosalie, too, remained quiet; deep in thought about how she'd handle the situation.

If only I could speak to Sigmund.

When they arrived, Mr. Johnson got out and opened the back door for her. Before she could gather her books, he said, "Leave them in the car. I'll wait and drive you home."

He walked with her toward the building. As she went through the double doors, she noticed he remained outside, lighting a cigarette.

She glanced his way one last time and when he looked her way, she made a small waving gesture. He smiled, nodded and took a long drag on his cigarette.

A woman met her at the reception desk.

"Hello, Rosalie. Please, come with me."

Judy Mason escorted her to Dr. Bennett's office and opened the door. He was seated at his desk. He waved her in.

"Sit. What's is it, Rosalie? What can I do for you today?"

"I didn't know Mr. Johnson worked for you."

"He's my man in the field. His job was to - - ,"

"Spy on us?"

"No, well, yes, on Dr. Lowe. These are important matters, child."

"Yeah, right."

"And to protect your family. With the kind of work we're doing, you needed someone on site to protect you. Surely, you cannot find fault with that, can you?"

"I'm not sure how I feel about it other than betrayed. I'm not so sure I trust you anymore."

Dr. Bennett laughed.

"Oh, Rosalie DeLuca, you are a funny one. Please, for now, can we put the matter of Elwood Johnson aside? When this is over, we can discuss it at length. Now, tell me, what is so important that you had to speak to me?"

Rosalie hesitated, wondering if she should share what she'd learned. Then, realizing she had no one else she could trust, she spoke.

"Okay, but you better not trick me," she said, leaning forward in her chair. "I didn't tell you about this before because Sigmund told me not to, but I had a visit from another entity, a woman. She said she's peace and that the man is chaos."

Dr. Bennett's jaw seemed to hang open as he scratched his bald head. He leaned back in his chair and looked to the ceiling.

"We have quite the dilemma here," he said as he lowered his head and looked her in the eye. "The question is this, who should *we* trust? Yes, Rosalie, we. I am in the same boat as you. Should we trust the woman or the man, or neither?"

"Exactly. I trust Sigmund, but I can't get to him, to ask him what I should do."

"Well, perhaps we can disturb him just this once."

Rosalie was surprised that he was so cooperative. He stood and walked around the desk. Rosalie stood, too.

"Come, follow me."

They headed down the long corridor that led to the steps she'd used on her initial visit. Once in the basement, they followed another corridor and, finally, reached Sigmund's private laboratory.

"We're here," he said. "Now, let's see what the good doctor is up to, shall we?"

Something was wrong. The male entity from the parallel dimension tried to contact Rosalie. After several attempts, his frustration mounted. Each time, he discovered that the way had been blocked. Somehow, the woman had surrounded the girl with negative energy.

The only portal available was through the one in the dark corner of Sigmund's office. He could see Rosalie, but it was as though a thick cloud had been constructed around her and he couldn't approach.

Somehow he had to get through.

He deliberately reviewed his actions. He'd received his orders from a higher being, one to whom he owed his allegiance. His assignment was to give Rosalie DeLuca the formulas Sigmund Lowe and his colleagues needed to enter the space-time continuum in order to stop a catastrophe. It had appeared easy enough.

"But, why the girl? She's but a child."

"It's easier to reach the girl because her thoughts are spread out in a random fashion. It will be easy to appear to her and communicate. Dr. Lowe, on the other hand, has great mind control. Contact the girl, give her the information and, hopefully, it will enable us to reach Dr. Lowe."

After Rosalie had delivered the information, the male entity tried on several occasions to reach Sigmund Lowe. He couldn't get through. That was until the first portal had been breached, the one achieved by Otto Kramer. He was then able to summon Sigmund Lowe.

It was there that the entity was able to bring Sigmund up to date on these matters of great importance. However, since that day, the scientist's mind was overcrowded with ways to breach the second portal, the one that led to the time continuum.

"I gave him the key. Of course, he would be thinking of little else."

Sigmund Lowe was, indeed, able to create the second portal. He was now in a position to adjust the trajectory of the bell and return to his realm.

The woman entity, however, had seized the opportunity to fully infiltrate Rosalie DeLuca's environment. She was now in control. She'd attached herself to Rosalie the day she was born. She watched as the girl's head and heart were filled with hatred.

Rosalie had almost overcome it, realizing she was being used in a game of thrones, a game where the dark mistress would gain millions of souls. These souls one day would be so grateful to her for releasing them from the abyss, they would do her bidding, causing havoc over many worlds in many dimensions. Humankind was but her first step toward creating chaos throughout the Universe.

Although the man was granted permission to view the material world from other portals, he was unable to break through. She was manipulating the girl, and there was no way to warn her.

The man felt a deep sadness. Rosalie was but a fourteen-year-old whose life was stained from the beginning. He didn't blame her. However, he had to stop her. She was instructed to destroy the device and, perhaps, leave Sigmund stranded in another dimension, one in which he'd be trapped. Of this, the man was certain.

He tried to break through to her. He watched in dismay as she retrieved the marble notebook from Sigmund's office. She read each page, renewing her mission to uncover the plot against the government.

"Rosalie, Rosalie, she's tricking you."

Rosalie had no idea she was being summoned. Night after night, he'd watch as she slept, knowing she was being manipulated in her dreams. Day after day, he'd watch as she tried to contact Sigmund.

Finally, after ten days, she made the decision to call Armand Bennett.

The man watched as the agent, Elwood Johnson, delivered the girl to Dr. Bennett's office. He listened as she explained why it was imperative she speak to Sigmund.

What he didn't know, he realized, was what she had planned.

Was she going to destroy the device?

Would she abandon Sigmund in another dimension?

Time was running out. In desperation, he faced the fact that he had but one option. He had to retrieve Otto Kramer from prison.

"What makes you think I'd do anything to help you?" Otto asked, his voice filled with anger. "You put me in Hell, a worse Hell than the fire and brimstone I'd been taught as a child."

"I sent you there so you could see for yourself what the female entity has planned for all humankind. She is a powerful source of evil."

Otto remained silent, his arms folded tight across his chest.

"I want you to go to Sigmund Lowe's laboratory and stop the girl. I need you to save humankind. I cannot do it. You are our only hope."

Otto's mind remained a closed trap. The man couldn't get a feel for what thoughts filled his head.

Was he looking for revenge?

Was he still romancing the idea of becoming the most powerful man in the world with his device?

Was he thinking he'd join forces with the woman?

He had no answers. He knew it was a gamble but, as the humans liked to say, it was the only game in town.

"Will you help me, Dr. Kramer?"

Otto didn't agree or disagree. He merely asked, "Where's the box?"

Sigmund followed the TIMEE for what felt like a long time. Finally, they stopped.

"We're here," the being said.

"Where?"

"1945."

"Germany?"

"Yes."

A portal opened and the laboratory where he had worked loomed before him, like a billion shards of information in tiny specks of light, each fitting together until it became real. The past was at hand.

Rosalie watched as Armand Bennett used his pass key and opened the door to Sigmund's office. He approached the middle of the room where a flow of energy created what appeared as a portal hinged like a curtain between two bright copper pillars.

"Sigmund, are you here?" he called.

Rosalie stepped in front of him and called out, too. There was no sound except for the low hum of the box situated on the floor near the pillars.

"What's that, Dr. Bennett? Did Sig build it?"

Armand Bennett looked over the device.

"Yes, I believe so. I think it creates a portal, a doorway between dimensions."

Rosalie jumped back as shards of electricity danced between the pillars.

"I've been through one of these. I went to a real nice place. The man who gave me the formula was there."

"This is similar, but I think this one will take a traveler into the time and space continuum. This is what Dr. Lowe has been working on for the last ten days. He left me a note asking to be left alone. I agreed, of course. I knew he was on to something big."

213

Rosalie remembered the warning she'd received from the woman.

This device, left in the wrong hands, could mean the end of existence for humankind.

"What do we do now? Should we go through?" Rosalie asked.

"No, no. It's too dangerous. You stay here and let me take a look beyond the portal."

"Will *you* go through?"

"Yes. Go and lock the door and don't let anyone in, no matter who comes knocking. Do you understand, Rosalie?"

She nodded and made a hard swallow. This, she realized, was the exact opportunity the woman had promised; the opportunity to confiscate the time travel device and deliver it to her.

"Yes, I understand. I'm to wait here."

"And touch nothing. I'm sure Sigmund is on the other side of that curtain and, by God, I won't come back without him."

She watched as Dr. Bennett approached the portal. She recognized the familiar crackling sound that always accompanied the passage from one dimension to another.

Dr. Bennett patted her shoulder.

"Stay vigilant, dear girl; stay vigilant."

He was just about to step through when, as he lifted his foot to break the barrier, another crackling sound to his left caught his attention. In an instant, he was thrown across the room, landing on the floor by the window, unconscious.

"Dr. Bennett, are you okay?"

"Leave him, child. Go, take the box."

Rosalie saw the outline of the angel, her wings like giant feathers. Her face became visible, her eyes were soft, and her mouth displayed a gentle smile.

"Is he alive?" Rosalie asked.

"He's fine," the angel said, her voice soft and comforting. She continued, "Rosalie, my darling girl, the fate of humankind is at hand. I need you to shut down that device, remove it from this facility and destroy it. Suceed and the world will owe you a great debt of gratitude."

Rosalie nodded and, just as she approached the device, she heard a loud banging on the door. How, she wondered, would she escape with the device with someone just outside. She stopped and turned toward the door.

Again, the banging sound shook the room. She could see the doorknob being tested.

"Rosalie! Rosalie! If you're in there, open the door."

She recognized the voice.

It was Otto Kramer.

Chapter 29

Sigmund reached the place in time where the bell had awaited its dangerous launch. He found it odd that no matter how long it took him to reach this point, the portal remained at his side. At any point, the manager informed him, he had the capability to step into another time period.

"The problem would, of course, be your location. We've set out on a journey that will take us to 1945 at your laboratory in the German countryside."

He was glad when TIMEE stopped.

"We're here."

"Do I simply go into the laboratory and reset the coordinates?" he asked.

"If only it were that simple. No, you have very specific guidelines you must follow and follow them to the second. Stay in this time period too long and I promise nothing but chaos will follow."

Sigmund didn't like the sound of that, a second was not long enough for a mistake.

"Chaos? The man calls the woman chaos and she calls him chaos. What, exactly, is it? I mean, is it something tangible?"

"It's more a state of being. It incorporates itself in people. Oftentimes, it comes in the form of a holy man; one who can lead. In the past, several leaders have represented themselves as working for the good of mankind. They have not. They have caused the destruction of mankind several times, almost to the point of extinction.

"Somehow, and much to your credit, mankind finds a way to come back. Your universe has been around for billions of years. I have lost count of the number of times humans, for example, made it back from the brink of extinction.

"Nevertheless, chaos comes in many forms and can control whoever has hate or fear in their hearts. And chaos will come back again and again. It will prompt mankind to perform genocide because of religious beliefs, color of skin, gender, any number of distinctions that separate one man from the other. If only humans could see themselves as I see them."

"How do you see us?"

"I see a mass of multi-colored lights, similar to what you call a crystal. Your kind is quite beautiful, all of you. Sadly, you identity each other from your differences instead of your likenesses.

"But, alas, it is time to correct your latest attack. Are you ready to change history?"

"Yes. Tell me what I must do."

TIMEE stopped and appeared to point to the curtain.

"We are at the point in time where you witnessed the death of your colleagues. There is but ten seconds between the time you witnessed the killings and returned to the laboratory to send the bell into the future. Ten seconds."

"Why can't I go in earlier, when there is more time?"

"As you know, when you arrived, you were met with Dr. Holtz, who'd excused himself so he could shower.

At that point, the New York coordinates had already been set. Otto Kramer did it the night before. At no point during the time he'd set the coordinates and your meeting with Dr. Holtz was the room empty.

"You went in and looked around, then you heard something outside and you went to the window and looked out. Do you remember that?"

Sigmund nodded.

"It is at that point, after you witnessed the killings, that you went into Dr. Auman's office. You were in there for a few seconds, ten to be exact. And it is during those ten seconds that you must change the coordinates and return through the portal."

"Why can't I go in when the 1945 version of myself is there?"

"Think about it, Dr. Lowe. Just think about it."

Sigmund scratched his chin, now in its liquid form. Shards of beautiful crystal lights seemed to explode in front of his eyes.

"Wow, that's amazing."

"Yes, it is."

"So, back to my task. I do see what you mean. Had I stopped, precious moments would have been lost."

"Precious moments that saved your life. Also, it is possible that if you came face to face with that version of your body, you could meld with it. You most likely would be killed. If you remember, Otto Kramer and the others were close by."

Sigmund pondered the implications of that encounter.

"So, how many seconds do I have? Did you say ten?"

"Yes, no more than ten. Less would be preferential. You don't have time to change anything but the space coordinates. The numbers you *now* have coordinate with a rural section of Pennsylvania. In 1965, there is nothing constructed at that location. I can see that. It is thick with sturdy trees. The bell will come down and crash in the woods. I anticipate no one will be there."

"When in 1965?"

"That, Dr. Lowe, is the only uncertainty since only Otto Kramer knows that date."

Sigmund allowed the importance of succinct action. He had to enter the laboratory, reset the space coordinates and return. If he allowed anything to distract him, his life was in danger. The lives of his children were at risk.

"I hope I can do this," he said.

"Don't doubt yourself. You must do this."

Sigmund looked to the luminous figure beside him.

"I'm ready. Just say the word."

The being seemed to stop its fluid-like movements. Sigmund realized he had stopped the flow of time long enough for him to step into the past. In his mind, he heard the command.

"Now."

He stepped through and found himself in the laboratory. From the corner of his eye, he saw his former self in Dr. Auman's office. Memories rushed into his mind, filling it with dread.

"Stop," he told himself.

With distinct and accurate movements, he approached the vibrational accelerator. The sound of gunshots rang out. He knew it was the moment the soldier killed Dr. Auman. Without hesitation, he pressed the new coordinates into the device. He sensed the 1945 version of himself heading back into the laboratory. With a full leap, he sprung into the portal, landing on his knees.

"I did it," he said. "I did it."

The being began to move again.

"Look, see what you've done."

Sigmund was able to peer into the past, his past. He watched as the former version of himself pressed the launch sequence. He saw himself climbing out of the window. A minute later, Otto and two soldiers burst into the room.

The bell was shaking, sending shards of electricity in every direction. Someone was screaming from outside the laboratory door.

"Stop that launch, immediately."

Otto feigned an effort. He turned to his captain with a look of frustration on his face.

"I'm sorry, sir, it was set to launch automatically. We've lost the bell. It's gone."

Sigmund stared into his friend's face. He wondered how he could be so wrong about another human being. They'd grown up together. They attended school and church as children. How had two boys who were raised alike end up so different?

"It's time to return," the being said. "And there's trouble."

"Trouble? What kind of trouble?"

"I sense that someone is trying to close the portal. In order for your actions to be completed, you must return to your own time. You must close the portal yourself. Time acts like fluid circles. One event affects another, but all must be complete."

"Who's trying to close it, Dr. Bennett?"

"No, it's not him. It's your sister-in-law."

"Rosie? No, she would never do that."

"Come, we must hurry. As your people like to say, time is of the essence. Even here, we must respect the frailty of time and space. Let's hope she doesn't close it before you return. And, as you will see, moving forward in time will be more difficult than moving in reverse. It's never easy moving forward, but one must persevere."

Like thick liquid moving over a rocky stream, they labored to move forward.

Rosie, please, trust in me. Trust in me.

Rosalie remained frozen with fear. The banging continued, accompanied by frantic shouts. Suddenly, the door burst open.

"Rosie, don't," Otto cried. "She's tricking you. She only wants to destroy mankind."

Rosalie looked from Otto Kramer's terrified face to the delicate features of the angel.

"No, she's peace. She wants to help mankind," Rosalie said.

"No, she's not peace. She's not even a woman, she's nothing but pure evil. She's a thing, the personification of disorder. It only wants to see humankind destroy itself."

"How do you know?" Rosalie cried. "Are you sure?"

The angel spoke in a soft, lilting tone.

"Rosalie, ignore him. He's a liar. You know he is evil. You know all about him and his evil plan to rule the entire planet. Don't listen to his lies. He's nothing but a Nazi turned Communist."

Rosalie bit her bottom lip. She could hear Anna Mary's and Mr. Pinella's warning. Surely, if they were present, they'd add Communist to their list. She thought about Aunt Ruthie who found it in her heart to forgive. She thought about Mr. Johnson, a soldier who was able to see his enemy as a friend.

She knelt on the floor in front of the device. Otto Kramer leaped into the room, landing a foot from her. The angel sent a bolt of electricity that sent him back several yards.

"Rosie, don't touch it," he begged. "I can't move. This thing has paralyzed me. But, I have to tell you something. I've been imprisoned in the abyss, the dark place. I now realize how my actions could have placed mankind in danger. The man, the other visitor, has opened my eyes. I was wrong. I know now that I was wrong.

"I beg you, Rosie, don't touch that device or we will all perish."

"Shut up!"

Rosalie jumped at the loud demand of the angel. When she turned to face it, she could see its form filling the room from floor to ceiling.

Otto's voice became frantic.

"Look at it, Rosie. Look close. You can see it is not an angel. It is not a being. It is evil. It is chaos. It is that part of man that tells us to hate. It is tapping into your distrust.

"Rosie, honey, it knew from the moment you were born that you were an ideal candidate to carry out its evil deeds. You've been taught to hate.

"Hate Germans. Hate the Japanese. Don't let hatred settle in your heart. What's next? Should you hate all Russians? All people of color? All Jews? Anyone who isn't like you?"

Rosalie thought about his words. Tears streamed down her face, a salty taste slipping into the sides of her mouth.

Never trust, Rosie, never trust.

The words repeated themselves in her mind.

She looked at Otto.

"Yes, it's true, I think I was taught to hate from the day I was born. And the lady did say that I was her agent."

"That's right, honey," Otto said as he continued to plead. "I went to Sunday School with Sigmund. But I was fed a steady diet of hatred for Jews. It encompassed my soul. But now I know how wrong that is. This thing is nothing more than a mental virus, a germ that slips into our hearts and minds and eats away at all the good."

"Shut up!"

This time, when Rosalie turned, she could see that the being was changing from an ethereal angel to a mass of brown and gray matter, swirling around like a muddy stream. Rosalie shivered at the sight.

"Rosalie, clear your mind," Otto begged. "Think of all the good you've found in Sigmund. He is a good man. You know that."

"Shut up!"

This time, when the angel sent a second bolt of electricity, it was so powerful it lifted Otto clear off the floor and sent him flying into air, across the room and into the far wall.

He hit it with a loud thump. His body seemed to hang on the wall for a few seconds. Then it slid to the floor, lifeless, a mass of blood and matter where the back of his head hit the wall.

"Oh, no," Rosalie cried. "Dr. Kramer. Dr. Kramer."

"Child, I had to do it. He's wrong. Listen to your heart, yes, do that. You know what Sigmund Lowe is. You've always known."

Rosalie remained still. She realized it was only she who could press the silver button. Only she was capable of shutting down the device. The angel, or whatever loomed above her, needed her to do it. Once again, her ire became inflamed that someone or something was trying to manipulate her.

With that realization, Rosalie discovered her inner power, her strength.

"You're not an angel at all, are you? You're something else, right? Is Dr. Kramer right? Are you just a virus, a mental virus?"

The being became quiet and shrank into a familiar form.

Rosalie's eyes filled with tears.

"Mama," she said.

"Honey, I tried to teach you about evil. Please don't be fooled by false kindnesses. You know what Sigmund Lowe was and still is. You know of what he is capable. Shut down the device. Don't allow him back into this world."

Rosalie remembered something the other visitor, the man, had told her. He said that when other-dimensional beings enter her world, they have the ability to shape-shift. That, he explained, was because they were nothing more than though patterns.

"Do it now," the woman said in Anna Mary's voice. "Go ahead, my darling little girl, shut it down."

As much as Rosalie understood what was happening, something inside urged her to obey. Years of hatred fought a battle in her mind; years of mistrust.

She thought about Otto's words. Hatred? Was it hatred that made her vulnerable to this creature?

She only knew of one thing, one weapon she had in her mental arsenal. She stood tall, her chin poised in indignation, and faced the woman who, without the ability to feed on Rosalie's fears, began to transform back into the muddy form.

Rosalie's tone became calm and sounded so much like an adult, she barely recognized her own voice.

"I love my brother-in-law. He is kind. He is good. I love him and I'd never do anything to harm him. I love him and I'm bringing him home. Do you hear me? I said I love him."

As she spoke those words, the being became smaller. Her voice, however, remained angry and harsh.

"You are a fool if you think this will stop me. One day I will return. Many are raised on hatred. One day I will find another who will kill anyone who doesn't believe in his ideology. It won't be difficult. I've done it many times in the past and I will do it many times in the future. You say you love, but I tell you this, humans love to hate."

Rosalie repeated her words, compartmentalizing her thoughts as Sigmund had taught her. She could sense she was blocking the being's anger.

"I love him. I love him. I love him."

The being shrank to nothing more than a spark and, as she continued to profess her love, the spark grew so small, it disappeared right before her eyes.

"I love Sigmund," she shouted. "Don't you ever freakin' forget that!"

The familiar crackling sound caused her to turn around. Sigmund stood in front of the portal, a smile on his face.

"Thank you, Rosie. I love you, too."

Dr. Bennett stirred and climbed to his knees, rubbing the back of his head. He looked at the lifeless body of Otto Kramer.

"Christ, what happened?"

"We saved the world, Dr. Bennett," she said. "Love, instead of hatred, saved the world."

Chapter 30

It was after midnight. Rosalie was asleep in her dorm room at Pennsylvania State University in State College, Pennsylvania.

The adamant ring of the telephone crept into her dream. It was the one where she was flying over the west coast again, diving downward to the water and then soaring toward the sky with wild abandon.

She'd had that dream often throughout her life. When she experienced visits from the other-worldly beings, she learned flying was natural.

"You're held down by gravity when you live on Earth," the man had said.

That sufficed. She believed she could soar and in her dreams, at least, she did oftentimes over the next seven years.

At twenty-one, it still took her a while to adjust to the reality of her life upon awakening. She wanted to keep flying, but the telephone demanded answering. She grasped the receiver, took a deep breath and, with her eyes still closed, whispered, "Hello."

"Rosie, it's Sigmund. Rosie, wake up. I have news for you."

When she heard the sound of his voice, his accent now more distinct than ever, she got up on one elbow, her heart pounding.

"What? Is it Carlotta? Stanley? Catherine?"

"No, no, they're all fine. They're still in Florida with Mama and Papa." He paused, then said, "It's something else."

"What?"

"I cannot speak of it on the telephone. You must come quickly."

"Where?"

"Johnson will come for you. You remember him, yes?"

She remembered the tall African American well. She also remembered how sad she was to see him leave his apartment above the garages. She remembered how, when she went inside to say goodbye, he was packing up all sorts of surveillance devices. She smiled at that memory.

"Yes, of course."

"Can you be ready in twenty minutes?"

"Sure."

She replaced the receiver of her princess telephone in its cradle.

She was annoyed that her dream of flying had been interrupted. She loved that dream. But this, she assumed, could be the discovery she'd waited for since she was a teenager.

Her thoughts, like her dream of flying, soared above the past seven years. As she showered, she pictured the beings who had visited her; the man, a good soul, and the woman who she eventually realized was evil incarnate.

Chaos, as she called the female entity, had fed on the hatred that had been instilled in her as a child. When the climax of the events peaked, she was forced to choose between love and hatred.

She shook her head, remembering the sight of Otto Kramer lying dead, the back of his head nothing more than a splatter of blood and matter on the wall. He had given his life persuading her to trust Sigmund.

"Poor Dr. Kramer," she whispered.

As she dressed in a pair of black slacks and a green sweater, she recalled what had followed.

"Sigmund," Dr. Bennett had said, "take the girl home."

Sigmund had hesitated. He later told her he was uncomfortable leaving his time-travel device in the hands of the government.

"Go," the doctor had insisted.

He picked up the telephone and told the person on the other end to come to the laboratory. Sigmund didn't seem agreeable, she recalled.

"Let me shut it down first," he said.

Dr. Bennett had nodded and Sigmund knelt beside the device and, after turning a few knobs and adjusting a lever, the curtain that separated the laboratory from the place where time and space was managed had closed. The room had become eerily quiet when the crackling noise dissipated.

"Keep this in a safe place," Sigmund warned. "It has the capability to create more chaos than anyone could imagine."

"Not to worry, my boy, it will be kept in a secret location."

Elwood Johnson entered with two uniformed men Rosalie had never seen before. Dr. Bennett told them to remove the device.

Sigmund had wrapped his arm around Rosalie and led her to the door. Rosalie felt him slide something into her hand.

"Wait," Dr. Bennett said. "Is this everything?"

"Yes," Sigmund had replied.

Dr. Bennett nodded to Johnson. The agent approached Sigmund and began to pat him down, checking the pockets of his lab coat.

"I'm sorry, Dr. Lowe, but I need you to empty your pant pockets, too."

Sigmund complied.

Rosalie smiled as she recalled the feel of the small square item that sat hidden in the palm of her hand. She slipped it into the slot behind the fuzzy poodle on her skirt, her secret pocket.

"He's clean," Johnson said.

"Me, too?" Rosalie asked.

Johnson had turned toward Dr. Bennett, who nodded.

He checked her hands and the deep pockets on the sides of her skirt. "She's okay."

"You go home, honey, and try to forget what has happened here today," Dr. Bennett said.

She nodded innocently.

"Thank you, Dr. Bennett."

Sigmund later told her that Dr. Bennett had the time travel device moved to a secure location. No one knew where he had it stored.

"Could somebody bad get their hands on it?" she'd asked.

"Trust me, Rosie, it's safe."

She knew Sigmund wanted to destroy it but, as he explained, he was kept out of the information loop.

"How do you think I feel about it? I created the damn thing and I have no idea where it will end up."

That was how the whole time travel adventure had ended for Rosalie. Or, so she thought. Here she was, seven years later getting dressed in the middle of the night and, hopefully, possibly, to see the infamous bell.

She slipped her feet, covered with green socks, into her knee-high boots and stood, catching a glimpse of herself in the mirror by the bathroom.

She was taller, five feet and seven inches. Her hair was cropped close to her head with small wisps framing her face.

After the incident, she was accepted at a private school. She studied long and hard, skipping two full years. She spent the last four years at Penn State, as everyone called it. She smiled now, realizing why Sigmund insisted she choose that school. She was only six months away from her masters in science degree. After that, she was promised a position working alongside Sigmund.

She stood in her kitchen gazing out the window as she gulped down the last of her instant coffee. She placed the cup in the sink, ran some water into it, and shut off the faucet. It dripped. She tightened the spigot.

A car horn blared from somewhere outside. It was so loud she heard it through the closed window of her third floor dorm room. She couldn't see the car as her windows faced a central courtyard, but she knew it would be the ordinary dark sedan of the agency.

"Mr. Johnson," she whispered as she headed down the stairs.

If he only knew that she had hidden the key to the device in her poodle pocket, he probably wouldn't have been so gracious to her over the course of the years that followed.

When she and Sigmund had arrived home, he took the square object.

"It won't work without this. This little piece of the puzzle is what opens the portal."

"I'm glad you have it and not them," Rosalie had said.

"You trusted me today and I'm trusting you now. This doesn't exist. You understand, yes?"

Rosalie had nodded. He placed it in the safe in his office. She never asked about it and he never spoke of it after that day.

She glanced at her watch. It had been a half-hour since the call from Sigmund. Johnson was outside waiting.

She donned her coat, a heavy pea coat in navy blue, and wrapped a thick red scarf around her neck. The matching hat was hanging on a hook by the door. It was early December and she had a feeling she'd be spending a lot of time outside.

"This better be what I think it is."

By the time she reached the car, her fingers were already turning cold. Johnson was standing at the passenger side door. He opened it as she approached.

"Hello, Mr. Johnson. So where are we heading?"

"I'm sorry, you know the rules. You're are on a need-to-know basis."

"Yes, need-to-know," she mumbled as she climbed in. "Are you going to slip a black sack over my head, too?"

Johnson let a soft rumble of laughter creep into the night.

"No, Miss Rosie."

At least, she thought, the man still maintained somewhat of a sense of humor. Within minutes, the car sped along one dark road after another. Mr. Johnson seemed to know the two-lane highways that snaked through Pennsylvania like she knew Silver Peach Acres. All the time, they headed west.

She felt a tinge of excitement. Sigmund had informed her he was able to reset the coordinates somewhere in the Pittsburgh area, deep in the woods.

She let out a small shiver.

This is it. This is it.

"Are you cold, Miss Rosie?"

"No. Mr. Johnson, but thank you."

After two hours, he announced, "We're almost there."

Johnson followed a smaller road that was equally as dark and stopped at a remote spot. Rosalie could see some activity ahead. Several vans were parked along the road and people mulled about.

Rosalie didn't wait for Johnson to come around and open her door. Instead, she got out and walked to Sigmund, who was standing by the last van talking to two men.

She called his name. When he turned, the reflection from the headlights caught the gleam in his eyes. He rushed to meet her.

"Rosie, this might be it."

"The bell?"

He smiled, his handsome face lighting up as though someone shoved a one-hundred-watt light bulb down his throat.

"Yes, the bell, Rosie. I think the bell has landed."

"Really? Where?"

"Right here in Kecksburg."

"Oh, is that where we are?" she said with a chuckle. "So, when did it land?"

"A few hours ago."

"How do you know it's the bell?"

"Several people saw a bright, actually brilliant, object moving across the sky. There's a boy who reported that he was playing outside and saw the object fall into the woods close to his house."

"Well, it could be anything. What makes you think it's the bell? Did anyone else see it?"

Sigmund grinned.

"Yes, many people. The police, the newspapers, and all of the radio and television stations in the area had their phone lines jammed with calls about the thing."

"What about the government? Are they involved?"

"Yes, they're already there; the Army and Air Force."

"Well, once they get involved, we're going to be out of luck. Remember Roswell?"

"Not true. They've agreed to let us have a peek."

"Me, too?"

"Yes. As a matter of fact it was Dr. Bennett's idea to send Johnson for you. We wants you to see it for yourself. You're as much a part of this as any of us."

"Sir, Dr. Bennett said we're leaving now. You can get in this van," Johnson said.

A few seconds later, Dr. Bennett climbed into the front seat. He turned to them as he spoke, his round face appearing years younger. Rosalie had never seen him smile so much. He was almost giddy.

"They're going to allow us to examine it. This is most exciting. I know it's your bell, Sigmund. I just know it."

Rosalie smiled, too, shaking her head. He reminded her of Stanley when he received his first two-wheeler at Christmas.

"Where?" Sigmund asked.

"Haven't you learned anything since you arrived here? They never tell us *everything*. The lead van driver knows where he's heading, no one else. Even Agent Johnson doesn't know. Isn't that right, Elwood?"

"Yes, sir," he said, laughing. "I just have to keep up with him."

Rosalie laughed and said, "Gee, it's nice to see even you guys get the whole 'need-to-know' treatment, too."

Dr. Bennett laughed, too.

"Yes, indeed."

They drove for more than an hour, staying mostly to dark two-lane highways. She looked through the back window into the black of night. Wherever they were heading, she thought, was most likely a secret government installation.

225

Just as that thought crossed her mind, they stopped at a high gate trimmed in barbed wire. A guard approached the lead vehicle. He perused the documentation and the gate slid open, allowing the van to pass. He followed the same protocol for each.

Johnson followed the procession along another dark strip of roadway for a minute. Rosalie kept her eyes ahead. Then, as though appearing out of nowhere, a low flat building sat in front of them. It was inconspicuous, long and gray.

Johnson stopped the vehicle and Dr. Bennett opened the door to jump out. As he did, he said, "Come on now. We're here."

Sigmund let out a small laugh and tapped Rosalie's hand.

"He shows his excitement," he whispered. "But, Rosie, make no mistake, inside I am even more excited."

Rosalie already knew that. She got out of the van and followed the men along a cobblestone walkway to the front doors, two iron monsters that looked formidable.

Johnson remained by the van. Whatever waited inside the building was not within the need-to-know criteria for the agent. He didn't seem to mind.

The door on the right opened and they entered.

A man in a dark suit greeted Dr. Bennett.

"Follow me," he said.

There were steps that led to a lower level, wide and inviting. As they descended, she discovered several people garbed in white lab coats scurrying about.

"This way," the man said, leading down a long well-lit corridor.

They came to a dead end where the man pushed a panel on the wall, a panel she hadn't noticed. It receded into the wall much like the doors on Sigmund's office. As it did, another part of the wall opened and there, sitting in the middle of the room, was the strange object that fell from the sky.

It was on the deck of a flatbed truck, a heavy tarp disguising its identity, but not its shape. She instantly recognized it. It looked to be more than twenty feet long and ten feet wide. It took up most of the truck's bed.

"Here it is, Sigmund," Dr. Bennett whispered.

To Rosalie, it seemed Sigmund had stopped breathing.

"Are you okay?" she whispered.

"I feel amazing," he said, smiling.

The man who led the way nodded and three others grabbed the edges of the tarp and pulled it off the object.

There it was, the bell, the vehicle that traveled through time in another dimension. Rosalie looked it over. It had strange writing around the edges that were worn from the entry into Earth's atmosphere. The emblem on the front was worn, too; almost invisible, but still present.

Rosalie recalled how the beings explained how they used the skies as a means of entry and egress because it was safer. Obviously, the bell's coordinates had been adjusted with that in mind. Also, she knew, Otto Kramer wanted it to appear as though it came from the sky.

"Go ahead, Dr. Lowe, touch it."

Sigmund ran his hand over the surface, caressing its re-entry scars.

Rosalie walked around the truck, inspecting every inch of the object. It appeared just how Sigmund had described it.

Finally, she let out a long sigh. Sigmund, hearing her, turned.

"Well, it's your bell, all right," she said. "Lion's bell."

The End

Made in the USA
Middletown, DE
19 September 2015